Praise for the work

Three Reasons to Say Yes

This was a really easy story to get into. I sank right in and wanted to stay there, because reading about other people on vacation is kind of like taking a mini vacation from the world! It's sweet and lovely, and while it has some angst, it's not going to hurt you. Instead, it's going to take you away from it all so you can come back with a smile on your face.

-The Lesbian Review

All the Reasons I Need

This is book two of the 'Paradise romance' series by this author. I absolutely loved book one, *'Three Reasons to Say Yes'* which was one of my favorites of 2018. Even though these are standalone romances, the reader will catch up with the story of Julia and Reed from book one, so I recommend them in chronological order to enjoy it fully...Overall, a good friends to lovers lesbian romance book with quite a bit of drama and angst.

-LezReviewBooks

What a fantastic follow up to what was one of my favourite books from last year. I hope this isn't the end for this series. I'm so invested now and can't wait to read more from these characters.

-Les Rêveur

Just One Reason

Just One Reason by Jaime Clevenger is a great age gap, workplace romance that kept me entertained and invested in a happily ever after for both main characters...The storyline glides along with ease and Clevenger's great dialogue lets the reader see how Sam and Terri are hardwired. The story is told from both Sam and Terri's points of view so getting to know them happens naturally. This is the third book in the Paradise series, but it works as a stand-alone…This book checked all the boxes on my list of what I want in a good book. I got to bond with two intriguing main characters. The plot had enough angst to make me question if there'd be a happily ever after (Hint: it's a romance), and the sex was hot. From any way you look at it, this story's a winner.

-The Lesbian Review

Party Favors

Like the old CYOA (choose your own adventure) books, *Party Favors* is written in the second person so that the reader is the main character… I'm not sure what I expected when I started this book, but it ended up being way more fun and hot than I'd imagined. All paths head towards some kind of sexual encounter, and no two encounters are the same…If you like erotica and books that are seriously fun, definitely check this one out, and even better—read it with a friend.

-Smart Bitches, *Trashy Books*

One Weekend in Aspen

Who'd have thought a book about a sex party would be full of suspense? I couldn't put One Weekend in Aspen down. I had to know what would happen next. I would have read it in one sitting if life had let me, but as it is, I had to stop reading for a whole day. Yet, now that I have turned the last page, I'm sad it's over. I really didn't want it to end…With this book, Jaime Clevenger did something that I didn't think was possible, not to that level: she wrote an incredibly hot story that will, at the same time, give you all the feels. —Les Rêveur

Jaime Clevenger is on my automatic list of authors to read so when I realized she had a new release, I already knew that I was going to read it. But when I read the blurb, it definitely caught my attention. I'm happy to say that I wasn't disappointed...I knew that Clevenger can write awesome sex scenes since I've read her erotica book Party Favors followed by her Paradise Romance series. So I wasn't surprised to see that One Weekend in Aspen was seriously hot. No, scratch that, this book is smoking, sizzling hot...So, if you are looking for some serious steam in your romance you should add this book to your list.

-LezReviewBooks

Praise for the works of Aurora Rey

Twice Shy

"[A] tender, foodie romance about a pair of middle aged lesbians who find partners in each other and rediscover themselves along the way. ...Rey's cute, occasionally steamy, romance reminds readers of the giddy intensity falling in love brings at any age, even as the characters negotiate the particular complexities of dating in midlife—meeting the children, dealing with exes, and revealing emotional scars. This queer love story is as sweet and light as one of Bake My Day's famous cream puffs."

-Publishers Weekly

"This book is all the reasons why I love Aurora Rey's writing. It's delicious with a good helping of sexy. It was a nice change to read a book where the women were not in their late 20s–30s..."

-Les Rêveur

The Last Place You Look

"This book is the perfect book to kick your feet up, relax with a glass of wine and enjoy. I'm a big Aurora Rey fan because her deliciously engaging books feature strong women who fall for sweet butch women. It's a winning recipe."

-Les Rêveur

"The romance is satisfying and full-bodied, with each character learning how to achieve her own goals and still be part of a couple. A heartwarming story of two lovers learning to move past their fears and commit to a shared future."

-Kirkus Reviews

"[A] sex-positive, body-positive love story. With its warm atmosphere and sweet characters, The Last Place You Look is a fluffy LGBTQ+ romance about finding a second chance at love where you least expect it."

-Foreword Review

Ice on Wheels—Novella in *Hot Ice*

"I liked how Brooke was so attracted to Riley despite the massive grudge she had. No matter how nice or charming Riley was, Brooke was dead set on hating her. A cute enemies to lovers story."

-Bookvark

The Inn at Netherfield Green

"I really enjoyed this book but that's not surprising because it came from the pen of Aurora Rey. This is the kind of book you read while sitting by a warm fire with a Rosemary Gin and snuggly blanket."

-Les Rêveur

"[Aurora Rey] constantly delivers a well-written romance that has just the right blend of humour, engaging characters, chemistry and romance."

-C-Spot Reviews

Lead Counsel—Novella in The *Boss of Her*

"Lead Counsel by Aurora Rey is a short and sweet second chance romance. Not only was this story paced well and a delight to sink into, but there's A++ good swearing in it and has lines like this that made me all swoony because of how beautifully they're crafted."

-The Lesbian Review

Recipe for Love

"Recipe for Love by Aurora Rey is a gorgeous romance that's sure to delight any of the foodies out there. Be sure to keep snacks on hand when you're reading it, though, because this book will make you want to nibble on something!"

-*The Lesbian Review*

Autumn's Light

"Aurora Rey has a knack for writing characters you care about and she never gives us the same pairing twice. Each character is always unique and fully fleshed out. Most of her pairings are butch/femme and her diversity in butch rep is so appreciated. This goes to prove the butch characters do not need to be one dimensional, nor do they all need to be rugged. Rey writes romances in which you can happily immerse yourself. They are gentle romances which are character driven."

-*The Lesbian Review*

Spring's Wake

"[A] feel-good romance that would make a perfect beach read. The Provincetown B&B setting is richly painted, feeling both indulgent and cozy."

-*RT Book Reviews*

"Spring's Wake has shot to number one in my age-gap romance favorites shelf."

-*Les Rêveur*

"Spring's Wake by Aurora Rey is charming. This is the third story in Aurora Rey's Cape End romance series and every book gets better. Her stories are never the same twice and yet each one has a uniquely her flavour. The character work is strong and I find it exciting to see what she comes up with next."

-*The Lesbian Review*

Summer's Cove

"As expected in a small-town romance, Summer's Cove evokes a sunny, light-hearted atmosphere that matches its beach setting. ...Emerson's shy pursuit of Darcy is sure to endear readers to her, though some may be put off during the moments Darcy winds tightly to the point of rigidity. Darcy desires romance yet is unwilling to disrupt her son's life to have it, and you feel for Emerson when she endeavors to show how there's room in her heart for a family."

-RT Book Reviews

"From the moment the characters met I was gripped and couldn't wait for the moment that it all made sense to them both and they would finally go for it. Once again, Aurora Rey writes some of the steamiest sex scenes I have read whilst being able to keep the romance going. I really think this could be one of my favorite series and can't wait to see what comes next. Keep 'em coming, Aurora."

-Les Rêveur

Crescent City Confidential

"This book blew my socks off… [Crescent City Confidential] ticks all the boxes I've started to expect from Aurora Rey. It is written very well and the characters are extremely well developed; I felt like I was getting to know new friends and my excitement grew with every finished chapter."

-Les Rêveur

"Rey's frothy contemporary romance brings two women together to restore an ancient farmhouse in Ithaca, N.Y. ...[T]he women totally click in bed, as well as when they're poring over paint chips, and readers will enjoy finding out whether love conquers all."

-Publishers Weekly

Winter's Harbor

"One of my all time favourite Lesbian romance novels and probably the most reread book on my Kindle. ...Absolutely love this debut novel by Aurora Rey and couldn't put the book down from the moment the main protagonists meet. Winter's Harbor was written beautifully and it was full of heart. Unequivocally 5 stars."

-Les Rêveur

Love, Accidentally

Books by Jaime Clevenger published by Bella Books

The Unknown Mile
Call Shotgun
Sign on the Line
Whiskey and Oak Leaves
Sweet, Sweet Wine
Waiting for a Love Song
A Fugitive's Kiss
Moonstone
Party Favors
Three Reasons to Say Yes
All the Reasons I Need
Just One Reason
One Weekend in Aspen

Published by Spinsters Ink
All Bets Off

Books by Aurora Rey published by Bold Strokes Books

Cape End Romances
Winter's Harbor
Summer's Cove
Spring's Wake
Autumn's Light

Built to Last
Crescent City Confidential
Lead Counsel (Novella in The Boss of Her collection)
Recipe for Love: A Farm-to-Table Romance
Ice on Wheels (Novella in Hot Ice collection)
The Last Place You Look
Twice Shy
You Again
Follow Her Lead (Novella in Opposites Attract collection)

About Jamie Clevenger

Jaime Clevenger lives in Colorado with wife, Corina, two daughters, two very hairy cats and one golden retriever. When not working as a veterinarian or writing romance, Jaime enjoys family adventures, fostering furry animals, swimming, and practicing karate. Jaime has published many books with Bella Books and has won a Golden Crown Literary Award for the romance *Three Reasons to Say Yes*. Listening to rain and eating chocolate are two not-so-secret pleasures, but Jaime also loves walks on the beach and reading.

About Aurora Rey

Aurora Rey is a college dean by day and award-winning lesbian romance author the rest of the time, except when she's cooking, baking, riding the tractor, or pining for goats. She grew up in a small town in south Louisiana, daydreaming about New England. She keeps a special place in her heart for the South, especially the food and the ways women are raised to be strong, even if they're taught not to show it. After a brief dalliance with biochemistry, she completed both a BA and an MA in English.

She is the author of the *Cape End Romance* series and several standalone contemporary lesbian romance novels and novellas. She has been a finalist for the Lambda Literary, RITA® and Golden Crown Literary Society awards but loves reader feedback the most. She lives in Ithaca, New York, with her dog and whatever wildlife has taken up residence in the pond.

Jaime Clevenger

and

Aurora Rey

BELLA
BOOKS
2021

Bella Books, Inc.
P.O. Box 10543
Tallahassee, FL 32302

Printed in the United States of America on acid-free paper.

First Edition - 2021

Editor: Heather Flournoy
Cover Designer: Kayla Mancuso

ISBN: 978-1-64247-239-4

PUBLISHER'S NOTE

Acknowledgments from Jaime Clevenger

Jaime Clevenger would like to thank Corina for being both a rock star beta reader and amazing partner on so many life adventures. Thank you, Laina Villeneuve, for trading beta reads and encouragement. Thank you, Aurora Rey, for being a fabulous co-author. This project was even more fun than expected. Also many thanks to editor Heather Flournoy as well as everyone at Bella Books and Bold Strokes Books for bringing a two-book co-authored project to readers. And thank you, dear reader, for picking this story.

Acknowledgments from Aurora Rey

Aurora Rey would like to thank Jaime for the adventure of turning these wacky ideas into two really fun stories, and for proving her wrong about group projects. Huge thanks to Heather Flournoy for the stellar editing and praise sandwiches. Also, much gratitude to Bella Books and Bold Strokes Books for letting us team up on these projects. And, as always, deepest gratitude to the readers who make it all worthwhile.

CHAPTER ONE

Amelia Stone closed one eye and surveyed the contents of her U-Haul. Mismatched boxes, a few pieces of furniture, and more duffel bags of clothes than she cared to admit stared back at her. Something about being thirty-five years old and having the entirety of her life fit in a fifteen-foot moving truck was enough to make a girl feel bad about herself.

She straightened her ball cap, adjusted her ponytail, and shook off the malaise. Not anymore.

After a string of false starts and commitmentphobes, she'd finally found a woman who was smart and attractive and wanted the same things she did. Who loved her and couldn't get enough of her. She wasn't about to waste any time or take any chances. Not this time.

"Is that everything?" Nana appeared next to her in the driveway, giving her a start.

"I think so." She'd loaded the meager contents of her apartment before driving over to her grandmother's house for a few final boxes and the antique desk that had been living in

Nana's garage. Things that hadn't fit in her share of the eleven hundred square feet she shared with two other people. Things she'd have room for now.

"Are you sure this is what you want to do? It all seems so fast."

If part of her wanted to dismiss the question as outdated and old-fashioned, she knew better. One, Nana would put her in her place faster than Percy appeared any time a tuna can was opened. Two, it was fast. Even by lesbian standards, she and Veronica had made the decision to move in together pretty quick. Not third-date quick, but not too far from it. "I know what I want, and I've finally found someone who wants the same thing. And we're not getting any younger."

Nana sniffed. "You've never been on vacation together. You've never even had a fight. How can you know she's the one for you?"

"I don't yet. That's the point." She'd practically memorized the speech. "We're not getting married. I'm moving in with her. We're fast-tracking the compatibility test."

Another sniff.

"You only think it's a bad idea because you don't like her. But you barely know her." She'd brought Veronica over exactly once. Nana had spent all day in the kitchen making ravioli from scratch only to have Veronica take one bite and launch into a tirade about how the camera adds ten pounds and women are held to a different standard than men. It might have been a point they could rally around, but Veronica had gotten a call about the chance to cover a fire at a shopping mall and taken off.

"You're right. I don't know her well enough to have an opinion and I'm pretty sure you don't either. That's my issue."

They'd had this conversation a dozen times since Amelia announced her plan. It sucked, really, because Nana was both her best friend and a stand-in for her flashy, never-around mother. She'd hoped Nana would start to come around by now, but no such luck. "She's really busy at work. You'll have plenty of time to get to know her soon."

"Tell me again why isn't she here now, helping you? On what should be such an important day for you both?"

Amelia blew out a breath. Her feelings had been hurt when Veronica announced she needed to be out of town the day they'd picked—together—for Amelia to move. But the truck was scheduled and so were guys to help unload and carry her possessions up the impossibly narrow staircase to Veronica's gorgeous loft apartment. "Mom got her an invite to this Women in Media event in New York. It's a once-in-a-lifetime networking opportunity."

Nana rolled her eyes. Whether it had to do with Veronica's priorities or mention of her daughter, Amelia couldn't tell.

The truth of the matter was that Veronica had said all the right things. She loved and appreciated how much Amelia supported her career. She couldn't wait for Percy to explore the apartment and check out his new cat tree. She couldn't wait to come home, knowing Amelia would be there waiting. "I'm supporting her. She'd do the same for me. It's what we do for each other."

Nana lifted both hands. "I'm not going to argue with you."

What she meant was she wouldn't argue right now. Nana wouldn't hesitate to make her opinions known. Hopefully, things with Veronica would go well, so well that Nana's opinions would change. And hopefully, that would happen very quickly.

"Good. Okay. I just need to get Percy in his carrier." She'd brought him over that morning to save him from the stress of being locked in a bathroom while she loaded the truck, but the movers assured her they'd have everything unloaded in an hour.

"You could leave him here until tomorrow, you know."

She could. She'd need to come back to pick up her car anyway. But she was a little freaked out by the prospect of spending the night in Veronica's—wait, strike that—*their* apartment alone. Not that eleven pounds of orange fluff would do much in the way of protecting her from an intruder, but his presence made her feel better. "I want him to acclimate and settle in before Veronica gets home."

Nana sighed. "All right."

Amelia hefted herself onto the back bumper and grabbed the handle of the rolling door. She got it closed and latched, then followed Nana into the house. Inside, the aroma of chocolate and sugar and butter surrounded her. "Oh, my God. Did you make brownies?"

"I thought I'd bake them for the two of you. I was trying to be nice." Her tone made it abundantly clear she considered it a herculean task. Not the baking, of course. Nana could bake circles around people half her age and twice her size. No, it was the being nice about Veronica part.

"She'll be home Friday. I'll share." Even though Veronica shuddered at the thought of carbs. "Maybe."

"Hmpf."

"Your brownies are amazing." She wrapped her arm around Nana's shoulders and gave them a squeeze. "And so are you."

"Well, someone has to keep you in line."

To a casual observer, having her eighty-six-year-old, four-foot-eleven grandmother say such a thing might come across as comical. But Amelia knew better than most that Nana meant every word. Edith Stone was a force to be reckoned with. And Amelia, despite her above-average intelligence and good intentions, didn't have the best track record when it came to taking chances and going after what she wanted. But like she said, all that was about to change.

She left Nana to wrap up her famous sugar bombs while she hunted for Percy. It didn't take long to find him. He was curled up on Nana's bed, making himself right at home. She felt a little bad about coaxing him into the crate with treats and closing the door before he caught on. He was a cute cat, but not the brightest.

He let out a meow of protest. Amelia brought her nose to the door and peered in. "We're heading to our new place, P. You're going to love it."

Back in the kitchen, she accepted the perfectly wrapped foil package and set Percy down long enough to give Nana a real hug. When Nana let go, she grasped Amelia's arms firmly. "You text me when you get settled."

She was driving all of twenty minutes away, but her heart softened at the tone. So much more maternal than her own mother had ever been. "I will. And I'll see you tomorrow. And the day after that."

Nana frowned. "Are you sure? I could take a taxi, you know."

"No, you can't. Because the doctor's office won't let you." It was standard cataract surgery protocol and a far more effective argument than working the sentimental angle.

"Fine."

"I love you."

Sniff. "I love you too."

Amelia took Percy and her brownies out to the truck and realized then she'd checked off her last to-do item. All of her anxiety about logistics gave way to excitement. She was really doing this—really moving in with Veronica.

Percy let out a perturbed meow as she buckled his carrier into the passenger seat. "Not long, buddy. You'll be in your new digs faster than you can say catnip."

After a final wave to Nana, she climbed into the driver's seat and turned the key. The engine rumbled to life, making the whole truck vibrate. Percy was not amused. She attempted to inch the seat forward again, but again, it didn't budge. Oh, well. She scooted herself forward instead and put the truck into drive.

This was her third time driving a U-Haul and by far the most exciting. She'd gone from college to a brief stint at Nana's to the apartment she shared with two friends so they could all save for down payments on houses. The three-year plan had stretched to five and now they were going on twelve.

She couldn't speak for Maya and Sneha but buying a house at thirty—alone—had felt like tempting the fates of spinsterhood. So, she kept renewing her lease, hoping Ms. Right would come into her life. She finally had, and Amelia couldn't be happier. She and Veronica would live together for six months and, if all went well, they'd spend the spring planning a wedding, looking for a house, and researching potential sperm donors. Who said efficiency couldn't be romantic?

Just like today. It was the end result, not the process, that mattered. Nana would come to see that eventually.

Amelia turned up the radio and drove west. Veronica's place was across town in a converted warehouse. Right as she was congratulating herself on being sassy and independent, a dump truck pulled out in front of her. She slammed the brake, but nothing happened. Well, not nothing. The truck probably slowed a bit. But it was too little, too late to do much good.

She'd always thought it cliché when people said things happened in slow motion, but as the inevitability of crashing registered, the whole scene seemed to play out frame by frame in her mind. Each fraction of a second had its own accompanying thought. Would Percy's seat belt hold? Good thing she'd sprung for the extra insurance at the truck rental place. Did U-Hauls have air bags? How bad was this going to hurt?

She even had time to close her eyes and brace herself.

The sound registered first. The grinding crunch of metal contorting in on itself and the pop of shattering glass. Smell came next. Not quite burning, it reminded her of a firecracker or a lit match. How strange.

Pain followed. A blow to her forehead, a wrenching in her leg. And then the darkness closed in and she felt nothing at all.

CHAPTER TWO

Finn Douglas hopped out of the driver's seat. Gravel littered the road and the smell of brake fluid cut the air. "I'll take the U-Haul, you check on the dump truck."

"Got it, boss."

Finn narrowed her eyes but didn't waste time chewing Toni out for the boss comment. No doubt her adrenaline was racing and she wouldn't listen anyway. Toni had been an EMT all of six months and still got a thrill being first on the scene, but a wail of sirens promised they wouldn't be alone for long.

By the look of it, the dump truck had pulled into oncoming traffic and clipped the front of the U-Haul. Unfortunately, it was one of the little U-Hauls and the dump truck had what looked like a full load of gravel. Depending on the speed, the impact definitely could have been enough for serious injuries.

Glass crunched under her boots as Finn stepped up to the driver-side door. She did a quick assessment of the vehicle before reaching for the handle: front windshield shattered and airbags deployed. The driver, a white female, maybe mid-thirties and easily someone Finn could carry if she had to pull her out before more help arrived, slumped against the seat belt. No other passengers, but a cat carrier was belted in next to the woman.

"Hey, can you hear me?" When the woman didn't respond, Finn lightly touched her eyelids. Her eyes fluttered open and she briefly met Finn's gaze before closing them again.

"I need you to keep your eyes open. Can you do that for me?"

"No."

Finn smiled. A cranky patient had a much better prognosis than an unconscious one. "How 'bout you try?" There was an abrasion above the woman's right eyebrow and a red welt on her forehead that would be a nasty bruise later. The airbag, or the woman's hands coming up to protect her face, could have caused both. Hopefully more serious head trauma wasn't part of the picture, but it was unlikely she'd get out of a CT.

It didn't escape Finn's attention that the ball cap the woman had been wearing, now pushed far back on her head, was emblazoned with the HRC logo. Between that and the wavy brown hair pulled back in a ponytail, the olive complexion, and the fit but curvy build, Finn would definitely have noticed her walking down the street. But now was not the time to think about that.

"It's important you keep your eyes open. Can you do that for me please?" The woman shook her head. Even better than a cranky patient was one who could move her head normally. Finn brushed the woman's cheek. "Please? I need you to talk to me."

When she opened her eyes again, she blinked a few times as if the glare of the sunlight was too much. After a moment, things seemed to come into better focus as she glanced from Finn to the cat carrier next to her. "Oh, shit."

"That's better. Can you tell me if you think you're injured?"

"My leg hurts. And my head hurts." She took a shaky breath. "It hurts to take a deep breath."

"You okay if I help you?"

"Mm-hmm. Something's wrong with my leg. I can't move it."

"We'll get to that. What's your name?"

"Amelia."

Finn checked Amelia's pulse and slipped on her stethoscope. Her lung sounds were normal, but when Finn pressed lightly against her left side, she cringed. Possible broken ribs. Maybe contusions. The other problem was that her right foot appeared to be jammed under the brake pedal. Pulling her free would hurt like hell.

Finn scanned the cab again, making certain she wasn't missing any detail that would matter when they tried to move her. An orange cat peeked out between the bars of the carrier, wide-eyed, and she made a silent promise to check him out later.

"Okay, Amelia, I'm gonna put something on your neck and then we're gonna get you out of here. You okay riding with me to the hospital?"

"Yeah. What about my foot?"

"We'll take care of you. I promise." That foot would hurt a lot more in a minute, but she didn't need to tell her that part. "You're pretty banged up but you're gonna be okay."

"I don't like hospitals."

"Why not? They're full of cute doctors and nurses. Plus, the outfits are hard to beat."

Amelia actually smiled, which gave Finn more hope than anything else. She glanced around for Toni. FD and CHP had both shown up and the fire captain was heading in Finn's direction. Toni popped around the far side of the dump truck and Finn motioned to her.

Jogging past the fire captain, Toni got to Finn first. "Whatcha need, boss?"

Finn didn't even bother glaring. "We're gonna need to stabilize this one and get her loaded up. How's the dump truck driver?"

"Grumpy. No injuries and refused to let me check him out. I bet ten bucks this was all his fault."

"Not our call to make. Grab a C-collar for me?"

Toni hustled back to the ambulance and Finn turned back to her patient. She'd closed her eyes again. "Amelia? I still need your eyes open. Can you tell me what happened?"

"Veronica asked me to move in with her."

"I mean the accident."

"Oh. That."

Finn smiled. "Yeah. That." Toni returned with the C-collar and a backboard to stabilize the spine. Finn slipped the collar into position on Amelia's neck. "Do you remember what happened?"

The fire captain and a CHP officer were both standing next to Finn now, waiting for the story.

"Veronica—"

"The accident."

"Right...that. The dump truck pulled out in front of me. Came out of nowhere. I was going straight, then I was going sideways."

"Been there," Toni murmured.

The fire captain chuckled and even the CHP officer grinned. Finn slid the board into position behind Amelia's back. She figured there'd be more jokes later back at the station. The all lesbian EMT-Paramedic team with the hot lesbian patient. Go figure. But timing mattered. They needed to focus and get her moved.

She eyed the captain and the officer. "Head trauma, possible broken leg—looks like her heel slipped under the brake pedal—and I wouldn't be surprised if she's got a few broken ribs. Real tender on her left thorax."

"But you're ready to move her?" the fire captain asked.

"Yep."

"Then let's make it happen."

The fire captain hollered to one of the other firefighters. Finn didn't mind accepting the help and she'd let Toni watch over the transfer to make sure the guys didn't screw up. She headed back to the ambulance to gather supplies and to radio dispatch with an update.

She'd barely finished by the time Amelia was loaded in the back and hooked up on oxygen. The clock never stopped running and she loved it when they had a patient ready for transport before dispatch figured they would.

"Can I drive?" Toni practically bounced on her toes. "Come on, you know you want to ride in the back. Did you see her hat?"

"I saw her hat."

"And she's hot. Even you gotta admit that. I've got a girlfriend, but you don't."

"She's a patient." No way would she ask a patient out. Besides, after the ride to the hospital, Finn would never see her again.

"You can still flirt. It'd be good for you." Toni tried to snatch the keys from Finn's grip and then made a face when she missed. "Please? You never let me drive."

They were wasting time arguing. And the truth was, Finn did want to ride in the back even if she'd never see Amelia again. "Fine. But watch the potholes." She handed over the keys. "Oh, shit. The cat."

"The cat?"

"Give me two seconds." Finn raced back to the U-Haul. She'd nearly forgotten the ball of orange fluff scrunched in the back of the cat carrier, silently hoping to hide from everyone. Throughout everything, the cat hadn't made a peep. Now, she heard a plaintive mew when she unlatched the seat belt and pulled the carrier free.

"All right, little buddy. You get to ride with us too." It wasn't the first time she'd brought along someone's pet. Although the rules didn't allow for it, exceptions were made. And Finn had never been much of a rule follower anyway.

She set the carrier in the back, climbed in, and eyed Toni. "What? You driving or not?"

"You brought her cat?"

"You want me to leave it in the U-Haul?" Finn shook her head. "Come on. Let's move."

Toni grumbled but closed the rear door. The engine revved and Finn turned her focus to Amelia. She'd closed her eyes again but was breathing comfortably through the oxygen mask, and with the monitors on, Finn didn't mind letting her rest. She placed an IV with only a small complaint from Amelia about the pinch and started fluids.

Toni took a corner a little fast and Amelia's eyes snapped open.

"New driver. Don't worry. She hasn't crashed yet."

Amelia tugged the oxygen mask off her face and glared at Finn. "What is that? You're not going to poke me, are you? I hate needles."

"I already placed your IV. No more pokes." Finn checked the syringe for air and then pushed the contents into the IV port. "This is something for the pain. How you feeling?"

"My leg still hurts."

"It'll feel better in a minute." With luck, the CT would show no brain injury and Amelia would get out of the mess with nothing more than a cast. "Can you keep that on your finger? It's showing me your oxygen levels."

"My oxygen levels are fine." Amelia fidgeted with the sensor. "This thing itches."

"Your oxygen levels were better when you were breathing through the mask." Finn held up the mask, but Amelia shook her head. "Okay, fine. We can leave it off for now. But the sensor stays on." In a few minutes, the opioid would kick in anyway. No sense having a fight now.

The ambulance lurched and a look of panic crossed Amelia's face. Finn reached for her hand and gave it a gentle squeeze. "Potholes. You can complain to the city."

"I work for the city."

"Perfect. You're the person I've been waiting for. Can we set up a meeting to discuss potholes?" Finn chuckled when Amelia gave her a stink eye.

"I think my foot feels better." Amelia yawned. "You're cute. Married?"

"No."

"Why not?" Amelia's words were starting to slur.

"Waiting for the right woman."

"I'd date you. But I've got Veronica."

"Right. Veronica." The drugs had definitely kicked in. "How long have you two been together?"

"Six weeks."

"And you're moving in with her already? Are you serious?"

"Mm-hmm. She's the one. She's perfect."

"How do you know she's not crazy? You barely get to know someone in six weeks."

"Oh, I know her."

Amelia's overly confident tone pushed Finn to go further. "Okay. Does she floss?"

Amelia hesitated. "I'm sure she does."

"Do you know if she votes?"

"You sound like my nana." Amelia's eyes closed and a yawn followed. "Of course she votes. Everyone votes. Anyway, her teeth are perfect."

"You feeling sleepy?"

"Nope. Wide awake."

Finn glanced at the oxygen monitor. Levels were steady, which was lucky because she didn't want to force Amelia to wear the oxygen mask. "Not everyone votes. She could be the one who doesn't. Or she could vote for the wrong side."

"Not possible. She's perfect. Beautiful, smart…" Amelia's voice trailed. When they hit another pothole, she seemed to be jostled alert. She shifted and looked right at Finn. "More than that, she likes me. And we want the same things."

"Anyone would like you."

Amelia's head bobbed side to side. "Do you know how long I was single? Too-too-too long." She sang the *too*s and Finn couldn't help laughing.

"You need a Veronica. She has friends. I could hook you up. What's your name?"

"Finn."

"Like Huckleberry?"

"You'll be surprised to know that's not the first time I've been asked that."

Amelia breathed out a long moan. "I like that name. I like huckleberries too. They're too-too-too good." Again she sang. "Have you ever had huckleberries, Finn? You should. You'd like them."

"I'll remember that." Finn chuckled. The ambulance pulled to a stop, and for the first time she wished the ride had lasted a little longer. But the sooner Amelia got a CT the better. "Okay. This is where you get off."

"What if I don't want to go? Nothing hurts anymore."

"Oh, it will. Trust me."

Toni popped open the rear door and nodded at the cat carrier. "What are we doing with that? You know the nurses are gonna hate us if you pass that on to them."

"We'll take him to the vet to get him checked out," Finn said. She glanced at Amelia to see if she'd be okay with her plan, but Amelia was snoring.

"Then what?" Toni asked.

"What do you mean?"

"How are you going to get the cat back to her? You gonna keep the cat?"

She looked down at Amelia. If only there was no Veronica… "I'll figure it out."

Toni chuckled. "You know I'm gonna give you shit about this later, right? So much shit."

CHAPTER THREE

Amelia woke slowly, like coming out of a fog. It registered as strange, because how often did she really notice waking up? Not as strange as the dream she'd had. Lying in a bed but also being in motion. This gorgeous butch smiling at her, holding her hand. And something about huckleberries.

Wait. Not huckleberries. Huckleberry Finn. Finn. The paramedic. Fuck.

Her analysis of the dream that wasn't a dream faded away as the other details of her surroundings registered. Something beeping. A weird smell. And why did it taste like something crawled into her mouth and died?

She opened her eyes. Yep, definitely a hospital room. Oh, this was bad.

She tried to shift, only to realize her right leg weighed about a hundred pounds. And her head throbbed like the worst hangover she'd ever had. But she was alive. That had to count for something.

What exactly had happened, again? It freaked her out more than a little that she couldn't piece together all the details.

There was a U-Haul. Veronica in New York. Arguing with Nana about Veronica being in New York. Then Finn. Everything else blurred together.

She needed to call Veronica. Nana, too, for that matter. She attempted to turn her head. The throb became a sharp pain, but it turned. She knew enough to know that was a good thing. Where was her phone? And her purse? Percy. Oh, God. What happened to Percy?

The monitor next to her bed started beeping more erratically and a nurse appeared in the doorway. "Ms. Stone. You're awake."

The nurse seemed pleased, and Amelia's instincts to put others at ease kicked in. "Amelia, please."

The nurse smiled. "How are you feeling, Amelia?"

"Like I've been hit by a truck." The second she said the words, the memories flooded back—the dump truck, trying to hit the brake, Finn asking her to open her eyes. "I was. I was hit by a truck."

"I'm afraid so."

As much as that reality sucked, it made her feel infinitely better than having gaps in her memory. "Do you happen to know what happened to my phone?" She cringed. "Or my cat?"

The nurse gave her a sympathetic look. "I can't help you on the cat front, but we plugged your phone in at the nurses' station so it would be charged when you woke up."

"How long have I been here?" She tried to keep the panic from her voice but failed epically.

"Only a few hours. The pain meds knocked you out, nothing more."

She appreciated these nuggets of good news, but they weren't enough. "Okay. That's good. Thanks…" She frowned. "I'm sorry. I didn't even ask your name."

That earned her another sympathetic smile. "I'm Shanisse, and don't apologize. I just need to take your vitals and then I'll go grab your phone."

Amelia mustered a smile in return. "Thank you."

A few minutes later, she had her phone, assurances her injuries were not life-threatening, and a promise that the doctor would be making rounds soon. Since she didn't yet have a missed call from Nana, she decided to start with Veronica. Not that she had a call from her either.

After five rings, she was prepared—disappointed, but prepared—to be sent to voice mail. But then Veronica's voice came through the speaker. "Baby. How are you? All settled and happy?"

For some reason, the upbeat tone made her eyes prick with tears. Or, maybe, it was knowing that Veronica and all her upbeat energy were two thousand miles away. "Not exactly."

"Don't tell me the movers were jerks. Or didn't show. I told you we should have gone with a full-service company."

Amelia closed her eyes. She'd thought getting a U-Haul would be fun. And with the money they saved, she'd feel better about that long weekend in Aspen Veronica wanted so badly. "I crashed the truck. Or, I think someone crashed into me."

"What? Are you okay?"

Hearing the pitch in Veronica's voice made her feel better. "I'm not sure. I'm in the hospital and my leg is all wrapped up. But the nurse says I'm okay and the doctor will be around soon."

"Okay, good."

When Veronica didn't say anything else right away, Amelia thought perhaps she was calculating how quickly she could make it back to Colorado. That made her feel better too.

"Babe, I wish I could talk more but I have to go. Miranda invited me to drinks with some of her colleagues. I want to hear everything later, though, so can I call you?"

Amelia felt herself deflate. The shift was so fast, the sensation so palpable, she had a moment of wonder that it didn't make an audible hissing sound. "Yeah. Sure."

"Do you want me to tell Miranda? I can give her the highlights so she doesn't worry."

"Um…" She tried to imagine her mother worrying about her and came up blank.

"You sound really groggy. You should rest. I love you and I'll talk to you soon."

Before Amelia could contemplate a reply, the call ended. She pulled it away from her ear and stared at the screen as though it might offer the reassurances Veronica hadn't. She couldn't decide whether to be upset or tell herself it wasn't that big a deal. Since trying was making her headache worse, she gave up. Nana would make her feel better, especially if she didn't tell Nana about her conversation with Veronica.

"Knock, knock." The greeting came with a gentle rap on the door.

She thought maybe it was the doctor, but the voice felt strangely familiar. And did doctors say, "Knock, knock"? "Yes?"

As soon as the woman stepped all the way into the room, Amelia felt her breath catch. And it had nothing to do with the pain in her chest.

Finn looked even better standing in the doorway of the hospital room than she had when she'd been only inches away, promising to get her out of the crashed U-Haul. Partly it was her confidence that Amelia had felt in the ambulance and could see in her expression now, but her uniform didn't hurt either. Dark navy cargo pants, white button-down shirt with Denver Paramedic patches on both shoulders, and a trim navy vest perfectly suited Finn's taller-than-average build. Professional and undeniably sexy. Especially when she smiled right at Amelia.

"Hey, there. It's good to see you with your eyes open."

"You too. I mean, your eyes were open before but…It's good to see you too." As nice as it was to have a second chance to appreciate her, Amelia couldn't help wondering what Finn was doing in her hospital room.

"How are you feeling?"

"Like I was hit by a truck." It felt like a joke now, which was maybe a bit macabre, but whatever.

"I bet. You took a pretty nasty hit."

Details of riding in the back of the ambulance took shape. Embarrassment wasn't far behind. Should she apologize? Pretend her dotty ramblings never happened? And had she sung to Finn? Hopefully she'd imagined that part.

"I don't usually check on patients I transport, but I wanted to let you know about your cat."

Percy. She'd been worried about him and forgotten all about him in a matter of minutes, like her brain wasn't firing on all cylinders. At least now it made sense why Finn was here. "Where is he? Is he okay?"

She must have looked on the verge of a meltdown because Finn crossed the room and took her hand. Either that or Finn was about to deliver awful news. "He's fine."

For the first time since waking up, relief washed through her. "Really?"

Finn perched on the edge of the bed and nodded. Amelia tried not to notice the tattoo that encircled her forearm or the way her muscles shifted under it. "I took him to the vet just to be sure. They're going to keep him until you can have someone pick him up. They do boarding and I took my cat there before she died, so I can vouch for them."

Whether it was knowing Percy was safe or hearing that Finn's cat had died—at some point—she couldn't say. Or maybe it was Finn's kindness. Whatever it was, it opened a torrent of emotions, complete with tears, that she could neither explain nor contain.

"Shh, it's okay." Finn scooted closer and pulled her into a gentle hug. "You're okay. He's okay. It's all going to be okay."

For a second, she let herself sink into the embrace. Finn's grasp wasn't firm, but her body was. It was nice. Maybe a little too nice. Amelia sucked in a breath and tried to get a grip. First, because crying in front of a gorgeous woman who'd literally come to her rescue was next-level pathetic. Second, because crying made her head, her ribs, and any number of vital organs protest in pain. "Sorry."

Finn pulled back and looked at her with an intensity that, under other circumstances, would make her insides melt. Even under the current circumstances, Finn's bright blue eyes broke past all her defenses.

"You don't need to say you're sorry. You've had a really crappy day."

She had. And somehow this complete stranger understood that, not to mention what she needed, better than her own girlfriend. She took a deep breath and shoved that fact aside. Later. She'd deal with that later. "I really can't thank you enough."

"I was happy to help. Just don't tell my boss. Animals aren't supposed to ride in the bus." Finn's smirk said more than her words.

"Let me guess, Percy wasn't your first?"

Finn brushed a finger across her lips and winked. "I don't know what you mean."

A small giggle escaped before she could stop it. "Your secret is safe with me."

"So, how are you? Have you seen the doctor yet?"

Amelia shook her head. "The nurse said they'd be by soon. Mostly I'm worried about my leg."

"Yeah, I'm guessing you're looking at surgery. But this is the best hospital in town. They'll take good care of you."

She felt herself blanch at the word *surgery.* "Do you really think that might—"

"Amelia?"

"Nana?" She'd know Nana's voice anywhere, even if her being there didn't compute.

"Oh, Sweet Pea. Are you okay? I got here as fast as I could."

"How?" In addition to knowing where to find her, there was also the matter of her not driving.

"Some veterinarian called me. They somehow got my number through Percy."

Either the story made no sense or her brain was more addled than she thought.

Finn stood and Amelia tried not to notice the loss of her warm, solid proximity. "Oh. I suggested they scan for a microchip."

The dots connected. "And I have Nana's number listed." Because Nana's landline was pretty much the most unchanging thing in her universe.

"Maybe also don't tell my boss I disclosed where you'd been transported in the event they got a hit." Finn's casual shrug was quickly becoming one of her favorite things.

"I'm sorry, I don't believe we've met." Like a sensor picking up a new target, Nana's attention shifted. "I'm Edith, Amelia's grandmother."

"Finn. It's a pleasure to meet you." Finn stuck out her hand and Nana shook it like they were meeting at a cocktail party.

"And you are?"

Finn smiled. Amelia seriously needed to stop noticing her smile. "I'm the paramedic who responded to the call."

"Oh, I do love meeting a hero." Nana offered a sly smile of her own. If Amelia wasn't mistaken, she also batted her eyelashes.

"Just doing my job." Finn glanced at her watch. "Which I definitely need to get back to."

Nana looked Finn up and down. "That's a shame. Do you have a card?"

Finn looked confused. "A card?"

"So we could track you down to offer a proper thank-you."

Finn blushed, and it was almost as attractive as her smile. "You really don't have to…"

She trailed off in the wake of Nana's withering stare. Amelia chuckled. Finn looked around, then grabbed the pen and notepad next to the bed. She scribbled off her information and handed it to Nana.

"Thank you." Nana nodded with satisfaction.

Amelia wasn't sure whether to be delighted or mortified she now had the ability to stay in touch with Finn. "And thank you for everything. I'm pretty sure you went above and beyond."

Finn's smile was playful this time. If Amelia didn't know better, she might even call it flirtatious. "My pleasure. I hope your recovery is quick."

She left and Amelia found herself staring at the doorway, almost sad to see her go.

"Well, she seems nice. Cute too."

"Nana." Even if her thoughts weren't so very different, she used her scolding tone on principle.

"What? I'm only expressing an opinion." Nana waved a hand back and forth. "But what am I doing, talking about cute paramedics? How are you? What hurts? Is anything broken?"

Right. She was in the hospital, injured. "I think my foot is, but I'm still waiting for the doctor. And it hurts to take a deep breath."

Nana tutted. "My poor girl. At least you are, and were, in good hands. Have you spoken to Veronica yet?"

With Finn's visit and Nana's arrival, she'd almost managed to forget about her conversation with Veronica. "I tried calling her but…I think she was busy at a reception or something."

She hated even a partial lie, but it would save both her and Nana some grief. Nana made a face but didn't say anything, which was enough to assure her she'd made the right decision. Besides, they had more important things to focus on. Like figuring out when she could go home.

As if summoned by her impatience, a petite dark-haired woman in glasses and a white lab coat appeared. "Ms. Stone. I'm Dr. Singh. How are you feeling?"

She refrained from making her hit-by-a-truck joke, even though she planned to do so at least a few more times before this was all said and done. "I'm okay, I think."

"That's the pain medication talking." Dr. Singh smiled.

Amelia cringed. "How bad is it?"

"You have a mild concussion, which means I don't want you watching TV, reading on a screen, or even being on your phone if you can avoid it. But that should be the only rule for the next three days. I doubt you'll have problems after that. With your head, anyway. Unfortunately, your ankle is a different story." She took a deep breath. "You have a complex fracture. We're going to need to put in a couple of pins for it to heal correctly."

Pins. That had to mean surgery. She gulped and tried not to look like a terrified little kid.

"It's routine but does require general anesthesia. We have you on the schedule for tomorrow unless there are complicating factors we're not aware of. Any chance you might be pregnant?"

Despite the spike in her anxiety, the question made her snort. "No. No chance."

"Okay. I'll order the standard bloodwork and we'll be good to go. If you want to see the X-rays, the orthopedist will be happy to show you them when he stops by to go over the plan."

Did she? For some reason, that didn't freak her out the way blood sometimes did.

"Any questions?"

So, so many questions. But none the efficient Dr. Singh could answer. "I don't think so."

"Is this your next of kin?" Dr. Singh angled her head toward Nana.

"Yes." She didn't hesitate for a second.

"Good. She'll be able to come and go to see you with the exception of the OR and recovery."

Amelia nodded. Everything about her situation was becoming uncomfortably real. "How long before I drive?"

Dr. Singh looked at her with sympathy. "If everything goes well, the cast will come off in three to four weeks. Then you'll move to a fancy boot for at least another three. And you should anticipate a month or two of PT before you have your normal range of motion back."

Fuck. "Okay. Thanks."

Dr. Singh offered her and Nana a smile and nod, then left. Amelia shook her head, her mind racing. A cast probably also meant crutches. How was she going to manage all the stairs at Veronica's place?

"I can see your wheels turning. You're going to give yourself a headache."

She didn't have the heart to tell Nana that ship had sailed. "You're supposed to have cataract surgery and I'm supposed to drive you there. And my new apartment—on the third floor— doesn't have an elevator. And I have no clue where any of my things are."

Her voice cracked on the last bit and tears once again threatened.

"You'll stay with me. No arguments. I'll bake a pie for my neighbor, Henry, and he'll be my chauffeur for the surgery. That man will do anything for pie."

"Everyone loves your pies, Nana, but—"

"No buts. Then I'll be cleared to drive a couple of days after that. I'll get Percy and bring him home with me and we'll track down your things."

As it so often did, Nana's no-nonsense approach to get through problems gave her courage. She hoped one day to have half the grit Nana did. "I'm so lucky to have you."

Nana squeezed her hand. "We're lucky to have each other."

She wasn't sure truer words had ever been spoken. She let herself trust, for at least a moment, that everything was going to work out. "Yeah."

"Now, not to be a Negative Nancy, but you look terrible. I'm going to go so you can get some rest. I'll be back in the morning."

If she weren't struggling to keep her eyes open, she might have argued. Whatever they'd given her for the pain was good stuff. "Okay."

Nana smiled, clearly pleased with having her plan taken at face value. She crossed the room and pressed a gentle kiss to Amelia's temple. "I love you, Sweet Pea."

The pet name made her smile. Nana had given it to her as a kid—before she knew it was a flower and thought being called a vegetable was the funniest thing ever. "I love you too, Celery."

When Nana left, she took a moment to take stock of herself. The aches were definitely there. And she couldn't wiggle her right toes. What a mess.

She closed her eyes and tried to think happy thoughts. Like being curled up in bed with Veronica or drinking coffee together in her—their—ultra-modern kitchen. Sitting on the sofa with a book in one hand and Percy curled up in her lap. It didn't take long for her to drift toward sleep. Her body relaxed and the worries faded. But instead of all the images she'd managed to conjure, it was Finn's smile she carried with her to sleep.

CHAPTER FOUR

"Earth to Finn. You want the yerba mate or the kombucha?"

Finn snapped out of her daydream when Toni dropped an ice-cold bottle into her lap. "Christ, what the hell is this?"

"Kombucha."

"I thought you were getting us coffee."

Toni motioned to the unfinished report on the console between them. "And I thought you were writing up that last call. Try it. It's better for you than coffee."

Finn picked up the bottle and turned it sideways. She had been writing up the report but her mind wandered to Amelia. Again. "There's something floating in this."

"Supposed to be like that." Toni popped the lid on her drink and took a sip. "Mmm. Mah-tay." She drew out the word as she closed her eyes.

Finn snagged the yerba mate out of Toni's hands and tossed her the kombucha. "You get the drink with the floaties. And tomorrow—real coffee. With donuts. I can't handle all this healthy stuff."

"You know you'd be able to lift more if your body wasn't running on carbs and processed sugars. Might even be better on the slopes."

"I do fine on the slopes, thank you very much." Finn took a sip of the mate and struggled to swallow. She stuck out her tongue. "Do you actually like this?"

"Yes."

"Your hippie girlfriend is starting to rub off on you."

"Call her what you want—at least I have a girlfriend." Toni dodged Finn's half-hearted shoulder jab and laughed. "I might be eating healthy, but I'm also getting laid every day. When's the last time you got some?"

"I'm not answering that." It wasn't that she was a prude. In fact, after her breakup with Nadia, she'd gone on a six-month spree that left her wondering who she *hadn't* slept with. But now she was in a holding pattern. And although she wasn't certain what she was looking for, or if she was even looking, she'd needed a break from the pickup bars and the dating apps. "You seriously have sex every day?"

Toni took a big swig of the kombucha and smacked her lips. "Don't knock hippie-chicks. You know Sierra's got friends. I could hook you up. Blind date?"

"Thanks, but no thanks." It wasn't the hippie part. Toni was twenty-three and Finn guessed that her girlfriend was close to the same age. She had almost a decade on them. The one time they'd all gone out for drinks, she'd felt like the chaperone. A little too old and not nearly cool enough. Aside from not wanting any part in a blind date, she wanted someone at least as mature as she was. Hopefully more so. But she was still on the fence about dating at all. "I like my life the way it is. I don't need a girlfriend."

It sounded rehearsed, but still felt true. Mostly, anyway.

People her age were supposed to be married. That's what everyone, including her parents, told her. And it'd been long enough since her breakup with Nadia that she ought to be putting herself out there. Still, she argued she didn't need anyone. Her life was full: good job, circle of friends, and Rascal, who gave her unconditional love in a way that only a cattle dog rescue could. Plus, any time she wanted, she could hop in her truck and take off for the mountains to spend the day skiing. Or biking, depending on the season. She didn't need anything more.

"You don't miss the sex?"

Finn sighed. "That I miss." And maybe that was why her body kept reminding her how good it had felt to sit next to Amelia. Considering how brief their encounter had been, she'd thought of her way too many times since she'd said goodbye in the hospital room. Simply sitting next to someone shouldn't have been enough to give her warm fuzzies that distracted her for the rest of the day. Of course, she'd also held her hand. And hugged her. Probably she shouldn't have done that, but she hugged plenty of patients.

"What about the cat lady from that U-Haul accident? You two had something going on…"

Toni had a sixth sense sometimes. Annoyingly so. "She had one cat. I don't think that makes her a cat lady."

"Did you get her number?"

"No. I'm not going to ask out a patient." Finn hesitated. "But I did give her mine."

Toni hooted, nearly spilling kombucha as she threw her arms up in the air. "Give it up for da' boss! Damn, I knew it. Soon as I saw her, I thought, 'Oh, this chick's for Finn.' There was something about her. I knew she'd be your type. So what happened? She asked you straight up for your number?"

"Not exactly. Her grandma asked for it."

"Oh." Toni's face fell. "Huh. Grandma got your number?" She scratched her cheek and her brow furrowed.

Finn wished Amelia had been the one to ask. It would have made for a better story. "Hey, don't hurt yourself thinking too hard. Grandma wanted to send me a thank-you note. That's why she asked."

"That's all? You sure?"

"Yep." No point denying it. The radio light blinked and the voice of dispatch crackled. "Ready to get back to work?"

"Guess so." Toni latched her seat belt and pulled the location dispatch sent up on the screen. "After we get off, I think you should go check on cat lady. See if she's still stuck in the hospital."

Finn zipped in front of a car, switching on the sirens. "Why?"

"You're a catch. Seeing you again will remind her of that. I'm telling you, boss, I got a feeling about this."

A little part of her wanted Toni to be right, but she knew better. Although she didn't need to follow up on the case, she'd asked around and found out that Amelia had been scheduled for surgery on the ankle. Other than that, she'd only had a mild concussion. Chances were, she'd be discharged by the time their shift finished. Not that it mattered since Amelia wasn't single anyway. "She's got a girlfriend, remember?"

"Right. The one she met six weeks ago. You and I both know that won't last."

"Well, I'm not getting in the middle of it. I'm not that person."

"Yeah—you're the person who's single all the time."

Finn chuckled. "Nice. What else you got?"

"All right, I didn't want to do this, but it's for your own best interest." Toni cleared her throat. "I dare you."

"You dare me? To do what?"

"I dare you to go check on her. See if she got discharged or if she's still there. You do that and I'll buy you a donut."

"And if I don't?"

"No donuts."

Finn chuckled again. "Damn. And I really wanted a donut. Oh, well."

"Ugh. You're impossible. Fine. Don't have sex for the rest of your life. See if I care." Toni folded her arms and slumped in her seat.

"You're cute when you sulk." And if Finn had ever been attracted to anyone as masculine leaning as she was, working with Toni might be a problem. Fortunately, she liked femmes. But she could still appreciate someone attractive. Between Toni's deep brown complexion, perfect pair of dimples, and lanky build, she had no shortage of admirers. "Really brings out the whole baby-dyke-crossed-with-a-tough-stud thing."

"I don't even want to talk to you right now."

Finn laughed. "I'm sorry I'm letting you down."

"Whatever. It's your donut."

* * *

By the end of their shift, Finn wanted pizza more than a donut. Unfortunately, it wasn't easy finding a slice at nine in the morning. She'd tried before and ended up disappointed.

Their last call was a transfer—some guy had a heart attack during a routine physical and needed a ride from one hospital to the other. Finn thanked her lucky stars for an easy end to the night and tried not to think about the fact that since she was at the same hospital as Amelia, she could easily check in on her.

"Man, I'm beat." Toni rubbed her eyes. "All I want to do is take a long shower and crash on my bed."

"I'll take that and a slice of pepperoni pizza." Finn pressed the elevator button and watched the numbers light up.

"Pizza sounds good. Have you tried a cauliflower crust?"

Cauliflower anything got a nope. "Let me guess—your hippie girlfriend put you onto that?"

Toni pulled out her phone. "I'm gonna find us a place with cauliflower crusts that's open early. I really want pizza now."

"Please let me keep something sacred. Just pepperoni pizza. No cauliflower."

"It's delicious. You'll see."

"Y'all having pizza for breakfast?" Shanisse raised an eyebrow. She'd come up behind them to wait for the elevator. "Don't get me wrong—I love pizza. But I'm with Finn on the cauliflower crust. Just no."

"Thank you. I need some backup with this one." Before Finn could say more, Toni started in on the merits of cauliflower and Shanisse laughed when Finn groaned. "Last night you wouldn't let me have donuts and now you try and take pizza away from me?"

"What's wrong with you?" Shanisse playfully batted Toni's shoulder, which earned her a wide smile. "You know you can't say no to someone who needs a donut."

Toni tried her line about the dangers of processed sugars, but Shanisse gave her a withering look. Finally, Toni raised up her hands in surrender. "All right, let's all go get pizza and donuts."

Shanisse winked at Finn. "I got your back, hon."

Shanisse was one of the nurses who had a thing for Toni. Not only was she hot, she was one of the best nurses Finn had come across. If Toni didn't already have a steady girlfriend, Finn would have encouraged her.

When the elevator door slid open, Shanisse popped in and pressed the button for the third floor. "Which floor?"

"Lobby." Toni stepped in and made room for Finn. "You know it's dinnertime for us."

"You still trying to make excuses for cauliflower pizza?" Shanisse laughed. "Wish I was going out with you two instead of just coming in. Now you got me thinking about pizza...mmm."

Finn straightened up, aware that she'd been included in Shanisse's gaze and remembering then that Shanisse had winked at her too. Maybe she'd read the situation wrong and Shanisse was into her instead of Toni? She smiled but didn't have a quick comeback to keep the flirty vibe going. Six months off sex and her mojo checked out right when she needed it most.

The elevator stopped on the third floor and Shanisse stepped out. She looked back at Finn and said, "Y'all don't have to be strangers, you know. Come say hi."

As soon as she'd gone, Toni clapped Finn's shoulder. "That makes two women this week who've got the hots for you."

"You think Shanisse likes me? I thought she was into you."

"Oh, come on, boss. She practically spelled it out."

Finn warmed to the idea. She'd noticed Shanisse for a while now but didn't figure the attraction went both ways. "Huh. Okay."

Toni pressed her palm to her forehead and gave an exasperated groan. "That's all you got? For someone so smart, you can be completely clueless sometimes. Plenty of women would go out with you. *If* you asked. Do you even want a girlfriend?"

Finn lifted a shoulder and Toni seemed to take that to mean she needed more prodding. "It'd be good for you to ask someone out and you know it. It'd be good for me too—you'd be less grumpy if you were getting laid. And I'm not talking about a hookup. You need a real date with someone who's got more than sex to offer."

Finn didn't respond. Saying she didn't know how much more she had to offer would only get Toni going on a psychoanalysis kick. She hadn't told Toni about Nadia, or about how she hadn't had a girlfriend since. Because she knew a therapy session would follow if she admitted any of it, all she'd told Toni was that she liked being single.

Over a year had passed since Nadia had moved out. Plenty of time for her to get past Nadia's cheating and their six years together that had amounted to nothing. She hadn't thought she'd ever get over it, but months of messing around with strangers in clubs had helped quite a bit. Well, it'd helped her ego anyway. It hadn't helped convince her that relationships were a good idea. The problem was, only sex wasn't that satisfying. She craved the emotional connection too. Which was why her clubbing days had petered out.

Her mind wandered to the feel of Amelia cuddling up to her. When Amelia had met her gaze, eyes wet with tears, her heart had leapt to her throat. Their connection—however brief—had been undeniable.

Toni pressed the button for the second floor.

"You got someone to see on the second floor?"

Toni ignored the question and stared at the ceiling.

The door opened and Finn eyed Toni. "Are you getting out?"

"No. You are. Cat lady got moved to the second floor after her surgery." Toni pressed the hold button and the doors remained open.

Finn eyed the hall. The second floor was a bustle of activity in the mornings. Nurses scurried every which way and patients were whisked in wheelchairs off to the surgical suites. "She's probably long gone."

"Go find out."

"What's the point?" She couldn't actually ask Amelia out on a date even if she got up the courage to do it. "She's not single."

"Not now. But would it hurt to be someone she remembers when her U-Haul disaster ends?" When Finn only shook her head, Toni pushed her out of the elevator. "Go check on her. We both know you want to."

It wasn't until the door was closing that she realized Toni had snagged the keys off her belt. She spun around and Toni held them up, a smile so big her dimples showed. "This is for your own good. Meet you out front in twenty."

She could chase Toni down but didn't have the energy for it. She looked up as a woman stepped forward to press the elevator call button. It wasn't Amelia, but how much she'd hoped it was spoke volumes.

She glanced at the nurses' station and debated if Toni's advice meant crossing a line. The problem was, she'd felt a connection to Amelia she couldn't seem to ignore. It was like their paths were meant to cross. But no way would she get involved with a woman who was already in a relationship.

An older man in a hospital gown limped past her, face downturned like he had the weight of the world on his shoulders. Finn watched him disappear into one of the rooms and made up her mind in that moment. The memory of being stuck in a hospital room for weeks had faded but it was still there. A friendly face could change a whole day. And she could certainly be a friend without crossing any lines.

Decision made, every step felt like a shot of adrenaline charging through her. By the time she made it to the counter, she didn't feel the least bit tired. "Could you tell me if a patient's been discharged? Amelia Stone. I think she had surgery on her ankle yesterday."

She tried not to tap her foot as she waited for the nurse to check her computer. The nurse squinted and then ran her finger along a line on the screen. "Looks like she got discharged this morning. Do you need me to pass on anything to the doctor on the case?"

"No, it's fine."

Finn stepped away from the counter, wishing the fact that she'd missed out on seeing Amelia one last time didn't make her chest feel hollow. At least Toni would get off her back and she could try forgetting about any connection. She started back to the elevator but stopped before she'd gone more than ten feet.

Amelia sat in a wheelchair in one of the rooms, purse in her lap and a phone in hand as if about to make a call. Her gaze, however, was on Finn.

"Hey." Finn walked up to the doorway. Out of the hospital garb and wearing a skirt and blouse, Amelia looked almost ready to face the world. But Finn couldn't help noticing the bruise on her forehead, only partially concealed by the way she'd brushed her hair, or the red abrasion on her cheek. "Nice cast."

"Thanks. I try to stay up with the latest trends." When Amelia smiled, the tension in her face tugged at Finn's heart.

"How are you feeling?"

"Tired but not awful. Grateful, really. Could have been a lot worse." Amelia pushed back a lock of hair that had fallen forward and the bruise on her forehead was more noticeable.

"That's a good attitude." Finn knew the energy it took to pretend to be fine and she wanted to tell Amelia she didn't need to pretend with her. "You waiting for Veronica?"

"You remembered my girlfriend's name?"

"You did say it quite a few times."

"Right." Amelia's blush came quick. She opened and closed her mouth. "My memory of the ride is a little fuzzy. I hope I didn't say anything too embarrassing."

"Not too embarrassing." Finn didn't need to tell her that she'd called her cute. Or said she'd date her if Veronica wasn't in the picture. None of that mattered since Veronica *was* in the picture.

"Thanks again for everything. You made one of the worst days of my life a little bit better. And, according to my nana, saved my life."

At least Grandma was a fan. "That might be going a little far but I'm glad I could help." Probably more than Amelia realized, in fact. "Anyway, I should go."

"Watch out for distracted dump truck drivers."

"I will. Good luck with your ankle." Finn started to leave but chanced one look back at Amelia. She'd dropped her gaze to her phone and her brow furrowed. "Is Veronica running late?"

"She couldn't get her flight changed." Amelia straightened. "It's no big deal. She'll be home Friday."

"Oh…do you have another ride coming?"

"I had one." She glanced at her phone again. "I'm working on Plan B. Or maybe it's Plan C at this point."

"Do you want me to give you a lift?"

"No, no, I'll be fine. I don't need another trip in an ambulance. Like everything else in my life at the moment, I'm sure it will work out somehow. It just sucks temporarily."

"At least you're moving in with Veronica. That's good news, right?"

Amelia hesitated. "She lives in a loft. Third floor. It's gorgeous but there's no elevator."

"Oh." Finn eyed the cast. Amelia's toes stuck out, but it went all the way up to her knee. No way was she climbing stairs. "Where are you going then?"

"My nana's house. But she had cataract surgery yesterday and can't drive. I thought I had a friend coming but they got tied up. Which is why I'm working on Plan C." Amelia forced a smile. "Anyway, today I'm not going to look pathetic in front of you. Or cry. Since I already did that."

"You got hit by a dump truck. Give yourself a little slack. That"—she motioned to the cast—"is temporary. But what happened to the rest of you is going to take a while to heal."

Amelia tilted her head. "What do you mean?"

"I mean that you're gonna feel like crying for no reason at all. An accident like the one you went through messes with your head. And even if everything seems minor now, the recovery will take longer than you think. You'll be mad at your body and you'll feel like your ankle is never quite the same. You'll probably have nightmares and you'll be scared the first time you drive again."

"Wow. You're a ray of sunshine this morning. You always like this?"

Finn chuckled. "Pretty much. I've also been through something similar. No dump truck. Just me, my skis, and a tree. But I got a pretty cast too."

"Pretty?"

"That's what my counselor called mine." Finn smiled. "I do recommend talking to someone. Even if you don't think you need to now." She'd needed it for sure, though she hadn't wanted to admit it. "You know, I really could give you a ride. In my truck—not the ambulance. My shift's over anyway."

"I can't ask you to do that."

"Then don't ask. I'll volunteer and all you'll have to say is okay. It's no hassle at all. After I drop off the ambulance, I have to drive this way to get home anyway."

Amelia didn't agree or disagree, and Finn wondered if she'd pushed too hard. She'd already blurred the lines between professional and personal.

"But if you don't feel comfortable—"

"It's not that." Amelia pinched the bridge of her nose, clearly trying to hold back tears. "Ugh. I think the pain meds are making me emotional."

Finn nodded. "That's real."

Amelia sniffed and met Finn's gaze. "Thank you for offering, really, but I'm sure you have better things to do."

"Actually, I don't."

Amelia laughed. The sound seemed to burst out of her and Finn couldn't help smiling. "You're only saying that to make me feel better, but thank you. You're a genuinely nice person."

A ping of guilt mixed with the stirrings of attraction. Maybe it was a problem but not one she couldn't handle. "So, is that a yes?"

"Yes. But you have to promise to let me make it up to you."

CHAPTER FIVE

Amelia sat in the wheelchair and did her best not to fidget. Why had she said yes to Finn? She could have gotten an Uber. But then a stranger would be jostling her in and out of their car. And what if the hospital wouldn't discharge her without a more legit ride? Even having to ask felt humiliating.

It was fine. It would be fine. It was only a ride. So what if her girlfriend wasn't the one helping her? So what if the way Finn looked at her made her pulse kick up a notch or two? None of that had to mean anything.

She looked at her phone again, as though Veronica might have texted that she'd been careless and insensitive and was on her way to get her right this very second. The only thing staring back at her from the screen was Percy's sleeping face. She blew out a breath and tried to shake herself out of it. No crying on the paramedic. Not today at least.

"You ready?"

She looked up and found Finn offering her an encouraging smile. She plastered on one of her own and nodded. "Yep."

Per hospital protocol, she had to be wheeled out to the waiting vehicle. Something about liability. Finn shouldered the small bag Nana had brought with her change of clothes and handed Amelia the standard-issue pair of crutches. "Please keep your arms and legs inside the ride at all times."

Amelia laughed in spite of herself. Outside, a handful of cars lined the circular drive. One old guy and two women holding newborns seemed to be in the same boat as her. She found that oddly reassuring. Only when Finn brought the wheelchair to a stop did she look at the vehicle waiting for her. The truck was big, beautiful, and navy blue. Funny, she'd never thought of trucks as beautiful before. "This is yours?"

"Don't be intimidated. It's got more legroom than a sedan."

It wasn't the legroom she was worried about. No, it was hauling her clumsy ass up into the passenger seat with only one good leg. "Um."

"Here, hand me those." Finn took the crutches and tucked them, along with Amelia's bag, in the back seat. Once that was done, she came around to Amelia's side. "Okay. Hold on to this arm and I'm going to wrap my other one around you."

Her throat went dry. Even if she'd wanted to protest, there were no words. Just the feel of Finn's muscular forearm under her hand and the sensation of being lifted. Oh, and Finn's smell. Something she shouldn't be noticing at all and definitely shouldn't be attracted to.

The next thing Amelia knew, she sat perched in the passenger seat. Finn came around and climbed in next to her. "All right?"

She wasn't entirely sure but nodded. "Uh-huh."

Finn started the engine but didn't put the truck in drive. "I don't know where we're going."

Amelia resisted a facepalm. "Right. Sorry."

She rattled off Nana's address and Finn, who'd been holding her phone, set it down. "That's right down the road from my apartment. We're practically neighbors."

"Small world." What an inane thing to say. But for the life of her, she couldn't think of anything more interesting or clever. Hopefully, this fuzzy-brained state would prove temporary.

"So, I know you mentioned you worked for the city. But what do you do?" Finn asked as she pulled into traffic.

When had she told Finn she worked for the city? Maybe on the ambulance ride? Which raised the question, what else had she admitted? "I run the Office for the Aging."

"Oh, that's cool. Those programs and services make such a difference for so many people."

The enthusiasm in Finn's voice seemed genuine, which caught her off guard. She couldn't help but smile. "They do."

They pulled onto the freeway and Finn focused on the traffic. It wasn't until after they'd exited and started down Nana's road that Finn spoke up again. "I do meal delivery for hospice. I bet there's some overlap in our people."

It was possible, but it wasn't like she'd ever run into Finn in real life. "Are all paramedics as knight-in-shining-armor as you?"

A hint of color rose in Finn's cheeks and Amelia wanted to kick herself. She'd only meant a gentle tease. Before she could apologize, Finn pulled into Nana's driveway. She cut the engine and came around to Amelia's side, lifting her down like a princess out of a carriage.

Amelia shook her head. What the hell was wrong with her?

Finn handed her the crutches and grabbed her bag. She hobbled up the front walk, feeling absolutely, positively not at all like a princess. Unfortunate, but much more what she was used to. She needed Finn's help again opening the front door, but as soon as they stepped inside the aroma of Nana's brownies wrapped her up like a warm hug. One sniff and she didn't know whether to laugh or cry.

"You okay?" Finn's look of sympathy almost pushed her over the edge.

She managed a nod and then lifted her head a little higher. She'd get better with the crutches. It would take time, but she'd gotten through worse. "Nana?"

Nana rushed in from the kitchen, wiping her hands on a dish towel. "Oh, you're home. I've been so worried about you trying to catch a ride."

"Should you be baking?"

Nana tutted. "My eyesight is blurry. I'm not an invalid."

She did laugh then. "Really? That's the card you're going to play today?"

Nana shrugged. "You started it." She glanced behind Amelia and her face lit up. "Finn, what a pleasant surprise! What are you doing here?"

"I happened to be getting off shift right when Amelia was discharged. I offered her a ride."

Nana beamed. "Oh, that's so kind of you."

"It was no problem at all." Finn lifted the bag a few inches. "Where would you like me to leave this?"

"Anywhere is fine." Amelia tried to shift out of the way and only ended up teetering awkwardly on the crutches. "Thank you again for the ride."

"You can't drop the bag and run." Nana gave Amelia an admonishing look as if she was responsible for Finn even considering that plan. "You have to at least stay for a cup of coffee. And a brownie. I'm taking a batch out of the oven now."

Finn looked to her. Most people simply got bowled over by Nana, but Finn seemed to be checking in with her first and Amelia had to give her credit for that. "Nana does make amazing brownies."

"If that's what I'm smelling, I don't actually want to say no. Thank you, missus…"

"No missus here. Call me Edith."

Nana hustled back to the kitchen. Amelia eyed the sofa, then the bag still in Finn's hands. "You really can put that down anywhere." If part of her wanted to protest about Finn staying any longer than was necessary, part of her was quietly celebrating. Simply standing next to Finn did things to her libido that would have made her embarrassed under normal circumstances. Fortunately, this wasn't a normal circumstance and she could blame the pain meds. At least she was home in one piece and Finn staying for a brownie might count as the requisite thank-you. Then they could part ways with nothing owed.

As it occurred to her she'd likely never see Finn again, she had to fight back a wave of sadness. Again, what the hell was wrong with her? She was in a satisfying and happy relationship with Veronica.

"You should sit, get that foot elevated to keep the swelling down." Finn gestured to the sofa.

"Right." She inched her way toward it and, lacking any graceful alternative, dropped herself onto the cushions with an oof.

"Do you remember the last time you took meds? You definitely want to stay ahead of the pain."

She looked at her wrist, only to realize she wasn't wearing a watch. "Huh."

"Where are your discharge papers?"

Her purse was on the other side of the room. She sighed, then pointed. "There."

Finn didn't seem to mind being her gofer, grabbing it from the table and handing it to her. "Here you go."

She riffled through, pulling out the paperwork and the two bottles of pills. Only she couldn't quite get her eyes to focus. "I hate to be this pathetic, but…"

Finn reached for the paperwork. "I got you."

Amelia closed her eyes. She'd officially reached peak pathetic. "Thanks."

After skimming the pages, Finn looked at each of the bottles and shook one of the pills free. "Let me get you some water."

"Got it, got it." Nana reappeared from the kitchen with a glass of water and the plate of brownies. She moved more like an agile waitress than someone recovering from cataract surgery. "Here you go, dear."

Amelia took the pill while Nana bustled back to the kitchen for the coffee. Finn studied Amelia for a second. "It sucks, but it's going to be okay."

She appreciated the kind words, more than she wanted to admit. "Your bedside manner is better than all the doctors at the hospital."

Finn flashed a grin that packed a serious punch. If she were single, she'd have half a mind to… Amelia shook off the thought and cursed the painkillers. She wasn't single. She had an amazing girlfriend who loved her and would be home soon.

She situated herself sideways on the sofa, leg propped on a pillow, and reminded herself to focus on that. Not on Finn sitting close enough to tickle her toes if she wanted to. Nana returned with the coffee and then offered up the plate mounded with more brownies than they could possibly eat. Which was saying something, given the number of brownies she could put away on a bad day.

Finn accepted one and took a bite. She let out a moan of pleasure that had Amelia thinking about anything but brownies. "This might be the most delicious thing I've ever put in my mouth."

Nana waved off the compliment. "You've led a deprived life, then."

"Apparently." Finn turned to Amelia. "It's too bad these don't have pot in them. They'd help you forget all about your foot."

"Ha ha. Very funny."

"You know what they say. When in Colorado…" Finn licked a crumb from her finger and Amelia had this flash of wishing it was her finger between Finn's lips. She shook it off. Definitely the painkillers.

"I've never baked with pot before." Nana tapped a finger on the arm of her chair. "Maybe I should."

"I'm not eating pot brownies." It came out a bit more petulantly than she would have liked.

Finn got a serious look on her face. "You might not, but the hospice patients I visit sure would. I've been trying to recruit folks to bake for the program I volunteer with, but I'd never thought about that angle. Pot brownies would be a win-win."

Nana raised her hand like an eager student. "I could bake them."

"Nana." If she'd been petulant before, now she had a scolding tone.

"What?"

"Where are you going to get pot?" It was a dumb question. They were in Colorado, after all. Still.

Nana gave her an exasperated look. "The marijuana store, obviously. They have those now, you know."

Finn made a noise that was definitely a snort of laughter, even if she tried to cover it up with a cough. Amelia glared at her. "You aren't helping."

Finn had the decency to look cowed. "Sorry. She's right, though. It's like walking into a drugstore. Or, maybe a candy shop is more accurate."

"See?" Nana offered Finn a nod of thanks and Amelia a look of vindication.

"If you'd be willing to do the baking, I'd be happy to bring you what you need. I already deliver edibles to some of the hospice patients, but a lot of them don't have great appetites and don't like the packaged stuff. Homemade brownies would give them the benefits of pot and make them feel loved at the same time."

Well, that was that. No way could she argue with making terminally ill people feel loved. And it wasn't like she had moral objections to marijuana. Honestly, she couldn't figure out why she was being so uptight about the whole thing.

"I do want to be sure I'm using the right stuff. In the right amounts."

Finn nodded with enthusiasm. "Absolutely. I can get some recipes and bring you the ingredients. The program has a budget for supplies, and I don't mind pitching in a little of my own to help with this."

Nana waved her off. "No spending your own money on this."

Amelia's gaze bounced from Finn to Nana as they ironed out the details of days and quantities and THC levels. She couldn't decide if she felt relieved at being left out of the conversation or annoyed. Either way, the back-and-forth gave her a second to think.

Maybe Veronica's opinions had rubbed off on her. She wouldn't begrudge hospice patients, but her general sentiment was that legalization made the state both lazier and stupider. Veronica had patience for neither.

"So, it's settled, then. We'll see you day after tomorrow. Dinner at six." Nana stood, looking satisfied with herself.

"Wait. What?" When did dinner get put on the table?

"Finn's going to have dinner with us when she brings my weed."

That managed to clarify things and confuse the hell out of her at the same time. "I don't understand."

Finn studied her with what looked like concern. "You're probably still a little disoriented from the meds." She nodded as if convincing herself too. "I'm sure you haven't been sleeping well at the hospital. You might want to try taking a nap."

Was that it? She hoped so, because none of this made any sense. Not the least of which, the little bubble of excitement in her chest over the prospect of seeing Finn again. "Maybe you're right."

"I put nice clean sheets on your bed for you," Nana said.

"Can I give you a hand?" Finn asked. "If you're woozy, you don't want to chance taking a spill on those crutches."

She looked at the crutches, propped against the arm of the couch, then at Finn's outstretched hand. "Sure."

Finn helped her up and wrapped an arm around her waist. Like at the hospital, it was hard not to lean into her and soak up the warm certainty of her body. This time she didn't care whether it was the painkillers talking or not. She let herself appreciate how strong Finn felt, and how sexy that was.

In her room, Percy dozed in the middle of the bed. At the sound of them shuffling in, he lifted his head. Finn smiled. "Hey, Percy. It's good to see you, buddy."

Finn remembering Percy's name struck her. Sweet, but personal too. Intimate in a way. She frowned. Maybe Finn was simply one of those people with a photographic memory.

"You're looking a little shaky. Let's get you settled."

Without letting go, Finn pulled back the covers. Percy shifted but didn't jump off the bed. Which was funny considering he pretty much hid anytime she had Veronica over to try to get them acquainted. She hardly noticed being guided into bed but there she was, complete with Finn pulling up the covers.

When Finn sat on the edge of the bed, Percy walked right up to her, pushing his head into the hand she extended for him. "He doesn't like strangers."

Finn's shrug, complete with a playful smirk, didn't help with the thoughts she absolutely should not be having about Finn. "We bonded during a crisis. I'm not a stranger."

No, she wasn't. She'd seen more of Finn in the last week than she had her girlfriend. Even with Veronica in New York, the reality of that didn't sit well. But holding it against Finn wasn't fair either. "Thank you for the ride. For everything."

"My pleasure. Truly." Finn stood and gave Percy a parting pet. "Get some rest. I'll see you Friday."

"Friday?"

"For dinner."

Right. She was supposed to be annoyed about that, but somewhere between the sofa and her bed the irritation had vanished. And even though she hadn't been groggy, her lids felt heavy and her eyes gritty. "Okay."

Finn left and she closed her eyes. And for the second time in as many days, she conjured thoughts of Veronica but carried images of Finn with her to sleep.

CHAPTER SIX

Picking out clothes shouldn't be a big deal. Especially considering her dinner date was an invite from Amelia's grandma, not Amelia. Still, Finn changed twice before settling on blue jeans and a striped button-down that necessitated pulling out the iron, and even then agonized over her choice. The problem was, she couldn't get it out of her head that she was seeing Amelia, not simply having a dinner to discuss pot brownies.

She wanted to look sharp but not dressed up. Anything besides a sweaty uniform would be an improvement, but rather than analyze why she wanted to impress Amelia, she focused on ironing the shirt. Once she'd finished, she slipped it on and then added the leather belt her dad had made for her—complete with the family ranch buckle. She contemplated her reflection in the mirror and didn't hold back a goofy smile that somehow rallied her spirits. She looked ready for a date. Or, if she had her cowboy hat, a barn raising.

At least Amelia wouldn't be expecting her to flirt or act like a smooth cocky butch. All she had to do was relax. *Easier said than done*. She took a deep breath and pocketed her wallet and keys.

Even stopping to pick up a bottle of wine, she made it to Edith's house in under twenty minutes. She knocked on the front door. Did wine imply a date? Hopefully Amelia would think it was simply polite.

Edith opened the door with a warm smile. "Hello, hello."

The house smelled like Italian spices and Finn's stomach rumbled awake. She gave Edith a hug and then glanced around for Amelia. She'd hoped Amelia would be the one to answer so she could gauge if she was really okay with the whole dinner thing. Edith hadn't exactly asked Amelia's opinion when they'd set everything up.

"Amelia's in the back. I've got her helping with the vodka sauce."

Apparently, Edith could tell she'd wanted to see Amelia. Could she also tell she was fighting a crush? It didn't matter, though, since nothing was going to happen. "Vodka sauce?"

Edith took the bottle of wine, nodded approvingly, and patted Finn's cheek. It could have been weird, but it happened so fast Finn didn't have time to do anything more than wonder if when she got old, she'd pat people on the cheek too.

"You've never had vodka sauce?" Edith clicked her tongue. "So deprived. Did you bring the weed?"

Finn took a bottle of what looked like plain cooking oil out of her coat pocket. She felt like a dealer given the way Edith excitedly snatched it out of her hands. It was all legal. She'd even run the idea past her friends who worked in hospice and gotten the go-ahead. Plenty of patients had already been cleared for medical marijuana but the expense—and failing appetite—often meant they didn't try it. "All the recipes say a little of this goes a long way."

"Good. We'll discuss it after dinner." Edith patted her arm this time. "I can't believe you've never had vodka sauce. It's one of Amelia's favorites."

"How is she?"

"Still figuring out the crutches and feeling sorry for herself."

"It's not easy getting around on those. Plus, she's probably still in pain from all the other places that got banged up in the crash."

"I can hear you two, you know," Amelia called. "And I'm not feeling sorry for myself. I just hate these damn crutches."

Amelia appeared in the hallway. She flashed a smile at Finn, balanced on her good foot, and held her crutches up in the air. "See? I'm nearly ready to do a pirouette."

"I don't know what that is, but I wouldn't recommend it."

Ignoring the advice, Amelia hopped on her good foot until she'd completed a spin and awkwardly curtsied. She clearly hadn't meant to be graceful and when she laughed at herself, Finn's heart skipped a beat.

Edith tutted. "Finn, please tell this girl she's going to break her other leg. Then you'll have to throw her over your shoulder and carry her everywhere."

Finn laughed as the pair wagged their fingers at each other. Edith's scolding was as playful as Amelia's pirouette, and Finn felt her nervous energy slip away. What had she been worried about? Tonight would be fine. Like a dinner with friends. Or family, even.

Amelia positioned the crutches back under her arms. Edith grumbled that she'd be the death of her and headed down the hall to the kitchen. Finn glanced from Edith's retreating steps to Amelia. A smile turned up the corner of her lips and instead of looking away or saying something, Amelia held Finn's gaze.

"Hi."

"Hi yourself." Amelia's eyes sparkled. "Thanks for coming tonight. Nana loves to cook for company."

"The house smells amazing. I might like vodka sauce better than brownies."

Amelia gasped. "Blasphemy. There's no better smell than brownies."

"I can think of a few."

"Well, Finn, we might not be able to be friends."

Finn chuckled. "Don't get me wrong, I love chocolate. I even had a dream about you and your grandma's brownies."

"Dreaming about me, huh?" Amelia teased.

"I didn't mean it like that." Finn rushed the words. "It was a totally innocent dream." Maybe it was innocent, but now a blush was heating up her neck and heading right for her cheeks. "We were sitting…somewhere…and there was this big platter of brownies and you were talking."

"Should I ask what I was talking about?" Amelia winked, clearly enjoying her discomfort.

"Um…"

Amelia laughed. "Everyone was dressed in this dream, right?"

Finn's embarrassment melted away as she laughed too. She was certain that Amelia felt the attraction, too, but it had to be a good sign that they could joke about it. Anyway, nothing was going to happen.

"I'm sure we were dressed. Though don't ask me what we were wearing. All I can remember is you and the brownies."

"Not sure that gets you out of trouble."

Amelia laughed again and Finn was swept up in the sound of it. She loved the sound of Amelia's laugh almost as much as how happy she looked in that moment.

"Oh." Amelia pressed her hand to her side. "As nice as it is to laugh, it still hurts."

"Right, bruised ribs. Sorry."

"Don't be sorry. I needed that. But you can't make me laugh again for the rest of the night."

"Lucky for you, I'm usually very serious."

"Very serious, huh? That sounds like a challenge." Amelia leaned on her crutches, her eyes still creased with a smile. "So, you really haven't had vodka sauce?"

"Nope."

"Good. I like being someone's first."

Finn half coughed, half laughed, and Amelia only waggled her eyebrows. It didn't seem fair that Amelia had a girlfriend. Yet that didn't mean they couldn't be friends. Flirting was innocent as long as they didn't take it further. *Right?*

"I'll give you a little taste before dinner to make sure you like it. If you don't, we've got some Alfredo I can heat up instead."

Before she could insist she'd like it, Edith hollered from the kitchen, "This is good wine you brought, Finn. If you two want any, you better hurry."

"Fair warning." Amelia lowered her voice. "Nana can drink anyone under the table." She turned to the kitchen and waved for Finn to follow.

Between the smells of dinner cooking and the clink of dishes as Edith set the table, Finn felt a wave of nostalgia for family meals back home. Edith's farmhouse-style kitchen table was even similar to her mom's. Along with the white cabinets in need of a touch-up coat of paint, older appliances, and countertops more useful than pretty, Finn felt right at home. "How can I help?"

"You don't get to help." Edith pointed to one of the chairs. "Tonight, you're the guest. If I invite you back a second time, you wash dishes."

Amelia quickly added, "Those are the rules. Sit."

Finn took a seat and the glass of wine Amelia handed her. While Edith buzzed between the pantry and the fridge, Amelia sidled up to the stove. She balanced on one crutch, lifted the lid of a pot and sniffed, then reached for a wooden spoon and stirred.

"You sure we can't break the rules this one time? I like being helpful and it looks tricky cooking on one leg."

Amelia waved the spoon. "Unless you're secretly a famous chef, I got this."

"What if I were a famous chef?"

"We'd ask you to leave," Edith piped up.

Finn chuckled. "Definitely not a chef. Honestly, I'd probably only be in your way but it's weird not helping."

"You can handle it one time." Amelia sampled the sauce, nodded her approval, and then set the lid back on the pot. She leaned against the counter and took a sip of wine, regarding Finn as if about to pose a question. When she didn't say anything, Finn fought back the impulse to ask what she was thinking.

"Do you like to cook?" Edith asked.

For a moment, Finn had forgotten it wasn't only her and Amelia in the room. She turned to Edith, reminding her brain she wasn't here for Amelia at all. "Beyond toast and coffee, I don't know how to make much in the kitchen. Mostly I reheat frozen food."

Edith glanced at Amelia, and Finn was aware of some silent communication passing between them. Had she said the wrong thing? Before she could ask, Edith was complaining about a finicky temperature setting on the oven and pulling out a tray of puffy golden pastries. She scooped them off the pan and onto a platter, which she promptly set on the table.

Since her stomach had been rumbling since she'd arrived, Finn didn't hesitate when Edith gestured for her to try one. She popped one in her mouth and then barely held back a moan. A savory blend of cheese, herbs, and crab perfectly complemented a flaky, buttery pastry shell. "Mmm, that's good. What is it?"

"*Amuse-bouche.*" Edith smiled. "It's French for 'eat what the chef puts in front of you.'"

"Don't mind if I do." Finn ate another, this time not holding in her moan.

"Nana, don't fill her up on those. She won't have room for dinner."

"I'll have room. I went to the gym after I finished work this morning. Besides, no one could resist these things. Have you tried them?"

Edith held the platter out for Amelia to take one. She made a moan, too, and closed her eyes. "Nana, I forgot how good those are. Why haven't you made them lately?"

"We didn't have anyone over I wanted to impress." Edith shrugged like that ought to be obvious. "Besides, sometimes you need a little *amuse-bouche* so everyone pays attention to the good thing right in front of their nose."

Amelia's face reddened, but she didn't say anything. Meanwhile, Edith murmured about needing a serving dish and disappeared into the pantry.

Finn wondered if she should say something. Clearly Amelia was uncomfortable. Honestly, so was she. She hadn't agreed to dinner to try to snare Amelia away from her girlfriend. One minute she was certain they had a chance at being friends and the next it seemed they were only tempting disaster. After a moment of indecision, she stood and went to the stove. "Should I not be here? I know you have a girlfriend and I'm not trying to—"

"Ignore Nana. She likes to imagine there's something when there's nothing." Amelia shook her head. "While we're on the subject, I shouldn't have teased you about your dream earlier. I was only joking but…Obviously I'm in a relationship and I shouldn't make those sort of jokes."

"No worries. I get that you weren't serious."

"But I was serious about wanting to thank you for everything you did for me. Coming to check on me was sweet. Giving me a ride home from the hospital was above and beyond. So was taking care of my cat. When you dropped me off here, I was so out of it I can't remember if I even said thank you." She held out the wooden spoon. A dollop of creamy red sauce steamed on the end.

Finn opened her mouth and Amelia raised the spoon to her lips. Tomatoes, spices, and heavy cream had never tasted so good. "Oh. Damn." She closed her eyes and focused on the flavors. When she opened them, her pulse quickened as Amelia stared back at her.

"Is that a good damn?"

"If you didn't have a girlfriend, I'd ask you to marry me." Finn winked so Amelia would know she was joking. Mostly joking.

Amelia smiled. "I'll take that praise. And, since you approve, I think we're ready to eat."

Getting seated was a process. Amelia insisted she didn't need help but dropped her crutches as she tried pulling out her chair and nearly tipped over her wineglass. She finally accepted Finn's arm with a sigh. Edith, to her credit, didn't have anything to say about the fumbles or how Amelia leaned against Finn for maybe a moment too long. Then again, maybe it was nothing. Maybe, like Nana imagining something between Amelia and her, she was also seeing—and feeling—something that wasn't there.

"Finn, how long have you been an EMT?" Edith asked, passing her a basket of warm bread.

"Technically I'm a paramedic." Finn took a slice, grateful she'd spent an extra twenty minutes on the rowing machine. She had every intention of maxing out her carbs with this meal. "And ten years."

"A paramedic is different than an EMT?"

Finn nodded and passed Amelia the bread. "More training, more years in school. But I get to do more fun stuff."

"Like poke people with needles." Amelia shuddered.

"You didn't even feel it."

"You're right. So either you're good at your job or I was distracted by how much my leg hurt."

"Both, probably." Finn smiled. "It's not a job for everyone, but I like it."

Edith handed Finn the bowl of penne covered in Amelia's sauce. "Is your family here in Denver?"

"No, South Dakota. I've got four sisters. All younger than me—and all married except the youngest who I don't think will ever settle down. She's twenty now and as much trouble as when she was two."

"Big family," Amelia said. "And five girls?"

"Yeah, my parents had it rough for a while. Only one bathroom too. We used to have some crazy sister fights over who got the shower first." She grinned. "What about you? Any siblings?"

"No." Amelia glanced at Edith. "Just me. Fortunately. Nana definitely didn't need more than one of me to raise."

"Truer words have never been spoken." Edith patted Amelia's arm.

Finn laughed even as questions about Amelia's parents swirled in her brain.

"I was mostly a very good kid, Nana."

"Oh, you were. Mostly." Edith's eyes glinted mischievously. "Remember that time you invited your entire softball team over while I was gone for the weekend? Lord, the places I found panties." She swirled a finger overhead as if to include the lamp over the table as well as the rest of the house.

"Can we please not talk about the softball weekend?"

Edith laughed. "I suppose you get one pass. I'll let you off the hook and go after Finn."

"Me?" Finn straightened up in her seat.

"Yeah, don't look so smug over there." Amelia lifted her glass and sipped. "I warned you about her."

Undaunted, Edith cleared her throat. "If your family is all in South Dakota, why are you in Colorado?"

"Once upon a time, I wanted to be a professional skier. I came to Colorado to try my luck." She lifted a shoulder. "Ended up liking it here enough to stay."

"What happened to being a professional skier?" Amelia asked.

"I hit a tree. I was working ski patrol at the time and was out in a blizzard. Didn't see the tree until it was too late. Anyway. I knew the dream of making it professionally was gone and my girlfriend was done living in a little cabin two hours from anything but snow. We moved to Denver and that was that."

"Didn't you say you were single?"

"I should have said ex-girlfriend. We didn't work out." Finn didn't want to talk about Nadia. Not tonight. Or ever, really.

"That's too bad."

Finn shrugged. "Things worked out for the best. We weren't right for each other. I'm happier now."

Edith clinked Finn's wineglass with her own. "You'll be even happier after you try the pasta."

Finn appreciated the change in topic. She could talk about Nadia now without feeling like an idiot, or worse, hopeless, but that didn't mean she enjoyed it. She picked up her fork and took a bite. The sauce was delicious—not quite as good as when Amelia had fed it to her right off the spoon, though little could compare to that. "This is officially my new favorite pasta sauce."

Amelia's smile was even better than the sauce.

"Think you could sell me some in a little jar?"

"She could do even better. She can teach you how to make it," Edith volunteered. "And then we can all learn how to make pot brownies."

Amelia set her fork down. "I don't know about this, Nana. I know marijuana's legal and all, but experimenting with it doesn't sound exactly safe."

"I have friends who cook with it and I got some recipes," Finn said. "We won't be experimenting."

"Okay, fine. But who's the taste tester?"

Edith's hand shot up and Finn couldn't help but chuckle.

Amelia shot a look at Finn that stopped her mid laugh and then turned to Edith. "Seriously?"

"Getting old's not for sissies and these bones ache every morning."

Amelia shook her head, but Edith continued, "A little nibble won't hurt me."

"Uh-uh. No way." Amelia pointed to Finn. "She can try them. I'm not letting my eighty-six-year-old grandma be the guinea pig."

"I can't. I get random drug tests for my job."

Amelia seemed about to say something, but a doorbell chime interrupted. She glanced at the clock on the wall above the sink and then at Edith. "Are you expecting someone?"

Edith waved a dismissive hand. "Probably a solicitor. Let's pretend we're not home."

Finn eyed Amelia when the doorbell chimed again. "Want me to check?"

"Don't be silly. You're our guest."

"Yeah, but she's not budging," Finn said, motioning to Edith who was busy chewing and clearly intent on ignoring the doorbell. "And remember how long it took you to get in that chair?"

Amelia dropped her chin. "Okay, fine. Thank you."

"See, that wasn't hard, was it?" Finn stood up and grinned. "Pretty soon you're gonna like asking me for help."

"If I could do it gracefully, I'd swat you right now."

"What happened to me being the guest?"

"You've annoyed me enough to make the friend list. Go get the door." Amelia laughed, managing to swat Finn's arm as she edged around her chair.

Finn laughed too, but the sensation of Amelia's hand on her skin sent a bolt of electricity to her brain. She was glad she had an excuse to leave the room and was still processing how Amelia made her feel as she opened the front door.

A gorgeous blonde in a dark gray pencil skirt and high heels narrowed her eyes at Finn. "Who are you? Where's Amelia?"

Instantly Finn knew she was in the crosshairs of Amelia's girlfriend. *So this is Veronica.* She swallowed and pulled back her shoulders. "Hi. I'm Finn."

When she held out her hand, Veronica made no move to clasp it. Veronica looked her up and down, distaste obvious in her expression, and Finn let her hand fall. So much for starting out smooth. "Amelia's in the kitchen with Edith."

"I'm sorry, I didn't get why you were here?"

"Edith invited me." Finn hated feeling like she had to explain herself but even more hated that the line was only a partial truth.

"Oh." Veronica's brow creased. Now she looked properly annoyed. "Well, can I come in?"

"Oh, yeah. Sure." Finn stepped back from the doorway. "If you're hungry, dinner's on the table. The vodka sauce is delicious. I'd never had it before tonight but it's my new favorite." She knew she should stop talking, knew she sounded like an idiot, but added, "It's nice to meet you."

Veronica stepped past, pulling a carry-on behind her. "I'm sorry, this is just a little weird. I wasn't expecting anyone to be home but Amelia and Edith. Are you friends with Edith or something?"

"Sort of. I had to bring some pot over for—"

"You brought pot? As in marijuana? Are you like a dealer or something?"

"Veronica?" Amelia called from the kitchen.

"Yeah, sweetie, it's me." Veronica gave a tense, clearly fake smile to Finn. "I'm going to go say hi to my girlfriend. If you were leaving, can you close the door behind you?"

Finn realized her mouth was still hanging open several seconds after Veronica had disappeared from the entryway. She heard Amelia's squeal of happiness and Veronica's sugary-sweet response.

"Oh, you poor thing, I'm so sorry that dump truck driver hit you," Veronica cooed. "Does your foot hurt?"

Finn smacked her forehead. What the hell was she doing? She eyed the door but couldn't simply walk out. And yet going back to the kitchen would be totally awkward.

Edith appeared in the hallway. She cocked her head. "Did you get lost coming back to your seat?"

Finn met Edith's gaze. "I did, apparently."

"She rubs me the wrong way too," Edith said in a lowered voice. "And don't ask me what Amelia sees in her. But I still need that brownie recipe."

CHAPTER SEVEN

Amelia basked in Veronica's attention. She'd been silly to worry. The woman adored her. She'd been busy in New York is all. And they were both better at showing affection in person instead of over the phone. "I'm really glad you're home."

Veronica stroked Amelia's hair, then took the empty chair next to her. "I've been worried sick about you. I caught an earlier flight so I could see you instead of getting in after midnight."

"Thank you."

"Of course. If these meetings in New York hadn't been so important, you know I would have rushed right home after the accident."

Amelia nodded, ignoring the little stab of disappointment at Veronica's choice of words. She was being too sensitive. But hadn't Veronica said she'd tried to change her flight two days ago and couldn't? She brushed away the question a moment later. Probably she'd misunderstood. "You're here now. Have you eaten? Will you join us?"

Veronica eyed the pasta left on Amelia's plate with a faint curl of her lip before smiling. "You know I don't eat pasta, sweetie."

"I know…I thought you might make an exception. I made vodka sauce."

"So, carbs and cream?" Veronica waved a hand. "I'm fine. You enjoy your exceptions while you still can."

"That sounds ominous." Finn had returned to the table but seemed reluctant to sit. And she hadn't said a word until then. As soon as she did, a look passed over her face that made it clear she hadn't meant to, at least out loud.

Amelia suppressed a snicker while Veronica glared. "Amelia is excited to embrace a healthier lifestyle after we move in together, aren't you, sweetie?"

Excited might be a bit of an overstatement. She was mostly interested in working out more and feeling stronger. Oh, and stretchier. She definitely wanted to be more limber. She had no real intentions of giving up carbs. Yet, in that moment, saying so felt like she would be taking Finn's side over Veronica's. That shouldn't feel dangerous, but it did. Since she didn't trust herself to look at Finn, she gave Veronica an enthusiastic nod. "I signed up for those belly dancing classes I told you about."

Veronica smiled. "Those will be great for your off days from real workouts. I'm proud of you."

She caught Nana and Finn exchanging a look and did her best to ignore it. "Tell me all about New York."

Veronica's eyes lit up, making her feel much better. "It was phenomenal. Your mom knows everyone—and everyone, of course, knows Miranda Stone. She introduced me to so many people. The whole gala was a whirlwind."

"I'm so glad you had a good time." Despite the trip's terrible timing, she was happy Veronica had enjoyed it. Not only did she love that Veronica got to benefit from her mother's media connections, but it gave Miranda someone to bestow her contacts on. That, in turn, made it easier for Miranda not to be disappointed in her daughter's choice of an unglamorous career in human services.

"And I have big news you're going to absolutely love. I'd planned to tell you when we were alone, but it's so good I can't wait."

Veronica's enthusiasm was infectious. Amelia felt her own excitement grow. "What is it?"

"One of the introductions Miranda made led to an interview. And that interview turned into a job offer. Literally. I got off the plane and the message was waiting."

"Wow. That's…amazing." Even as she said it, a thousand questions and red flags bounced around in her brain. Most of them under the heading: East Coast.

"They want me to be the newest personality on *Wake Up*, the biggest morning show in the metro New York market."

Within the broad range of her questions and fears, subcategories formed. These included, but were not limited to, New York City in general, the panic of a possible relocation, anxiety over attempting to keep things together long-distance. "Oh, my God. Congratulations."

"I know, right? Can you believe it? I mean, I can. I've got exactly the experience and talent they'd want. But to have it all fall into place so perfectly. It's a dream come true."

Amelia nodded and tried to think of something more concretely positive to say. It was harder than she cared to admit.

Finn coughed lightly. "Edith, why don't I help you clear the table and we can go over those recipes we were discussing?"

"That would be good. Thank you." Nana stood rather abruptly and gathered plates.

Amelia glanced between Finn, who was already at the sink rinsing dishes, and Veronica. "Maybe we could go to the living room for a minute?"

Veronica nodded. Her brow furrowed as she watched Amelia gather herself up with the crutches. "Do you need me to do something?"

"I've got it."

Once they'd reached the living room, Amelia wondered if they should have stayed in the kitchen. Veronica seemed taken aback by her hoofing it on the crutches and maybe the reality of the accident was only now setting in.

"I promise I'm fine," she said, hoping to reassure Veronica.

"It's a lot seeing you like that. The cast and the crutches…"

"Yeah. The accident sucked. And the surgery after was no picnic." Seconds ticked by. The moment alone with Veronica should have made her happy, but it didn't. She wasn't even sure what to say next. "So…"

"You don't seem excited about New York." Veronica frowned.

"I am." She mustered a smile. "Just overwhelmed. It's really big news."

Veronica gave a little toss of her head, flipping her gorgeous, perfectly straight, blond hair over her shoulder. It wasn't hard to imagine her on TV. Or, fancier TV than the local affiliate in Denver where she worked. "The biggest. I know we planned to settle down here, but obviously this is something I can't pass up. The salary is good enough that we'll be able to get an apartment in Manhattan and you won't have to worry about working right away. I even get a clothing allowance and a driver."

"That's great." She tried to match Veronica's enthusiasm but couldn't seem to. The news seemed surreal. "You want to move to New York?"

"I hadn't exactly planned on it, but the offer is amazing, right? Sweetie, are you okay? Are you hopped up on Vicodin or something?"

She'd skipped her afternoon dose so she could have a glass of wine with dinner. Between her perhaps ill-advised pirouette and the headache now simmering behind her eyes, she was seriously questioning that decision. "No. Like I said, I'm a little overwhelmed is all. It's, well, it's big news—like you said."

Veronica smiled. "It is. That's why I meant to tell you when it was just us. But I simply couldn't hold it in another second."

At the mention of "just us," Amelia braved a glimpse toward the kitchen. She could hear Nana and Finn still busy cleaning up. "I really am happy for you. But I can't seem to stop my mind from racing ahead."

Veronica took her hand and gave it a squeeze. "We have all the time in the world to figure it out. They don't need me to start until Thanksgiving week."

Maybe it was the weirdness of the last few days, but in her mind, that felt really, really soon. "Okay."

"I'm sure you're not feeling yourself and I'm beat from travel. Why don't I head home and we can grab drinks tomorrow? Or dinner?" Veronica stood.

Was it just her, or did the casualness of the invite not at all go with the woman who was supposed to be her girlfriend heading to the apartment that was supposed to be theirs? "Um, sure. I'm planning to go into the office next week so I might as well get practice with my crutches."

The look of concern on Veronica's face made her feel slightly better. "Maybe it's too soon to be leaving the house. You know what they say. You shouldn't rush your recovery."

Nana had basically said the same thing, so she took the question as caring and not patronizing. She'd promised to start back slow to make sure the concussion symptoms were gone, but she was really looking forward to getting back to her office and her staff. "I'll take it easy. I promise."

That seemed to satisfy Veronica. She offered a decisive nod. "Okay. I'll text you in the morning."

"Sounds good."

"Sleep well, sweetie." Veronica leaned down and kissed her forehead and then she was gone.

Amelia sat for a moment before blowing out a breath. "You two can stop hiding out in the kitchen."

"We weren't hiding." Nana appeared in the hallway. "We were simply taking our sweet time doing the dishes."

She rolled her eyes. "Same difference."

"We had important matters to discuss." Nana's matter-of-fact tone made her smile.

"We did need to discuss the brownies," Finn offered, looking almost sheepish.

"Maybe don't discuss that in front of Veronica, okay?" She directed the comment mostly to Nana since Finn and Veronica were unlikely to cross paths again.

"Does she hate pot, brownies, or the specific combination?" Finn asked.

Nana let out a sniff. "All of the above."

"Sounds like a barrel of fun." Finn made a face, but like before, she seemed to catch herself. "Sorry."

"Don't be," Nana said before Amelia could reply.

Amelia pressed a thumb to her temple. The headache had spread, leaving her longing for darkness and quiet.

"I should go," Finn said.

"I'm sorry that was weird." A weak apology, but she couldn't bring herself to admit Veronica had been rude.

Finn waved a hand. "It's fine. None of my business."

Finn was right. So why did her words make things feel even worse? Because Amelia wanted to be Finn's business? *That isn't problematic at all…*

Nana turned to Finn. "I'll plan to see you on Wednesday for pickup, yes?"

"Sounds good. Call me in the meantime if you need anything." Finn glanced at Amelia. "You too. I know your girlfriend is back, but if you need a friend for something, like a ride to the store or whatever, I've got the next few days off."

After Veronica's news and the awkwardness of the night, being friends with Finn seemed unlikely at best. And yet temptingly nice.

"That's sweet of you to offer," Nana said. "She tries to overdo it on those crutches and could stand asking for help every once in a while. We'll repay you for any help, of course, with home-cooked meals."

"I like that deal." Finn turned to Amelia. "You've got my number. Call if you need anything. But no pressure. I know it's not easy asking for help, and maybe it'd make things more complicated."

Had Finn read her mind? Amelia wasn't sure what to say. Fortunately, Nana piped up first. "Well, it would be helping you out as well. Amelia would be getting you a free meal."

Finn smiled. "Good point."

Amelia watched the interaction play out with a mixture of fascination and confusion. She didn't want this to be the last time she saw Finn, and Nana seemed to be working to guarantee that wouldn't be the case. But she should be thinking about Veronica and New York.

"Speaking of help, would either of you like a hand with anything before I go?"

Before Amelia could turn her down, Nana said, "No, we're fine. But I wanted to send you home with some leftovers."

"I won't say no to that."

As Nana disappeared to the kitchen, Finn met Amelia's gaze. "I'm sorry if me being here made things weird with your girlfriend."

"I don't think it was you. I think it's me." Amelia raised her casted leg. "I'm feeling a little off because of this."

"I get it. Everything's harder when some part of you is broken. Even conversations."

Amelia clenched her jaw, overwhelmed and worried she might cry. She didn't want to break down now.

"If you want a friend to talk to about it, text me anytime. And, really, don't hesitate to ask for help. I like to be useful." Finn paused. "Us being friends doesn't cross any lines with you and Veronica, does it?"

"No. Not at all." It shouldn't, anyway. But at the moment, Amelia wasn't sure what the tangle of emotions in her chest meant. Finn offering to help drove home the fact that Veronica hadn't. She also hadn't really asked how Amelia was feeling or what she might need.

"Also, Edith mentioned you skipped your afternoon pain pill. I'm guessing you're pretty achy. I'm obviously not a doctor, but you only had a half glass of wine at dinner, so you should be fine to take one before bed."

Being thoughtful and reminding patients about pain meds was second nature to Finn. Probably nothing more. She was a paramedic, after all. Comparing Veronica to someone like Finn wasn't fair. "I think that pirouette earlier was a mistake."

"If it's any consolation, you looked good in the moment."

Amelia smiled. "That's the important part, right?"

"Definitely. Seriously, though. Take it easy on yourself."

The thoughtfulness, paired with Finn's affectionate look, sent a ripple of warmth through her. Which probably wasn't a good sign. Maybe being friends with someone who made her feel like Finn did was a bad idea.

Nana reappeared with a Tupperware container and handed it to Finn. "I'll walk you out."

Amelia let Nana take over the hostess role and headed for the sofa. She flopped down on the cushions and closed her eyes.

As exhausted as she was, her mind wouldn't stop spinning. One minute she was turning over Veronica's news and the next she was thinking about Finn.

With Veronica, the problem was wanting to be happy and also feeling generally steamrolled by the whole conversation. She wanted Veronica to have the job of her dreams, but everything about her accepting it threw a wrench in their plans. Worse, Veronica didn't seem to have even an inkling that might be the case. Well, that or she didn't care. Neither of those scenarios sat well. Nor did it bode well for their future.

The problem with Finn was how everything felt right when she was with her. Even when things were a complete mess, one minute alone with Finn and she was happy. And more herself than she ever was with Veronica.

"Do you want to talk about it?" Nana handed Amelia a mug of tea and sat in her recliner.

"Thanks." Amelia breathed in the chamomile and lemon. How did Nana manage to know what she needed even when she didn't? "And I'm not sure."

"Do you think one of the reasons you like Veronica is that she reminds you of your mother?"

Where the hell did that come from? Yes, they shared a certain ambition, worked in the same field. But the idea she'd fall in love with a woman who… No. "That's a little creepy, Nana."

She waved a hand. "I don't mean in some Freudian way. But maybe the idea that someone like Veronica would choose to build a life and a family with you is something you need on some level."

Yeah, definitely next-level creepy. "Not helping."

"I only thought that spending time with someone like Finn might get you thinking."

"Thinking about what?" That Finn was her type in pretty much every way imaginable? Way more her type than Veronica? She shook her head. There was no chance Finn would have the life goal of settling down in a cute house and making babies. Veronica did.

"I've seen the way you look at her. And the way she looks at you, for that matter." Nana punctuated the statement by tapping her index finger on the arm of her chair.

"I think that's a problem, actually." Amelia willed herself to go on. She had to say it aloud. "I need to focus on me and Veronica right now." She was supposed to be living with Veronica, planning her wedding, and talking about sperm donors. Even as she thought it, the prospect of doing it felt a little hollow. "Finn's been racking up hero points for the last week. It's been nice, but it isn't real. And I already have a girlfriend."

Nana shook her head and her teasing expression fell away. "Is it any less real than convincing yourself you're in love with Veronica because she claims to want all the same things you do?"

She knew better than to call low blow, even if she wanted to. The truth of the matter was that moving in with Veronica was one of the rashest decisions she'd ever made. She'd spent her entire life being the sensible, practical one. She didn't rush into relationships or anything else. And what had that gotten her? A whole lot of nothing. "I feel like life is passing me by and I'm terrified that I'm going to miss my chance at happiness."

Nana's features softened. It would have made her feel better if it didn't make her feel pathetic. "You don't just get one chance."

"I know." She did. But it didn't make the prospect of starting over any easier.

"A bad girlfriend in the hand is not worth two in the bush."

"Nana, that might be the worst analogy ever." But even as she argued, she smiled.

"Is it?" Nana stood and took Amelia's now empty mug. "Well, what do I know?" She kissed Amelia's forehead. "Good night, dear."

"Good night, Nana."

She watched Nana head off to bed but kept her place on the sofa. She wasn't quite ready to call it a night. Or, perhaps more accurately, she wasn't ready for the thoughts that would dance around her brain in the darkness. Or the dreams that might echo things she shouldn't be thinking about in the first place. She didn't want to take a break from Finn, but she knew she had to do it.

CHAPTER EIGHT

"Your hands are too far apart." Jess leaned over Finn's head and tapped her finger on the bar. "You know, you've been lifting the same weight for the past year. When are you moving up?"

Finn shifted her grip and pressed another five. She rested with the weight on her chest and stared up at Jess. "Don't you have somewhere you're supposed to be right now?"

"My next class doesn't start until nine. Besides, I'm spending quality time with my roommate who's hardly ever home anymore."

"I've been working." In the last two weeks, she'd only had one day off.

"The question is, why are you picking up all the extra shifts? Trying to keep yourself out of trouble?" Jess stuck out her tongue when Finn fumbled for an answer. "You could add another twenty pounds and hardly notice. Want me to grab the weights now?"

"No." Finn started another set. Having a roommate who was in notably better shape was one part inspiring and one part annoying. She rested again, trying to slow her breathing. "Why do you keep looking at me like you're waiting for me to say something?"

"Because I am." Jess made a show of looking put-off. "Whatever happened to that woman you had dinner with? Amelia, right? You couldn't stop talking about her and now— nothing. Did she turn out to be an ogre?"

"An ogre? You mean like Shrek?" Finn smiled. "I do love ogres."

"Come on. Tell me. How'd dinner go? I never got the scoop."

"One more set."

Finn had hoped she'd hear from Amelia after the dinner. But no call or text came. Now nearly three weeks later, she had to accept that Amelia had weighed the risk and benefits of a friendship and decided it wasn't worth it. Probably that was for the best for both of them. Still, it stung. "Dinner was delicious. Have you ever had vodka sauce?"

"Yes, but not the point. So things went well? Did you set up a second date?"

"I'd never even heard of vodka sauce."

"You eat mac 'n' cheese with peas and think you're being adventurous." Jess scrunched up her nose.

"It's good. You should try it sometime."

"Focus, Finn, or I swear I'm going to find this woman's number and call her up myself."

"She's not your type. Too girly."

Jess stretched out her hands and pretended to squeeze Finn's neck. "Why do I have the most frustrating friend in the entire universe?"

"Maybe that's something to consider for self-reflection?"

Jess finally laughed. "Tell me already. How'd it go? When's the second date?"

"There's no second date because there was no first date. Amelia's got a girlfriend."

"So that's why you've been working so much," Jess guessed. "You've been trying to forget about her." She poked Finn's arm until she nodded. "You didn't tell me she had a girlfriend. Only that her grandma was the one who'd invited you."

"I did tell you it wasn't a date. And that I was only going to talk about pot brownies and the dinner was their thank-you." She thought of the moment Veronica had knocked on the door and how dinner had gone downhill from there. "Ever see two people together and know they're completely wrong for each other?"

"And that I'd be a much better choice for one of those people?" Jess raised an eyebrow.

Finn pressed on. "This girlfriend—Veronica—is completely wrong for Amelia."

"Mm-hmm."

"If you'd met this woman, you'd understand. Totally self-centered and all about appearances. She wouldn't stop talking about this fancy job offer she got. Hardly even asked Amelia about the accident. And she bashed the meal without even trying it."

"Wait, so this thank-you dinner was you, Grandma, Amelia, and her girlfriend?"

"Veronica showed up as a surprise. Anyway, I'm telling you Amelia's making a mistake with her."

Jess rubbed her temple. "What are you doing getting your heart messed up in this, Finn?"

"My heart's not messed up in anything. I've been keeping my distance since that dinner."

"But you're friends with her grandma, right? Isn't she the one who's making the pot brownies for the hospice patients?"

"I pick up the brownies when Amelia's not there. My point is, I think Amelia could use a friend."

"To tell her that she's making a mistake with her girlfriend?" Jess shook her head. "Finn, is this some kind of exercise in self-control?"

"Hypothetically speaking, do you think two people who are attracted to each other can be friends?"

"Hypothetically speaking, I don't think it's a healthy plan. Someone's going to get hurt." Jess sank down on the weight bench next to Finn. "I don't want to bring up Nadia, but…"

"Nadia was a mistake. I'll give you that."

"If it was only her, I wouldn't say that you have a pattern. The thing is, I've seen the other women you've brought home since Nadia. None of them were long-term options and you know it. Do you want to talk about why?"

Before she had a chance to answer, or argue, for that matter, Jess held up her hand. "Because in your head, Colorado is temporary. Even after ten years, you're not ready to plan your life here. Nadia knew that. And I'm not saying that's why she cheated, but I do think she sensed you weren't all in. If something happened to one of your folks, or one of your sisters, she knew you'd be in South Dakota in a heartbeat. After your mom's stroke, after your sister crashed her car, after your other sister got in a fight with her husband, after your other *other* sister needed someone to watch her kids for a week…

"And we both know you're planning on taking over the ranch when your parents are too old to run the place. Your family's your priority and you know it."

Finn hung her head.

"I'm not saying it's wrong, but taking care of everyone in South Dakota means you don't plan your future here."

"I don't see how this applies to Amelia. I'm not planning a future with her. I'm talking about being her friend. Hypothetically."

Jess bumped her shoulder. "Nadia was with someone when you met her too."

"I had no idea she wasn't single. And Amelia's not Nadia."

"I know. But I'm standing by what I said. I think you're subconsciously drawn to women who aren't available because you know you aren't all the way available either."

Finn face-palmed with a groan. "I don't think I can handle lifting weights and a therapy session all in one blow."

"You're not lifting anymore." Jess's look was more sympathetic than critical. "I'm sure Amelia is amazing and interesting and all that. Probably she'd make a great friend. But you're signing up for a heartbreak."

"I'm not signing up for anything."

"You know what you need to sign up for? My barre class."

"What? No."

"Yes." Jess caught Finn's hand and dragged her up. "You need a focus reset."

Finn took a long shower after Jess's class. At least for a solid hour, she hadn't thought about Amelia once. But now, as she leaned against the cool tile, hot water pounding her back, her mind replayed Jess's words. Was she drawn to Amelia because she wasn't available?

It was true that she hadn't dated seriously since Nadia. And she'd purposefully slept with women who weren't interested in anything more than a one-night stand. But that was to get over Nadia. Wasn't it? Or was she living with one foot in Denver and one boot on a ranch in South Dakota?

As she got out of the shower, a yawn caught her off guard. She rubbed her towel vigorously over her body, trying to shake off the exhaustion more than dry off. Whenever she made the switch from working nights to working days, the key was a solid workout, plenty of sleep, and no caffeine. Her brain knew it, but her body didn't like it even after years of training. Nadia had griped about how awful the schedule was. One more reason to pick up women at clubs instead of finding a steady girlfriend.

She glanced at the time as she dressed and realized she needed to hurry. Edith had mentioned Amelia was working half days this week and she'd scheduled today's brownie pickup at noon to avoid a run-in. Her conversation with Jess had confirmed it was the right decision even though her heart didn't like it.

Thanks to traffic, Finn reached Edith's house ten minutes after the hour. She jogged up the front path hoping Amelia would leave work a little later than usual.

Before she could knock, the door cracked open. Edith peered out at the empty street, clearly pretending to look for someone. "You sure you weren't followed?"

Finn smiled. "I took the necessary precautions."

"Good." Edith stepped back from the doorway. "In that case, *entrez s'il vous plaît.*"

"French again? I looked up that word you said for those appetizers. *Amuse-bouche*. Something little to amuse the mouth." Finn entered and took a good long sniff. The house smelled of brownies once more.

"I had a fling with a very handsome French man. Had to learn a few things."

If younger Edith was anything like the spitfire she was now, her boyfriends had been the ones to learn plenty. Finn almost said as much, but when they got to the kitchen she found herself at a loss for words. The kitchen had been transformed into a laboratory. Along with a set of scales, Edith had dozens of flasks in different sizes, cylindrical glass measuring tubes, and for some reason, a Bunsen burner. The brownies, individually packed in clear plastic wrap as usual, were stacked in a tray on the table.

"What's with the Bunsen burner? And all these flasks?"

"Oh, those are for decoration." Edith waved dismissively.

Before Finn could ask more, she heard a thump behind her. Amelia stood in the hallway on her crutches, a wry smile on her lips.

"Decorations to scare Veronica," Amelia said. "Hi, Finn."

"Hi." Finn glanced between Edith and Amelia. She shouldn't be happy that Amelia wasn't at work, but her heart danced in her chest all the same. Well, there was dancing and then there was more of a clenching sensation that made it difficult to breathe. All the desires she told herself to ignore, the second-guessing, and three weeks of missing someone she'd barely gotten to know hit at the same moment. A tentative smile from Amelia made Finn think at least some of her emotions were shared.

Finn swallowed. Staring at each other was going to get awkward in about five seconds. "So did the decorations work?"

"Hard to say." Amelia gave Edith an admonishing look. "She didn't stay long."

"We'll see if I get a visit from the police later." Edith's tone was decidedly unapologetic.

Finn moved to the side so Amelia could come into the kitchen. "I thought you'd be working."

"I am. I decided to work from home today in case Veronica—" Amelia stopped short. "Never mind." She turned her attention to Edith. "Nana, you know Veronica wouldn't call the police. She was concerned is all. You shouldn't mess with her like that."

"Oh, it was only a little fun. No harm done."

Amelia shook her head and gave Finn a look that seemed to say she was in the doghouse too. "Nana told Veronica she was considering options beyond pot brownies. Veronica took one look at this kitchen and jumped to something illegal."

"She thinks your grandma is cooking up meth in a kitchen full of pot brownies." Edith broke into a peal of laughter as she shook the Bunsen burner in the air.

Finn couldn't help laughing too. "Where'd you even get that thing? It looks straight out of my high school chemistry class."

Amelia cleared her throat. "My grandpa was a chemistry teacher. Nana has some of his old stuff still around. The flame works great if you want to make fondue."

"Or any number of other things," Edith added, finally sobering as she set the Bunsen burner back on the counter. "Finn, would you like something to drink? Coffee maybe? I'm still packing the second box."

"No, thank you. I'm off caffeine for the day. Schedule switch… Can I help?"

Edith nodded. "Gloves are over there. I'll cut, you wrap. Amelia, you can warn us if there's any uniformed officers at the door."

"You can cut the act. Veronica's gone." Despite her scolding tone, a smile edged her lips. She dropped into one of the kitchen chairs, a more practiced move than when Finn had seen her last. "It's nice to see you, Finn. How have you been?"

"I've been okay. And you?" Nothing about Amelia's question, or her response, felt weird. She wanted a recording of it so she could prove as much to Jess. Maybe they could be friends.

Amelia motioned to her cast. "You can probably guess how exciting my life has been with this thing."

"It gets old fast, doesn't it?"

"Understatement, but yes. Getting anywhere on crutches gives you a different perspective on what accessibility means."

"I bet. You didn't give yourself much time to let the rest of you recover, either." Edith had been providing updates on

Amelia, and Finn knew she'd struggled getting right back to work. "But you'll be out of the cast soon, right?"

"Thursday. I can't wait."

"That's great."

"It is. Everything's going according to plan." Amelia's downturned expression didn't match her upbeat tone. Finn nearly called her on it, but she followed Amelia's gaze to Edith. Edith's back was turned and yet there was no doubt she was listening. Amelia clearly wanted her grandmother to think she was doing better than she was.

Finn put on the gloves Edith had set out and picked up the roll of plastic wrap. "You know, there's a lot to be said for seeing the world from a different perspective. I gained a huge respect for folks in wheelchairs after spending some time in one."

"When were you in a wheelchair?"

"After my skiing accident."

"That one you mentioned with you and a tree? Must have been a bad accident."

Finn nodded. She didn't want to list all the bones she'd broken with one bad judgment call. Instead, she picked up a brownie, tempted by a whiff of rich chocolate, and set to wrapping. "People treat you differently. They might not even mean to. I think everyone should have to spend one day in a chair to see how it feels."

"Crutches for three weeks are nothing." Amelia sighed.

"That's not what I meant," Finn said quickly. "What I meant is that it's good to realize everyone brings something important to the table. No matter how we get there."

"You a philosopher on the side? Or is this Finn, the therapist?"

Finn grinned. "I'm just a paramedic."

"Just?" Amelia cocked her head in a way that made it clear she didn't agree with the assessment.

Finn held her gaze. She swallowed as heat seared through her, way too aware that Amelia wasn't looking away.

Edith set another brownie in front of Finn. "Ahem. You're getting behind over there."

Thank God for Edith. All of a sudden, Finn didn't trust her self-control. There were so many things she wanted to say to Amelia—things she had no business saying. She picked up a brownie and started wrapping. "Or someone's getting ahead of themselves."

"Are you calling me fast?" Edith slapped another brownie on the counter in front of Finn. Her mischievous smile creased her eyes. "Now I have a reputation to uphold."

"You're trouble," Finn said.

Amelia shook her head. "You both are. I'm starting to wonder who's egging on who."

"Speaking of," Edith said, pointing at Finn. "You haven't told me your schedule for next week. You know I like to keep tabs on my pot dealer."

"Starting tomorrow I'm back on day shift."

Edith shook her head. "You work too much."

"I've been picking up extra shifts, but I'll have some time off soon."

"When?" Edith went over to her wall calendar. "I'm going to put it on the calendar because I want you to come over for dinner then."

"Nana, I'm sure Finn has a life outside of work. She's got better things to do than have dinner with us."

Edith ignored Amelia. "How about Friday?"

"I don't think I can." It was the truth. If she couldn't be cool for five minutes around Amelia, how would she survive dinner?

Amelia cleared her throat. "Nana."

Nana shrugged, all innocence. "I wanted to make a cake for that woman with brain cancer who you mentioned was having a birthday on Sunday."

"Oh. Right." Finn recalled the conversation they'd had and how she'd promised two pickups this week to accommodate Edith's special cake delivery. "How about Saturday afternoon? I traded shifts so I could volunteer at the fire station's Halloween festival. I could swing by after."

"I love Halloween festivals," Amelia mused. "I worked a booth at one when I was in high school. My softball team ran the dunk tank."

"You could come." The words came out before Finn could stop them. She scrambled to add, "With Veronica of course." Almost smooth. Actually, it wasn't a terrible idea. She'd be there with Jess, and what better way to test the friend waters than have Veronica join them?

"The festival raises money for the Children's Hospital," she continued. Now she might as well sell it. "The cider and hot dogs are famous—at least according to the firefighters. But the best part is seeing all the kids running around in costumes."

Amelia shook her head. "Maybe if we had a kid. Without one, I don't think Veronica would be up for it."

"She's not into hot dogs?"

Amelia made an are-you-actually-surprised face. "Or costumes."

As much as she wanted to, Finn couldn't suggest Amelia come without Veronica. "I get dressed up every year. This year I'm going as a banana."

"A banana?" Amelia let out a snort of laughter. "Why'd you pick that?"

Finn grinned, only now thinking how ridiculous she'd look. "I guess I hadn't really thought about it. My friend Jess offered to pick up a costume for me when she got hers. We do the festival together every year. She's going as a pineapple, so I guess she figured we'd match."

Edith patted Finn's shoulder. "Ignore Amelia. You'll make a lovely banana."

"I agree," Amelia said, though she seemed to be having trouble not laughing still. "You'll be an amazing banana. And your friend sounds cool. I wish I could see both of your costumes."

"If you can convince Veronica, we'll let you both play a round of ring toss on the house."

"That's hard to pass up." Amelia smiled. "Well…I can talk to her."

CHAPTER NINE

Amelia shifted in the passenger seat as her friend, Cody, pulled up to a stoplight. "Thanks for doing this with me. Showing up alone would have been pathetic."

Cody chuckled. "It's a Halloween festival, not prom."

"Yeah. For kids. Showing up without a date or a child would have been twice as sad." Ever since Finn had mentioned the festival, she couldn't get the idea of going out of her mind. Not surprisingly, however, Veronica had shot it down the moment she'd suggested it. And going alone wasn't an option.

"Well, we always enjoy company, don't we, Ben?"

"We love company!" Ben bounced around in the back seat as much as his seat belt, booster seat, and Clifford costume would allow.

Amelia smiled back at him. "I love your company too."

"Now, who are we hoping to bump into again?" Cody asked.

She felt herself blush. "No one."

"Wait, I remember!" Cody slapped the steering wheel. "We're coming to check out the paramedic who responded to your accident."

Amelia shook her head.

"The one who visited you in the hospital and drove you home, right?"

"That's Finn, yes, but we're not checking her out. We're friends. Sort of." She'd briefly mentioned Finn to Cody, but she hadn't said anything about the dinner that had ended on rocky footing or the unlikely friendship that seemed to be forming between Finn and Nana. Or that she'd decided not to contact Finn while she figured things out with Veronica.

Figuring things out with Veronica hadn't gone as well as she'd hoped. One week after getting back to Denver, Veronica flew back to New York and then to LA. All for work. In between, nearly every time Amelia suggested doing something, Veronica was too busy. They'd gotten together for a handful of lunches—that oddly felt like work meetings—and dinner twice. Amelia had mentioned a night together, but Veronica wasn't interested in being at Nana's house and Amelia still couldn't manage three flights of stairs. They'd had no time to reconnect.

Seeing Finn unexpectedly in Nana's kitchen had brought a torrent of emotions. She'd read enough self-help books to be convinced that because Finn had helped during the accident and was there for her through a crisis, her response to her was amplified. It made perfect sense. She'd even convinced herself that a friendship with Finn wouldn't throw things off with Veronica as long as she kept everything in perspective. But that didn't mean she was ready to be alone with Finn.

"Have we discussed whether she's hot? I can't remember." Cody shot her a teasing look.

"I may have gushed about Finn after the accident, but I was on pain meds and not thinking clearly. Her hotness is irrelevant."

"Hotness is never irrelevant."

Amelia gave her an exasperated look. "It is when you have a girlfriend."

"We've been friends for twenty years, don't pull that crap on me." Cody's voice dropped to a whisper for the word *crap* without missing a beat. "You like Finn, right? It's not like you're engaged to Veronica or anything. Have you two even had the commitment talk?"

"Well, no, but…it's complicated."

Cody cocked her head. "I have a PhD. Try me."

She and Cody weren't best friends, but they'd been friends since high school and even dated briefly in college. She'd been calling Amelia on her shit almost as long as Nana had. "If the accident hadn't happened, I'd be living with Veronica right now."

"But the accident did happen. You know, there's plenty of good reasons not to commit."

"Just because you're terrified of commitment doesn't mean the rest of us are." Amelia folded her arms.

"What's commitment?" Ben asked from the back seat.

"A grown-up word you don't need to think about for a very long time," Cody said.

Amelia rolled her eyes. "It's not a four-letter word, you know."

"And I'm not terrified of it," Cody argued. "But why be tied down if you can avoid it?"

"Maybe I want to be tied down."

Cody quirked a brow. "Kinky."

"What's kinky?" Ben asked.

"Nothing." Amelia and Cody answered in unison as Cody pulled into the lot next to the fire station. Cody cut the engine but pointed a finger at Amelia. "This conversation is not over."

They'd see about that. In the meantime, there were plenty of other things to demand her attention. Kids ran around in every kind of costume imaginable. Cowboys chased ninjas, Disney princesses pranced and curtsied, and Kylo Ren seemed to be in a fierce lightsaber battle with a taco. The squeals and giggles added to the chaotic energy and made her smile.

"Are you sure you're up for this?"

Amelia thought about the dark cloud that had settled over her mood the last couple of days and looked down at her foot. At least she'd been upgraded to a walking cast. She wouldn't last long if they had to do a lot of walking, but the prospect of soaking up a bunch of kid energy lifted her spirits. "It's exactly what I need."

The fire trucks had been pulled out and the cavernous space filled with games, food stalls, and a pumpkin-painting station. Amelia scanned the crowd for Finn but didn't see her. Then she remembered what Finn had said about her costume. A second look brought her gaze squarely to one of the game stalls, where a banana and a pineapple were running the ring toss. She smiled again.

"Okay, Miss Goofy Grin, where is she? Point her out." Cody looked at her with an amused expression.

She chuckled at being so transparent. "Banana. Two o'clock."

Cody's gaze moved in that direction. "Definitely your type."

"Bananas are my type?"

Cody laughed. "You know what I mean."

"I'm testing out a friendship here." Even if her dreams the last few nights begged to differ. "Nothing more."

"Well, the way she's staring at you makes me think she's not on the same page."

"Wait. What?" Sure enough, Finn's eyes were on her. Finn lifted her hand in a wave. Amelia took a deep breath and told herself to relax before doing the same.

"Go say hi. We're going to start with lunch. Want a hot dog?"

"I don't need to—"

Cody gave her a nudge. "Go. Mustard?"

"Yes, please."

"Come on, Clifford. Time to eat."

Ben woofed his agreement and off they went. Amelia made her way across the room, past the apple-bobbing station and the kettle corn stand. Why was her heart beating so fast?

Finn whispered something to the pineapple and stepped out from behind the booth. "Look at you, out and about."

She lifted a shoulder. "Have boot, will travel."

"Makes such a difference, doesn't it?"

"It does. I like your costume." Even if it hid most of Finn's sexy body, the outfit was endearing. "I didn't know what to expect, but you rock the banana look."

Finn held up her hands. "It's completely ridiculous, but the kids seem to get a kick out of it. That's what matters."

The way Finn's smile went all the way to her blue eyes did nothing to help Amelia's racing pulse. "That's sweet."

"Did I see you come in with someone? And maybe a Clifford?"

It was hard to tell what she enjoyed more—Finn noticing her come in or her knowing the children's book character. "My friend, Cody, from high school. And her son Ben."

"Nice."

"Yeah, she single parents so I try to help out when I can." The occasional babysitting had nothing to do with her tagging along today, but Finn didn't need to know that.

"Good practice for when you have your own."

Had her biological clock started ticking out loud? "Something like that."

"I'm glad you made it."

"Well, I don't want to keep you." She tipped her head in the direction Cody and Ben had gone. "And I think there's a hot dog with my name on it."

"If there's a hot dog waiting, I don't want to keep you either." Another smile, as gorgeous as the first one. "Maybe swing by our booth though? You can assure Cody we're giving away coloring books and not goldfish or anything else requiring care and feeding."

Amelia laughed. "Noted. We'll be over in a bit."

"Excellent."

Finn returned to the booth. Amelia watched her engage a gaggle of princesses for a second. It would have been one thing if Finn had just been good-looking. Or good-looking and charming. Did she have to be both those things and great with kids too?

She headed over to the picnic tables to console herself with company and carnival food. Ben talked a mile a minute about all the things he wanted to do, and Amelia found herself caught up in his enthusiasm. At least mostly. A little part of her worried that she was counting down the booths until they'd be at Finn's ring toss. And another little part of her worried that she was glad Veronica hadn't been at all interested in coming to a Halloween festival.

* * *

It was nearly five when Cody dropped her off. She chatted briefly with Nana before hurrying to her room to get ready for the swanky museum party Veronica had gotten them tickets to. She'd just finished her makeup when Veronica poked her head in.

"How's my sexy date?"

Amelia hobbled over to the door. "Better now that you're here." She expected a kiss, or maybe hoped for it, but Veronica swept right past her.

"How do you like my outfit?"

The suit—a nod to a tuxedo but cut very much to show off Veronica's feminine frame—complemented the dress perfectly. "You are beyond gorgeous."

Veronica did a spin and struck a pose. "It's perfect, right? Totally worth the insane price tag."

Even as she appreciated how stunning her girlfriend looked, the fatigue she'd been denying drummed behind her eyes. She sat and picked up the one stocking she'd be able to put on. A sigh escaped before she could stop it.

"What's wrong?"

"Any chance I could talk you into a quiet night in? I could probably hobble my way up the stairs at your place and we could watch movies and cuddle." Saying it aloud made her want it even more, but disappointment flashed on Veronica's face. "I'm not sure I'm up for a museum gala. And the nightclub after. Maybe we could pick one?"

Veronica didn't seem mad, exactly. She looked at Amelia's boot and seemed to contemplate the options. "I invited a bunch of friends to join us at the club. And I made the gala reservations weeks ago. It's going to be the hottest night out until New Year."

"I know. And I was really excited for it too." Not a total lie. "But this afternoon tired me out more than I thought."

"Of course it did. Kids are exhausting. I still don't understand why you went to a party for children in the first place." Veronica's voice took on a trace of an edge.

Amelia felt a pang of guilt. She should have thought about how much walking she could handle. But it wasn't only that. "I want kids. I like spending time with them. And it was a chance to catch up with a friend I haven't seen in a while." It really was all those things, way more than the prospect of seeing Finn.

"I don't want to drag you out if you're not going to have a good time."

The knot of tension in her chest eased slightly. "Thank you. I don't want to go and wind up being a wet blanket either."

"But I'm not going to bail on my friends. I haven't seen them since I got back from New York."

So, no cozy romantic night in. "We've hardly seen each other either."

"Babe, you know I've been busy." Veronica lowered her head. "I was really looking forward to having my friends get to know you."

Even though the comment felt a little manipulative, Amelia had been pushing for them to spend more time with each other's friends too. "You're right. We should go. And I'm sure it will be a blast."

Veronica crossed the room and stroked her hair. "That's better. Why don't I help you with your dress?"

The thought of Veronica's hands on her back, touching her skin as she slid the zipper up, helped counter the last of her indecision. "Yes, please."

Amelia hauled herself to her feet and adjusted the garter on her stocking. Veronica offered her a sexy smile before slipping the dress from the hanger and over Amelia's head. Amelia turned and Veronica inched the zipper up and kissed her shoulder. "I'm going to enjoy taking this off you later."

"I'm going to enjoy letting you." They hadn't had sex since the accident and Amelia was relieved to feel a rush of arousal. The truth was, she'd spent too much time lately thinking of what it would be like to have Finn touching her instead of Veronica. Now she'd like to fast-forward to the part where she and Veronica were slipping into bed, which was good.

Veronica took her hand and led her through the house, out the front door, and to her car. The spirit of it was sexy, even if the thump of her walking cast killed the mood slightly. She wasn't quite in second-wind territory, but she was no longer dreading the evening.

When they got to the museum, Veronica pulled right up to the valet. Although it usually made Amelia uncomfortable, tonight she was grateful. Inside, low lighting and shimmery decorations in black, silver, and orange turned the normally minimalist space into a sleek and sophisticated take on Halloween. Such a far cry from the firehouse that afternoon.

Veronica put a hand under her arm. "We're meeting my friends in the bar. Liz and Dion from my CSU days, but you'll also get to meet Maddie and Claire. They texted to let us know they got a table. After drinks, we can walk around a bit. I've heard this place really gets going after ten."

After ten? And the nightclub after that? Amelia held in a groan. She let herself be led and said a silent prayer of thanks that they had a table. Her gratitude was short-lived—Veronica's friends were clustered around a tiny high top with no chairs.

A couple of the women squealed when they spotted Veronica. She turned to Amelia and smiled, then let go of her arm to give them hugs. After an uncomfortable amount of fanfare, the attention turned to Amelia's boot. There was some tutting over Denver drivers, then U-Hauls, but the conversation quickly shifted back to Veronica's job offer.

Despite having a drink, it wasn't long before she found herself shifting uncomfortably from foot to foot. Not only did she have to face walking around the museum, it would be hours probably before they got to the after-party. Chances of finding a place to sit would be slim to none. Focusing on the pain wouldn't help pass the time, but she couldn't participate in a conversation about people she'd never met and parties she'd missed. And the truth was, she couldn't seem to make herself care.

Veronica offered to get the next round of drinks and Amelia followed her. "I don't want to be a downer, but my foot is killing me."

"Aw, sweetie, that's terrible. Don't you have any Vicodin left?"

Amelia shook her head. "I've been trying to lay off the pain pills. I just can't stand for this long."

Veronica made a face. "Do you want to go? Is that what you're saying?"

"I'm saying I'm not sure how much longer I have in me." She added a smile to show she was trying to be a good sport. "Could we maybe go somewhere with some chairs?"

Veronica pursed her lips. "I really don't want to leave yet. We haven't even walked around to see the exhibits."

"I know." Maybe she could push through the pain a while longer.

"I don't think my friends want to go somewhere else either. I won't get to see much more of these girls, so I want to get in as much time as I can."

The irritation and disappointment of the evening gave way to a deeper dread. "What do you mean you're not going to see much more of them?"

"When we move to New York." Veronica's left eye twitched ever so slightly. "If. You know what I mean."

She did. She hadn't wanted to. In fact, she'd been going out of her way to avoid, ignore, or flat-out deny what her gut had known since Veronica had announced the job offer. Maybe even since the accident. "What are we doing?"

Veronica offered her a bright smile. "I thought we were out for a fun night with our friends."

Veronica's friends, technically. "Sometimes I'm not sure how well we really know each other."

"You could put in a little more effort to get to know me. Beyond what I like in bed, and that I want kids, you haven't really asked. I have goals you know." Veronica straightened. The move was subtle but meant she was looking down on Amelia and the feeling of her condescending attitude was only amplified.

"I have goals too." But were their goals as similar as Amelia had once thought? Suddenly she wasn't at all sure. "Maybe we moved too fast. Maybe we weren't ready to move in together."

"Actually, I've been thinking the same thing." Veronica took a deep breath. "I think it'd be good if we slow things down. Or take a break for a while." She didn't seem to be thinking out loud. In fact, the words felt rehearsed.

"You want to see other people?"

Veronica lifted a shoulder. "It might be a good idea. At least for a while—it might help us figure out what we really want. But we don't have to talk about it now. We're here to have fun."

"I'm not feeling very fun at the moment." It wasn't only the fact that she had a broken ankle and Veronica clearly didn't care. The part that really hit home was that Veronica could gloss over their conversation of seeing other people as if it were nothing important. Still, she wasn't one to cause a scene, even in a moment that maybe called for it. "My foot really is killing me."

"I'm sorry your foot hurts, but you made the decision not to take pain meds."

Amelia clenched her jaw. "Yeah. I'm ready to go home."

"Come on, babe. Can you not be like that tonight?"

"Like what? You basically just told me you want to break up."

Veronica shook her head. "No, I said a break. Not break up. And you said you thought we'd moved too fast too."

She couldn't meet Veronica's eyes with tears pressing at her own. She looked back at the table where Veronica's friends were laughing and probably gossiping about people she didn't know. "Your friends seemed to know more about your New York trip than I do. And about the job offer."

"They're excited for me." Veronica's tone was icy. "It's more than I can say about you these days."

Amelia swallowed the retort on the tip of her tongue. It wasn't a lie. She'd tried to muster enthusiasm but couldn't get past what it meant for their relationship, their future. "Because you taking this job means we break up or I uproot my whole life. And because even though those are the options, you clearly made this decision already without any input from me."

"I told you it wasn't a hundred percent settled."

She folded her arms and tried for a withering stare.

"Okay, I may have accepted. It's the opportunity of a lifetime and I didn't think you'd be so wishy-washy about it."

"Wishy-washy? Every time I've tried to have a conversation about the pros and cons of us moving, you've changed the subject." Her voice pitched louder, but she didn't care. "Now I know why. You decided three weeks ago and didn't care what it meant for me. What if I don't want to go?"

"Because you don't want to leave your grandmother? Or is it your high-powered career of planning bingo nights for old people?" The vitriol in Veronica's voice had nothing on the condescension.

Amelia looked down at her boot. "Turns out I'm not even up for bingo tonight."

"I didn't mean that the way it came out."

So many things she didn't want to believe settled in her chest like a lead weight. "I think you did. But this isn't the time or place to fight."

To her credit, Veronica nodded. "You're right."

"I'm going to go. Let's agree to talk after we've cooled off?"

She thought maybe Veronica would protest, or at least insist on driving her home. But she didn't. She nodded stoically, turned around, and went back to her friends.

Amelia stood for a moment, surprised and yet not. She started for the door, only to realize her purse remained on the table where Veronica stood laughing like the argument they'd just had didn't even happen. She took a deep breath and walked toward the group as subtly as her lopsided gait would allow.

"Excuse me." She reached into the pile of clutches and bags in the middle of the table.

Conversation stopped, but no one said a word to her. Not one. She grabbed the one that was hers and bit the inside of her cheek, willing herself not to cry.

Outside, people continued to arrive. The night was just getting started for the hip and childless crowd. She realized how much that wasn't her, kids or not. Fortunately, it meant she didn't have to wait ages for an Uber.

On the ride home, she did her best not to stew. Was it unreasonable to expect Veronica to take her feelings into consideration before making such a huge decision? Maybe it was. Maybe Veronica's priorities were exactly where she wanted them to be and it was foolish for Amelia to want something different.

No, not foolish. She refused to doubt her desire for love and family first. But maybe she'd been foolish to think Veronica felt the same. She took out her phone and pulled up their recent text exchanges.

I think you're right about seeing other people. Hope you have fun tonight.

The text was nothing like anything she ever thought she'd say. And yet it felt right. She didn't want to hold Veronica back. Especially not when she wasn't even sure she liked her. She let out a derisive sniff and hit send.

When the car pulled up in front of Nana's house, she thanked her driver and extricated herself from the back seat. Packs of kids had started making their way up the street, along with toddlers in wagons pulled by parents. Laughter and the occasional squeal filled the air. She wondered what Veronica would say if she admitted handing out candy to trick-or-treaters was much more her speed—regardless of her broken foot—than a fancy museum gala and late-night after-party.

She found Nana dumping bags of candy into a giant bowl. "You're home early, dear. Veronica didn't turn into a pumpkin, did she? Or fly off on her broom?"

A snort of laughter came from behind her. Amelia turned and found herself face-to-face with Finn, who made a show of covering her mouth and coughing. "What are you doing here?"

Finn glanced at Edith. "I came to pick up a birthday cake."

"Oh, right. For that woman with the brain tumor." Amelia felt a rush of guilt. Her own bad day was nothing in comparison.

"And then the trick-or-treaters started coming…"

"I asked her to help with door duty when we got a rush of little ones." Nana shrugged. "I thought you'd be out late."

Amelia closed her eyes and tried for a calming breath. There was no reason she should be mad at Finn. Finn was simply in the wrong house at the wrong time, being helpful. And also everything Veronica wasn't.

"I'll go."

"No, no. Don't do that."

"It's fine, really." Finn looked down, then at Amelia. "I didn't think you were going to be here."

"Well, I wasn't supposed to be home." As much as she didn't want to parade her fight with Veronica in front of Finn, making her feel bad would be next-level bitchy. "Veronica and I had a fight."

Nana set her hand on Amelia's arm. "I'm sorry, dear. Do you want to talk about it?"

Amelia took inventory of her feelings once again. "You know what? Not even a little."

Nana nodded, understanding in her own way, but Finn still looked painfully uncomfortable. Before anyone could say more, the doorbell rang.

"More customers." Nana handed Finn the bowl of candy. "Finn, will you do the honors?"

Having a task seemed to help Finn relax. She headed to the door and Amelia eavesdropped as she greeted the trio of kids and their designated grown-up. Just like at the carnival, she chatted up each one and got some laughs. It drove home just how much Veronica wasn't that and didn't want to be.

Amelia turned from the door and caught Nana's gaze. Her sympathetic look made Amelia even less sure of what she should do.

When Finn greeted a new group of kids—the door hadn't even closed after the last bunch—Nana came over and wrapped her arm around Amelia. "You know I'm not a Veronica fan, but I'd never wish you unhappiness. I hope you know that."

"I know." She took a deep breath. Nana gave her a hug and then let go right as Finn closed the door.

Finn looked back at Amelia with uncertainty. "I really can go."

Amelia shrugged. "Honestly, I could use a little distraction."

"I bet you could also use a nice stiff drink." Nana winked.

Being off the painkillers had some benefits. "I think that's a fantastic idea."

"That's my girl. Finn?"

Finn ran a hand up the back of her neck. "I'm going to go with yes."

"What's your pleasure?" Nana asked.

Finn angled her head toward Amelia. "I defer to Ms. Stone."

Amelia smiled. "Gin martini, extra dirty?"

It was hard to tell if Finn was surprised by her choice or impressed. Either way, she offered a nod of approval. "Works for me."

CHAPTER TEN

"The Tootsie Pops are going like hotcakes. We only have two left." Finn shook the bowl, scattering the miniature Snickers and Butterfingers and unearthing a few remaining bags of Skittles.

Amelia reached past her and snagged a red one. "You mean we only have one left."

"Hey—you're supposed to say Trick or Treat."

"Treat." Amelia unwrapped the lollipop and dropped onto the couch. She popped the cherry-red candy into her mouth, twirling the stick as she eyed Finn, then let it slip out of her lips. "Were you hoping I'd say trick?"

"Maybe."

"Well, you can't always have what you want."

Amelia's tone was decidedly flirty now that she'd polished off her second drink. The way she handled the lollipop didn't hurt either. But Finn wondered how much of her attitude was a cover. She'd come home looking like she was about to cry, though her mood had decidedly improved over the past hour. The question was, what had happened with Veronica? Clearly, they'd had a bad fight if Amelia was upset enough to leave the party.

Amelia held Finn's gaze, her tongue dancing over the round red knob for longer than necessary. "What?"

"Nothing. Just that you're trouble." Finn knew she was loosening up herself. Edith sure didn't go easy on the gin. That was probably why she'd called it quits a half hour ago and gone to bed, leaving Finn and Amelia to finish out the candy dispensing.

"Me? Trouble?" Amelia feigned innocence. "Because I don't ask first?"

Finn smiled. "Sometimes it's better not to grab the first thing you see."

"Why?"

Finn didn't let her flirty answer slip out. Even if they'd had a fight, Amelia was still with Veronica. She set the bowl of candy on the coffee table. It was after nine and the stream of trick-or-treaters had noticeably slowed. She wanted to sit, but Edith had left a pile of recipe books in the rocking chair and Percy had claimed the love seat. The only open spot was the couch where Amelia sat. She settled in a foot away from Amelia, telling herself friends could sit next to each other. Besides, they weren't close enough to touch. Only close enough for her to think about it. And close enough to notice how good Amelia smelled.

"You still thinking of your answer?"

"To why you shouldn't grab the first thing you see?" Finn leaned back. "Well, you might think you like what you see. It might even taste sweet. But who knows what you would have gotten if you'd waited and asked?" She'd tried to keep her voice even and any hint of flirting out of it, but she was feeling hot under the collar all the same. Especially with Amelia's gaze dancing over her body.

"What would you have done if I'd said trick?"

"Uh-uh. Too late. You already got your candy."

Amelia laughed. "But maybe I want more than candy."

"We all want more than candy." Finn reached into the bowl for a Snickers, mostly for a distraction. When she looked back, Amelia was still working on the lollipop, but her tongue paused long enough for Finn to notice. They were on the same page. The page that could get them both into a lot of trouble if things kept going in the direction they were headed. Finn cleared her throat. "Anyway, it is what it is. We eat the candy we pick and tell ourselves we're happy."

"Says Finn, the great philosopher." Amelia nudged Finn's leg with her stockinged foot. "Tell me. What would you have done if I'd said trick?"

"You'll never know." Finn unwrapped the Snickers and popped it into her mouth. If only she could be satisfied with chocolate, peanuts, and chewy nougat. But now Amelia's not-so-subtle toe stroke up her shin had her imagining the same move with no clothes to get in the way. And, damn, what she would do to trade places with that lollipop…

Percy yawned, making an adorable squeaky cat sound, and she pounced on the chance to change the subject. "Cats are so cute. It's like they sit around and practice."

"Truth. And Percy is the cutest. But don't tell him that. He prefers 'handsome.'" Amelia paused. "Do you have a cat?"

"No, but I've got a cattle dog who thinks she's a lap cat. She may not be as cute as Percy, but she can ride a skateboard."

"Seriously? I want to see. Percy, you hear that?" Amelia made a chirping sound that got a tail flick from Percy but nothing more. "Finn's dog rides a skateboard. What tricks can you do, lazy boy?"

"Aw, he only needs to sit around and look good."

"So, basically same as you?"

Amelia's smirk seemed to dare Finn to take things one step further. And she so wanted to. Unfortunately, the refrain about Amelia having a girlfriend wouldn't leave her head. "What are we doing?"

"Right now? Talking. Is this something new for you?"

Finn rolled her eyes. "You know what I mean."

"Do I?" Amelia's tone remained playful, but she breathed out and a moment later looked almost pensive. "I don't know what we're doing exactly. But I'm glad you're here and I don't think we need to worry. We're both adults."

"Adults can get into a lot of trouble. Especially after two of your grandma's martinis." Finn didn't want to, but she forced herself to go on. "Amelia, I like you, but you have a girlfriend and I want to respect that."

Amelia met her gaze. "Duly noted, adult friend."

"I'm serious."

"So am I. And since you said it first, I like you too. But you're right. I've got a girlfriend. At least I think I do."

"What do you mean?"

Amelia shrugged. "You know, I was kind of annoyed at first that you were here. After everything with Veronica, I wanted to go to my room and mope. But I'm glad that didn't happen."

"Did you two have a big fight or a little fight?"

"Little fight, but I think it's a big deal. Veronica already made up her mind on the New York job. She pretended she wanted to know my opinion, but she already told them yes."

"So, you're going to New York?"

"I'm not sure. I don't know if we have as much in common as I thought we did. And we're both realizing that we jumped into things too soon." Amelia held up her hand. "Please don't say I told you so."

"Wouldn't dream of it."

"The hard part is, at first everything was so amazing with her. Now I'm wondering if she even likes me. I think she likes the idea of me. And the idea of the life we could have. She might like my mother more than me, which is weird. But also not." Amelia sighed. "We both got carried away, I think."

"You've had a crazy month. With the accident and moving in with your grandma…Your whole world turned upside down. And now Veronica's world is completely changing too. Maybe you could still be amazing together."

"Maybe." Amelia took a deep breath and exhaled. "She suggested that we take a break. See other people. I didn't like the idea at first, obviously, but now I think maybe she's right."

"How's that make you feel?" Finn asked because she wanted to know, and because if she didn't focus on Amelia's feelings, her heart might leap out of her chest.

"Weirdly relieved. I don't know what I want. I don't even know what I'm doing here." She looked around her grandmother's living room and shook her head.

"Right now, you're talking to a friend." Finn held out her hand. Amelia clasped it and warmth spread through her. A minute passed, and then another.

"Thanks for being here." Amelia shifted closer, narrowing the gap until their legs were touching. "Turns out I needed you again."

Finn tried to concentrate on their entwined fingers and not Amelia's leg against hers. Or the overwhelming desire to stroke her hand up Amelia's arm. She could do the friend thing even if it was torture, but it'd be easier if Amelia moved a little farther away. Not that she was going to tell her that. And damn did Amelia's hand feel good in hers.

"Finn?"

"Yeah?" Finn looked up and Amelia leaned toward her.

She didn't pull back when Amelia's lips touched hers. A roaring sound filled her ears, blocking all thoughts save one— Amelia was kissing her. The taste of gin mixed with sweet cherry candy and she pressed forward. When Amelia parted her lips, wanting her to deepen the kiss, it was exactly what Finn wanted too. Amelia's acquiescence, the gentle touch of her tongue and then the feel of her hand on Finn's chest, was everything. Everything she needed. That one thought snapped her out of the moment like a rubber band against her skin.

She pulled back. Amelia stared at her, breathless and clearly confused. Her lips tingled and all she wanted to do was kiss Amelia again, make the moment that had gone wrong right. But more kissing wouldn't make it right.

"I can't kiss you. And you shouldn't kiss me." She stood and the room spun around her. "I need to leave."

"Fuck." Amelia covered her face with her hands.

Finn fought the urge to comfort her. She wanted to take back her words and let her body, instead of her head, make decisions for the rest of the night. And yet…she couldn't. "I'm sorry."

Amelia shook her head. "I'm sorry too."

Finn waited, half expecting Amelia to say more. To say the kiss had been no big deal and she was freaking out over nothing. She expected it but knew that would only make everything worse. When Amelia didn't even meet her eyes, Finn found her jacket and slipped it on. She patted her pockets, making sure she had her keys and her wallet, and without a word, let herself out.

* * *

"I don't know why you're so upset," Jess said again. "She kissed you. It might have been a mistake, and a bad call on her part, but it's not the end of the world. You know, I did warn you this would happen."

"Can you please not lecture me?" Finn wondered now why she hadn't thought to call an Uber. Or even better, she could have walked the mile to her apartment. Instead she'd called Jess, thinking her best friend would be sympathetic.

"Is the problem that you don't want to be her rebound?" When Finn didn't answer, Jess pressed on. "Ever since you met this woman you've been whining about how you weren't sure how she felt about you. Now you know. She clearly wanted to make out with you and her girlfriend basically gave her permission. So why did you ditch right when it was getting good?"

"I haven't been whining," Finn argued, distinctly aware that her voice had a slight whine to it.

"Oh, there's been whining. But that's not the point. Why'd you call me to come pick you up?"

"Because I drank too much and it's Halloween. I don't want to hit some kid."

"I mean, why didn't you spend the night with her?"

Finn shook her head. "First off, it's her grandma's house. Second off…I'm worried it's partly my fault that she isn't trying to fix things with her girlfriend."

"You're the one who told me they were completely wrong for each other."

"Yeah, well, maybe that's because I want to be right for Amelia."

Jess cocked her head. "Do you? If you really want her, why aren't you still there?"

Finn threw up her hands. "Oh, I don't know. Maybe because she's not single?"

"Or maybe because of your issues. Maybe Amelia is perfect for you and you're scared because deep inside you know it."

"You're the one who told me not to spend time with her. Not to get my heart messed up in something that wasn't going anywhere."

"And did you listen?" Jess let out a frustrated growl. "Finn, clearly you like her. The question is, why are you in my car? Is it because now that you know she's available, you're scared? Scared she's going to trample on your heart like Nadia? Or scared she's going to make you have to choose between a life here in Denver and always being able to run home to South Dakota?"

Finn stared out the window at the passing streetlights. "She hasn't broken up with her girlfriend yet. And maybe it's about to happen but it's not going to be because of me. She only kissed me because she was upset and a little drunk."

A car darted in front of Jess's Mini Cooper and Finn slapped the dash. "What the hell is wrong with people? It's Halloween. Doesn't that guy know there are kids everywhere? I hate drivers that think they're the only ones on the damn road." She grumbled again when the driver zipped around another car and then revved it through the intersection a fraction of a second before the light turned red. "Slow down, asshole."

Jess turned halfway in her seat. "Since that dude's already in the next state, can we please focus on you?"

"People are dumb."

"True. You have your moments too." Jess cleared her throat. "Okay. Let's recap. Amelia's basically breaking up with her girlfriend. Maybe that's partly your fault, or maybe it has nothing to do with you. But she kissed you. Was it a good kiss?"

Finn shrugged. *Hell, yes* wouldn't do the kiss justice.

"Finn—I know feelings are hard for you, but this isn't rocket science. When Amelia kissed you, how'd you feel?"

"More alive than I've felt in a long time." Finn closed her eyes, her mind immediately picturing Amelia the moment before the kiss. In that one second, she was certain her heart stopped beating. Then Amelia's lips touched hers and she forgot everything else. "Her lips felt exactly right. Like she's the one I'm meant to be kissing or some cheesy bullshit like that. But she's still with Veronica and who knows if it would even work with us—like you said, I come with issues."

"Everyone's got issues. Veronica is her gorgeous girlfriend who's probably gonna be famous someday?"

Finn nodded. "Your light's green."

Jess turned her attention back to driving. "You know what? I agree with you for leaving."

"You do?"

Jess nodded. "Aside from what I said about you needing to figure out what you want—and if you even want a relationship—you're a catch. Whoever gets you has to deserve you. I hardly know her, but Amelia's done zip to earn one of the coolest people I know."

She could argue Amelia was too good for her, but what was the point? Finn rubbed her face. The day had caught up with her finally and she couldn't wait to tumble into bed. If only she could go straight to sleep without thinking of Amelia or the kiss that definitely shouldn't have happened. Jess parked on the street in front of their apartment but didn't turn off the car.

"I have an idea."

"Please tell me it doesn't involve that banana costume."

Jess grinned. "You made an adorable banana, but we don't need costumes for this. The clubs are still open. Let's go out. You need a hookup and I need to find a willing partner for 'The Cuffing Chronicles.'"

She didn't even try to hide the cringe. "I'm not sure which part of that to take issue with first."

"How about none of it?"

"On one condition."

CHAPTER ELEVEN

Over a week had passed since Halloween and still no word from Veronica. Not a call, not a text. Nothing. Amelia had cried herself to sleep the night of their fight—the night she kissed Finn, who then bolted faster than she could say boo—then settled into a state of restless, edgy irritation.

At least that's what Nana called it every time she pointed out how foul Amelia's mood had become.

She was starting to think maybe Veronica expected an apology. Or maybe she was so busy packing for New York, she wasn't thinking about her girlfriend at all. The girlfriend she'd assumed would pick up and move across country with her.

But even as she stewed about Veronica, it was Finn who occupied the lion's share of her thoughts. Had she ruined any chance at a friendship with Finn?

Finn and her teasing about grabbing the first thing. Finn and her intense blue eyes that reassured her and riled her up at the same time. Finn and her perfect mouth and the kiss that still had Amelia brushing her fingers over her lips in an attempt

Jess laced her fingers together. "What's that?"

"Please don't make me go out."

"Fine." She cut the engine. "I still think you need to get this girl out of your mind or you're going to end up in bed with her."

Finn didn't argue. With Amelia's kiss still making her lips tingle, she couldn't.

to hold on to just how perfect it was. Finn, who now seemed to be going out of her way to avoid her. And, honestly, she didn't blame her.

Still, she couldn't bring herself to completely regret the kiss. Yes, she felt guilty about it. Yes, she'd put Finn in a terrible position. But maybe a kiss that good was a sign they weren't meant to be friends. Exactly like crashing the U-Haul was a sign she wasn't meant to move in with Veronica. Or maybe those were only her excuses and she was a total mess that no one should date.

She'd gone round and round, analyzing and overanalyzing her actions and Veronica's and Finn's to the point where she wanted to scream. The whole situation was infuriating. It was demoralizing. It was—

"Are you around today, dear?" Nana's question pierced her thoughts.

"Huh? What?"

"You. Are you home this evening after work?"

She'd done nothing but go to work and come home to mope in days. "Probably. Why?"

"Just asking."

Amelia narrowed her gaze. "You never just ask anything."

Nana rolled her eyes and let out a huff. "Fine. Finn is stopping by later to pick up brownies and wanted to know if you were going to be home."

"She did?" Both her voice and her mood perked up at the prospect.

"Yes, she was worried about running into you."

"Oh." She didn't think she could feel worse but now she did.

"What happened between you two? You were perfectly fine when I went to bed on Halloween and now you're not speaking to each other?"

Amelia blew out a breath. "I kissed her. I was tipsy on your martinis and she was being so nice and things got flirty and…I kissed her."

"Ah." Nana nodded and seemed not even the tiniest bit surprised.

"Really? That's all you have to say?"

Nana shrugged. "I figured you'd either kissed or fought. It's nice to know which."

Amelia pressed her fingers to her temples. "We didn't fight, but she booked it out of here like she'd learned I was carrying the plague."

"Well, you can't really blame her for that, can you, dear? You do have a girlfriend. Or has that changed?"

"I don't know." It was all one big, gigantic, colossal mess. She didn't know where things stood with Veronica, didn't know where she wanted them to stand, and on top of that, she felt bad for putting Finn in the awkward position of being in the middle of it.

"What are you going to do?"

Such a simple question. Why did the answer feel impossibly difficult? Because her relationship with her actual girlfriend was in free fall and she couldn't stop thinking about kissing someone else. A very attractive, smart, funny, and kind someone else. Someone who wasn't looking to move across the country. "I have absolutely no idea."

She headed to work, relieved to have somewhere to channel her energy and attention. She reviewed statistics from the Smoke Alarms for Seniors program and drafted her grant proposal for the spring while the information was fresh. At the staff meeting, plans for the community Thanksgiving dinner were in full swing. And if her thoughts drifted to Veronica's impending departure or what Finn might do for the holiday, well, her staff had the kindness not to call her out.

When she got back from her weekly check-in with the county manager, the first thing she did was grab her phone. Still nothing from Veronica, but she had a message from Finn.

Can we talk? I want to apologize.

Amelia stared at the words for a full minute before responding. What did it say that the woman she wasn't even dating was more invested in making up than her girlfriend? Nothing good, that was for sure. *I'd like to talk. But you don't need to apologize. If anyone does, it's me.*

She expected a text conversation, or maybe a suggestion they grab coffee, but a few seconds later, her phone rang. Finn's name appeared in the caller ID. "Hello?"

"Why do you seem surprised to hear from me?"

She laughed at being caught. "Who talks on the phone anymore?"

"Uh, I do. Do you not?" Finn sounded genuinely confused.

"I mean, I do. I work in a government office and with old people. It's required."

Finn laughed. "I'd never thought of it that way. Anyway, is this a good time?"

She didn't have any more meetings for the day and, thanks to Veronica's radio silence, no plans for after work either. "Sure."

"Okay, good. So, I wanted to apologize for taking off on you the other night."

Wow. She really didn't beat around the bush. "I guess that means I should apologize for kissing you."

Finn made a sound that could have been a sigh but might also have been a growl. "You don't need to apologize for that."

"No?" It sure as hell seemed like it.

"Was it a mistake? Probably. But I can't bring myself to regret it."

Oh. It was harder to say what she found more attractive in that moment—Finn's directness or the idea that Finn didn't regret their kiss. "How about I apologize for the timing, then? Or doing it while tipsy?"

"I'll take that."

"Thank you." She wanted to accept Finn's apology just as readily, but wanted—needed?—to understand the why behind it. "I think—"

"I left because I wanted to kiss you again. And if I kissed you again, I would have wanted a whole lot more than a kiss."

Amelia's heart started to race. Finn wanted her. Like, really wanted her. Something about the admission, sober and in broad daylight, felt more real than when they'd discussed it before. "Really?"

"Yes, but I couldn't allow myself to go there. I can't be with someone who is already in a relationship. And I can't be the reason someone's relationship falls apart." Finn's voice had an edge to it, making Amelia wonder about her past relationships.

"I get that. I swear I do. I hope you know I'm not the kind of person who makes out with other people while she's seeing someone else. I've never done anything like that before." For some reason, it mattered that Finn believed her.

"But something made you. Something you need to figure out."

"Is this your way of telling me we can't hang out anymore?" The thought made her inexplicably sad.

"Maybe. Unless…I was kind of hoping we could put it behind us and agree to be friends." Finn waited a beat before continuing, "But I understand if that makes you uncomfortable."

Amelia closed her eyes. Might as well be honest. "The idea of never seeing you again makes me uncomfortable."

Another pause. Eventually, Finn said, "So, friends?"

Relief and something akin to joy rippled through her. "Friends."

Yes, part of her might want to be way more than friends with Finn Douglas. But her life was sort of a disaster at the moment, and she'd just managed to sort one little piece of it out. For now, she'd take what she could get.

* * *

Talking things through with Finn drove home the fact that she needed to do the same with Veronica. Even if part of her dreaded the outcome, it couldn't be worse than the limbo state they'd landed in. With that unease fueling her, she swallowed her pride and sent Veronica a text. More specific than Finn's simple request to talk, but the sentiment remained the same. Unlike with Finn, it took some back-and-forth to arrange a conversation. Though, to be fair, she insisted this one be in person.

The following afternoon, after reminding Veronica twice she needed a ride, she found herself at the café where they'd had their first date. It felt at once nostalgic and surreal, like some mystical combination of ages ago and the couple of months it had actually been.

Veronica offered to get their drinks and Amelia scouted a table, settling in next to a guy who appeared to be having a tea date with his preschool-age twin daughters. Veronica passed them just as one of the girls toppled her drink. Watching the dad attempting to console her while he sopped up the mess made her smile.

Veronica set down their matching almond milk lattes and rolled her eyes. "Dramatic much?"

Amelia shifted her attention to Veronica, more irritated perhaps than the situation warranted. "Do you like kids?"

Knowing she didn't want the answer meant she really needed it. Even if this wasn't how she planned to start the conversation.

"What are you talking about? Of course I do."

Amelia shook her head, the dots she'd been trying so hard not to connect creating a picture nonetheless. "I think you like the idea of kids." When Veronica didn't argue, Amelia pressed on. "And you like the idea of a perfect little family that complements your professional image. A wife you can take to events, kids whose pictures you can show on-air and tell charming stories about."

"I mean, yes. I do want those things. You make it sound so shallow, though."

Because it was shallow. Was everything about Veronica shallow? She'd picked up on a few things early on—like her obsession with perfect appearances and having the right friends—but she'd brushed it off as coming with the territory of her job. At worst, a sign of insecurity. And who was she to judge when it came to that? But now it felt less like a foible and more like a gaping chasm between them. "I'm not ready to go to New York."

"I figured." Veronica reached across the table and took her hand. "You're upset about me accepting the job without telling you."

"A little, yeah."

"When do you think you'd be ready?"

"I'm not sure…You were right about us needing a break. But I think it might be more than that. I'm not sure we make sense together."

Veronica didn't respond immediately. She let go of Amelia's hand and shifted back in her seat. "You shouldn't be making such a big decision when you're upset."

The delivery and the tone Amelia had once convinced herself was adoring now reeked of condescension. "Maybe not. But—"

"There really is no rush for you to come to New York," Veronica interrupted. "I need to be there before Thanksgiving. There's a chance I'll get to be one of the correspondents for the Macy's parade. But you could take a few months to settle things here. It could be after Christmas, even. I'm sure I'll be busy with parties. Miranda has already invited me to three engagements—nothing you'd enjoy."

"Of course she has." Amelia realized she didn't actually care about missing any party Veronica and her mother would be at. One beat later, a second realization hit her. "Oh, my God."

Veronica regarded her with concern. "What? What is it?"

"You asked me out because of my mother."

Veronica's brow bunched. "That's ridiculous."

"If you love someone, you want to be with them. You want to spend Christmas with them. You want to do things they want to do. But you don't care about all of that because you love the idea of dating me, the idea of us together, more than the reality of it." And the reality of their situation, and the terrible choices that had gotten them both there, landed heavy on Amelia's chest. "The only reason you picked me for this perfect life you've created in your head is because it includes Miranda Stone."

"Okay, now you're being more dramatic than Miss Can't Hold Her Own Beverage."

The insult, and the underlying dig on unwieldy children, landed, but Amelia plowed on. "Maybe I am, but it's the truth." Even if that wasn't Veronica's initial, or even primary, motivation, she knew without a shred of doubt her mother—and her mother's connections—were a part of it. How could she have been such an idiot?

"Look, I appreciate everything Miranda has done for me. She's made me feel welcome and she's bent over backward to help me. I thought you liked that she and I hit it off."

She had, at least in the beginning. Now, though, she realized she'd been little more than the thing that brought them together. And somehow she'd become a third wheel in the process. Snippets of conversations flitted through her mind. Warning signs she'd gone out of her way to ignore. All of Nana's reservations.

Amelia shook her head. She'd been so very foolish.

"Why don't we—"

"Break up."

Veronica frowned. "No, that's not what I was going to say at all."

"It's what I'm saying. Veronica, I don't want to move to New York, but even more, I don't want to be with you. I don't need a break to figure it out." Saying the words aloud drove home just how much she meant them.

Veronica didn't say anything. The silence felt unnatural and made her realize how often Veronica talked around her. Over her.

"Don't worry, I'm sure you and Miranda can still be friends. She's lacking that mama bear instinct." She'd resented it as a child, but at this point, it didn't even sting.

"You're really doing this?" Veronica shook her head with what appeared to be disbelief. "You're breaking up with me?"

"I am."

"We could have had it all, you know."

She'd thought so too. It was the reason she threw logic and caution to the wind and agreed to move in together in the first place. But in her attempts to be bold and decisive for once, all she'd managed to do was make a mess. "Even if that's true, I don't think our versions of having it all are the same."

Veronica stood. "I'll box up the things you left at my place and send them over."

Amelia started to apologize but caught herself. She straightened her shoulders and tried to rustle up all the dignity that could be had given her current state. "Thank you."

After Veronica left, she stayed at the table, staring at her now empty cup. She expected tears, but none came. Only relief.

Relief until she realized she was stranded. She could get an Uber. She'd gotten quite good at that in the last few weeks. But the fact of the matter was she could use a friendly ear as much as a ride. She took out her phone and pulled up the thread with Finn. Nana had invited Finn to join them in a pie-making extravaganza and that had led to a text exchange on the merits of savory versus sweet pies. She read Finn's last text. *I'm not saying apple isn't awesome but I'd take a shepherd's pie any day.*

The back-and-forth had been easy and light and not at all flirtatious. The conversation, even over text, had made her feel good when everything else felt awful. Which meant they were officially in the friend zone, right? Anyway, Finn wasn't the reason she'd broken up with Veronica. She took a deep breath. *Any chance you're free?*

Amelia didn't really expect an immediate reply, but one came.

Leaving work now. What's up?

Should she tell Finn about breaking up with Veronica in a text? Or should she do that in person? Did it even matter? They'd agreed to be friends, after all. Not being with Veronica didn't change that. *Sad singleton needs a chauffeur and you come highly recommended.*

You're hiring me out to other people now? A smiley face emoji followed.

Nope. I'm the sad singleton. That was one way to do it.

Oh.

The brevity of the reply made her smile. Which was saying something. *Yeah.*

Where are you? I'll be right there.

Fifteen minutes later, Finn's truck pulled up in front of the café. As she hauled herself up and hobbled out, she told herself it was simple relief she felt. But when Finn got out to open the door and help her up—with a smile that said she wouldn't ask questions unless Amelia wanted to talk—she had to admit, at least to herself, it was a whole lot more.

CHAPTER TWELVE

"You're making pies with her?"

"Yeah. Why is making pies weird?" Finn tugged the zipper on her coat all the way up to her throat. The sun hadn't risen yet to warm the day but both Jess and Rascal had a bounce in their step.

"It's not weird to make pies. What's weird is *you* making pies."

"Well, I think it's weird to enjoy a walk when it's nine degrees out." She'd almost let Jess take Rascal out alone, but guilt got her out of bed.

"I love the first real cold snap." Jess took a deep breath as if trying to pull the ice into her lungs. "Makes me feel energized. After pies, what's your plan?"

Finn shook her head. "I don't have a plan. We're friends. We'll probably hang out until the pies are done and then I'll leave."

Jess's look was skeptical. "Friends who kiss when they hang out."

"We kissed one time." She shouldn't have told Jess about the kiss in the first place, but she'd needed to talk about it and, well, Jess was her person for things having to do with feelings.

"You know it won't last, right?"

"What won't last?"

"You two pretending to only be friends. Friends who don't want to kiss."

Finn knew Jess was right. Before she decided on a way to change the subject, Rascal spotted a squirrel and whined. The sound was so much like a plea that Finn wanted to give in and let go of her leash. The squirrel studied Rascal for a moment before skittering across the sidewalk and bolting up a tree. Unable to help herself, Rascal lunged forward and yipped.

"Sorry, girl." Finn pulled back on the lead. It might not be the same one, but they walked the same block every morning and more often than not a squirrel was waiting at that exact tree to taunt Rascal. "One day I'll let you chase that little nut head. Promise."

Jess ignored the shift in conversation. "I bet you're sleeping together by Christmas."

"That's not happening. First off, she just broke up with the woman she'd planned to have kids with. She's not ready for another relationship. Second, we make good friends. And third—"

"And third, you're scared she's the real deal."

"I'm not scared." Now she really wished she'd let Jess take Rascal alone. To be back in bed, snuggled under her down comforter and enjoying a quiet morning, sounded even more appealing. "Maybe I don't jump into things but that's different than being scared. I like to have a plan and know what's going to happen."

"So much self-control, Finn. It'd be impressive except I don't buy it. You're scared you like her too much already."

Finn didn't respond. She whistled when Rascal pointed her nose toward the park. Some days they took a longer walk and circled it, but today she wanted a cup of coffee and a shower. Or to go back to bed. "Can we talk about you now?"

Jess rolled her eyes.

"What happened with your date last night?"

"Wasn't a date. It was research."

Finn chuckled. She felt the knot in her stomach ease. She liked girl drama in other people's lives better than her own. "Okay. How'd the research go?"

"Fine." Jess was clearly trying to sound impartial, but she couldn't hide her smile.

"That sort of fine, huh? Did you sleep with her already?"

"What? No. This is for my column, Finn. I'm not even sure I'm going to sleep with her."

"Okay, but did you at least talk about who's wearing the handcuffs?"

Jess groaned. "Cuffing has nothing to do with handcuffs. I already told you that. Cuffing is a temporary relationship, generally over the fall and winter. Hence the phrase 'cuffing season.' And the only reason I'm doing it is because my boss asked me and I'm getting paid to write about it in my column. Straight people have been doing it for ages. Lesbians need to catch up."

"Okay, but, if you do have sex, are you going to be thinking about the fact that you're doing it for an article?"

"I'd only have sex because I wanted to. Never because of my column."

"But you're gonna write about it after. That's a lot of pressure. Especially with handcuffs being involved..." Finn laughed when Jess gave her side-eye.

"Since you've got so much interest in handcuffs, maybe you should ask Amelia if she likes that sort of stuff."

No way was she going to ask Amelia something like that. "I'm leaving the cuffing to you, Jess. In all its connotations."

"Whatever." Jess snagged Rascal's leash. "Go get ready for your pie date. Rascal and I want to go for a run around the park. I think it's sweet, by the way, that Amelia's teaching you how to make pie. Even if we both know you're only going because you want to eat some of hers."

Finn shook her head. "Your mind's in the gutter."

"Spend the day with her and then tell me you don't want to eat her pie."

* * *

"Hi." Amelia's smile lit up her face. "You always right on time?"

In fact, she'd worried about being too early, and too eager, so had gone to the gym first to work off some energy. Then she'd worried about being late. "I try to be on time, but I seem to run into a lot of emergencies."

"Says the paramedic. How long have you been working on that terrible joke?"

Finn grinned. "That one just came to me."

Amelia pushed the door open wider. "Come on in. Nana's gone to the store for sugar. I told her we'd have enough but she hates running out in the middle of a project."

"I could have picked sugar up on the way here."

Amelia nodded. "I told her that. She insisted you wouldn't know what to get."

"She doesn't think I can buy sugar? And she's letting me help make pie?" Finn took off her coat and hung it in the closet. She'd been over enough times to know that if she didn't make herself at home she'd get scolded by either Edith or Amelia.

"Nana buys special sugar. Trust me, you don't want to get between her and a grocery store aisle. Besides, you are going to be under close observation throughout the pie making. No chance she will leave you alone in the kitchen."

"Probably a good idea." Finn wouldn't trust herself to do more than throw a potpie in a microwave.

Amelia led the way to the kitchen. She was getting around better, but Finn wondered how much pain she was still dealing with. The accident was likely still playing games on her mind as well—and now on top of that she had her breakup with Veronica to weather.

"Coffee?"

"Yes, please."

Amelia poured two mugs and nodded at a platter on the kitchen table. "We also have day-old donuts if you aren't picky."

"Not picky at all." Finn helped herself to a maple bar. "Toni—the EMT who helped when you got hit—won't let us get them anymore. She's dating this hippie chick who's turned her into a health freak."

"I'm sorry for your loss."

"Thank you for understanding." She took the mug Amelia handed her, added cream, and sat. Amelia joined her. She started to reach for a glazed old-fashioned but pulled back her hand and sighed.

"You don't like day-old donuts?"

"The calories won't be worth it. Not with this thing on my foot." She raised her boot in the air and gave it a shake. "I can't work out and everything I eat goes right to my...ugh. Never mind." She took a sip of coffee, her brow furrowed. "I sounded like Veronica there for a minute."

"It's okay, you know, to feel bad about the boot. And the accident." Finn shifted in her seat. "It won't be long before that thing comes off and you can go back to your old routines. Do you work out?"

"If you count trying to walk up steps with this thing."

"That counts for sure. Ramps should be everywhere. But I meant are you someone who works out. Like before the accident."

Amelia sighed. "I used to."

"Want me to stop pushing?"

"You're not pushing. It's fine."

Finn wasn't certain she trusted Amelia's answer, but she knew how important it was to not get stuck thinking things weren't going to change. Or, rather, to think that an accident ruined everything. Her skiing accident had changed her life, but some of that change was for the better. It took her a while to see that, though. "What's your favorite workout?"

Amelia eyed the boot again. "I like group classes. Preferably with music, but I'll try anything—spin, CrossFit, Zumba, kickboxing. I even took pole dancing for a while. That was a blast, but I couldn't take myself seriously whenever I saw my reflection in the mirror." She looked up at Finn. "I'm not one of those people who hates working out. I love it, actually. And I sound pathetic right now, but I miss it. I miss so many things that it's driving me a little crazy."

Finn broke off a section of the maple bar and handed it to Amelia. "After my run-in with the tree, I really got into lifting weights. At first, I was only trying to get the muscles retrained, you know? But then it was retraining my head too."

Amelia stared at the donut for a moment and finally took a bite. "Still good… After your accident, when did you start working out again?"

"Before I was even supposed to get out of bed, I started with hand weights. Couldn't help myself. I had to do something."

Amelia's brow creased. "My ankle still hurts. Wakes me up sometimes throbbing and I can't walk for long. At my last checkup, I wanted to ask if the pain is supposed to be gone by now. But I couldn't bring myself to. When my doctor asked if I needed more pain meds, I lied and told her it wasn't hurting."

"We all want to feel fine. And we want to be all healed before we are. Pushing through the pain isn't always the best idea. Sometimes the pain is telling you to go slow." Finn hesitated. "Or eat a pot brownie."

Amelia laughed. "Don't think I haven't considered it."

"Edith does make amazing brownies."

"And I'm sure the pot makes them extra amazing." Amelia sighed. Two more bites and the donut was gone. She wiped her fingers on a napkin but a bit of maple icing stuck at the corner of her lip.

"You've got some icing…" Finn touched the corner of her own lip, but Amelia swiped the wrong side of her mouth. "No, here." She reached out to touch the spot, but Amelia tensed and Finn quickly pulled back her hand. "Sorry. I'll let you get it."

"It's fine." Amelia patted her lips with the napkin as a blush colored her cheeks. "Apparently I can't even eat a donut without making a mess of things."

"Some things are better messy."

Amelia held Finn's gaze. A smile tugged up her lips. "You're pretty good at making me feel better, you know."

"After I make you feel crappy?"

"Exactly." Amelia reached out and touched Finn's cheek. The caress was light and only lasted a moment but sent a rush through Finn's body.

"Did I have donut on me too?"

"No." She paused. "You touched my face and I wanted to touch yours."

"That's fair. That's what friends do, right?" Finn tried to keep the joking tone, but her chest felt tight and she longed to close the distance to Amelia's lips. So much that she couldn't think of anything else.

"We should get started on the pie crusts."

"Yeah. Okay." Finn didn't move but neither did Amelia.

Amelia tilted her head. "Finn, if Nana comes home and you're still looking like you're about to kiss me, you get to explain things to her."

Finn eyed her coffee. "Do you think we can't be friends?"

"I think you need to decide what you want." Amelia paused. "And probably we need to keep our hands to ourselves. I'll try if you will, but it's hard when every time we're together I feel like you want to kiss me."

"You kissed me first."

"Yeah. I did. And then you freaked out and I admitted it was a mistake. Help me out here, okay?"

Finn didn't want to help. Not with that. But she didn't want to leave either. Did she have another choice?

"Let's move on. First things first. We need pastry flour. Do you want to look for that in the pantry?"

"Sure." Finn didn't get up. There were so many things she wanted to say, starting with—maybe she was the one who'd made a mistake. Maybe the kiss was the right thing and being friends was the bad idea.

CHAPTER THIRTEEN

"Are you getting the flour or not?" Amelia crossed her arms. She'd joked about Finn looking like she wanted to kiss her to lighten the mood, but it clearly didn't work. Now Finn looked like she wanted to kiss her, but also like she wanted to leave—intense and sexy and uncomfortable all at the same time.

"I do want to kiss you again," Finn said eventually, without breaking eye contact.

She imagined Finn pulling her to her feet and doing exactly that. Backing her up against the counter and pressing their bodies together. Threading her fingers into her hair and—

"But if I do, I'm pretty sure we can't be friends."

As quickly as the fantasy took hold, it vanished, leaving her in a metaphorical cloud of dust. "Yeah."

"And since I don't want to be some bad idea rebound you wind up regretting, I think we need to stick with friends for now."

Even as it made perfect sense, it left a hollow feeling in her chest. Still, she couldn't bear the thought of losing Finn from her life completely. "I hope you know you'd never be just a rebound. You're—"

The back door swung open and Nana marched in, a canvas grocery bag in each hand. "I swear half the population of Denver was at Safeway today."

Amelia froze, realizing she'd been on the verge of confessing all sorts of things she had no business confessing. Things that went a whole lot further than admitting how much thought she'd given to kissing Finn again. Disappointment gave way to relief, and she stood. "Thanksgiving shoppers already?"

"Must be." Nana looked from Amelia to Finn and back, then narrowed her gaze. "Am I interrupting something?"

Amelia glanced at Finn, who seemed to be deferring to her on the matter of how much to share. "Finn and I were talking about how glad we are to have become friends."

"And how funny it is that good things can come out of bad circumstances." Finn stood as well and locked eyes with Amelia for the briefest of moments.

Amelia swallowed the words and feelings and questions that remained on the tip of her tongue. She wasn't sure she and Finn were done with this conversation, but it wasn't the time or the place to press on. Which was maybe for the best. "The universe likes to play games with us sometimes."

Finn offered her a wink before turning her attention to Nana. "I'm sorry you didn't ask me to stop at the store on my way over. I'm not a baker, but I'm very good at following directions."

The gesture, paired with the comment, didn't chase away the tension entirely, but it helped. Even if Finn's ability to flip the energy in a room managed to make her all the more attractive. Amelia shrugged. "I told her you were extremely picky when it came to ingredients, but she didn't believe me."

Nana set down the bags and waved her hand. "I am. I'm also perfectly capable of managing the fray of the grocery store."

Finn placed a hand on her chest and gave Nana an almost comically earnest look. "I promise it had nothing to do with doubting your abilities."

Nana looked Finn up and down, then lifted her chin. "All right, smooth talker. How about you wash your hands and we get to work?"

Finn straightened her shoulders, made a saluting gesture, and went to the sink. Amelia sighed. This whole situation would be a hell of a lot easier if Finn didn't have to be so fucking perfect.

"You, too, missy. No loafing. We've got a dozen pies to make and no time to waste."

Amelia did as she was told, scooting in close to Finn and bumping her with her hip. "Don't hog the sink, cowboy."

Finn regarded her with a raised brow before hip checking her back. "Cowboy?"

Amelia tipped her head in a way she hoped came across as playful and not I-want-to-get-in-your-pants. She wet her hands, then lathered them up. "It seems to suit you."

"Mm-hmm."

Being this close to Finn made her body do all sorts of things it shouldn't, but Amelia stubbornly refused to notice. She rinsed her hands, then took the towel Finn held out. "Friends?"

Finn smiled. Not some forced, let's-get-through-this sort of smile. A real one. The one that had gotten Amelia into this predicament in the first place. "Friends."

In the ninety seconds or so it took them to clean up, Nana had arranged an entire setup at the kitchen table: two large bowls, the crock of flour neither of them had managed to get from the pantry, blocks of both butter and lard. Amelia smiled at the efficiency.

"Now, Amelia, you know your way around a crust. Will you school Finn while I get started on fillings?"

Amelia couldn't help but smirk. "I'll school her all right."

She walked Finn through the proper way to measure flour, stirring in the salt and sugar, and working in the fat. Finn gripped the pastry cutter like a weapon and stared at it. "I always wondered what this was."

"Did your mother not bake when you were little? Or did you just not help her?" Only after the words were out of her mouth did she realize how personal the questions were. "I'm sorry. You don't have to answer that."

Finn's face seemed more curious than offended, and she smiled. "I don't mind." She took a minute, seeming to think, before continuing, "She baked a lot but…On the ranch there was a lot more outside work to be done. As soon as I was old enough to follow after my dad, he put me to work. I think he liked that I wasn't girly and didn't complain about the dirt. And I liked being outside chasing cows. I guess when I was supposed to be learning to bake, I learned how to ride a horse to check the fence line instead."

"You really are a cowboy."

Finn rocked her head side to side. "I don't know if I'd go that far."

"Well, I'm calling you cowboy from now on." Amelia could tell by the hint of a smile on her lips that Finn wasn't going to object. The image of Finn in a plaid shirt and a pair of Wranglers wasn't something she'd object to either. "Do you miss life on a ranch?"

Finn raised a brow. "Which part? I definitely don't miss waking up before the sun's up when it's minus fifteen with wind chill and going out to crack ice on the water troughs."

"What about the rest?"

"Parts I miss…I miss the openness of the land, the quiet, being outside all day around nobody but cows and horses. And I miss my family. But I love what I do here."

Amelia wanted to ask more questions, but before she could, Nana came over to inspect their progress.

"Not bad, not bad." Nana nodded her approval. "Now pick up the pace. We've got to get all these pies baked before dinner."

Amelia explained the next steps then demonstrated, carefully adding the iced water and blending the dough until it just came together. When Finn tried her hand at it, her brow furrowed in concentration. She managed to be distractingly adorable and sexy at the same time. Amelia wished that wasn't a problem.

Soon they had dough divided into pieces, wrapped in plastic, and ready to chill. After she'd taken the dough to the fridge,

Finn started measuring and cutting for the next batch. Amelia narrowed her eyes, but Finn only shrugged. "You're better at the making. I'll measure."

"You'll get better if you practice."

Finn shook her head. "That part's a little too precise for me."

"Says the woman who places IVs. Come on, you can't kill it."

"Not kill, but ruin."

Amelia smirked. "Chicken."

"Hey, now. There's no need for name calling." Finn gestured with the pastry cutter as she spoke, sending a bit of flour flying at Amelia.

"Well, there's no need to throw things." Amelia took a pinch of flour and cast it in Finn's direction.

Finn looked at the dusting of flour on her shirt. "You know, what I did was an accident."

Amelia bit her lip. She'd done it mostly without thinking. Mostly. "Sorry."

"I don't think you are." Finn grabbed a handful of flour.

"I am. I swear I am." She put both hands up in defense. Finn wouldn't start a full-blown food fight. Would she?

Finn didn't throw the flour, but she didn't move to put it down either. "Prove it."

How was she supposed to do that? And perhaps more importantly, why did it feel like they were back in flirting territory? "Um."

"What are you two doing?" Nana, who'd gone down to the cellar for apples, appeared in the doorway with a basket of them in her arm.

"Nothing." The simultaneous answer did more to imply guilt than the flour on both their clothes.

"Looks to me like you're behaving like a pair of kids without adult supervision."

Finn released the handful of flour onto the table and dusted off her hands. "Not at all."

Nana set down the apples and let out a sigh. "That's too bad. People your age are way too serious."

The comment didn't surprise Amelia, but Finn let out a snort, which in turn made Amelia giggle. "Well said, Nana."

"Now get back to work. Remember, we need everything baked before dinner. You'll stay for dinner, won't you, Finn?"

Finn hesitated only a moment before saying, "I'd love to."

Did the hesitation come from their earlier conversation or Finn's not wanting to impose? Or maybe she had plans—or possible plans—with someone else. Not that she could ask. Not that it was any of her business. She knew Finn didn't have a steady girlfriend but presumably she dated. As she considered who Finn might go for, she finished the last batch of crust. Once that was wrapped and in the fridge, she pulled out the crusts that had been set to chill first. "Ready to roll?"

Finn turned to her and smiled. "Absolutely."

They rolled. They poured in pumpkin filling and then moved on to peeling and slicing Nana's apples. No more serious threats of a food fight, although there was some friendly flinging back and forth of apple peels. If some part of Amelia wished it had a flirtatious edge, the sane part of her knew it was better this way. Ending things with Veronica might have been the right thing to do, but it didn't mean she was ready to date someone new. Even if she knew in her heart Finn would never be only a rebound, she also cared enough about Finn's feelings not to press it.

Nana drifted in and out of the conversation, offering direction and little nuggets of praise. Finn, clearly an amateur at pie baking, took it all in stride and seemed to be genuinely having a good time. Each variety got assembled and baked according to Nana's strict instructions. A bit of a slow-moving assembly line, but they made steady progress.

After showing Finn how to pinch the edges of a double-crust apple pie, Nana stepped back to watch her work. "Finn, what are you doing for Thanksgiving? You said your family was in South Dakota, right? Are you driving up there to see them?"

At Nana's question, Amelia held her breath. She'd been wondering the same thing but hadn't wanted to seem intrusive. Or, maybe more accurately, she didn't want to seem too invested in the answer.

Finn looked up from crimping the edges of the crust. "I always work Thanksgiving so I can have time off around Christmas."

"So, you'll be in town." Nana clearly didn't have the same reservations. "And do you have plans for dinner?"

"No plans. I'll be on the day shift, and with the holiday there's no telling how late we'll be working. Probably dinner will be takeout, to be honest."

Nana tsked. "You'll come here after your shift."

"I—"

"Ah. No arguments. I insist. It will only be Amelia and me and we don't have our hearts set on eating at a specific time. We'll time it for whenever you can make it."

Finn looked her way, eyes questioning but also a little helpless. Amelia smiled. "There's no point arguing with her once her mind is made up. Surely, you've figured that out by now."

Finn hesitated still. "It might be way past dinnertime."

"But you'll need to eat." Nana wasn't giving up.

"Well, yeah."

Nana clapped her hands together. "Fantastic."

Finn returned her attention to the pie, giving it perhaps a bit more focus than was necessary. Amelia did the same with hers, opting for a lattice top instead of a full crust. The two cherry pies came out and the two apple went in. Nana set the timer and declared the day a success.

After an entire afternoon of baking, Amelia suggested ordering from the Indian restaurant down the street instead of cooking. Nana grumbled, but Finn pounced on the idea and Nana was less inclined to argue with her. Nana opened a bottle of wine—so much safer than martinis—and half an hour later they cozied up at the kitchen table, passing around cartons of saag paneer and chicken tikka masala.

Maybe it was the way Finn joked with Nana or the way she tore a piece of naan in half and offered it to Amelia, but somehow it felt like they'd been sharing meals for years. More than once Amelia caught herself looking at Finn and wishing they were dating. They weren't on a date, but the whole day was better than any she'd shared with a girlfriend in as long as she could remember.

If only she could have more of Finn in her life, platonic or otherwise. She got up to load their plates in the dishwasher while Finn and Nana packed up leftovers and wasn't surprised at all when Nana insisted Finn take the leftovers home. The two of them argued about what Finn could bring for dinner and then exchanged hugs before Finn patted at her pockets and looked around, readying herself to leave.

"I'll walk you out."

Finn glanced down at Amelia's boot. "You don't have to—"

"Only out to the porch. I could use some fresh air."

"Okay." Finn nodded, then got her coat on while Amelia did the same.

Amelia opened the door and swept her hand. "After you."

Finn stepped out and Amelia followed, pulling the door closed behind them. "I want to thank you for today. Nana can make pies in her sleep, but a dozen is a lot for her, even if she won't admit it. And I'm only so much help."

Finn ran her fingers through her hair, making Amelia itch to do the same. "I should thank you both for including me. I had a lot of fun. And I'm pretty sure I could make a pie now, should the need arise."

"You absolutely could." She could let it go at that. Wish Finn a good night and see her for Thanksgiving dinner. But she didn't want to. She took a deep breath. "Thank you for this morning too."

"What do you mean?"

"The pep talk I didn't think I needed but clearly did." She looked at her hands, then into Finn's eyes. "And for not holding that kiss against me."

"I'm pretty sure pep talks are part of the friend package."

"Well, I appreciated it. The thing is, I'm glad you're in my life. The last couple of months have been, hands down, the craziest of my life. I swear I'm not usually this much of a mess."

"You're not a—"

Amelia lifted a hand. "You've been kind and patient and supportive, but you've also reminded me what it feels like to have someone like being around you with no expectations for you to be anything more than what you are." She stopped and shook her head. "Maybe that sounds weird."

"It doesn't sound weird. I get it."

"Honestly, with Veronica I thought I liked the challenge of living up to her expectations. But I never made it close. And trying was exhausting." When Finn nodded, her expression understanding, Amelia wanted to go on. "I got so swept up in the fantasy of having this life with her that I didn't stop to think if I wanted that life, if I was happy. You make me happier than I ever was with her."

Finn's eyes managed to look both intense and wary. "Amelia, you don't—"

She shook her head. "Let me finish. I totally get why kissing me or acting on your attraction or whatever feels like the worst idea in the world. I respect it and I promise I'm not going to throw myself at you. But I'd hate myself if I didn't own that it was the best kiss I've had in as long as I can remember and I want you to know that I like being around you. That's all."

Finn opened her mouth to speak, but Amelia pressed a finger to her lips.

"You don't have to say anything. In fact, it probably would be better if you didn't. But if we're going to be friends, I thought we should clear the air." She smiled and pulled her hand away. Then, before she could overthink it, she pressed a kiss to Finn's cheek. "See you soon."

She opened the door and hurried inside, closing it quickly behind her. Through the frosted glass of the front door, she watched Finn lift her hand and once again run fingers through her hair. She lingered for a moment but didn't knock or attempt to come back inside. Eventually, her blurry form went down the porch steps and disappeared from view.

"Well, that happened." She hadn't planned to say those things to Finn, but she felt lighter than she had since the night of Halloween. That was a good sign, right? It had to be.

CHAPTER FOURTEEN

"You got your wish. Is this enough snow for you?"

"This is not what I had in mind. I asked for fresh powder. In the mountains." Finn hunched against the wheel, straining to see shapes in the whiteout. The winter weather advisory had been in effect for the past six hours but that hadn't stopped Thanksgiving travelers from hitting the roads. And hitting each other. She'd lost count of the calls they'd run.

"Did you tell your lady you're not making it for dinner?"

Finn eyed Toni long enough to make her irritation clear. "She's not my lady."

"Fine. The *cat* lady. You should at least text her. You're gonna be late."

"We've been through this—she only has one cat. And Percy's cool. When I die, I want to come back as a big fat orange house cat."

"So you can sit in some pretty lady's lap and get petted all day?" Toni chuckled. "I've always thought I'd want to come back as a dolphin. Women love dolphins. But a pussy cat wouldn't be a bad deal either."

Finn tapped the brakes when she spotted the flashing lights of a fire engine. PD had beat them to the scene as well. She'd barely parked before Toni hopped out.

"Catch ya later, boss. I'm off to save lives."

Finn radioed dispatch. Single car, stuck in a snowbank. By the looks of it, the driver had simply hit a patch of ice and lost control. Before Toni reached the car, one of the officers waved her over. Finn couldn't hear the conversation, but he didn't look particularly perturbed, so she guessed there weren't any injuries. Still, they had to check, and injuries or not, she wasn't making it for dinner.

After ten minutes freezing on the side of the road, Finn got a statement from both the driver and the passenger declining rides to the hospital. A few bumps and scrapes but nothing serious. Neither of the men were sober and chances were good they'd be longing for another drink after their trip to the police station.

"You should call her." Toni buckled her seat belt.

"I already texted her." Finn started the engine, rubbing her hands together and blowing into her palms as she waited for the defrost to kick in. "Told her I was sorry, but dinner wasn't happening."

"What'd she say?"

Finn reached for her phone. She hadn't checked, guilt waylaying her. Today was a perfect example of why she shouldn't try to date. Trying to be friends was hard enough. She couldn't make any plans. Couldn't be counted on. And she'd miss every holiday. Nadia had been quick to point out all of those things. That, on top of her schedule changing from days to nights and back with little warning, was Nadia's excuse for why she'd gone looking for companionship elsewhere.

Though it had all started when Finn had gone to South Dakota after her mom's stroke. She'd stayed for two weeks taking care of her mom and helping her dad cope. When she got back, Nadia seemed happier than before she'd gone. Rather than analyze it, she'd enjoyed that there was less tension between them. Nadia hadn't even minded when Finn had to take another trip to South Dakota. It was a full year later when she realized Nadia had been a month into a new relationship.

Nadia, who didn't know which end of a hammer to hit a nail with, met the woman in a hardware store. Finn didn't ask what she'd been doing in the hardware store in the first place. She'd simply taken the blame for not being around when Nadia needed her, accepted that she couldn't be what Nadia needed, and walked away.

Nadia was tangible proof that she shouldn't do relationships. Everything Jess had said was true—she'd drop everything if her family needed her in South Dakota. And if her job needed her, she'd work late.

Toni snagged Finn's phone and read Amelia's text out loud in a falsetto voice: "'I don't care how late it is. You'll still need to eat. Come whenever.'" She gave Finn a wide grin. "I know what she wants you to eat."

"She's talking about food, Toni. Why does everyone seem to think two lesbians can't be friends?"

"Whoa, boss. You don't have to bite my head off. I'm only messing with you. Sure, you can be friends. But I know you like her."

Finn didn't respond, and after a long moment Toni asked, "What's going through your head right now?"

"Mostly I'm wondering how I got paired with such a nosy partner."

"Ah, you love me and you know it."

Finn sighed. "I do."

That got a dimpled smile from Toni. "And for some reason, I put up with you. Like your cat lady. Although she probably doesn't do it 'cause you've got amazing catheter skills and can talk down angry drunk assholes." She held up Finn's phone. "Come on, we've gotta text her back. What are we going to say?"

"*We* aren't going to say anything."

"Fine. Be that way." Toni grumbled and tossed Finn's phone back on the console. "What are you worried about, anyway? That she's not ready 'cause she just went through a breakup? I'll let you in on a secret—'come whenever' means she's ready. Wet and ready."

"It's not only the breakup. Yeah, I don't want to deal with the rebound thing, but…Your girlfriend rolls with this job because she works nights too. She doesn't care when you get home. Amelia's got a regular job with normal hours. She's ready to have a family and she wants someone stable. Someone who's gonna make it home for dinner every night." And what were the chances Amelia would ever consider moving to a ranch in South Dakota?

"Has she told you that?"

"Not in exactly those words, but I know what she wants." Finn cussed as the dispatch voice crackled through the speakers. Everyone was working overtime. That's how holidays were. And this was her life. She wanted to explain that to Amelia. It wasn't only that she didn't want to be a rebound. Things were more complicated than that.

"Hey, what are you doing with my phone?" Finn reached for it, but Toni pressed a button on the screen.

"Sent!"

"What'd you say to her?"

"Exactly what you should have said an hour ago when she texted you back." Toni smiled smugly. "That you'll be tired, but you can't wait to see her."

"You shouldn't have told her that."

"Is it a lie?"

"No, but that's not the point."

"What's the point, then? Face it, Finn. You. Like. Her. And reality is, she's perfect for you." When Finn said nothing, she added, "Okay, here's the plan. You shower at the station and then show up at her front door with those big blue eyes of yours. Don't talk too much but make sure you apologize about missing dinner. Then don't think about what's supposed to happen next. Just relax and enjoy her company. As soon as she kisses you, you'll thank me for texting her back."

Finn hadn't told Toni they'd already kissed. And agreed it was a mistake. "Jess thinks I shouldn't get involved. She thinks it's too soon for Amelia, and I should try dating other people for a while. Give us both some space to figure out what we want."

"Jess—your single roommate who's in that fake relationship? You're taking advice from her over me?" Toni shook her head. "I'm practically married. And happy. How long has she ever stayed with someone? Hell, right now she's pretending to date someone for an article. Cuffing, my ass."

"Don't tell her that." Finn imagined the sparks that would fly if Jess could have overheard this conversation. "Cuffing's a temporary relationship, not a fake one. She's already given me that lecture. And, so far, she really seems to like the woman."

"Uh-huh. Sure. Bet the sex is good too."

Jess mentioned there were a few roadblocks in the sex department, but she guessed it wouldn't be long before they were hot and heavy. They were spending all of Thanksgiving break together. Something was bound to happen. Meanwhile, Finn was stuck working. And when she finally got off, she either went home to her empty house—she'd sent Rascal to a friend's because she'd anticipated a long shift—or went to Amelia's.

Turning down turkey and mashed potatoes wasn't easy. And there'd be a slice of pie waiting for her. Maybe Toni was right. Maybe she needed to stop overthinking the whole thing.

* * *

When Finn finally got to Amelia's, it was after ten. She debated knocking but decided to text instead. *You awake? I'm outside.*

Her rumbling belly and annoying hormones both cheered at Amelia's reply: *Be right there.*

The door opened a moment later. "You look like you've had a hell of a day."

Finn looked down at her boots. "I did shower, but—"

"Relax. You're still plenty sexy."

Finn met Amelia's gaze. "You don't look half bad yourself."

Amelia leaned against the door. "Not half bad, huh? Careful, that's almost a compliment."

Not half bad was a far cry from the truth, but the word *beautiful* stuck in Finn's throat. The oversize flannel shirt and leggings couldn't hide how attractive Amelia was. Instead, the casual outfit only captivated Finn more. Amelia couldn't look bad if she tried.

"Notice anything different?" Amelia stuck her slippered foot out and gave it a little shake. "I'll give you one hint."

"Hey, look at that. No boot!"

"Three weeks in a cast, four weeks in that damn boot, and finally I can wear cute shoes again—so of course it snows." She sighed. "But I feel more like me than I have in a long time. Come in. It's freezing out there."

"Below freezing, actually." Finn stomped her feet on the welcome mat. She tugged off her boots in the entryway and hung her jacket. When she straightened, Amelia was eyeing her with a curious expression. Finn wanted to ask what she was thinking but stopped herself. Asking would be too personal. Too much like something she'd ask a girlfriend. "I'm sorry I'm so late."

"Don't be sorry. I would have been mad if you didn't show at all. I've been thinking about you all day and worrying about you out there working in that storm. Hungry?"

"Starving, actually." Finn tried to push Amelia's comment out of her head but it stubbornly settled in. *Thinking about you all day…* Could she admit the same thing?

"You came to the right house. Nana made so much food. She made me promise to fill you up and send you home with a care package."

"Is she asleep?"

Amelia nodded and Finn wondered at the happy dance her hormones did. She wanted time alone with Amelia—she could admit that much. But friends could want time alone too. Although probably friends wouldn't want naked time alone. She followed Amelia to the kitchen wondering if she should follow Toni's advice or Jess's.

"We made you a plate with a little of everything. Give me a minute and I'll heat it up."

Finn stood in the kitchen with her hands jammed in her pockets. She ought to be tired. After she'd showered and changed at the fire station, a wave of exhaustion had hit her. But watching Amelia swish from the fridge to the microwave with a brimming plate of food, she wasn't tired at all. Relaxed, yes. Not thinking clearly, maybe, since all she wanted to do was catch Amelia's hand, pull her close, and then press her lips against hers.

"Was it rough out there with all the snow? Lots of accidents, I'm guessing?"

Finn nodded, her thoughts far from work. One step and she could close the distance between them. Now that she knew what Amelia's kiss was like, she wanted it more than ever. What was wrong with her tonight?

"You okay?"

Finn swallowed and nodded again. *Focus.* She tried to recall Amelia's earlier question. "You asked me something about snow?"

Amelia laughed. "You clearly need to eat before I make you try and talk."

"I had a long day. With not enough food."

"Well, as I said, you came to the right house."

"I didn't come here only for the food. I mean, I wanted to see you on Thanksgiving because we're friends."

"We are." Amelia held her gaze, a hint of a smile on her lips. She looked as if she were about to say more when the microwave beeped. "Want to eat in the living room? I'm about an hour in on *The Princess Bride*."

"Sure."

Amelia handed Finn the plate, seemingly careful to avoid any accidental touching. They made their way to the living room and again Amelia noticeably kept her distance. Maybe the tension between them was normal after not seeing each other for a while. They also hadn't spent much time alone together with Amelia officially single. Maybe they needed to recalibrate the friendship. Which would only work if Finn stopped thinking about kissing.

Amelia started the movie where it had left off, then stretched her legs out on the ottoman opposite the couch. Finn let her gaze wander from her plate to Amelia's feet. It was strange seeing a pair of socks instead of the boot or the cast on her right foot. Between the ankle socks and the start of the leggings was a bit of exposed skin. Nothing that should have turned her on and yet a humming started in her body all the same. She glanced at the TV, trying to force her attention onto something else, but a moment later she was pulled back again. Her gaze silently traced the curve of Amelia's calf and then farther up her leg to the inside of her thighs.

"It's a good thing Nana's not here. She'd freak out if she saw how little you're eating."

"Huh? Oh, yeah." Finn eyed her plate. A few bites had gone into her mouth, but she'd hardly thought about what she'd eaten. "It's all delicious. I'm just a little distracted."

"Why?"

She couldn't lie. Not outright. But she couldn't exactly admit she was too horny to eat because she'd seen five inches of exposed leg.

Amelia studied her. "Are you sure you're all right?"

"Yeah. I'm good. Sometimes at the end of a long shift, I have trouble focusing on anything…Even food." She took a bite of the stuffing and tried to pay attention to the flavors. In fact, it was possibly the best stuffing she'd ever had. She took another bite. "Edith outdid herself on this meal. Especially the stuffing."

"I made that," Amelia said. "One of my specialties."

"What else did you make?"

"Only that and the pies."

Finn finished the last bite of stuffing and glanced at Amelia. "You're looking at me funny again. What is it?"

"You've been looking at me funny since you got here." Amelia raised her eyebrows and turned back to the screen. "I didn't eat pie earlier because I wanted to have mine with you. I made pumpkin and pecan."

Finn took a bite of turkey and chewed, but her body wanted more than food. "Which one's your favorite?"

"Both." Amelia smiled. "What do you usually eat on Thanksgiving?"

"Other than fast food?"

Amelia inclined her head. "Back home. What sort of Thanksgiving meal does your family have?"

Finn felt a rush of longing. Not for the food, but for her family. She wondered what Amelia would make of a big meal at the Douglas house. Would Amelia like her folks? Would she get along with her sisters? And what would she think about the ranch? "This food's like what I get back home. Only better. Don't tell my mom."

"Lips sealed." Amelia kept her gaze on the screen. She seemed to be avoiding looking at Finn. "Do you miss your family?"

"I do. Tonight, I miss them a lot." Finn set down her fork. "I miss seeing everyone together…And all the hugs. It's always way too loud but I love it anyway. I've been missing the ranch lately too. I even miss the smell of the cows."

"Will you go there for Christmas?"

"If I can swing it with work. Every year it's a challenge even when I work Thanksgiving. Is it always just you and Edith for the holidays?"

Amelia nodded. "My mom doesn't really do family stuff. Every so often she makes an appearance on Christmas but…I can tell she doesn't like being here. She doesn't even like pie."

"You sure she's not an alien?"

Amelia smiled. "Not completely sure."

"I knew there was something a little different about you. Half alien, huh?"

"I wish I were that cool."

"You're cool enough for me. And now you have me wanting pie." Finn got up from the sofa, shaking her head when Amelia started to get up too. "You can stay here. I'll get us a slice of each to share."

Amelia shifted back on the cushions. "Sounds perfect."

Finn took a deep breath when she got to the kitchen. In a way, it was a relief to have a moment to refocus. She'd never had to fight so hard against her body's desire, and Amelia was testing every limit she had.

"There's whipped cream," Amelia called from the living room. "It's in a glass mixing bowl in the fridge."

Finn located the whipped cream and the pies. She dished a slice of each pie onto one plate, added dollops of cream, and headed back to the living room with two forks in hand.

Amelia's eyes went right to the plate and she gave a little moan. "Oh, I've been waiting so long for that."

Finn chuckled. "That's a good line. And the moan isn't half bad either. How long have you been practicing?"

Amelia took the plate. "For teasing me, I shouldn't even share with you."

Finn dropped down on the sofa, sitting closer this time with the excuse of sharing pie. She handed Amelia a fork. "You could try fighting me off, but I think I'd win. Besides, you want me to try a bite."

Amelia arched an eyebrow. "How do you know that?"

Finn's knee was only an inch from Amelia's. She wanted to bump against it but didn't dare make contact. "Because you're one of those sharing types."

"I'll have you know I'm perfectly happy to eat both of these slices all by myself." Amelia laughed and pulled the plate back when Finn tried to snag a bite of the pecan.

"Okay, fine. Enjoy your pie." Finn shifted back on the sofa, pretending to watch the movie. She'd seen *The Princess Bride* enough to quote lines, but at the moment it was only a blur on the screen. All her attention was focused on Amelia. Out of the corner of her eye, she watched Amelia carefully balance a bite of the pecan on her fork. The swirl of cream was mouthwatering.

"Hey. You. Over here."

Finn didn't turn her head. "What?"

"I want to share my damn pie with you."

"Trying to pretend you're a sharer now?"

"Whatever. I've always been a sharer." Amelia paused. "But you know how to test my patience."

"Hmm. I see." She kept her gaze focused on the screen despite how much she wanted to turn to Amelia. "First you want me to share your pie, then you don't, then you do…Why are women so difficult?"

"Finn Douglas, try my damn pie."

She laughed at that and finally glanced over at Amelia. The brown eyes looking back at her said so much without a word. Amelia wanted her. She could hardly breathe as the weight of Amelia's desire hit her full on. Amelia held out the fork.

Finn shifted forward and opened her mouth, catching Amelia's wrist to steady her hand as she took the bite. She was acutely aware that Amelia was close enough to kiss, and the feel of Amelia's smooth skin under her thumb threatened to push her over the edge. But she focused on the pie. Nutty pecans mixed with sweet filling and the buttery crust all topped with a light kiss of whipped cream.

"I think I like it. Maybe I should have another bite to be sure."

A smile creased Amelia's eyes. "And you call me difficult."

"You can't expect a full review with only one little taste."

"Hmm." Amelia took a bite for herself, moaning a little as if for the theatrical benefit, and then poked her fork at the pie as though considering whether or not to share more. "I could give you a review, you know, and I only had one little taste."

"A review of what?" Finn knew exactly what Amelia meant but she was trying to keep the teasing vibe going. When Amelia looked at her, choosing not to answer because they both knew the truth, there was no use trying to make a joke of it. Arousal flooded her senses and it was all she could do to not close the distance to Amelia's lips.

Amelia held out another bite. Finn took the fork this time. She chewed, hardly tasting, and Amelia's eyes didn't leave hers. "Your pie's not as good as your kiss."

"You're a tease."

"No, I'm not," Finn returned. "I was being honest. I'm having a hard time being only your friend."

"Well, you know where I stand on that."

Amelia's declaration only made Finn want to kiss her all the more. But for them to have any chance staying friends, she knew she couldn't.

"There you go again—looking like you're about to kiss me." Amelia set the plate on the coffee table and stared at the TV. After a moment, she turned to Finn. "What is it you want? Do you really want us to only be friends?"

"I don't want to make things complicated."

"That's not the same as telling me what you want." Amelia touched Finn's knee, and the light caress sent a flare through her body. "I can handle complicated. Can you?"

Finn didn't want to answer. She was done talking. Done holding back. She leaned forward and met Amelia's lips.

CHAPTER FIFTEEN

Amelia had spent most of the day and the entire evening thinking about kissing Finn and wanting Finn to kiss her. But she didn't actually think it would happen. She expected some teasing, another line about them needing to be friends. So, when it did, the brush of Finn's mouth over hers sent an immediate ripple of heat through her body. Good thing she was sitting down because no way would she have lasted on her feet.

As hot and full of desire as it was, the kiss ended almost as quickly as it began. When Finn pulled away, the absence of her lips felt like having the blankets yanked away on a cold morning. It was all she could do not to whimper in protest.

Amelia reluctantly opened her eyes and found Finn staring at her with an intensity that sent an entirely different sort of ripple through her. "I hope you aren't going to apologize for that later, because—"

Finn didn't let her finish. She pressed her mouth to Amelia's again. Only there was no brush of lips this time. Finn's kiss was hungry and demanding.

She grasped at Finn's shirt, pulling her closer. Finn's hands threaded into her hair, angling her head and taking the kiss deeper. Her tongue traced Amelia's bottom lip before nipping it with her teeth. Unlike their kiss on Halloween, there was nothing hasty or uncertain now. No, this kiss was all intention—hot, sexy, focused intention.

Finn angled toward her and Amelia shifted sideways, lying back against the sofa. Finn followed, bracing herself over Amelia with one arm. The length of Finn's body pressing into her, the weight of it, was at once everything she wanted and not nearly enough.

They continued to make out, a tangle of lips and tongues and teeth that threatened to short-circuit her brain. Finn's hand slid under her shirt, her fingers warm and rough against the softness of Amelia's stomach. Finn grazed along her ribs before moving higher, first to cup Amelia's breast, then to pinch her nipple through the lace of her bra. The sensation made her gasp. It also made her need to feel a hell of a lot more of Finn.

She tugged at the Henley Finn wore, yanking it over Finn's head before she could protest. Her broad shoulders were even more muscular in person than Amelia's overactive imagination. She ran her hands up Finn's arms, over the top, and down her shoulder blades. On the return trip, she scraped her nails lightly over Finn's skin.

"Fuck, you feel good."

The statement, and the expletive, made her smile. "I was thinking the same thing."

"But you're wearing too many clothes." Finn punctuated each word by undoing a button on Amelia's shirt. When it was completely open, she ran a hand from Amelia's throat to the waistband of her leggings. "There. That's better."

She should feel exposed, self-conscious about the softness of her belly. But she didn't. Something about the way Finn looked at her made her feel desired exactly as she was.

Finn's mouth traced the same line as her hand—the hollow of her throat, between her breasts, and down to her navel. Amelia arched in a combination of pleasure and longing. Finn kissed her way back up, more of a zigzag than a straight line. She paused at the clasp of Amelia's bra. "Well, that's convenient."

She flicked it open with one hand. The comment, along with the smoothness of the gesture, made Amelia giggle. But then Finn's mouth closed over one of her nipples and the giggle vanished. In its place, a moan. Finn sucked, then swirled her tongue. When she bit gently, Amelia cried out.

Finn lifted her head, concern in her eyes. "Sorry. Too much?"

Amelia shook her head, fumbling for anything resembling coherent thought. "Not too much."

Finn smiled, and a look of confidence returned to her face. "Good."

She turned her focus to Amelia's other nipple, lavishing it with the same attention. Back and forth, back and forth, until Amelia thought she might literally explode with wanting. "Please."

Finn looked up once more, right into Amelia's eyes. With no words, and probably fewer than five seconds, a whole negotiation happened between them—questions, answers, desire, consent. And then Finn's hand slid down her torso and under the fabric of her leggings.

The first stroke of Finn's fingers over her wetness almost made her come. She had a vague thought of wondering if she'd ever been this turned on before, but then Finn slipped inside her and all traces of thought vanished. Finn muttered an expletive against Amelia's neck, making her smile once again.

"More."

Finn added both a second finger and force to her thrusts. Amelia arched, rising to meet her. Finn's thumb stroked over her clit each time she filled her, making Amelia's panting breaths sound more like a cross between whimpers and moans. She managed a few yeses, along with Finn's name, as Finn pushed her, fucked her, harder.

The orgasm caught hold and spread before she could stop it, shockwaves of pleasure pulsing out from her core. She said Finn's name again, grasped at her shoulders. Finn held her as her body quaked, some inexplicable mix of possessive and protective that made her heart trip. Amelia let herself sink into it, taking comfort she didn't know she needed.

When her breathing returned to something resembling normal, she managed a, "Fuck."

Finn chuckled. "Yeah."

"That was amazing."

Finn kissed her neck. "You are amazing."

Amelia shook her head. "Nope. You are. I'm well-fucked."

Finn propped herself up enough to look Amelia up and down.

"It's a good look on you."

"I'm also dying to get my hands on you."

Without further comment or ceremony, she undid the button of Finn's jeans, slid the zipper down. She wanted Finn naked, wanted to taste her, but she couldn't wait long enough to make either of those things happen. She slid her hand into Finn's underwear, seeking her wetness with something akin to desperation. Finding it, along with Finn's rock-hard clit, was almost enough to make her come again.

Finn let out a groan and bucked against her. The response—raw and unrestrained—spurred her on. She made circles with her finger before dipping inside. The way Finn clenched around her made her own body tighten again.

But unlike her stretchy leggings, Finn's pants didn't give her much room to maneuver. She pulled her hand away, smiling when Finn mumbled in protest. She shifted out from under Finn and onto the floor. She grabbed at the waist, yanking both the pants and underwear down. Finn lifted her hips, making the task easier. She nudged Finn's knees apart. Now that she had the access, she wasn't about to waste it.

Amelia looked up to make sure Finn was on board, finding her lips parted and her eyes fixed on her. Without breaking eye contact, she moved closer. She paused for the briefest of moments, just to enjoy the view. And then she pressed her tongue to Finn's center.

Unable to stop herself, she let out a hum of pleasure. Everything about Finn—the way she felt, the way she tasted—

was like her fantasies on steroids. She stroked up one side, then down the other. Again and again and again. Finn's hips rocked with her, a hypnotic dance.

When she stroked squarely over Finn's clit with the flat of her tongue, Finn's hands fisted in her hair. There was something aggressive about it, something she hadn't gotten from Finn before that moment. She moaned her approval and smiled when Finn's grip tightened.

Part of her wanted to stay like that forever—on her knees and at Finn's mercy. But she wanted to feel Finn come undone, to come with even half the force of the orgasm Finn had given her. So she tightened her hold on Finn's thighs and increased her pace. Finn matched her, and when her muscles began to quiver, she didn't let up. Finn arched into her, held her head in place as she came.

Amelia stilled her mouth but didn't move away until Finn sagged back against the sofa. She rested her forehead on Finn's thigh, as breathless and spent as if she'd come again herself. She crawled up Finn's body and settled in her lap, straddling Finn's thighs and resting her head on Finn's shoulder. Eventually, her pulse slowed and the roaring in her ears died down. As it did, awareness of her surroundings returned.

Nana's sofa, in Nana's living room. The afghan Nana crocheted half on the coffee table, half on the floor. And the voice of Miracle Max, telling them to have fun storming the castle. She'd entirely forgotten about the movie. "Uh."

Finn nuzzled her neck and kissed right below her ear. "Yeah."

Amelia rubbed a hand over her face, only to discover her limbs felt like wet spaghetti. "Did we really just do that?"

"Yup." Finn's voice had an almost drunken slur to it.

If the location of their hookup freaked her out, Finn's sleepy and satisfied reply made that detail feel far less significant. She turned her head and blinked at the screen, where Westley was coming to terms with being mostly dead all day, and let out a contented hum.

Finn lifted her head as well and locked eyes with Amelia. "Wait, are you okay?"

"Oh, I'm much more than okay." She wriggled slightly, mostly to test the feel of Finn under her. "I'm pretty damn perfect."

Finn's gaze narrowed slightly. "Are you surprised? Is that it?"

She smirked. "Not the fact that we did. Just the where."

Finn's head swiveled. Confusion gave way to awareness; a horrified look quickly followed. "Oh, God."

Finn shifted and started to get up. Amelia squeezed Finn's thighs between her own, holding her in place. "Relax. It's okay."

"We're in the middle of Edith's living room. And she's right down the hall."

"I know. It's weird, but she sleeps like the dead. I think we're okay."

Finn didn't seem remotely appeased. "I'm supposed to pick up brownies from her this weekend. How am I going to look her in the eye?"

Amelia bit her lip. Finn sure was cute when she was freaking out. "I promise chances are high she didn't even hear us."

"But that means there's a chance she did."

"If it's any consolation, she likes you way better than she ever liked Veronica." She looked at the ceiling and curled her lip. "Or any of my other girlfriends for that matter."

"Yeah. Not helping."

Finn hadn't relaxed, but she hadn't made any further moves to get up either. That had to count for something. "You're not going to bolt again, are you?"

She'd meant it in sort of a teasing way, but Finn's expression turned serious. "No."

Amelia grinned and planted a kiss on her frown. "Good."

Finn's eyes softened, but the rest of her face remained firm. "I'm not bothered by what happened. Just, like you said, the where."

She nodded. "Good."

They sat like that for a long moment. Amelia's eyes started to get heavy and part of her wished she could just take Finn with her to bed.

"Things are going to be more complicated now."

Amelia found Finn's hand and clasped it. "Things were complicated the moment we met. I feel like they're getting less complicated now."

Finn seemed to consider. After a moment, she shifted and looked around the room. "I should probably go."

She didn't disagree, even if the idea made her want to pout. "I don't want you to, but I get it."

Amelia hauled herself off Finn's lap and Finn stood. She pulled her pants back on and looked around, ostensibly for her shirt. It had landed in Nana's chair, on top of a sleeping Percy. Amelia grabbed it and handed it to her. She rehooked her bra and buttoned her own shirt, though it did little to tame the sex-tossed and disheveled feeling.

Finn moved toward the front door, so she followed. "So, now that we've slept together, do I get to take you on a real date?"

She felt the corners of her mouth twitch. "You say that like you've asked and I've turned you down."

Finn folded her arms. "You know why I haven't asked."

Amelia mirrored the gesture. "Is this your way of asking?"

"If we're doing this, I want to do it right." Finn stood up a little straighter and lifted her chin. Not arrogance, exactly, but something akin to swagger. "Would you go out with me on Saturday? I know a great little place for a romantic dinner."

She couldn't have suppressed the smile if she'd wanted to. "I'd like that."

"I'll pick you up at seven."

A flutter of excitement zipped through her. "Is this a dress-up sort of place?"

"Mixed. You should wear whatever makes you feel good."

Not that she wanted to be in the business of comparisons, but she was pretty sure Veronica had never uttered those words to her. She let out a sigh.

"Sorry, that probably wasn't helpful. I won't wear jeans, but only because it's a date."

"I wasn't annoyed by your answer, for the record. But thank you for the clarification."

Finn slipped on her coat. "Thank you for waiting up for me. Dinner was fantastic. Dessert was even better."

The comment might be innocent, but the look in her eyes was anything but. As much as it made Amelia want to drag Finn to her room and not let her leave, it also reminded her about the plate Nana had wrapped up for Finn to take home. "Nana made you a plate of leftovers for tomorrow."

She hurried to the kitchen, pulling out the container and the plate Finn hadn't finished before. Finn appeared behind her. "Do I get pie too?"

"Depends. Are you talking about actual pie?"

Finn's eyes darkened with desire. "Like I said before, your kisses are better than your pie."

"Yeah, but pie is what you get to take home with you tonight."

Finn's arms came around her. "That's too bad."

Usually at this point, she'd get awkward and bashful. But something about Finn made her brave. "Maybe if you play your cards right…"

Finn nodded slowly. "I see."

"I mean, we're going on a date. Who knows what could happen?"

"Amelia?"

God, she loved the way Finn said her name. "Yeah?"

"When I pick you up for our date, you might want to go ahead and bring a bag."

The simple request, and everything it implied, had her turned on all over again. The prospect of a whole night with Finn—naked, in a bed—made her wish it was already Saturday. Not sure she wanted to own just how much the idea affected her, she quirked a brow. "I'll be sure to bring cuter pajamas than what you caught me in tonight."

Finn's hands drifted from her waist to her butt. "Don't go to too much trouble. You won't be wearing them for long."

Amelia wiggled free. "You keep talking like that and I'm not going to let you leave."

Finn let out a noise that was part sigh, part growl. "If I was still blissfully oblivious to Edith being here, I'd take you up on that."

She walked Finn to the door for the second time. "I'm really glad you came."

Finn tipped her head. "I'm glad you came too."

Despite her reckless abandon in the moment, Amelia blushed. She could get used to a smug, confident Finn. Especially when she was so good at taking charge. "I'll see you soon."

She opened the door and Finn stepped onto the porch. Finn turned back, leaned in, and kissed her. Nothing over the top, but not a quick peck either. "Good night."

She waited for Finn to get into her truck before closing the door and leaning against it for a moment. Wow.

In the living room, the movie credits had begun to roll. She shut off the television and tidied the sofa. She meant what she'd said to Finn. Chances were slim Nana had heard them or would have any idea what had happened. Well, she'd probably read it on Amelia's face in about two seconds, but Finn didn't need to know that.

CHAPTER SIXTEEN

"What's up with you today, boss? You know, you haven't yelled at me once for calling you 'boss.'"

"Don't push it." But Finn cracked a smile. "I'm in a good mood, that's all."

"All right, I'll bite. Why?"

"Keystone got three feet of fresh powder with yesterday's storm. The mountains are calling."

Toni cocked her head. "You're telling me the only reason you're happy is 'cause it's almost ski season? Bullshit."

"I happen to love skiing." Although not nearly as much as she'd loved her evening with Amelia. She'd been walking on clouds since and not even a long day on the job could change her mood. She couldn't stop thinking of how Amelia felt under her. How her kiss tasted like pecan pie and how her hands had been intent on mapping every inch of her. Amelia really wanted her—there was no doubting that now. When Finn closed her eyes, she could see Amelia going down on her and it was an image she didn't want to let go of anytime soon.

"Okay, now you're really weirding me out, boss. You're sitting over there smiling like you've smoked too much weed and I know you're not into that. What the hell is it? And don't tell me it's the snow."

Finn chuckled. "I can be happy about the snow."

"Spill."

"Amelia and I may have done more than eat pie last night." She felt sheepish admitting it, but Toni would get the story out of her eventually anyway.

"No shit! You two got it on? Hot damn." Toni held up her hand for a high five, laughing as Finn gave her a side-eye. "I knew it was gonna happen sooner or later. How was it?"

"Good—and that's all I'm gonna say."

"I'll take that." Toni thumped Finn's shoulder. "Right on, boss."

Even as Finn tried to act mature about the whole thing, Toni's excitement and her dimpled smile carried her along. She'd slept with Amelia. It was no dream. And as much as she'd enjoyed the fantasy of it happening, the real thing was even better.

"Did you already call her today to check in?"

"I thought about it, but I didn't want to bother her. Besides, it's not like what we did was a big deal or—"

"Stop right there. You have to check in. You like her and you don't want to mess this up. And don't try arguing with me because you know I'm right." Toni reached for Finn's phone on the center console and held it out. "You've been thinking about her all day. Let her know that."

Finn looked at her phone. She'd been wanting to talk to Amelia since the moment she woke up. "She's not going to think it's weird?"

"You *are* weird. She might as well get used to it."

"Whatever." But Finn pulled up Amelia's number. Then she hesitated. "We only have an hour left on our shift. Maybe I should wait. I could call her instead."

"You know how that last hour goes. We could be done in an hour or we could get stuck working another three. You might forget about her."

"Not possible." Finn stared at Amelia's name and debated what she wanted to say. Deciding against anything too gushy, she finally texted: *Hey. Thinking about you.*

Toni peered over her arm to read the text. "Not a bad start. Add something about how much you want to see her right now."

"That won't come across as obsessive?"

"No. She wants to be wanted. We all do."

The fact that someone ten years younger than her was coaching her on a texting conversation probably should have bothered her, but it didn't. With Amelia, she wanted to do things exactly right. And yet, the worry that what they'd done last night had been partly spurred by Amelia's need for a rebound still itched at her thoughts. She was holding on to the possibility that they had a chance for something real even if she wasn't sure how much more she could offer on her end.

Finn tapped the side of her phone. "I don't know what to say."

Toni raised a shoulder. "I like your tits?"

Finn burst out laughing. On second thought, she was definitely not taking advice from someone ten years younger than her. *Hope you're having a good day.*

Toni narrowed her eyes with obvious disapproval. "That's boring. You gotta make yourself unforgettable. With texts like those, she's gonna think you don't really like her. Or worse— that you think she's boring."

"She's definitely not boring."

"Then make sure she knows that."

Finn sighed. "As much as I like her tits, there's no way in hell I'm texting her that."

"This is why you don't have a girlfriend."

The remainder of the hour passed with one call from dispatch interspersed with Toni giving examples of why it was important to recognize and say out loud how much a woman's body was appreciated. Finn didn't stop her, but she soundly shut down every suggestion that she text Amelia anything regarding her body. Yes, Amelia was gorgeous. And, yes, she had amazing breasts. But there was so much more to what Finn felt than anything that superficial. She knew, even while she couldn't bring herself to say the words aloud, that she'd already gotten in too deep feelings-wise. That Amelia's body was exactly her type was only a bonus.

Amelia didn't text her back immediately, and it wasn't until Finn was leaving the station that she had time to check her phone. She smiled as soon as she saw Amelia's name.

I'd be having a better day if I were with you. Had a momentary lapse in judgment and went shopping. On Black Friday…Shoot me now. Can't wait to see you tomorrow night.

Amelia's tone hadn't changed—still lighthearted and joking. She wasn't sure what she'd hoped for instead. The gushy words she'd held back from writing herself?

After rereading the text three more times, she shoved her phone in her back pocket. She couldn't think of a funny quip and there was too much risk giving space to the feelings in her chest.

Rascal, at least, was thrilled to see her. As soon as Finn retrieved her from the neighbor's house, she howled in delight and leapt up to head height. Leave it to a dog to be better at expressing feelings. "Okay, goofball. Let's go. You need a walk."

Maybe they both did. Finn's mind cleared more with every block, and by the time they reached the park she'd decided that Amelia's text was exactly the right tone. Neither of them needed to be gushy or in too deep. Not yet.

Rascal found a snowdrift as tall as her and dove in headfirst. She emerged with a tennis ball that had seen better days and her whole body wiggled with glee.

"How'd you find that?" Finn couldn't help smiling. "I'll let you off-leash for a couple throws, but no chasing squirrels, okay?"

As soon as she unhooked the leash, Rascal dropped the ball and yipped. Finn raised her arm and she bolted toward the center of the field. Beyond the periphery of the streetlight-rimmed park, Finn lost sight of the ball, but it wasn't long before Rascal's triumphant return.

Finn tossed the ball again and felt her phone vibrate against her butt. She hoped for Amelia's name on the screen and tried not to feel let down when it was her dad instead.

"Hey, old man, what's up?"

Her father chuckled. "It's South Dakota. Nothing's up around here but the goddamn stars."

Finn smiled. She'd talked with her mom on Thanksgiving morning and asked her to pass on well-wishes to the rest of the family, but she missed everyone all the more hearing her father's voice now. "Did you spend today shopping all the Black Friday tractor deals?"

Another chuckle. "Don't reckon they have those deals at Ranch Supply."

"Probably not." Finn guessed that her father had spent the day puttering around his shop. She knew the stormy weather had headed from Colorado straight to South Dakota and it was unlikely he'd been out in the snow for longer than it took to feed the steers and crack any ice that managed to form on the heated water troughs. "You know you don't usually call unless something's wrong."

"I should probably change that." He sighed. "You talked to your sister lately?"

He didn't need to say which one, even if she had four. "What'd Dara do now?"

"She's pregnant."

"Shit." Finn hadn't guessed it would take long for her youngest sister—the daredevil and beauty of the family—to get knocked up, but even still she'd hoped Dara would have enough sense to at least finish junior college first. "How far along?"

"Far enough for Mel over at the gas station to notice. She's the one who mentioned it to me. Said Dara had come in asking for spare change so she could get enough gas to get to work."

Finn tried to remember how long it had been since she'd last spoken to her sister. A month, maybe six weeks? She'd been distracted with everything with Amelia and hadn't been checking in on her family as much as she usually did. And since Dara's falling out with their mom and moving out, she knew Dara hadn't gone home for Thanksgiving. "Dammit."

Her father's murmured "a-yup" made Finn wish she could drive up now and shake some sense into her sister. "Wonder if she even knows whose kid it is."

"Mel said she doesn't."

It wasn't that Mel was a stranger—her dad seemed to know everyone in a fifty-mile radius of the ranch—but that Dara had told someone at a gas station more than she'd told anyone in their family made Finn realize how bad things had gotten.

"You know Dara. She's juggled more than one beau at a time since middle school." Dad clicked his tongue. "I'm guessing that's somehow my fault but not sure how. Your mom's so upset she won't talk to anyone about it at all."

"It's not anyone's fault. Dara's always been someone who wanted the wild side." Finn couldn't help feeling guilty, though, that Dara hadn't called her for help when she was desperate enough to be begging for change. Nearly twelve years separated her from Dara but that hadn't stopped them from being close. She'd always tried to take care of her, check in on her, but Dara had made that difficult. She was always losing her phone, and after she'd left the ranch she'd bopped between friends' houses with no consistent address.

"I'll call Dara and then Mom. Those two need to talk." The fight between them had been over a year ago but there was no sign of either bending. Dara had been nineteen at the time. Old enough to move out and certainly old enough to make big mistakes. "Maybe now's the time to settle things between them. It's a baby, not the end of the world."

"Your mom's not listening to anything I have to say. Thinks I was never strict enough with Dara." He paused. "Maybe I should've given you all more rules?"

"You did fine, Dad. Rules don't stop anyone from getting pregnant."

"No, that's condoms." He chuckled. "Or sleeping with the same damn sex. You should've convinced your sister to be a lesbian like you."

For a while she'd thought Dara might be bi. Maybe she was and hadn't found the right girl. Finn smiled, stopping herself—but only barely—from saying as much to her dad. "I can try to talk some reason into her but that's a hard ask."

"I guess you are, or you aren't, when it comes to being gay, huh?"

"Well, there's some gray area."

"You sure were a lot less work at this age. At any age. You're coming home for Christmas, right?"

"I'm gonna try and make it. At least for a few days."

"Good. Bringing anyone?"

Finn immediately thought of Amelia. She wanted to invite her, but would Amelia think it was too soon to be meeting her family? Or that their relationship was that serious? "You saying I'm not enough company, Dad?"

He laughed. "Oh, you're good enough. That was my way of asking if you were seeing anyone."

The line went quiet as Finn debated answering.

"You're not still hung up on that Nadia woman, are you?"

"No, I moved on. There's been plenty of women since her. Trust me." But only one she'd want to introduce to her family. Finn bit her lip. Could she ask Amelia?

"Plenty of women and yet you haven't managed to get anyone pregnant. It's a fucking miracle."

Finn grinned. Her dad cussed like a sailor and had a sarcastic humor honed by the tough South Dakota winds, but he was all teddy bear on the inside. "No matter how hard I try. And trust me, I've tried."

"You gotta stop shooting blanks." He sobered after a moment and said, "Having your fun is all good, but I'd like to know someone was taking care of you. We all need that...even if we don't think we do. Keep your eyes open, okay? That's all I'm asking. Don't let the right one pass by 'cause you got your heart broke once."

Finn wanted to tell him about Amelia. Her heart told her Amelia was the one but doubt made her cautious. Amelia might feel perfect in her arms, but it was still early.

She wondered if Dara had been thinking about the long term the night she'd gotten pregnant. "I bet Dara's scared. If she's asking Mel at the gas station for money, she's gotta be desperate."

"Kinda hope she'll be desperate enough to know she ought to move back home. She used to love the ranch."

"I think she still does, Dad." She thought of Dara riding around bareback on Ranger, their old chestnut gelding, and singing about how much she loved sunshine and purple flowers and the smell of stinky cows. "Remember how she used to make little bonnets for the cows when it was cold?"

"That's Dara. Sweet as can be one minute and hell on wheels the next." He cussed again. "Pregnant and no father in sight. I want to help but I don't think she'll let me."

"I'll remind her she always has a home at the ranch."

Dad mumbled thanks, emotion making his voice break. "We miss you around here, Finn."

"Miss you too. I'll make it home for Christmas. Promise." With Dara pregnant, broke, and single, she needed to focus on her family. That's where her priority had to be. But her thoughts stubbornly returned to Amelia. Christmas at the ranch with Amelia would be perfect. Unless she was only a rebound.

CHAPTER SEVENTEEN

"Wait, so you broke up with the woman you were moving in with and slept with the paramedic who rescued you after you crashed the U-Haul? En route to said move-in?" Maya narrowed her eyes and stared at Amelia over the rack of dresses.

"Well, yes, but…it didn't happen quite like that."

Maya's faced morphed to a look of exasperation. "Am I missing something?"

"The two things aren't technically related. Veronica and I broke up because I shouldn't have been with her in the first place. Finn and I happened to connect around the same time." At least that was the story she kept telling herself, even if the spark with Finn had given her some of the courage she needed to end things with Veronica.

Maya abandoned the wrap dress she'd been considering and came around to stand right in front of Amelia. "And you got to know the paramedic because she started hanging out with your grandma. Which isn't weird at all."

Amelia smiled at Maya's sarcasm. "That part really isn't."

"You don't think the paramedic made friends with Grandma to get to you?"

She thought back to the first few times Finn came to the house. She and Nana had certainly clicked, but had Finn come to see her? Maybe at first. But after that thank-you dinner, she knew from Nana that Finn had done her best to only come over when Amelia wasn't home. She'd hated it at the time and respected Finn all the more for it.

"Am I wrong about that? Because if I am it might be less weird."

She tried to press her thighs together in a way that wouldn't draw attention. "I mean, she and Nana are friends, but that's kind of a separate thing too. They have this whole pot brownie thing that they do."

Maya shook her head. "I don't understand lesbians. At. All."

Amelia folded the dress she wanted to try on over her arm. Maya was one of her best friends. They'd been housemates first, then both got jobs working for county agencies. Not only did they like the same kinds of books and movies, they both enjoyed going out for a glass of wine after a crazy week. But Maya was straight and a party girl and completely perplexed by lesbian mating rituals. Although, to be fair, Amelia had been rocking some pretty extreme versions of them lately. "I broke up with someone and hooked up with someone new. It's not that foreign a concept."

"Oh." Maya's eyes lit up. "You're rebounding. I get it now. Why didn't you just say that in the first place?"

Because even though that word had crossed her mind several hundred times since she and Finn first kissed, she didn't want to consider that might be exactly what was happening. "It's not a rebound."

"It sounds a lot like a rebound."

She ran a hand through her hair. "I'm going to try this on."

"You know I'm not going to magically forget this conversation if you run away for five minutes." Maya's voice, a little louder than Amelia would have liked, followed her in the direction of the fitting rooms.

Amelia closed herself in and, for a moment, let herself slump against the door. Was Finn a rebound? The thought made her heart ache. Not because she thought rebounds were necessarily a bad thing, but because she really didn't want Finn relegated to that role. The idea of hurting Finn put a knot of anxiety in her stomach. But even worse than that was the notion that things with Finn would inevitably blow up and she'd never see her again. Argh.

"Does it fit? I wanna see." Maya's voice came through the changing room door.

"I don't even have it on yet. Give me a second." She pulled the sweater she had on over her head and slid her jeans down her legs. She slipped the dress from the hanger and put it on, tugging the fabric into place and adjusting her boobs in the bodice. It was a little tighter than what she usually went for. Lower cut, too.

"What exactly are you doing in there?"

Maya's impatience with everything was a running joke between them, so she didn't take it personally. "Changing my clothes like a normal human being."

She opened the door and Maya let out a low whistle. "I know I said all that stuff about lesbians being weird, but I'd totally go gay for you in that dress."

Amelia laughed. "It doesn't work like that."

Maya shrugged. "Maybe not, but damn. You look amazing. I have no idea where you're going to wear it, but you have to buy it."

She thought about her date with Finn. She'd picked it up with that in mind. "Are you sure it's not too much?"

"Too much what? Hotness? Confident sex goddessness?"

"Cleavage." She looked down. If she bought it, she'd need a new plunge bra too.

Maya angled her head. "For work? Sure. But not for a date. Your breasts are one of your best features. You shouldn't hesitate to put the girls on display."

She laughed again. Straight or not, Maya was her perfect match for doing all things girly. "It doesn't look like I'm trying too hard?"

"It looks like you're confident. And maybe looking to get laid."

She wasn't sure about the former, but the latter was definitely true. She turned back to the mirror and angled herself one way, then the other. "Okay. I'm trusting you on this."

"You should. The cut is perfect for you and the color is great for your complexion and does amazing things for your eyes."

She turned back to Maya. "You're the best."

"You are." Maya held up a slinky black halter dress. "I'm going to see if I can pull this off and then we can go."

They each left the mall with a dress, new lingerie, and at least a few Christmas gifts. They grabbed dinner at a Thai place nearby, where Amelia managed to shift the conversation to Maya's recent adventures in dating. She worked in a few straight jokes because fair is fair, and they exchanged hugs in the parking lot, wishing each other good weekends and great sex.

Amelia started her car and let it warm up. After so many weeks of being unable to drive, simply sitting in the driver's seat made her happy. Not to mention no longer having to rely on Nana or a rideshare to get her everywhere. She had an image of riding around in Finn's truck. Yes, she'd hated being an imposition, but maybe it hadn't been all bad.

She drove home, smiling at the snowflakes that danced in the air but weren't enough to accumulate on the roads. In the driveway, she cut the engine but didn't rush to get out. She'd started thinking about Nana's house as home. Not that she didn't love spending time there, and she was beyond grateful to have it as an option, but she was going to have to start looking for a new place of her own soon.

She would have expected her thoughts to go to Veronica, to the apartment that was supposed to be her home. But they didn't. Instead, she found herself wondering about where Finn lived. She'd mentioned a roommate, but she also had a dog, so it couldn't be too transient an arrangement. Did Finn want a place of her own? A little house with its own yard and no shared walls?

Christ. Getting ahead of yourself much?

Annoyed with herself, Amelia headed inside. Nana had already retreated to her room, so she made a cup of tea and settled on the couch. The couch Finn had fucked her on the night before. It somehow felt like ages ago, even though she could close her eyes and conjure the way Finn tasted, how it felt to kneel between her legs.

Her phone chirped, pulling her from the daydream. She had a second of thinking—hoping—it was a text from Finn. But it was Cody's name on the screen. *How was Thanksgiving with your sexy paramedic?*

Amelia smiled. She couldn't help it. *Pretty fantastic.*

Cody: *Can we call her your girlfriend now?*

Not yet. But I want to. After her mistakes with Veronica, she knew she couldn't rush things with Finn. Even if she wanted to. *How's the family holiday with your fake girlfriend?*

Cody: *She's not my fake girlfriend. We're legit dating. With an expiration date.*

The reply made her snicker. *Right, right. You still think she's going to break up with you on Valentine's Day?*

Cody: *Got a minute to talk?*

She confirmed that she did, and a minute later her phone rang. "Hey. What's up?"

"I wanted to check in." The casualness in Cody's voice didn't match her request to talk.

"What happened?"

"Jess and I slept together."

Amelia laughed.

"Okay, it's not that funny."

"I'm only laughing because Finn and I did too. And I'm happy for you. Or should I not be?" Cody had mentioned that she wasn't anticipating any alone time with Jess—since Ben would be with them—but apparently, they'd found a way.

"It was so good. I forgot how much I like sex."

Amelia laughed. "So, what now? Does this mean you want out of cuffing and aren't going to break up on Valentine's Day?"

"I'm not sure. We haven't gotten a chance to talk about it yet. Being surrounded by Jess's family and Ben makes it tricky."

"I bet." Amelia bit her lip to stifle a laugh. "Yet that didn't stop you from having sex in the first place."

"Touché. We didn't have a lot of time, but we made the most of it. Honestly, I can't say much more because people are in the next room. I don't want to chance being overheard."

"Does Jess's family know you two are cuffing?"

"I don't think so. They're super nice to me—and awesome with Ben. I kind of hope they don't know. Is that messed up?"

"Not at all." Amelia took a sip of her tea to keep herself from laughing as Cody grumbled. "At least the sex is good?"

"Amazingly good." Cody made a little contented moan.

"I'd tease you for sounding so happy but I'm feeling pretty damn happy myself."

"So, what happened with Finn after you two decided on only being friends?"

Amelia filled Cody in, going into slightly more explicit detail than she had with Maya. When she was all done, she added, "But Maya thinks it's a rebound and now I'm freaking out because maybe it is a rebound and I really don't want that."

"You don't want a rebound, or don't want to rebound with Finn?"

"I don't want to hurt Finn. And I don't want this to be a rebound. But I'm worried a rebound is exactly what I need."

Cody made a clicking sound. "I think as long as you keep that in mind, you'll be fine."

"Huh."

"My advice is to relax. You've been so focused on wanting the wife and kids that you jumped into something you shouldn't have. It's okay to let go and have fun and see what happens." Cody's voice was calm and sure and almost enough to convince her.

"That's so not me." She wasn't high strung or anything, but she put a lot of stock in having a plan.

"Yeah, but that's kind of the point. As long as you can do that without hurting someone you care about."

She thought about the dress, with its plunging neckline, and Maya's comment about looking confident and ready to get laid.

Maybe this was her chance to go out on a limb in more ways than one. "Maybe…I don't know."

"Are you worried about letting go?"

"Letting go, taking charge, being too much. Any number of things, really." She didn't want to admit the extent to which being with Veronica had tanked both her confidence and her sense of self. But not admitting it didn't make it any less so.

"Can I let you in on a little secret?"

She had this image of Cody, tucked away, while her fake girlfriend's family celebrated in the next room. Lounging on the bed with her feet propped up, doling out relationship advice like some sage lesbian advice columnist. Which was extra funny since her fake girlfriend was a lesbian advice columnist. "What's that?"

"Butches love confident femmes who aren't afraid to say what they want and go for it."

Amelia wondered if Cody was only speaking for herself. In so many of her relationships she'd wanted to do exactly that, but she felt shut down whenever she'd tried to ask for what she wanted. Veronica was no butch, but she was case in point for making her feel terrible for wanting too much. She didn't want to make that same mistake with Finn. "I don't know if that's a universal rule."

"Okay, how's this: Insecure women can't handle a confident femme. The rest of us can."

She wasn't sure that was the case with Veronica, but maybe Cody had a point. "You really think Finn wants that?"

"I only met her once, obviously, but Jess talks about her a lot. They're pretty close, you know. Anyway, I think Finn could handle you being yourself and really going for what you want."

She'd only heard bits and pieces about Jess and felt a little jealous that Cody might be more in the know about what Finn wanted. "I don't know."

"If the way she was looking at you at the Halloween festival is anything to go on, she pretty much wants you anyway she can have you. Slow and steady nibbles or one greedy bite." Cody chuckled.

Amelia thought back to Thanksgiving. They'd gotten hot and heavy after agreeing not to. That kind of impulsive sex didn't happen unless both parties were really into it. "Maybe you're right."

"Is part of the problem that, when it's all said and done, you want her to be in charge?"

She laughed. Cody knew her so well. "Maybe."

"Then don't be afraid to tell her that too. Trust me, it's really fucking hot."

Cody was usually careful about swearing, so the expletive drove home the point. "You sound pretty sure."

"Oh, I am. Give it a try and see for yourself."

Sleeping with Finn, dating her, was already a potentially colossal mistake. What was one more risk added to the pile? "I'll do that."

"I gotta go, but I can't wait to hear all about it."

Amelia smiled. "Okay. But then you owe me a sexcapade story too. Don't think I'm going to forget."

"All the details next week. Promise."

"Or I could just read Jess's column." She'd taken to teasing Cody about her love life inspiring lesbians everywhere to give cuffing a try.

"Can you not remind me about that part?"

"You realized sleeping with her was going in the column, didn't you?"

"Goodbye, Amelia." There was a hint of a growl in her voice.

"Goodbye, Cody."

She ended the call and picked up her mug. The tea had gone cold, but she didn't really want it anyway. Cody's words hung in the air. Combined with, once again, thinking about what she and Finn had been up to the night before. Maybe a step outside her comfort zone was exactly what the doctor ordered. She stood and stretched, then brought her mug to the kitchen. In her room, she stripped and got ready for bed, all the while thinking about the dress and what she'd wear under it and the look in Finn's eyes when Amelia told her exactly how she'd like to be fucked.

CHAPTER EIGHTEEN

"That can't be the time." Finn squinted, trying to rearrange the numbers on the screen. "It can't be after seven." She cussed and then looked over at Toni. "We took that call at five thirty. How can it be after seven?"

"Well, you delivered a baby. But it went a hell of a lot faster than I expected. You weren't kidding when you said she was crowning. And I know you said you'd delivered babies before, but I wasn't totally convinced you could do it. But you did. *We did.* Which was awesome. Mom's pressure plummeting? Not so awesome. Thank God she finally agreed to go to the hospital." Toni rubbed her neck. "I think I'm gonna need a massage."

"It can't be seven fifteen. Damn, damn, damn." Finn pulled out her phone and found Amelia's number. She pressed the call button, her stomach clenched into a hard fist.

"Oh shit. I forgot. You got a date with your cat lady." Toni's face reflected either pity or concern. Probably both. "I was supposed to remind you to watch the time."

"It's not your fault." Finn listened to the ring, wondering if she should simply tell Amelia that it wasn't going to work. She sucked at dating. Plain and simple. Why had she set up a date for a night that she worked anyway? *Because.* Normal people went out on dates on Saturday night. And if she'd finished her shift at six like she'd been scheduled, it wouldn't have been an issue. She flashbacked to Nadia screaming when she'd come home two hours later than expected. That night she'd entirely forgotten about the concert they had tickets to. Yes, work had run late, but the truth was she'd blanked on their plans.

"Hi, Finn." Amelia's voice centered her back in the moment. She didn't sound upset. But Finn hadn't already disappointed her countless times. Nadia would probably tell Amelia not to waste her time. "You on your way?"

"No. We just finished a call."

There was a pause. "Does that mean you're not coming?"

Finn took a deep breath. "I'm sorry. I'm a huge flake when it comes to dating. I shouldn't have set anything up with you."

"Tonight? Or in general?"

Finn hated the disappointment in Amelia's voice, but she also hated what she had to say next. "I meant tonight. And maybe in general. Work got crazy, but honestly that's pretty much my normal. I hate canceling but I have to do it a lot. It's one of the reasons I don't date."

Amelia didn't say anything, and Finn's heart went into free fall in her chest. She squeezed her eyes shut, wishing they weren't having this conversation. If only she were five minutes away and calling simply to say she was running late. For the second time in a row, she'd messed up their plans.

"I shouldn't have asked you out to dinner on a day I was working. I don't think I was thinking clearly."

"For the record, I'm glad you weren't thinking clearly." Amelia paused. "You kind of turned my world upside down too. I'm less happy about you canceling now. But if you need to because you're tired, I get it."

"It's not that I'm too tired but our reservations are at seven thirty and there's no way I'm gonna make that." They were both skirting around the question of dating in general. Did that mean Amelia wanted this as much as Finn did and was willing to take on the ups and downs of her schedule?

"Give me the phone," Toni said.

Finn looked at Toni and mouthed, "No way."

Toni snatched it out of Finn's grasp. "Hey. This is Toni. Finn's partner. Look, Amelia, I'm not sure why she's got her head stuck up her ass at the moment, but she really wants to see you tonight."

"Give me back my phone," Finn interrupted.

Toni shook her head, scrambling to the edge of her seat and past Finn's reach. "She's real sorry about dinner but I swear she's not a flake. She was delivering a baby. That shit takes time." Toni paused, clearly listening to Amelia, and then said, "Yeah, we've had a hell of a day. Dispatch had it out for us and you know Finn—wants to help everyone. Before the baby thing, Finn brought some dude back after a full-on cardiac arrest and then his drunk wife tried to hit her—"

Finn managed to get the phone back in time to hear Amelia say, "Tell her I don't care about dinner. I just want to see her."

"Hey. It's me. I got my phone back." Finn gave Toni what she hoped was a meaningful glare. "I'm really sorry."

"I know you are." Amelia's voice was understanding but definitely not happy. "Do you want to see me tonight, Finn?"

She could almost feel Amelia in her arms. "You have no idea how much."

"Good. Then we're trying this, okay?"

"Okay." Chances were she'd still disappoint Amelia. The more attached they got, the harder it was going to hurt when they accepted it wasn't going to work. Unless somehow it did.

"Text me your address. I'll grab a pizza and meet you there. What time?"

"You're coming to my apartment with pizza?" Her mind spun. After dating someone like Veronica, Amelia was probably used to expensive meals at places where waiters were at your beck and call. And she deserved all that. Was she really okay settling for a pizza date? "You don't want to go out? I could make reservations for a late dinner at a different restaurant."

"I've been thinking about you nonstop since Thursday night and I promise my thoughts weren't about what we'd eat for dinner."

Finn opened her mouth but no words came out. Toni leaned over and said into the phone, "Pizza sounds great, Amelia. I'll get her home in an hour."

Amelia laughed. "Tell your partner I like her."

"I'm not telling her that. She's already got too many admirers." She stuck her tongue out at Toni, who only held up her hands and grinned. Then she turned back to the phone. "You sure about this?"

"I'm sure about wanting to sleep with you tonight. Is that admitting too much?"

She smiled into the phone. Her heart had gone from completely deflated to soaring. "I like you admitting too much."

"In that case, there's more. I get that you don't have a regular job. That isn't a problem for me. As long as you don't stand me up, we're all good. But you better tell me if you're having second thoughts."

"No second thoughts." Maybe she should be having them, or at least doubts on how it could possibly work long term, but all she wanted was Amelia. "I'll send you my address."

"Perfect. And Finn—you have no idea how much I want to get you naked."

* * *

Amelia's parting words followed Finn all the way home. She let Rascal out and took a quick shower, but the doorbell rang before she'd done more than pull on a clean pair of jeans. She snagged a black T-shirt from her closet and ran for the door. Unfortunately, Rascal beat her to it, howling with delight at the sight of someone running in the house.

"Just a minute," Finn said, tugging the shirt on. She caught Rascal's collar and opened the door. "Hey." One look at Amelia and she was thrown off-balance with a rush of desire.

"Cute dog."

"Yeah." Finn took a deep breath, trying to keep her body from jumping ahead. Amelia had said she wanted to get her naked but that didn't mean she wanted Finn to push her up against the wall the moment she walked in the door. She looked from the pizza box in Amelia's hands down to Rascal and tried to refocus. "This is Rascal. She has some manners but not many. And she's better after a run, which she did not get today."

Finn stepped back to let Amelia in. As soon as the door closed, she let go of Rascal's collar. Within seconds, Amelia got a full-fledged demo of Rascal's antics—after a mad dash for one of her stuffed animals, she tossed the toy in the air, caught it, then zoomed off to the living room. All before plopping down on her bed with a toothy smile.

"Is that a smile?"

"Yep. She's a total ham."

Rascal grabbed her stuffed animal again, yipped, and made another circle around the living room.

"A total ham with a lot of energy."

Finn ran a hand through her hair. "Jess usually takes her for runs and she's a little better behaved."

"You don't run?"

"Oh, I do. But I don't like it."

Amelia smiled. "We have that in common."

"Here, I can take the pizza for you. I've got plates and drinks set up in the kitchen. I'm guessing you're hungry?"

"I am. The smell of pepperoni has been tempting me for the past twenty minutes." Amelia handed off the pizza box and started unbuttoning her coat.

Finn headed to the kitchen mostly to stop from staring at Amelia as she took off her coat. She couldn't get out of her mind how good Amelia had felt under her, and now that she was here, she didn't want to wait another minute. But after flaking on the fancy dinner, the least she could do was serve up pizza first.

Amelia came into the kitchen. Her dark green dress dipped low enough to show cleavage and Finn's breath caught in her throat. She hadn't quite gotten used to the fact that they'd kissed, let alone had sex. And now Amelia had come over. To see her. It didn't seem real that someone as gorgeous as Amelia would be into her at all. But here she was, staring back at Finn with a playful look that said she'd noticed where Finn's eyes had gone—and where her mind had gone for that matter too.

"Wine?"

"Yes, please."

Finn poured two glasses of cabernet. "You look amazing."

"Thank you. I thought about changing when I found out we were staying in, but I felt like wearing this and it was already on." Amelia took the glass Finn handed her and reached out to touch the neckline on Finn's shirt. "You look like you got dressed in a hurry."

Finn's body zinged at Amelia's touch, but then she looked down at her shirt and realized she'd put it on inside out. "Oh man. Usually, I can at least dress myself after a long shift." She chuckled. "In case you were wondering, this is the real me."

"I like the real you." Amelia smiled. "But you know I'm going to be thinking about taking that off you all through dinner."

"Taking it off to turn it right side out?"

"We can say that would be my intention."

She liked that Amelia was already thinking about taking off clothes. A lot. "I could take it off now and fix it."

"I wouldn't stop you."

Amelia's tone was serious, and Finn nearly choked on the sip of wine she'd taken. She felt a blush hit her cheeks as Amelia's gaze went slowly down and then back up her body. Clearly, she didn't feel any need to hide her desire.

Finn knew a challenge when she saw one and had every intention of showing Amelia she could handle it. Setting her glass down, she pulled her shirt over her head. Before she could get it back on, Amelia stepped forward. The feel of Amelia's cool palm against her chest brought an explosion of nerves. Finn dropped her shirt and pulled Amelia into her arms. Amelia wasted no time bringing their mouths together. And when Amelia's lips parted, she wasted no time deepening the kiss.

Time stopped. Finn knew she should pull back. At least dish out the pizza and finish a glass of wine…but she couldn't stop kissing Amelia. Her lips felt too good. She spun Amelia around and pushed her against the counter. She ought to at least take Amelia to a bed. They were supposed to have a proper date at a fancy restaurant and here she was ready to fuck her on the kitchen counter next to a pizza box.

"I need you," Amelia breathed.

The three words buzzed through Finn. She hiked up Amelia's dress until her hands found smooth warm skin. Amelia's murmur of pleasure spiked Finn's arousal.

"We should find a bed."

"Okay." Amelia nipped Finn's neck. "Or how about right here…"

The graze of her teeth, the unmistakable need in her voice, pushed Finn past thinking. She kissed Amelia again, encircled her waist, and pulled her close.

Amelia unzipped Finn's jeans and slid her hand inside. Finn moaned. "I like the way you think."

Finn wanted to have Amelia first, but as her clit pulsed under Amelia's fingers, she had to allow that going second had advantages. Still, the more aroused her body became, the more desperate she was for taking Amelia. She pulled away and Amelia's whine only turned her on more.

"You'll get your turn." She hooked her thumbs under the waistband of Amelia's underwear and tugged them down an inch. "But I need something now. I didn't get to taste you last time and you have no idea how much that's been driving me crazy. Would you let me right here?"

Amelia nodded, biting her lip and moaning as Finn dropped to her knees. She tugged off Amelia's underwear and stroked her hands up Amelia's smooth legs. As soon as she bent her head to lick, Amelia arched into her.

One taste and she felt heady. Whatever Amelia let her do tonight wouldn't be enough. She knew that already. She pushed deep with her tongue to find Amelia's swollen clit. Amelia took one unsteady step, parting her legs farther. Finn followed, her hands wrapping around Amelia's butt. She pulled Amelia against her mouth, enjoying the sound of her low moans. The musky scent and taste were even better than she'd imagined.

Amelia took a step back, stopping when she was pressed against the counter. She gripped Finn's shoulders. "That feels so good."

Finn broke away long enough to meet Amelia's gaze. "We're just getting started."

She took Amelia into her mouth again and savored the moan she got in response. She worked faster, circles turning into firm strokes, as Amelia's fingernails dug into her skin. Amelia bucked but she didn't let up. Even when she felt Amelia shaking against her, she only pushed harder. When she slid a finger inside, the sounds of Amelia's climax pierced the air.

"Fuck." Amelia squeezed her legs together, a vise grip on Finn. She trembled and was still for a moment before another tremor passed through her. She breathed out and her knees slackened. Finn looked up and met her gaze. *God, she's beautiful.*

Amelia tugged Finn's arm. "Come up here."

Finn stood, wiping her lips and not hiding her smile.

"You should look so smug all the time. It suits you." Amelia stepped into her embrace. Soft kisses followed.

Finn held her then, enjoying how she relaxed completely in her arms and wanting nothing more than that moment.

"How'd you get so good at that?" Amelia shook her head. "Never mind. I probably don't want to know how much more experience you've had than me."

"That was only an appetizer. *Amuse-bouche.*"

"*Amuse-bouche?* Is that what that was?" Amelia laughed. "Would you believe it if I told you that's the first time I've had someone go down on me in the middle of the kitchen with all the lights on?"

"I did offer a bed."

"Mm-hmm. But I couldn't wait. I liked seeing you work, by the way. Maybe I'll have to keep the lights on more often."

Finn smiled, warm satisfaction filling her. Satisfied but still wanting more. She already had a plan for what she wanted when she got Amelia to her bedroom. If Amelia wanted it... "How do you feel about toys?"

Amelia tilted her head. "Depends on my mood."

"What's your mood tonight?"

"How about you tell me what you're thinking and then I'll answer?"

Finn wasn't sure if Amelia wanted to know more before making up her mind or if she was pushing her to say exactly what she wanted. She got the feeling it was the latter, and the challenge in Amelia's eyes made it all the more arousing. Spelling out the fantasy she'd imagined over the last few weeks wasn't easy, especially standing in the middle of the kitchen with Amelia sizing her up. And yet she wanted to prove she wouldn't back down. "I was thinking of a strap-on."

"Hmm. You like having sex that way?"

Finn sucked in a breath. From the look on Amelia's face, she was almost certain it was what Amelia liked too. But she clearly had no intention of letting Finn off with an easy answer. "I do. But I want to do what makes you happy. We don't have to go there. Fortunately, I like a lot of things."

"That is fortunate..." Amelia's words trailed and Finn wondered if she should say again that it didn't matter what they did together.

When Amelia spoke again, she seemed to be choosing her words carefully. "I haven't had sex with a strap-on in a while. The women I've dated lately haven't been the types to wear one. But I do like it." She paused. "I probably shouldn't admit this, but I've had more than one fantasy of you coming into my room, pinning me down, and having your way with me with a big cock."

Finn opened and promptly closed her mouth. What the hell could she say to that?

"You're sweet when you're tongue-tied." Amelia caressed Finn's cheek, a smile dancing on her lips. "I think you in a strap-on should be our dessert. First dinner. And wine." She handed Finn her glass. "Here. You look like you could use something to drink."

"I think I need more than wine." But Finn took a sip anyway. "You know, every time I decide I can't like you any more than I do, you say something to turn me on even more."

"That sounds tough." Amelia clearly wasn't sorry about the effect she had on Finn. "Speaking of being turned on, you should probably put your shirt back on. Otherwise I'm not going to keep my hands to myself." She reached past Finn to get a slice of pizza. After a bite, she held it out for her. "You might want to eat. I plan on keeping you up long past your bedtime."

CHAPTER NINETEEN

Amelia hovered just on the other side of Finn's door. They'd managed to sit down long enough to eat a couple slices of pizza and finish a glass of wine between them. But the air never stopped crackling and, when Finn pushed back her chair and stood, Amelia was happy she didn't suggest a movie or anything else.

"I'm going to go change."

The implication had been for Amelia to wait, either for Finn to return or summon her to the bedroom. As much as she tended to hang back, to do what she was told, something about Finn made her want to throw all that out the window. So here she was, seriously considering walking in uninvited. Well, not entirely uninvited. The way Finn looked at her all through dinner made it seem like all Finn could think about was fucking her. It was that look that spurred her on now.

She stepped through the door just as Finn was pulling up her pants. "You don't really need to bother with those."

Finn turned. "It felt weird strolling out to get you in my boxers."

"You getting shy on me?" She crossed the room. "The boxers aren't really necessary either."

Finn cleared her throat. "Not shy."

Amelia shifted her gaze from Finn's eyes to the bulge in her pants, then back to her eyes. She slid her hand in. The warmth of Finn's body, the weight of the cock, made her breath catch. "That's good."

Finn's gaze didn't waver, but her eyes darkened. "You keep doing that and I'm going to have to throw you on this bed and have my way with you."

That wouldn't be such a bad thing. But she had other ideas first. "Not yet."

Finn's expression turned quizzical. "No?"

She turned her hand, pulling the cock free. It sprang to life, making her entire body clench with wanting. She stroked it a few times, using the downward movement of her hand to press the base against Finn's clit. When Finn groaned, she didn't even try to suppress a smile. "Soon."

Without asking for permission or waiting to see what Finn might say in response, Amelia dropped to her knees. She wrapped her fingers around the cock and stroked it a few more times, running her hand up and down the shaft. Finn didn't break eye contact.

Amelia took a moment to enjoy the intensity of Finn's stare, the way she stood with her hips thrust ever so slightly forward. And then she did what she'd been thinking about from the moment Finn asked about her interest in toys. She took Finn's cock into her mouth.

"Amelia." Finn's voice was raspy. She grasped at Amelia's shoulders.

Amelia leaned back and looked up into her eyes. "Yes?"

"You don't have to do that." Finn half-heartedly pulled at her.

She flushed. A voice in her head told her she'd gone too far, been too pushy. But even as Finn spoke, the heat in her eyes didn't falter. "Do you not want me to?"

Another shake of her head. "It's not that. I—"

"I'd like to suck you off. And then I'd like you to fuck me. Is that okay?" She didn't even sound like herself. There was this confidence in her voice that bordered on arrogance.

Finn nodded. "Yes."

"Yes, that's what you want?"

She could see Finn swallow. So fucking hot. "Yes."

"Good."

She trailed her tongue down the length of the cock and back up, then swirled it around the head. Finn's eyes closed and her fingers threaded into Amelia's hair. "Fuck."

It was all the encouragement she needed. She placed a hand on either of Finn's hips and went to town. The silicone was warm now, and wet. She imagined it pressing against Finn's clit, and what it would feel like pushing into her. She could feel herself get even wetter. She wanted Finn inside her, but she didn't want to stop what she was doing.

She continued working the cock, wondering if she could make Finn come like this. Finn's grip in her hair tightened. Her breathing and the pumping of her hips intensified. Despite Amelia's position, it made her feel powerful.

"You have to stop."

She paused. There was a ferocity in Finn's voice now. A desperation. "Are you going to make me?"

Finn leaned down and put her hands under Amelia's elbows. "I need to be inside you."

"Hard to argue with that."

But she wasn't quite ready to let Finn take charge. Or, perhaps more accurately, she wanted to see if she could drive Finn to her limits, push her until she lost control, at least a little. Since they were near the bed, she gave Finn a little push. When Finn sat, she motioned with her finger for Finn to scoot back. When Finn obliged, without comment or hesitation, she had a fleeting thought that maybe she could get used to running the show.

"You should take your shirt off."

Finn pulled it up and over her head and tossed it aside. Amelia paused for a moment, enjoying Finn doing her bidding.

Then she lifted her dress over her head and dropped it to the floor. Watching Finn's eyes rake over her made her glad lingerie was one of her primary indulgences. She grabbed Finn's pants and worked them down her legs, then did the same with the boxers. The cock sprang back to attention.

"Better." Since Finn had already dispensed with her underwear, she slowly removed her bra, cognizant of Finn's eyes watching her every movement.

"You should come here," Finn said.

She climbed onto the bed and straddled Finn's thighs. "Like this?"

"Better." Finn's voice, the angle of her head, mirrored Amelia's from a moment before.

Two could play at that game. "I want you inside me."

Finn locked her gaze. "You want it, or you need it?"

"Both." She positioned the cock, then let herself sink down on it. As much as she'd been expecting it, the sensation of Finn filling her made her eyes close. A moan escaped before she could stop it.

Finn's hands came to her hips, guiding her up and then slowly back down. "I've wanted you like this. Been thinking about it probably more than I should. You make a good fantasy."

She didn't doubt that Finn wanted her at this point. But the idea that Finn fantasized about her, about fucking her—that was exactly what she wanted. "Thanks for telling me. I like that I'm not the only one having fantasies."

"Were your fantasies like this?" Finn's intense look made it clear an answer was needed.

"Like this…And other things." She felt the blush on her cheeks but pushed past it. "You've been doing all sorts of things to me every night for a while now." She started to move in a slow grind that made the cock hit her in all the right places.

"Oh. Yeah." Finn's hands slid up her thighs and over her ass. Her hips rose to meet Amelia's, adding an extra layer of friction. Amelia leaned forward, planting a hand on either side of Finn's head. Finn's hands moved up her back and then came around to cup Amelia's breasts. She pinched Amelia's nipples, rolled them between her finger and thumb. "Tell me what you want, exactly how you want it."

"I…" For all her bossiness a moment before, words escaped her. How could she articulate her deepest desire? To be fucked for someone else's pleasure more than her own. Even thinking the words felt strange. The sort of thing that came off as weirdly kinky instead of hot.

Finn's fingers stilled, along with the thrust of her hips. "Tell me."

"I want you to want me."

Finn's eyes narrowed. "Are you seriously doubting that right now?"

She shook her head. Gathering her thoughts wasn't easy at the moment, but it felt important and she didn't want to back down. Or get shy. "I want you to want me —so much you can't string a thought together. I want you so caught up in me and the moment, you're not stopping to ask what I might like."

"You want me to be selfish?" Finn looked genuinely confused by the idea.

"I want to make you lose control a little. I want you to let go."

"You sure?"

Amelia nodded.

"I can do that." Gone was the confusion. In its place, a look of hunger that held a trace of the rawness she craved.

"I know it's a bit—"

"On your belly." It wasn't a question this time.

Amelia obeyed, shifting off Finn and settling on her stomach. Finn's hands grabbed her ankles and pulled her down the bed. When she let go, Amelia's feet found the floor, leaving her perfectly bent over the edge. She braced her hands on the bed, holding herself up and waiting. All of a sudden, she was shaky and full of nervous energy—but in a good way. She liked not knowing exactly what to expect. Even more than that, she liked being at Finn's mercy.

Finn's foot nudged one of hers. "Spread your legs wider for me."

The firmness of Finn's directions only increased her arousal. She did as she was told, bracing her feet farther apart on the floor. Finn's fingers slicked over her only long enough to spread around her wetness. When the edge of the cock pressed against her, she thrust her hips back.

"That's a good girl."

The comment, paired with Finn filling her completely, sent her tumbling into the start of an orgasm. It caught her by surprise and made her gasp.

Her legs threatened to buckle, but Finn wrapped an arm around her. "Oh, no you don't. Not yet. You're not getting off that easy."

The assertion—closer to what she craved than what she'd had with most of her girlfriends and far more intense than anything she ever did with Veronica—made her breath catch. "I don't know if I can help it," she admitted.

"Good things will come if you wait. I have plans for you…"

She looked over her shoulder at Finn. "I'm yours, you know. All yours."

Finn's eyes closed and she let out a groan. Her grip tightened once again and she started to move. Slowly at first, long and languid strokes. Amelia rocked back against her. She should be sated at this point. Spent. But something about the way Finn touched her, held her, made her body do things she didn't think it could. She wasn't sure Finn was anywhere close to losing control, but she couldn't bring herself to be bothered.

It didn't take long for the thrusts to pick up steam. Finn let out another low groan. She held Amelia's hips even more tightly, controlling both the pace and intensity. She pulled out almost completely before driving back in. Each time she seemed to go deeper, making Amelia groan with pleasure when Finn filled her.

One of Finn's hands snaked up her back and fisted in her hair. Amelia arched her back and angled her head. She let out a hum of pleasure.

"You like that, do you?"

"I do. I really, really do." Finn didn't stop fucking her, so each word came out staccato, each thrust a punctuation mark.

"You drive me crazy. I hope you know that."

She was starting to believe it. Intellectually, sure. But this was different. The feeling of Finn inside her was a deeper sort of knowing. Cellular, almost. "Yes."

"I've never wanted anyone the way I want you."

Finn's words made her heart trip in her chest, made her whole body tighten with the pleasure of being someone Finn couldn't get enough of. "Show me."

Finn let go of her hair and held her hips once more. This time, her fingers dug in. There was something possessive about it, uninhibited.

Amelia continued to rock her hips back, but as Finn fucked her harder and faster, it became almost impossible to move in any direction but with her. She shifted onto her tiptoes but then lost even that purchase. She collapsed onto her forearms, pressed her forehead against the mattress. Anything to keep herself from slipping out of Finn's hold.

Finn's breathing ratcheted up and her noises pitched both louder and higher. The sounds hit her with the same force as Finn's cock. And then Finn's fingers were on her clit. Strumming, circling, gentle then rough. Finn only seemed to half pay attention to what she was doing and that only made the sensations more overwhelming. Finn hadn't stopped thrusting. If anything, she was pushing harder now. Pleasure bordered pain but, God, she never wanted it to end.

Breathless, she begged. *Don't stop. Please.*

She wasn't sure Finn heard, wasn't sure the plea had even left her lips. But Finn didn't let up. How much more could she take? As the thought crossed her mind that Finn might not stop, might keep going all night, riding her harder and asking more of her, the fire that had been gathering low in her abdomen spread.

Like a dam giving way, the orgasm rushed through her body, pulling her and everything in its path under. With it, a flood of liquid heat. She cried out, exhilarated and almost frightened by the sheer intensity of it.

Finn said her name, swore. A chorus of "Amelia" and "fuck," again and again. Amelia did her best to stay with Finn as her body quaked. Her orgasm seemed to go on and on. Amelia's body trembled with the force of it, the knowledge that she'd been the one to get Finn there.

Eventually, Finn stopped moving and collapsed on top of her. Amelia let her arms go and fell into the mattress. God, she loved the weight of Finn on her.

She turned her head so she wouldn't suffocate and tried to catch her breath. With Finn on her, she couldn't quite fill her lungs. "Could you...I can't..."

"Huh? What?" Finn's head lifted from her shoulder.

The shift gave her just enough room to take a deep breath. "Whew. It's okay. That's better."

"Oh, shit. I'm crushing you." Finn started to shift away.

"No, no. Please don't go anywhere." She pressed her thighs together in an effort to hold Finn close.

Finn didn't roll away, but she braced herself up on her arms. "You sure I didn't hurt you?"

"You didn't hurt me." Amelia clenched the cock a little tighter. She was definitely going to be sore tomorrow. The very best kind of sore. "You're good. So good."

"That's definitely you." Finn kissed Amelia's shoulder. "I'm getting off you now."

She let out a disappointed sigh, but it was probably for the best. She needed to see Finn's face, read her eyes. "Okay."

Finn eased away, gently sliding the cock out and flopping onto her back. Amelia's body protested, both at the loss and at how roughly she'd been fucked. It was all worth it. She rolled to her side and propped up on one elbow. Finn's eyes were closed and she had one arm flung over her head.

Amelia pressed a kiss to her shoulder. "That was really fucking hot."

Finn opened one eye, then the other. "I don't even have words."

"I'm taking that as a compliment."

Finn looked at her, but it took a second for her focus to settle on Amelia's face. "You're the sexiest woman I've ever met."

Heat rose in her cheeks and she shook her head. "Okay, let's not lay it on too thick."

Finn reached out and gently brushed back a lock of Amelia's hair that had fallen forward. "I mean it."

The gentleness, as much as the look of desire still in Finn's eyes, had Amelia stumbling for words. She wanted to believe Finn, but she couldn't get past the implication of what it meant. "I bet you say that to all the girls."

Finn shifted up on an elbow and leveled her gaze with Amelia. "I don't say it to all the girls because I wouldn't mean it and I go out of my way to only say things I mean."

Amelia swallowed. Finn fucking her was unlike anything she'd ever experienced, but this... This crossed the line into things she'd scarcely let herself fantasize about.

"This, what we have, isn't like what I've had with other women."

She nodded, still not trusting herself to form words.

Finn kissed her. The soft brush of her lips had Amelia's heart flipping in her chest. "Now, are you sure you're okay?"

"I'm so much more than okay."

"Good." Finn kissed her again then settled back next to her.

Amelia took a deep breath and rolled onto her side again. "It's the same for me, for the record."

Finn regarded her with a mixture of curiosity and post-orgasmic glow. "What's the same?"

"I might have wanted that, but I've never done it before. Not like that."

Understanding played across her face. "No?"

She shook her head. "No."

Finn smiled. "I like that."

The significance of it should give her pause, but she was too sated and sleepy for the worry to take root. "I do too."

"Do you want some water?"

She didn't really want Finn to get up, but she'd regret not having anything but a glass of wine come morning. "Yes, please."

Amelia sat up as Finn climbed from the bed. In spite of her multiple and earth-shattering orgasms, the sight of Finn—naked save the harness and cock—sent a ripple of longing through her. How on earth had she managed to capture the attention of someone that gorgeous and that amazing in bed?

Finn stepped out of the harness and stuffed it in a drawer. "What?"

Caught staring, she bit her lip and tried for a playful shrug. "Just admiring."

Finn came back to the bed and leaned in. "Are you not satisfied? Because if you aren't, there are plenty of other things I'd like to do to you."

She was pretty sure her body couldn't take any more, but damn if a little part of her didn't want to try. "You fucked me halfway to next week. I think I'm good."

Finn's knowing smile made her even sexier, if that was possible. "I hope that doesn't mean I have to wait until the middle of next week to have you again."

"I'm sure we'll be able to work something out."

"Good." Finn nipped her jaw then sauntered from the room completely naked.

Amelia had a moment of gratitude her roommate was still away while she waited for Finn to return.

"I'm going to let Rascal out for a quick pee," Finn called from the other room.

"Is there anything I can do to help?"

"All good. Be right back."

She looked around the room, taking in the details she'd not bothered to notice before: a pine dresser that appeared handmade, a headboard that matched, a chair in the corner buried under a pile of clothes. She heard the door open and close, then do so again a moment later. She had an image of Finn outside with the dog, naked. But when Finn appeared in the doorway a moment later, she had on a pair of faded sweatpants. At least she hadn't bothered with a shirt so Amelia could appreciate her shoulders and the muscles in her arms as she held out one of the two glasses of water she'd brought.

Amelia took a sip of water. "Please tell me you walked the dog like that."

"Sorry to disappoint. I threw on a coat."

She sighed. "Probably for the best."

Finn gulped down half her water, then set the glass on the nightstand. "Thank you again for coming over tonight, and for not being mad about not going out."

She had a fleeting thought about who in Finn's past put her so on edge over having to change plans last minute. She shoved it aside, preferring to focus on the now. "I have to say, I think I might be partial to staying in with you."

"You'll stay over, right? Let me make you breakfast at least?"

She set her own glass aside. "I got distracted ordering the pizza and forgot my bag, but yes."

"It's okay. You'll look good in my pajamas."

CHAPTER TWENTY

The morning light lengthened across the bed, but Finn didn't move to get up. She hadn't felt so content in months—no, years. It wasn't simply that she was overdue for a long night of sex, though maybe that helped. But Amelia sleeping peacefully next to her and looking as if she belonged under the blue flannel blanket was what sealed it. Everything about Amelia felt right. Even the sex, which usually came with a learning curve and some negotiation, was simply easy and fun. Perfect, really. That by itself felt dangerous—nothing perfect lasted long.

She pushed away that thought and shifted closer to Amelia, not caring that as she'd pulled the blanket, she'd exposed her backside. She was warm enough. Breathing in the faint scent of vanilla mixed with musk on Amelia's skin, she closed her eyes. A wet nose nudged her calf and she tensed, barely holding back an expletive. When she glanced over her shoulder, Rascal whined. One ear up and one ear down and a pleading look in her eyes only meant one thing.

With a finger pressed to her lips, Finn carefully slipped out of bed. She snagged a shirt and jeans off the floor as Rascal hurried her to the door. It wasn't until she stepped outside and the ice seared her bare feet that she realized how out of it she was. Not enough sleep combined with the best sex of her life and she'd forgotten shoes. She looked down at her feet and then at Rascal. "How fast can you pee?"

If Rascal could have answered in words, she probably would have lectured Finn about being forgetful in general but more absentminded than ever with Amelia around. That was true, of course, but she didn't have time for more than a disapproving look before a squirrel popped out of a nearby bush and she went bonkers. Only after the squirrel escaped through a neighbor's fence did Rascal stop to sniff her favorite tree.

"You gotta ignore those squirrels," Finn said, brushing a bit of embedded gravel off her heel. "They mess with you on purpose."

Rascal finished sniffing the tree and then looked back at the spot in the fence where the squirrel had escaped.

"We need our own yard, Rascal." It was one of the things Finn longed for. That and a little house to go with it. "And a dog door. You could chase the squirrels all morning. While I stayed in bed."

After a circle around the tree, she convinced Rascal back inside with a promise of extra kibble. All she could think about was how nice it would be to slip back under the covers with Amelia. Amelia, warm and naked and snuggled up in her bed. Did Amelia staying over make it official? Were they dating? She wanted to hope for that, but that didn't change the very real possibility of her being only Amelia's rebound no matter what they called it.

While Rascal had her breakfast, Finn headed back to the bedroom. Amelia didn't stir when she settled under the blanket. She tried to relax, but between the questions about her relationship with Amelia and freezing toes, she was more alert than ever.

She'd promised Amelia breakfast, but what would happen after that? Would Amelia want to spend the day together?

She didn't care what they did. All she wanted was more time together. They'd connected over the past few weeks, for sure, but there was still a lot they hadn't discussed. A lot they didn't know about each other.

Amelia rolled onto her back, bringing her closer to Finn. The sun had snuck its way across the sheets and now bathed Amelia in light, teasing out the amber highlights in her hair and kissing her cheeks in a warm golden glow.

Her eyes fluttered open and she smiled softly at Finn, then stretched. "How long have you been awake?"

"Long enough to let Rascal out and then lie here admiring you."

Amelia exhaled. "I'm sure I'm not much to admire at the moment."

"I'm sure you're wrong. You're gorgeous. And not just because you're naked and in my bed."

"Nice line. But you should really keep working on those." Amelia stretched again. "Do you have somewhere to be this morning?"

"It's my day off. I've got no plans except this."

Amelia murmured her approval and then reached for Finn, pulling her arm over her chest as she curled up close. "Why are you so cold?"

"I forgot shoes when I took Rascal out. I don't recommend walking outside barefoot in December."

"I like dogs, but cats are better. They pee in litter boxes."

When she yawned and closed her eyes, Finn wondered if she'd drift back to sleep. She'd been surprised at how fast Amelia nodded off last night. Only moments after they'd finished making out, she was softly snoring. And she'd slept, as Finn's mom often used to say, like someone who didn't have a single guilty thought. It wasn't guilt so much as stress, though, that often kept Finn awake. Probably Amelia had plenty of things to stress about too. She wondered again at how little she really knew about Amelia.

"You're not relaxed," Amelia murmured. She tugged Finn's arm tighter around her. "Is everything okay?"

"Everything's good. I was only thinking…"

"About what?"

"Lots of things. Mostly questions."

"Like what?"

Finn considered the rebound question and promptly discarded it. It wasn't fair to ask. "Like…what's your favorite thing to eat for breakfast?"

When Amelia didn't answer right off, Finn continued, "I also was wondering what your favorite color is if you'd rather tell me that." Amelia smiled, eyes still closed, so she went on. "And… when's your birthday? How old were you when you came out?"

"That's a lot of questions." Amelia brought Finn's hand up to her lips and brushed it with a soft kiss. "I like omelets."

"That's all you're gonna tell me? Omelets?" She chuckled. "Okay. I got other questions if you're too scared to tell me your favorite color. When you were a kid, what'd you want to be when you grew up?"

"I'm not scared to tell you anything—which is weird. I'm not usually this comfortable with someone I just started sleeping with." Amelia snuggled closer to Finn. "But you're different. I wanted to be an actress."

"An actress, huh? I could see that."

"You could?"

"Definitely. You're outgoing and fun and beautiful. I think you could do anything you wanted to do, really."

Amelia snuggled closer. "You say really sweet things. That one's not true, but it's still nice to hear."

Before Finn could ask why she thought it wasn't true, Amelia said, "Purple is my favorite color, but I also like orange— especially orange flowers. And March twenty-eighth is my birthday. Don't worry about remembering that date because I love to tell people my birthday is coming up. I'll even put it on your calendar."

"I appreciate that." Finn smiled. Even more than a reminder about the date, she appreciated that Amelia thought they'd be together still by then. "Purple's pretty gay, you know."

"Ha. You're pretty gay." Amelia kissed Finn's hand. "In the best possible way. On that note, I came out when I was fifteen."

"That's early. You knew what you wanted right away, huh?"

"Well, sort of. I dated a guy a year later and thought maybe I wasn't a lesbian after all. But then I got on the softball team. As it turned out, Scott was a fluke and I *was* into women. Haven't been with a guy since. Anything else you want to know? Or do I get to find out your favorite color now?"

"Blue. But I'm not done yet. Why didn't you go into acting? What changed your mind?"

Amelia's grip on Finn's arm loosened. She didn't say anything for a minute and Finn wondered if she should say taking a pass was okay.

"In second grade, our class play was *Goldilocks and the Three Bears*. I got the part of Goldilocks and my mom came to watch the performance." Amelia paused. "This is silly. Do you really want me to keep going?"

"Are you kidding? I'm hooked. Goldilocks is the original badass. I mean who else is brave enough to walk right into a bear's house and eat their damn porridge?"

Amelia laughed.

"So, what happened?"

"Apparently, I was amazing." Amelia sniffed, overplaying it a little but clearly enjoying it. "My mom made a huge deal about me getting the lead in the play. She'd never come to my school before or showed any interest in anything about me, honestly, so her showing up was huge. Then she took me out for ice cream after the play and went on and on about how talented I was. So that day I decided I wanted to be an actress."

"But it wasn't what you really wanted?"

Amelia lifted a shoulder. "It was in second grade. Did you really know what you wanted to do with your life when you were seven?"

"Sure. I wanted to be a bull rider. I was a little conflicted about the whole thing 'cause I didn't like how the rodeo guys teased the bull to make him mad. I thought I could make friends with the bull instead."

Amelia shifted to look right at Finn, probably to see if she was serious, and then smiled. "I love that. You were cute even at seven."

Finn shook her head. "Not that cute and I never did make friends with a bull…Do you regret it?"

"Regret what?"

"That you didn't go into acting."

"I did try…My mom wanted it so much and, honestly, I'd have done anything for her to pay attention to me back then. It took me a while to realize her paying attention to me wasn't the same as actually loving me. God, that sounds depressing. Oh, well. Whatever. I think she thought acting was something we could share. Some way she could connect with me."

"Your mom's an actress?"

"Miranda Stone." At Finn's obvious lack of recognition, Amelia added, "Most of her career was in daytime soaps but she had a few small parts in some movies. She's on an afternoon talk show now."

"That's cool. Wait, is it? I mean, are you happy that your mom's a famous actress?"

"I'm happy that she's happy. She loves being in the spotlight and she's good at what she does. The talk show isn't my cup of tea but I'm happy she's gotten the success she wanted."

"What's the talk show about?"

"Basically she and four other women sit around talking about trendy stuff and dishing on other celebs."

"Hmm. Yeah. Not my cup of tea either, but props to her."

"Right?" Amelia stroked a finger lightly over Finn's hand. "I kind of like that you haven't heard of her. Anyway. Acting wasn't for me. I do, however, have one claim to fame because of it. Want to know what it is?"

"So much."

Amelia laughed again. "Thanks for your enthusiasm. When I was nine, I had a talking part in a commercial for a furniture company."

"Do you still remember your lines?"

Amelia sat up in bed and cleared her throat. "If I get this desk, Dad, I promise I'll finish my homework *every day*."

Finn clapped. "Brilliant!"

Amelia bowed and then dropped back on the pillows, laughing. "Pretty much everyone in fourth grade thought I was cool."

"You're even cooler now."

Amelia shook her head but then found Finn's hand and clasped it. "I'm lucky you think so. Last night may have been the best sex I've ever had."

"May have been?" Finn's mock gasp earned her a cheek kiss.

"Yes." Amelia shifted on top of Finn and straddled her hips, a coy smile on her lips. "I don't want to say definitely in case you decide to stop trying so hard to win me over."

"Oh, is that what I'm doing?"

Amelia leaned over Finn, her breasts temptingly close. "I've had my suspicions about you, Finn Douglas, for a while now. Suspicions that you might like me. And the truth is, I like those suspicions. Because I like you back. So, did I answer enough questions to convince you to have more sex?"

Finn wanted to hold on to Amelia's smile, wanted to memorize the faint lines creasing the corners of her eyes and the way her skin glowed in the morning light, wanted to simply enjoy the moment. She did believe Amelia liked her. Everything with Amelia was written on her face. No hidden emotion or hidden agenda. But that meant Finn couldn't pretend there was more to the way she was looking at her now. All of this was simply fun. Nothing serious. One minute she was certain Amelia felt their connection and knew what they had was about more than sex, and the next she'd only confirmed this was all a rebound. "We could have more sex. Or we could eat breakfast first."

"I am hungry." Amelia rocked her head side to side. "But I like you eyeing my breasts as if you're about to do something naughty."

"Me? Naughty?" Finn reached up and caressed the line between Amelia's breasts. Should she simply enjoy the ride? Or get off before she got her heart broken? When she brushed over a perked nipple, Amelia closed her eyes and moaned her pleasure. "How much do you like omelets?"

"A lot. But not as much as I like your hands." She pushed forward, pressing both breasts into Finn's hands.

"I like orange flowers too. Poppies especially." Finn didn't stop plying Amelia's nipples and a hum started in her body that she found difficult to ignore. "And I don't really think purple is a gay color."

"I like that you were paying attention to my answers. I was wondering if I should quiz you later."

"I'd ace that test. I like paying attention to you." The problem wasn't the questions she'd asked but the ones she hadn't. "Ever been to Syrup?"

"No, but I've heard the food's amazing... The line is always way too long though."

"Some things are worth waiting for." Finn dropped her hands to the mattress and then pushed up to a sitting position. "If we leave now, we'll beat the brunch crowd."

Amelia laughed as Finn scooted out from under her. "I don't know why I thought I could get you to do what I wanted this morning. Should have learned my lesson last night about you being a top."

"Is that a problem for you?" Finn knew by Amelia's look that she wasn't really complaining.

Amelia narrowed her eyes. "Yes. And no. I like you in charge. But I also have trouble waiting for things I want."

"Poor you."

"Exactly." Amelia dropped onto her back in the middle of the bed. "God, last night was amazing. You really want to leave this bed?"

"I do. And I'm pretty convinced I can get you back in it later." She leaned close and kissed Amelia. "I won't be asking you to break other plans if I keep you for the day, will I?"

"No. But if I did, I'd break them for more sex with you."

Amelia's words should have made her happy. Instead, they were only a reminder of Amelia's transparent honesty. It wasn't fair to expect Amelia to be ready to jump into a new relationship. And maybe she wasn't relationship material anyway.

"Is it okay with you if I shower before we go?"

Finn nodded and Amelia headed to the bathroom.

Amelia turned on the faucet in the shower and then stepped back into the bedroom while the water warmed. "I feel like I should admit something…Last night was a complete departure for me."

"In a good way?"

"Definitely. But in the light of day, I'm feeling a little shy. And now I'm making myself more embarrassed admitting that. It's just that after last night, now I know how good sex can be when I let go and I want more. But I'm also a little intimidated."

"Intimidated? By me?" Finn could hardly believe it, especially given how forward Amelia had been last night, but her expression was serious.

Amelia dropped her chin. "Did you stop us from having sex just now because you really wanted breakfast, or was there something else on your mind? I hate to ask, but I want to know if…if I was a disappointment."

"Oh, fuck. No. Not at all." Finn crossed the room. She caught Amelia's hand and brought it to her lips. "I'm so sorry if that's how it felt. Last night was amazing. Truly." She knew the right thing was to leave it at that. But she couldn't. "I want more than sex with you but I'm not sure what you want. And probably the right thing to do is ask. But I'm not sure I want to know your answer."

"You think all I want is sex." Amelia closed her eyes. "Why didn't I think about that?" She shook her head and then met Finn's gaze. "I like you. A lot."

"But you just broke up with Veronica."

"Yeah. I did." She sighed. "And I don't want to rush things. Well, part of me doesn't anyway. The logical part that knows how much I screwed up U-Hauling it with Veronica. The other part of me wants to know where you plan on retiring."

Finn wanted to tell her all her plans right then. Talk about U-Hauling it—she was already imagining their rocking chairs on the back porch at the ranch. "How about you ask me that question in a month or two?"

Amelia nodded. She didn't seem to trust her voice and that tugged at Finn's heart more than anything else. They were both stumbling through this.

"We'll go slow."

"Are you okay with that? I think it is what I need but I hate to ask…"

"I happen to like slow." Finn smiled. "Then again, I like fast too."

"Thanks for being so flexible."

"No problem." Maybe it would be better for both of them to take it slow. Finn closed the distance between them and savored Amelia's kiss. It would work out. Somehow.

When she pulled back, Amelia's eyes opened slowly. Desire was there, but something else too. "What is it? Your wheels are still turning. I can tell."

Amelia glanced away for a second. "I have no idea what I'm going to wear to breakfast. I don't want to wear the dress I came over in but I'm not sure any of your clothes will fit me."

"Clothes I can handle. Do you trust me?"

Amelia tilted her head. "Yes."

"Then go enjoy your shower and I'll get you something to wear. It won't be anything fancy, but you're going out with me so you can relax."

"I don't need fancy." Amelia seemed about to say something more but then bit her lip and turned to go into the shower. She pulled the curtain closed and then poked her head out a moment later. "Finn?"

"Yeah?"

"Thank you for telling me what you were thinking earlier. I need someone brave."

CHAPTER TWENTY-ONE

Amelia pressed the back of her hand to her forehead and tried to catch her breath. "Whew. Okay."

"Okay?" Finn, who remained braced over her, leaned in and kissed her neck. "Are you saying you're okay or declaring that was just okay?"

Despite the struggle to get enough oxygen in her lungs, she laughed. "Me. I'm okay. More than okay. I didn't think I was going to come again. You proved me wrong."

"Good."

Finn rocked her hips a couple of times and Amelia put her hand on her chest. "But you need to stop. If I have another orgasm, I might actually die."

Finn stilled. Instead of worried, she looked proud of herself. "Ms. Stone, did I wear you out?"

She hadn't thought such a thing possible, but damn if she wasn't walking that line. Not once had Veronica brought her to that point. "Maybe. I definitely need a minute."

Finn shifted up and over, easing the cock out with her. She flopped onto her back and extended her arms. "Come here."

Amelia rolled onto her side and settled in next to Finn. One of Finn's arms came around her and her other hand stroked Amelia's hair. Amelia traced circles on Finn's chest with the tips of her fingers and let out a purr. "To be fair, you've found a limit I didn't know I had."

"I'm not sure I can bring myself to feel bad about that."

"You shouldn't. If anything, I'm tempted to give you a gold star."

That made Finn laugh. "Making you happy is all the reward I need."

"Happy. Satisfied. Maybe a little wrecked."

"Wrecked?"

She lifted her head to look into Finn's eyes. "Wrecked. Wrung out. Like, there is literally no come left in me."

"I like the sound of that. Assuming it's not a permanent state, of course." Finn reached for a water glass by the bed and passed it to her. "Fluids?"

"Thanks for knowing what I need."

"You know I was going to take you out to breakfast a few hours ago."

Amelia took a sip of the water and then held up her hand. "Okay, stop right there. Who jumped who when I stepped out of the shower?"

"Um, well…" Finn looked as guilty as a kid caught with a cookie.

"Yeah. And that was after I told you I wanted this to be about more than sex too."

"And that we were taking that part slow." Finn winked. "Want to go out to brunch with me?"

"I think it's more lunch, but yes." The idea of sitting across from Finn at a diner, with pancakes or omelets or whatever between them, sounded not quite as good as the prospect of staying in bed all day. But food was a good idea. And she did want what they had to be about more than sex. It already was so much more than that and it hurt her heart thinking that Finn had worried it wasn't. Yet it also made sense.

She thought back to Finn's questions that morning. Her wanting to know something as simple as her birthday and her favorite color shouldn't have come as a surprise. But it'd been so sweet. Simple and sweet. Exactly like Finn. So why was she worrying about falling for her? Because *maybe* it was too soon.

"I'd love to know what you're thinking right now."

"My mind is kind of a pile of mush at the moment." Which wasn't untrue.

"If you don't want to go out, I can manage toast and coffee. Oh, and there's cold pizza. Not classy, but satisfying, especially after what we've been doing."

Finn trying to be hospitable was adorable. She sat up and crossed her legs, turning to face Finn. "I'd love to go out to brunch with you. Even if we have to wait in a long line."

"Even if it's late lunch by the time we get there?"

"Yes. And for the record, earlier I was thinking that I liked how you asked me questions and wanted to know about me." And that everything with Finn felt completely different than with Veronica. When Veronica had heard—through her mom—that Amelia had once tried acting, she'd flat-out laughed. Amelia hadn't bothered telling her much else. But Finn wanted to know. She could feel her desire to connect and she wanted to run right into it. Even if she was scared. "I've got questions for you too. Not only where you plan on retiring."

"Maybe we could take a walk after and talk some more? Then maybe I could convince you to come back here and see if you're, you know"—she raised a brow and tipped her head—"replenished."

Amelia laughed. Finn trying to be silly still managed to be sexy. "I think we should try. For science."

Finn nodded, all business. "For science."

"Wait."

"What?"

She let out a sigh. "Clothes."

"Right. That." Finn climbed from the bed and returned a moment later with what appeared to be a pair of black leggings and a South Dakota State sweatshirt. She held them out to Amelia. "Diner attire."

She wasn't wrong. "Do I want to know why you own leggings?"

"The sweatshirt's mine but the leggings come courtesy of Jess." Finn lifted a hand. "But before you worry about it, she steals my hoodies all the time and I know she wouldn't mind. Especially given the circumstances."

That seemed reasonable. And the stretchiness would be both generous and forgiving. As for wearing Finn's sweatshirt, the prospect made her feel like Finn's girlfriend. They might not be there yet, but she could still enjoy it.

"Again, I'm dying to know where your mind is."

"Food." Not all of the truth but some of it. At least her stomach growled on cue.

After another shower—this time only to rinse off—she got dressed. Between no hairbrush and no makeup, she felt a bit disheveled, but Finn didn't seem to mind.

By the time they got to the diner, the line wasn't as bad as she'd feared. "I think more people are leaving than arriving."

"Good thing I let you talk me into having more sex before we left."

Amelia raised an eyebrow. "So, good things come to those who mess around."

Finn smiled and a warmth spread through Amelia. She held out her hand and Finn clasped it. When Finn shifted closer and brushed her cheek with a light kiss, Amelia didn't look around to see if the others in the line had noticed. She didn't care. Instead, she looked right at Finn. It'd be so easy to let go and fall for her all the way.

The line moved fast, and they soon had a table. The happy noise of well-fed diners and the energy in the space lifted her already high mood. On Finn's recommendation, Amelia ordered the Trail Runner omelet and agreed to split an order of waffle sliders. The sliders were topped with scrambled eggs and ham, but Finn insisted maple syrup made the whole thing even more delicious and she wasn't wrong.

Finn got pigs in a blanket—which she said was her favorite—and they ended up sharing everything. What seemed like too much food vanished quickly. Finn had a serious appetite and made Amelia less self-conscious about her own. Of course, they'd also burned off a whole mess of calories with the hours and hours of sex.

"So why are pigs in a blanket your favorite? All the fancy things to try at this place like Nutella-stuffed French toast or eggs Benedict with chorizo and you go for the little pancakes with sausages in them?"

Finn took a sip of her orange juice. "The Nutella-stuffed French toast is delicious—I had it last time I was here. But I guess I like the simple stuff best. Pigs in a blanket remind me of breakfast back home."

"On the ranch?"

Finn nodded.

"When you were talking about the ranch that day we were making pies, I had this image of it in my head but I'm sure it's not right. Do you have any pictures?"

"You want to see the ranch?"

"Why are you so surprised?"

Finn lifted a shoulder. "Most people aren't all that excited about a cattle ranch in the middle of nowhere South Dakota."

"Maybe I'm not most people. I want to imagine the place where you grew up. Plus, I happen to like cowgirls in tight jeans. Got any pictures of that?"

"Honestly? Maybe." Finn reached for her phone and brought up her photos, then scrolled for a minute before handing the phone over. "This was last summer. Me and my dad."

In the picture, Finn stood in a field of green grass, darker green rolling hills in the distance and a cloudless blue sky overhead. Her jeans weren't all that snug, but they had a worn look and fit her perfectly, as did the black cowboy hat pushed back on her head. She held the reins of a dusty brown horse that seemed to be trying to nibble her sleeve, and her easy smile went right to Amelia's heart. On the other side of the horse was a red tractor and sitting on the tractor was an older, well-wrinkled man wearing a baseball cap and a shirt that read "This is what a feminist looks like."

Amelia pointed at the man. "That's your dad?"

"Yep." Finn touched the screen and the picture disappeared.

"Hey, I wasn't done appreciating that cowgirl. Or that middle of nowhere South Dakota."

"Maybe someday you could see it in person."

Amelia wondered if Finn was serious. She wanted to jump at the offer, and what it might mean. But was she ready to meet Finn's family after agreeing that she needed to take things slow? "I like that shirt your dad was wearing."

"Christmas gift from me. He thought it was hilarious. And he is a proud feminist—kind of has to be with my mom. She's a spitfire."

"They sound amazing."

Finn nodded. "I didn't realize it as a kid, but they are."

Amelia reached across the table and found Finn's hand. "Kind of like you."

* * *

After breakfast they did end up in bed again. Then came a walk with Rascal. Then sex again. That's when they went for the cold pizza. And then cuddling with a movie. That maybe led to fooling around once more.

By the time Amelia got home, she was pretty certain she'd come more times in twenty-four hours than she ever had, not in a day, but a month. Not that she was complaining. She was sated, spent, and happy.

Nana was once again in bed. She felt bad about not really seeing her all weekend, but it was silly. Nana had more of a social life than she did. She found a note in the kitchen assuring her Percy had been fed and noting there was lasagna in the fridge if she wanted it. The whole thing made her smile. Yes, she needed to think about a place of her own, but she could do way worse in the roommate department than Nana.

Percy rubbed against her legs and followed her to her room. "I missed you, too, P."

She fell asleep literally seconds after climbing into bed and woke before her alarm. As she got ready for work, she noticed how limber her body felt—looser all over and better than she'd felt in months. There was also a lovely ache between her thighs that would be a nice reminder of how she'd spent her weekend for at least the next day or two.

In the kitchen, Nana puttered away, making what appeared to be scones. "Well, good morning. I was starting to wonder if I'd ever see you again."

Amelia hung her head. "I'm sorry I've been out so much."

Nana waved a hand. "I'm teasing you. I'm thrilled to see you getting out and about. I'd started to worry about you after that whole Veronica mess."

Veronica. The breakup wasn't that long ago but Veronica seemed like a distant memory. She should probably feel bad about that. If not Veronica specifically, what it said about her and relationships and what the hell she was doing with her life.

Even as those dark thoughts threatened to gather, memories of her time with Finn pushed them away. She'd never felt sexier than Finn made her feel. And Finn was genuinely interested in who she was and what she thought and how she felt. Rebound or not, it was good to be reminded of what that was like.

"I'm sorry for that too. I sure have given you lots to worry about lately."

Again, Nana waved her off. "It's fine. All my hair is already gray."

She poured herself a cup of coffee, then peered over Nana's shoulder. "Your scones look delicious. I mean it, though. I'm an adult and you're my grandmother. I'm pretty sure I'm supposed to be worrying about you."

Nana let out a pfft.

"Any chance those will be ready for me to steal one to take to work?"

"Fifteen minutes and you can take two."

She was beyond spoiled. "Can I help?"

"No, no. You don't want to get flour on your work clothes." Nana shot her a wink and slid the pan into the oven.

"I resemble that remark." Baker? Yes. Neat about it? No.

"So, things are going well with Finn?" Nana asked.

Nana knew she'd spent the night with Finn, so it was sort of a rhetorical question. "They are."

"Good." Nana piled dishes in the sink and started wiping down the counters. "I'm happy for you both."

Nana knowing that she'd slept with Finn didn't bother her. She didn't have explicit conversations with Nana about her sex life, but Nana was far from a prude. Nana had actually been the one to have the sex talk with her because Miranda was too busy traveling and working to be bothered. And when she'd realized she was gay, Nana was, without hesitation, the first person she came out to. Still, she wasn't sure she wanted to say much more about her weekend.

Nana smiled that knowing smile she had. "I could say I told you so."

"You could." Amelia sat at the table and sipped her coffee. "I'm not sure it's a good idea we got together so fast, but I'm also not sure I care. Is that bad?"

Nana didn't answer right away. She washed and dried her hands, refilled her own coffee cup, then joined Amelia at the table. She took a sip, closed her eyes for a second the way she always did with a fresh cup of coffee. Eventually, she said, "I think you should worry a little less."

"Seriously? That's your advice?"

She shrugged. "You're a worrier."

"Yet, when I was going to move in with Veronica, I wasn't worrying enough." Nana had been right about Veronica, of course, but it made this advice seem less than genuine.

Nana set down her coffee, dropped her elbow on the table, and pointed her finger right at Amelia. "Well, that was a mistake from the get-go. One you made because you were so busy worrying about having a family you forgot to listen to your gut."

How did she do that? "Touché, Nana. Touché."

"Finn's different. She's got substance and a good heart."

That was part of the problem. Everything about Finn screamed smart, thoughtful, and grounded. Paired with the amazing sex, it wouldn't take much for her to wind up in head-over-heels territory. And nothing screamed emotionally unstable lesbian than one who fell madly in love with someone right after a breakup.

"See? I can see you worrying already. You're about a thousand steps ahead of yourself. Enjoy Finn. She's something that doesn't come around very often." The oven timer beeped, and Nana went to check her scones. "You never know what could happen."

"True." Which was also the scary part. What if Finn was the one?

CHAPTER TWENTY-TWO

"I like your butt from this angle."

Finn looped the end of the extension cord around the drainpipe and glanced down at the driveway. "Well, I like you looking up at me." She smiled but didn't dare wiggle her butt. She'd had to go up to the last step on Edith's rickety ladder to reach the roof. "Wanna plug me in?"

Amelia found the trailing end of the extension cord and disappeared around the side of the house. A moment later, the rainbow lights blinked on. In an hour, when it was truly dark, the lights would look even better than in the dusky light now, but Finn was happy with her work.

"I love it. Absolutely love it." Amelia stood with her hands clasped together and a wide smile on her face. "I'm like a kid when it comes to Christmas decorations. A strand of twinkling lights and I'm all fuzzy and warm inside. How'd you convince Nana?"

"I promised not to break my neck." Finn started down the ladder. When she got to the last rung, Amelia was waiting for her. She wrapped her arms around Finn and took her breath away with a deep kiss.

Finn smiled as she pulled back. "Hi. That was nice."

"I love coming home to you looking all butch in cargo pants and work boots. You are so damn hot." Amelia leaned in for another quick kiss. "But seriously, what'd you say to Nana? She's got an irrational fear of heights. I can't remember the last time she let us put up lights or anything out here. Probably it was when Grandpa was still alive."

Amelia in a sexy business suit with a skirt made Finn long to talk about more than Christmas lights, but she reined it in. "I told her I painted houses every summer in college and knew my way around a ladder."

Amelia looked incredulous. "That's it?"

"I may have offered to touch up the trim on this place come spring."

Amelia laughed. "Nana has you wrapped around her little finger."

"She's not the only one in the family." Finn winked. "What are you doing tonight?"

"With any luck, I'm hanging out with you." Amelia entwined her fingers with Finn's. "Let's go inside. My ankle's killing me in these heels."

Edith had gone shopping and only Percy noticed that they went right to the bedroom.

"Do you want to go out for dinner?" Amelia asked.

"We could. Or we could eat here."

Amelia tilted her head. "With Nana?"

"Well, we both like spending time with her, right? I feel bad that I've only really been by to pick up brownies lately and haven't chatted much." Finn glanced at Amelia, wondering what her furrowed brow might mean. "If you'd like to go out, we totally can."

"No. I'd actually love to stay in. I'm beat."

"Then why were you looking at me like I have green legs coming out of my head?"

Amelia laughed. She reached out and tousled Finn's head. "No green legs here. I was just trying to figure out where you came from and how you could be so perfect. Can you help me with the zipper?"

She turned and presented her back to Finn. She'd taken off her heels in the hallway and stripped her coat as well. Every time something came off she got sexier, but this took the cake. Finn tugged the tiny zipper at the back of the skirt while Amelia undid the buttons on her blouse. She shed the skirt and one peek at her underwear was all Finn got before she stepped out of reach and right into a pair of jeans.

Amelia shot her a look. "Why the big sigh?"

"It's hard watching you get dressed. I like you better naked."

Amelia raised a brow. "Do you work on these compliments all day, or do they just come to you spur of the moment?"

"Spur of the moment."

Amelia turned back to the dresser where she'd laid the sweater and picked it up. Before she had it over her head, Finn stood up and closed the distance between them. She circled her hands around Amelia's waist, her body pulsing with sudden need. "Maybe we have time before dinner to test out your bed. It might feel nice to get off your feet."

"These ideas you have…" Amelia leaned into Finn's hand. "I will remind you we are at my Nana's house."

"Mm-hmm. But she's not home." Finn pushed Amelia's hair to the side and kissed her neck. "Did you have an important meeting today?"

"How'd you guess?"

"The outfit. Fancier than you usually wear. And your hair's down. I love how you smell, by the way."

Amelia turned and met Finn's mouth. She parted her lips, silently asking Finn to deepen the kiss.

"Well, there's no body outside so clearly you didn't die." Edith's voice stopped them both in their tracks. Finn stepped back and Amelia sighed softly. "Unless you did break something and they've taken you to the hospital…Finn? Amelia?"

"I guess I gotta make my move faster next time," Finn said.

"You sure you don't want to go to your place?"

"I'm sure I do." The sex would feel good and her body was strumming with arousal. "But I can wait. We really should spend time with Edith."

Amelia shook her head. "You agreeing with my conscience is weird." She reached for the sweater she'd dropped and slipped it on, then opened the bedroom door and called out, "Nana, we're in here."

"We'll be out in a minute and can help with dinner," Finn added.

Amelia opened one of the drawers of her dresser and pulled out a pair of socks. "After I left your house this weekend, I did some thinking."

"Uh-oh."

"No. It was good thinking. Mostly about how nice it is being with you. I can be myself when I'm with you." Amelia sat down on the bed and tugged on the first sock. The gray wool hugged her toes and looked cozy.

"I like that. But are you that different when you're with me than when you're with other people?" Finn realized she'd only seen Amelia around Edith. Well, and Veronica. But she didn't really know her friends and they hadn't gone on proper dates before they'd gotten intimate.

"I was different with Veronica for sure. And I know I'm not supposed to talk about exes but with Veronica, sex was…Well, it was fine. But not really earth-shattering, you know? And then you and I got together and everything was…well, the sex is fucking amazing. But I realized it's me that's different too. I'm not worrying about what happens next. I'm letting go and it feels awesome."

"So, I don't get to be earth-shattering?" Finn forced a playful smile. Sure, she wanted to hear that the sex they'd had together was better than what Amelia had with Veronica, but it felt like they'd spun right back to where they were before going out to brunch. The going-slow, not-girlfriend-yet, territory.

"Oh, you're earth-shattering all right. Like knock my socks off and I can hardly move after. In fact, I don't want to move or do anything in case I get lucky and you decide to come back and do it all over again." Amelia waved the sock she hadn't put on yet at Finn for emphasis. "My point is, you're good for me."

"Like a vitamin." Finn joked but reality hit like a slap to the face. Amelia clearly needed a good time more than another relationship. Why did she keep hoping this was the start of something real?

"A very sexy vitamin. Exactly what I needed after Veronica." Amelia finished with her sock and found her slippers. "Should we go make dinner?"

"Sure."

Amelia stood up and put a hand on Finn's chest. "I'm sorry Nana came home when she did."

"It's fine. Really."

"Can I make it up to you later?"

Amelia's kiss saved Finn from having to answer.

"I want you," Amelia murmured between kisses. "So damn much."

If only they both wanted the same thing. Finn pulled back and straightened up. "Maybe you'll get what you want later."

"Maybe?"

Finn reached for the doorknob without answering. Amelia could think she was playing, but she'd never felt so divided about sex. Unfortunately, there was nothing she could do but wait for Amelia to figure out what she needed.

* * *

Dinner didn't disappoint. Edith went all out with a chicken potpie that tasted as heavenly as it smelled, and Finn launched into it while Amelia and Edith argued the merits of a plastic tree versus a real one. Once they'd abandoned the conversation about the tree, they turned to the question of Amelia's mother coming for Christmas. It didn't escape her notice that Amelia tensed as the conversation hovered on her mom and didn't relax until the topic changed to which cookies to bake for the neighbors.

When it was time to clear the dishes, Amelia seemed to have returned to her earlier good mood. She bumped into Finn as she carried empty glasses from the table. "Sorry."

Finn smiled. "I think you intentionally bumped into me."

"Maybe I did." Amelia set the glasses in the dishwasher and turned to lean against the counter. Edith had gone to watch the news in the living room and now that they were alone, Finn wondered if she could keep pretending everything was fine.

"You okay? You got quiet during dinner."

"I may have eaten too much. Got a little sleepy there for a minute."

Amelia leaned close and kissed her. When she pulled back, her eyes sparkled. "Wide awake now?"

"Much better, thanks." Even without the kiss, which did feel nice, she could pretend everything was fine. How long had she done that with Nadia? The reasons were different, clearly, but she'd ignored problems then too. That thought sobered her.

Amelia's hands settled on her hips. "Penny for your thoughts, cowboy."

"I was wondering if you'd like to go for a drive and look at Christmas lights." It was one of her thoughts anyway.

"Instead of going back to your place?" Amelia seemed to consider it. "Could I have both?"

"What time do you have to be at work tomorrow?"

"Early. And if I go home with you, I'm not going to get a good night's sleep. But I want you too much to care."

"It's already after nine. What if we do lights tonight and tomorrow you come over to my place right after work? Then we can have the whole evening together." Finn kissed her lightly.

"Mmm. How is it possible that when you don't give me what I want, I want you even more?"

"My plan is to keep you wanting more for as long as I can." It was honest at least. Amelia pulled her close for another kiss and Finn didn't resist.

CHAPTER TWENTY-THREE

Finn slowed her truck and pulled over in front of an elaborately decorated house. Amelia leaned in, as much to get closer to Finn as to get a better look. She caught a whiff of Finn's woodsy cologne and let out a sigh.

"I know, right? I can't even imagine how much time that took to rig up." Finn's gaze was on the eight twinkling reindeer perched on the roof. Santa hung from the chimney in blinking red and white.

She bit her lip. "I wasn't really sighing over the lights."

"No?" A shadow passed through Finn's eyes when she looked at Amelia. "What's on your mind?"

"I was thinking about how nice it is, doing this with you." Not anything she ever did with other girlfriends, or even as a kid, really.

"You're not mad I didn't coax you back to my place for sex?"

"I mean, I do love having sex with you." She wanted to say the rest of her thought but stopped herself. Admitting she agreed with Finn about wanting their relationship to be about more than sex would only start her off to saying all the things she felt when they were together. Relaxed, happy, excited, hopeful… It all seemed great. Except she still couldn't reconcile all of that with how she'd jumped right into another relationship before she'd even sorted out the mess with Veronica.

"Getting interrupted earlier was hard," Finn said.

"For you and me both. Being able to recover from the accident at Nana's and having a place to live after everything with Veronica has been exactly what I needed. But I'm starting to itch for my own place. For lots of reasons."

"It'll happen." Finn pulled back onto the road. They made a loop of the neighborhood, pointing at the different displays and sharing a laugh over the placement of an inflatable Grinch pretty much in the middle of a nativity scene. They sang along to classic Christmas music on the radio and debated the sexual politics of "Baby, It's Cold Outside."

"It's creepy," Finn insisted.

Amelia folded her arms. "I get there are some seriously problematic lines, especially by today's standards. But I still think the spirit of it is sexual liberation."

"Uh…"

"She says she ought to say no, not that she wants to."

"Huh."

Finn's look of genuine confusion made her smile. "As a recovering good girl, I'm just saying there's something to be said for getting talked into being naughty."

"I see." Finn nodded slowly. "So, you're saying you'd like me to convince you to be more of a bad girl?"

She lifted a shoulder. "You seem to be doing a bang-up job so far."

Finn took a breath and seemed to choose her words carefully. "I like that side of you, you know. It's sexy as hell but it's more than that. It feels real. I hope you'll tell me if there's ever a point where that isn't what you want."

Amelia tried to suppress the flutter in her chest. One minute she'd managed to convince herself that dating Finn as a rebound was a good idea and the next…she felt like falling in love was a foregone conclusion. Finn was so different. So much more of what she'd always secretly wanted. Different from Veronica, different from the professional powerhouses she dated in her twenties trying to please her mother. "I'll tell you if something changes, but it's definitely what I want for now. I like that you get me to do the things I've always wanted to do."

"Can I take you somewhere?"

"Now?"

Finn nodded. "It's a bit of a drive, but I think you'll like it."

She couldn't imagine telling Finn no to anything she asked for. Not that Finn needed to know that. "Sure."

Finn drove them out of the neighborhood and then angled west to the mountains. "Tell me about your Christmases as a kid. What's one of your favorite memories?"

"Favorite memory?" The question momentarily stumped her. So many Christmases were tied to disappointment.

"Picking a favorite is a lot of pressure," Finn conceded. "How about this—what was one of the Christmas rituals at the Stone household?"

"My mother and I always spent them with Nana. My grandfather died when I was young and my mother is Nana's only child, so we were all we had."

"It's nice that she had you to celebrate with."

"It's nice that I had Nana. My mother isn't very maternal, and she often worked right through Christmas Eve night."

"That's too bad she had to work."

"She didn't. She was more comfortable with her job than with her family." She heard the trace of bitterness in her voice and shook her head. "Sorry."

"Don't apologize. I asked."

"Still. There's no need to get all dark. I do have good memories. Baking cookies and decorating gingerbread houses. Visiting the neighbors and bringing cards and little presents to residents at the nursing home." That had all been Nana's doing.

"Those are great memories. Is that what inspired you to work with seniors?"

"At least partly. I always thought old people were so underappreciated. And I wanted a job where I helped people, but I don't have the stomach for medicine." She also had a fondness for order and systems and making things work.

"It's not for the faint of heart, that's for sure." Finn paused. "For the record, I think what you do is really important. And I'm pretty sure I don't have the brains or the patience for the bureaucracy and all the moving parts."

She thought about the argument she'd had with the mayor earlier in the week. The one she'd won by managing to convince him her idea had been his all along. "Thanks. So, what about you?"

"My job or my Christmases?"

"Let's start with Christmases."

"Okay." Finn pulled onto the highway and focused on the other cars for a minute before saying, "I've always loved Christmas. My family is loud and we joke a lot when we all get together, but as kids…it was the best."

Amelia wondered where they were headed. She didn't want to worry about how she shouldn't be having a late night out. Instead, she wanted to forget about every other obligation and let Finn take her away. Anywhere would be fine.

Finn continued, "Christmas Eve we always used to stay up late playing card games. Then we'd hang stockings…We all woke up early Christmas morning. My dad and I would hurry out to do the feedings. On the ranch, you never eat breakfast until after all the animals are fed.

"We'd come back inside and the whole house would smell like maple syrup and sausage. It was always so noisy until we started eating." She paused and smiled. "My mom used to make this big spread for breakfast—fried bread, pancakes, hash browns, scrambled eggs, and sausage. Bacon, too, of course. I remember being excited about the presents but being more excited about the fried bread and bacon."

Amelia imagined Finn's family on the ranch. She only had the picture of Finn's father on the tractor to go on, but as she thought of Christmas morning with a full, noisy house, a deep sort of longing filled her. "That sounds amazing."

"Christmas is my favorite holiday. Mostly I love the family time, but I also like hanging stockings." She looked over at

Amelia. "Kid at heart, I guess. I missed last year because we were short-staffed and I had to work. Moped around for about a month after. Didn't realize how much I needed the time back home."

"It's important to be with family."

Finn nodded but focused on driving and didn't say more. They'd pulled off the highway and onto a narrow two-lane road. Amelia wanted to ask what Finn planned for herself— did she want a family to bring home for the holidays? A new set of traditions? When Finn turned off the road and into a clearing, Amelia tore her eyes from Finn's profile and looked straight ahead. The view was breathtaking. All the lights of Denver sprawled below them with the streetlights and traffic and buildings twinkling in a myriad of colors.

"Wait, where are we? This feels familiar but…Did you drive us all the way to Lookout Mountain?"

"Been here before?"

"Yeah, but never at night. Once upon a time I used to go hiking up here. It's gorgeous with the lights."

"It's not Christmas lights exactly, but it's one of my favorite spots."

"It's beautiful." She looked once again at Finn.

"I confess I used to bring dates up here when I first moved to Denver. I thought I was very suave and romantic."

"Oh, you're still pretty suave." Romantic, too, although it felt weird to say so.

"How about you scoot a little closer and let me try some of my moves on you."

She didn't argue. As much as she loved being in bed with Finn, being curled up with her was a close second. Finn's arm came around her and she rested her head against Finn's shoulder. "Mmm."

"See? Romantic." Finn kissed the top of her head.

"How are you not already hitched, Finn?" The question sounded ridiculous in her ears, but it was too late to take it back.

"You mean married? Wow, that's a loaded question." But if Finn was offended, she didn't show it. Instead, she seemed to think for a minute and then said, "I feel like I'm in a holding pattern at the moment. I had a serious girlfriend—Nadia—and I thought she was the one. After things ended with her, I wasn't sure what I wanted." She met Amelia's gaze. "I'm getting a better idea now."

As much as Amelia wanted to ask if that better idea might mean someone like her, she held back the words. "What happened with Nadia?"

Finn's head fell back and she stared at the ceiling of her truck. "We were together six years. I'd bought a ring and was planning how to propose when I found out she'd been sleeping with someone else for more than a year."

"Fuck." It came out as a whisper, elongated by just how much she wasn't expecting that to be the answer.

"Yeah."

"I'm really sorry."

Finn shrugged. "It is what it is. Kind of soured me on relationships, though."

Her ill-fated escapade with Veronica seemed insignificant in comparison. "I can see how that would happen."

"Being with you has been good for me. It's been complicated, sure, but it's also easy. I think it's helped that we were friends first."

Was that it? That despite having crazy chemistry, the foundation of their relationship came from a place of not acting on it? She'd not been able to put her finger on why things with Finn felt so unlike all her past relationships, but she was in complete agreement that they were. "Yeah."

"And I think you needing this to not be serious is letting me get my footing. With Nadia, I was always five steps ahead. Didn't even see it when we weren't on the same path anymore." Finn shook her head. "What about you? What did your life look like before Veronica and U-Haul crashes?"

Amelia shuddered. It sort of killed her that Finn's knowledge—okay, opinion—of her was based on a set of really, really bad choices. Not that her choices before Veronica had been all that stellar. She lifted her head and turned to face Finn. "I spent my twenties trying to please and be like my mother."

Finn regarded her with surprise. "Really?"

"I know. It seems funny to say that now because we're not even close anymore." That distance was part of her finally allowing herself to live her own life.

"Hey, I'm not here to judge."

"It's okay if you do. I do."

Finn's expression morphed from defensive to concerned in about two seconds. "I think you're probably too hard on yourself."

"Eh."

Finn reached over and squeezed her hand. "Want to tell me about it?"

"There's not that much to tell. My mother is obsessed with her career and raised me to be that way too. But because I didn't go into acting like she'd hoped I would, everything else was a disappointment to her. I've told myself I don't care what she thinks, and honestly, most of the time that's true. But I had goals for myself that have come and gone." She sighed. "I wanted to be a success at my job—even if it wasn't flashy—and I wanted my own family by now. Turns out having it all is harder than it sounds."

Another squeeze of her hand. "I think we get caught up in giving our plans a time frame. It's not a race, you know. And no matter what people think, you can't have all of everything. You have to pick what's important, what makes you happy, and then decide that's enough."

Finn's words could be taken as evidence she was jaded from having her heart broken, but it didn't feel that way at all. No, it felt genuine. And, perhaps strangely, wise. "I wish I'd met you ten years ago."

"Ten years ago, I was singing a very different tune."

Right. "Well, I wish I'd had your insight today ten years ago. I dated ambitious ladder climbers who either had no interest in having a family or who expected me to drop everything to be the stay-at-home mom."

"Seriously? There are lesbians who operate that way?"

Amelia chuckled. "Oh, yeah. It was one mistake after another, and I found myself approaching thirty without the family or the high-powered career."

"So, what happened?"

"Well, first I had a meltdown. I fondly refer to it as my pre-midlife crisis. Then I let myself be happy with the career I had and started thinking about having a family."

"And that's when you met Veronica?"

She wrinkled her nose. "And that's when I met Veronica. And instead of the sports car, I got the U-Haul."

Finn laughed. "I feel like I should say I'm sorry it didn't work out, but I don't think I can."

Like so many things Finn said, it was the exact right thing to say. Instead of making her feel worse about her choices, it made her happy she'd escaped relatively unscathed. "Don't worry. I'm so glad it didn't work out."

"Good. You deserve better than her."

"You're good for my ego." She didn't like to admit her ego needed the boost, but there it was. She closed the small distance between them and Finn's lips found hers. Before she could stop it, a small moan escaped. Did it have to feel this good every time?

Finn's mouth moved to her neck, just under her ear. "You can't make those sounds if you don't want me to make love to you right here in the front seat."

Amelia's heart flipped over in her chest. Whether it was the desire in Finn's voice or the way she said *make love*, it was hard to tell. But whatever arguments, stern talks, or rationalizations she'd been having with herself vanished. All that remained was desire and longing and the fact that she was about two steps away from falling head over heels for Finn Douglas.

CHAPTER TWENTY-FOUR

At ten after five, the business suits coming out of the gray office building went from a trickle to a flood. Finn stood at the corner of Colfax and 14th, her hands jammed in the pockets of her jacket and her breath an ice cloud every time she exhaled. She squinted at the blur of faces, worried she'd miss Amelia in the crowd, but a moment later, her heart sprang to her throat.

Amelia.

She'd stepped out of the building, seemed to realize the temperature had dropped, and stopped to button her coat. Before the long wool coat could conceal it, Finn took in the dress that clung to her body. As much she liked Amelia for more than her looks, damn, could she make business attire sexy. Her hair was done up in a twist that Finn immediately imagined undoing when they were alone, but the real kicker was her pair of knee-high boots. She'd like to help take those off later.

Amelia turned when a slim Black woman in bright red heels called to her. She'd come out of the building with something in her hand—Amelia's lunchbox, Finn realized as it was passed off.

They said goodbye, Amelia squeezing the woman's hand, and then turned to head in opposite directions.

Finn started up the sidewalk, knowing Amelia still hadn't spotted her and eager for the moment when she did. The stirrings in her chest ratcheted up in anticipation. When Amelia stopped ten feet from Finn, her mouth opened in a question that quickly turned to a smile.

"What are you doing here?"

"I came to surprise you." A pinch of worry made her wonder if she should have discussed that with Amelia first.

"Well, you accomplished your goal." Amelia's smile widened. "Any particular reason?"

"I wanted to see you." Finn closed the distance between them, wrapping her arms around Amelia. The feel of her pressed against Finn's chest took away the worry and brought back the memory of what they'd done the night before. Amelia, clinging to her shoulders, trembling under her as she begged Finn not to stop. Her arousal was immediate, but she tamped it down. Tonight, she wanted to show Amelia she could manage a proper date.

"Want to go out with me tonight?"

"I'd love to." Amelia touched the collar of Finn's shirt. "You look good dressed up. The tie's a nice touch. Did you know I love surprises?"

"I didn't. But now I won't forget it." She wouldn't forget the look of desire in Amelia's eyes either. Dinner first. Later they'd have time for all the other things she was thinking of.

Finn leaned close and Amelia melted into her lips. A rush of longing made her go in for another. She slid her hand behind Amelia's neck, pulling her even closer. Amelia parted her lips, a soft moan escaping. One deep kiss followed another as if they had the sidewalk to themselves.

They weren't alone of course, and as if in reminder, someone passing by loudly cleared their throat. Finn pulled back and noticed the blush on Amelia's cheeks. A wave of uncertainty hit.

"Is it not okay to kiss you here? I should have thought to ask first. I just couldn't—"

"Stop. It's definitely okay." Amelia pressed a finger on Finn's lips. "I love kissing you." As if to prove her point, when she pulled away her finger, she kissed Finn again. "It's the type of kisses you give me that's the problem. It's a good problem to have, don't get me wrong, but you make me think things I probably shouldn't be thinking in public."

"Such as?"

"How about I promise to tell you later? After you get me naked." Amelia's eyes sparkled.

"You make it hard to argue."

"I've gotten places in life being good at convincing people." Amelia hooked her arm in Finn's. "So, where are you taking me? I'm hoping it's somewhere warm. It's freezing out here and I'm pretty sure my nipples can't get any perkier."

"That sounds like a challenge." Finn chuckled at Amelia's eye roll. "Remember that dinner date I flaked on? The one where I was going to take you to a fancy restaurant?"

"You didn't flake. You were delivering a baby. And I do remember. Are we going there now?"

The hopeful excitement in Amelia's voice buoyed Finn's spirits. "We've got reservations in twenty minutes."

* * *

The food was delicious, but Finn hardly thought about the bites she put in her mouth. She was too distracted. Something about the realization that this was a real date, that they were out at a fancy restaurant and the waiter had referred to Amelia as her partner and Amelia hadn't corrected him, made her wonder at exactly how she'd ended up so lucky. She could connect the dots as well as anyone—a U-Haul accident, pot brownies, and now here they were. But despite that, or maybe because of those dots being what they were, it still all seemed so unlikely. Would it last?

"You look serious over there. Should I be worried?"

"I pretty much always look serious unless I'm smiling. It's kind of my resting expression."

Amelia smiled over her wineglass. "I've noticed. But this particular serious face usually means you're thinking about something important. And you're not eating very much. Something's up."

"You think you know me that well, huh?" Finn tried to focus on her food and took a bite of her roasted potatoes.

"I'm learning to read you—I think, anyway. Want to tell me?"

Finn considered it. She wanted to have the conversation about whether or not she could call Amelia her girlfriend. It shouldn't be a big deal, but maybe Amelia would feel it was too soon? Or, worse, she'd admit that she didn't want any commitment at all. If so, the question would ruin a perfectly lovely dinner.

"Did I talk too much about work? It's been crazy lately with all these year-end meetings…Or is your salmon overdone?"

"You're definitely not talking too much. I like hearing about your work. And the salmon's perfect. Want a bite?"

Amelia shook her head. "I'm not a big fan of salmon. Besides, this risotto is to die for." She pushed another bite onto her fork. "You sure there's nothing?"

"I'm happy being here with you."

"I'm happy being with you too. And with this risotto." Amelia took the bite, closed her eyes, and groaned with pleasure.

"I love when you make those little sounds. Although I like it better when I'm the one who inspires them."

"You and this chef could go toe-to-toe." Amelia took another bite with a mischievous wink. "So, you sure you don't want to talk about it? I can tell there's more on your mind."

"Oh, there's a lot on my mind. Especially with the way you enjoy that risotto."

"Finn, are you by chance thinking about sex?"

Finn laughed at Amelia's schoolteacher tone. "Well, now I am." She sipped her wine, enjoying the smile she'd put on Amelia's face. "I wonder how many times I've tried to surreptitiously imagine you naked, but you knew exactly what I was thinking."

"Let's just say you're lucky we both have dirty minds."

Finn thought of all the other little things they had in common—like how they both knew the lyrics to every Brandi Carlile song and how neither of them liked onions or pajamas. She poked at her food some more, thinking about how she shouldn't waste delicious fish, and then wondering where her appetite had gone. Except she knew why she wasn't hungry. Wanting to tell Amelia that she was falling for her had taken up all the space in her mind. She didn't have room for anything else.

After they'd finished eating, they ordered more wine and lingered at their table. It was a weeknight, and with the icy weather outside the place was half empty, so the waiter didn't seem in any hurry to shoo them out. "What should I get Edith for Christmas?"

"You don't have to get her anything. She's always saying how she has everything she needs. Maybe a card?"

Finn shook her head. "She has three presents already wrapped for me. I saw them with her pile of presents for you on the coffee table the last time I was over."

"You're going to laugh when you see what she made you."

"I can't even guess." Knowing Edith, it was probably better not to. Hopefully it would be something tame like a pair of socks. "Would she like something for her kitchen? Maybe some special gadget that whips up pie crusts or something?"

Amelia's smile made it clear Finn was clueless about kitchen gadgets, but she stretched her hand across the table, palm up, and said, "I like that you want to get her something. Maybe we can go shopping together for her? I need to find something too."

"That sounds perfect."

"I also really like you. And that has nothing to do with Nana or Christmas presents or this risotto."

"I like you too." Finn set her hand on Amelia's, her heart racing in her chest. *Like* wasn't the word she wanted to use.

"In that case, want to take me to your place and make good use of the rest of our evening?"

"Hmm. What counts as good use?" Finn let herself fall into the flirty banter that followed. Foreplay felt good and she didn't want to fight it. Besides, maybe they weren't ready for the other conversation.

When they left the restaurant, Finn gave Amelia a ride back to the parking garage. She waited for Amelia's car to pull out and then followed her through the city streets to her apartment. After parking on the street out front, Finn hopped out of her car and jogged over to open Amelia's door.

"Hey."

"Didn't want to be away from me for even a minute, huh?" Amelia caught the front of Finn's jacket and pulled her into a kiss. "I'd say you were being chivalrous, but I have a feeling you're just horny. And by the way, I like you all hot and eager. Your eyes have been working me up and down all night."

"Maybe I'm also chivalrous."

"Maybe." Amelia batted her eyelashes. "I do appreciate that you rescue me whenever I need it, but at the moment, I'm more interested in your sex drive."

"I'm glad it's not a problem."

"Not a problem at all. I love how much you like sex." Amelia bumped her hip against Finn's side as they headed up the path to the apartment. "You've made me realize I need that in my life."

"Sex?"

"Well, I always knew I needed that." Amelia hesitated. "Or at least needed a relationship where that was part of it. But… With some women I've been with, I've felt like I wanted it more than they did. With you, I don't feel bad about my needs." She slipped her hand around Finn's waist. "In fact, I think it's possible that you think about sex even more than me."

"I can tell you every time I think about sex and we can start counting. Although I already want to win this contest, so good luck. I'm pretty competitive."

Amelia laughed. "Competitive about sex? Or in general?"

"Exactly."

They fell into step and Amelia shifted her hand to the low of Finn's back when they reached the door of the apartment. As she waited for Finn to unlock the door, she leaned close and kissed her neck. Finn loved that Amelia didn't want to let go.

"Do you know how wet I am for you?"

"I hope you're going to let me find out soon."

She'd planned out their evening hoping to show Amelia that she was good for more than sex. But so far she'd let her hormones lead. She needed to do more talking than kissing and yet her body argued talking could come after kissing.

She unlocked the door but before she opened it, Amelia took the keys from her hand and pushed into her. The kiss was full of need, more so than Finn had ever felt from her. The debate over needing more talking than kissing was replaced with the thought that maybe she could show Amelia that this wasn't simply casual sex. Tonight she wanted to make love to her.

Amelia pulled back and caught the zipper of Finn's coat and tugged it down enough to slide her hand inside. "You have no idea how much I want you."

"I'm beginning to get the idea." Finn pushed open the door, pulse racing as her own arousal shot up. Amelia slipped past her and they didn't speak as they took off their coats in the entryway, nor as Finn hung them in the closet. But Amelia's eyes didn't leave Finn's until she bent to unzip her boots. The dress clung to her backside and Finn couldn't help stepping forward to press against Amelia's butt. She leaned down to help with the stubborn boot zipper.

"I thought about helping you out of these when I first saw you tonight."

Amelia's fingers faltered. "You're so helpful."

"I try."

Amelia stepped out of the first boot and let Finn take over with the second. Once the boots were off, Finn straightened up, still pressed against Amelia's back. Shared need pulsed between them. "You said yes to an all-nighter, right?"

"I wish." Amelia moaned when Finn's hands trailed up and down her arms. "Unfortunately, I need to sleep tonight. Another important meeting in the morning…You're going to have to make good use of your time and have me in bed by midnight."

"Have you in bed by midnight, huh? Does that mean I can have you on the kitchen counter at ten?" Finn kissed Amelia's neck as she undid the clip to let the twist slip away. She ran her fingers through Amelia's silky hair. "And the sofa at eleven?"

"As long as your roommate doesn't come home, you can have me in every room of this apartment. You know I like it best when you do whatever you please with me."

Finn's pulse quickened. *Whatever you please.* "And if my roommate came home?" She pushed Amelia's dress off her shoulder and kissed the bare skin she'd exposed. Even without touching herself, she knew her clit was swollen and ready.

"If your roommate came home, you'd cover me up because you're so chivalrous."

"Actually, I would." Finn chuckled as her bravado smacked against reality.

"I love that about you, you know." Amelia leaned back against Finn's chest, accepting her embrace. "You take care of me in the sexiest way."

"Would you let me take care of all your needs tonight?"

"Yes." Amelia turned to face Finn. She caught Finn's tie and her grip tightened on the narrow black strip. "I can't get enough of you."

"Good. I'm doing my job right."

Finn kissed Amelia even as she laughed. She kept Amelia laughing and stepping back with playful kisses until she had her pinned against the door.

"Here in the entryway, huh? Is that where we're doing this?" Amelia sucked in a breath as Finn kissed her throat and then moved down until she reached the line of her cleavage. "Too bad you have such a little place. I really would offer up in every room."

"As long as I'm done with you before midnight." Finn pushed the fabric down until she could feel Amelia's bra and ran a finger over the lace. "This is nice. Very pretty."

"Why is it that when you say sweet things about what I'm wearing, I get the feeling you want to tear them off me?"

"Are you worried I might ruin your pretty things?" Finn asked, all the more tempted.

"Worried, hopeful…I have trouble deciding."

Finn shifted her hand and stroked down the length of Amelia's dress. "This dress is nice too. And you're right. I do want to tear it off you." She tested the edge of the cloth with a light tug. "But I don't need to. Not for what I want to do at the moment."

Finn slid Amelia's dress up above her hips to get to the waistband of her tights. She hooked her thumbs under the elastic and tugged the tights down along with Amelia's pink-and-red striped panties. Amelia wasn't naked enough for her desires, but she shivered when Finn moved against her.

"You cold?"

"God, no," Amelia said. "I'm hot. And so ready for you."

"Maybe I should check."

"You should."

In one fluid move, Finn spun Amelia around and pressed up against her backside. Amelia put her hands on the front door, bracing herself and moaning as Finn slid her hands up her legs. She moved her feet apart, then shuddered as Finn moved against her.

"You said you weren't cold," Finn whispered, nipping at her earlobe. "You know I won't do anything you don't want me to do."

"I know…I'm a little nervous. But I like it." Amelia moaned as Finn stroked lightly up and down her arms.

"Why do you like it?" Finn wanted to keep Amelia talking. Her little sounds of contentment paired with their whispered conversation was making her hotter than ever.

"I like knowing that you could overpower me."

"I thought you liked me taking care of you."

"Mmm. I do." Amelia tried to turn, smiling when she felt the strength in Finn's hold. "This is you taking care of me," she whispered. "You know how to push me to the edge, but you'll stop if you find my limit. I love both those things."

"I love it when you whisper." Finn made circles with her thumbs on Amelia's butt, then shifted her hold from Amelia's hips to the smooth bit of skin around the triangle of short hair. She didn't slip inside despite how much she wanted it. "And, since we're admitting what we love, I love it when you're ready for me."

"I'm so ready." Amelia pressed against Finn. She didn't move her hands from where they were braced against the door, but a tremor went through her as Finn moved closer to her center.

The desire to push inside Amelia, to fill her and have her cry out with pleasure, blocked out all other thoughts. Still, she held back. Amelia rhythmically rocked against her, making her lose focus as her need pushed to the surface. She wanted to whisper, "I love you," but the words were dangerous and stuck in her throat.

"Please?"

"Please what?" Finn knew exactly what Amelia was asking for.

Amelia breathed out the words then pushed herself against Finn. "You know where I need you."

Finn sucked in a breath. She stroked down Amelia's thighs and then up to her breasts, the material of the dress tangling around her. It was thin fabric and maybe she would tear it. But that'd be on accident and she'd buy Amelia a new dress if it happened. Somehow that thought gave her desire permission and she grabbed at the zipper, ripping it down. The dress gaped, showing off more of Amelia's back and the straps of her bra. Finn couldn't wait any more. She unhooked the lacy bra and then moved to grab Amelia's full breasts.

She squeezed the nipples until Amelia gasped. She loved the weight that filled her hands, the fullness of each breast, but she loved even more how Amelia pushed right into her hands.

"I don't know how long I'll be able to hold back," Amelia murmured.

"You don't have to hold back. I'll let you come now…I know I can have you again when we get to my bedroom." Finn squeezed again and Amelia pressed forward, leaning against the door as she groaned.

"I want your hands other places too."

"Which places do you mean?" Finn knew but was savoring the wait.

"You know what I need."

"I do know. And I also like pushing you to say it. Or maybe I'll get you off just doing this." Finn rolled the pebbled tips. She had no doubt that they were harder than they'd been earlier outside in the cold. Now they were swollen with need. "I can save your wet pussy for later. I want something to do when we get to the bedroom."

Amelia bucked against her again and Finn's clit pulsed. Despite what she'd said, she desperately wanted to feel Amelia come on her hand. Shifting between her legs, she spread Amelia's folds. Amelia moaned as she circled her swollen clit.

As soon as Finn dipped inside, Amelia clenched around her fingers. Her orgasm was so close Finn could feel it rising as if it was her own body about to climax. When Finn started to pump her hand, Amelia tensed, shivered, then sank down on Finn's fingers. The pressure on her clit brought everything to the finish line in a dizzying rush. Finn had to brace one hand on the door to keep them both standing. She felt Amelia's climax roll through her own body, and when she sank her fingers in deeper, Amelia went up on her toes and Finn's whole body felt the release. A moment later, Amelia trembled and took a shaky step back against Finn.

Finn slid out, her fingers dripping with proof that Amelia wanted her as much as she'd claimed. When Amelia turned to face Finn, her eyes were moist.

"You okay?"

She nodded. "Better than okay." She kissed Finn, long and hard, but when she pulled back her chin quivered.

"You say you're okay, but it looks like you're about to cry."

Amelia shook her head. "I don't want to talk right now. I want to feel you on me. Will you take me to bed?"

CHAPTER TWENTY-FIVE

Amelia woke to the sensation of pins and needles. Her entire left arm was asleep. Well, had been asleep and was now returning to life in the most excruciating way possible. She rolled onto her back, attempting to extricate it from under Finn, who was snoring. Her whole body protested. The combination of what she and Finn had done last night and then falling fast asleep and not moving for hours made every muscle and joint ache. And then there was that entirely different ache between her thighs.

She smiled. A small price to pay, really, for the night they'd had. The sex had been off the charts. More than ever, she'd felt Finn's need for her. But it was more than that. Something was different in the way Finn looked at her, the way she kissed her. They hadn't talked about it exactly, but last night Finn had seemed to make love to her. So tender, loving, even when she was rough. Amelia had wanted to ask what was different, wanting the confirmation to what she was feeling, but she'd held back. *Again.* What was she waiting for?

She looked at Finn and knew the answer. It wasn't fair to expect Finn to say it first, especially when she'd been the one to say she needed to take things slow. But after Veronica, she couldn't be the one who jumped first. Not without knowing if someone would be there to catch her.

At least they'd finally managed a real date. That had to mean they were in the girlfriend category now. She'd thought Finn might want to talk about their relationship at dinner, but it hadn't come up. Maybe she needed to learn to be patient. She let out a contented sigh and glanced at the window, where a thin strip of sunlight slipped in through the gap in the curtains.

Wait.

The sun wasn't supposed to be out yet. She was supposed to be up and on her way home to get ready for work before it even hinted at being out. She rolled to the edge of the bed, looking for the phone that wasn't there. It never made it to the bedroom. It never even made it out of her purse.

She lifted her head and looked around. A trail of discarded clothes on the floor, a lamp and a stack of books on the nightstand. No clock. Where the fuck was the alarm clock? Gone the way of hers, likely: broken and not replaced after cell phones started doing the job just as well.

Since there was no sign of Finn's phone, either, she climbed out of bed and padded to the living room. A few more items of clothes were strewn about and her purse sat precariously on the arm of the sofa. She grabbed it and rooted around for her phone. She already knew she wouldn't like the answer but the screen told her it was even worse than she expected. 9:22.

"Fuck, fuck, fuck."

In addition to the time, a string of notifications bombarded her. Most were from her assistant, Lori. The first asked if she wanted coffee before her meeting. The second asked if she was going straight there. The third and fourth expressed concern, while the fifth gave way to panic. The county legislature's office had called when she'd not shown up for the nine o'clock budget hearing.

"Fuck, fuck, fuck."

"Is everything okay?"

The voice behind her made her jump. And it didn't belong to Finn. Amelia whirled around and found herself face-to-face with a gorgeous woman in a high-waisted pencil skirt and form-fitting blouse. They'd still not met, but this had to be Jess. "I'm late."

Jess nodded.

Realization dawned. "And naked." She grabbed for the closest piece of clothing on the floor—Finn's shirt—and held it in front of her. "Sorry."

Jess didn't seem nearly as mortified by the whole thing as she did. "It's okay. I teach fitness classes. I'm pretty comfortable with bodies. I'm sorry I startled you."

Flashes of what she and Finn had been up to the night before, and how much noise they'd made doing it, filled her brain. "I didn't think you were home."

"I wasn't. I came home this morning to get ready for work. Oh, and I'm Jess. I know we kind of met at the Halloween festival but I was dressed like a pineapple and, well, a lot has happened since then."

Amelia nodded, still clutching the shirt awkwardly in front of her. "Right. Nice to meet you. Again. I'm Amelia."

"I know. Finn talks about you all the time. Anything I can do to help? You seem more than your basic running-late sort of upset."

Right. She was missing one of the biggest budget hearings of the year. "I need to go. Sorry."

"No worries. Good luck. I'd love to have coffee or something sometime when you have more time." Jess seemed completely relaxed, and perhaps a little amused by their whole interaction. "And clothes."

"That would be great." If she weren't so mortified, not to mention panicked, she might have laughed. Instead, she gathered up the rest of her clothes and retreated, backward, in the direction of Finn's room.

Once there, she found Finn sitting up in bed, rubbing her eyes. She blinked a few times at Amelia and smiled. "I was wondering where you'd run off to."

"I was looking for my phone. It was in the living room, along with your roommate."

Finn snickered. "I thought I heard her come in a bit ago."

Her already frazzled nerves snapped. "And it didn't occur to you to wake me up? I'm late. Like, extremely late. For a crazy important meeting. You knew I needed to get up early."

Finn scrubbed a hand over her face. "Crap. I forgot."

"No shit." She started yanking on her clothes. "I shouldn't have come over last night. I should've been going over the meeting agenda and not fucking around." There was no time to look at the agenda now. She still had to go home and change since she couldn't very well saunter into the office wearing the same outfit as yesterday.

"But fucking around's fun, right? And you're cute when you're harried, so there's that."

Maybe Finn was trying to be sweet or lighten the mood or something else with the best of intentions. But all she could think about was the hit her professional credibility was about to take. Not to mention the programs she was supposed to be advocating for. "This isn't funny, Finn."

Finn lifted both hands. "Trying to help. Obviously failing. But I am sorry we overslept. Last night was so great it put us both in a coma."

That was just it. Last night had been great. It let her think—really start to think—that maybe there was more to them than just sex. But now, in the light of day, it felt like the opposite. Like she was indulging in a completely immature, completely unrealistic fling that had no legs and no place in her otherwise grown-up, responsible life.

"Was last night not okay?"

"Last night's not the point." She heard her voice rise but couldn't seem to temper her frustration. "I can't waste time on this. I have to go."

"Okay." Finn nodded, seeming at a loss for words. "Anything I can do to help? Coffee? Ride?"

"No." It came out harsher than she'd intended.

"Right, right. Not part of the fuck-buddy arrangement."

She stopped struggling with the zipper of her dress and looked at Finn. There'd been no anger in her voice. If anything, she'd said it almost as a matter of fact. The cool, detached look on her face only echoed the sentiment.

Right. Because while she might be falling in love with Finn, they hadn't even agreed to be girlfriends. Why should Finn take her or their relationship seriously? And while part of her couldn't blame Finn, she'd really hoped they were on the same page. No, worse. She'd allowed herself to believe they were. So now, on top of being late and irresponsible, she could add foolish to the mix.

She left without another word, or a kiss goodbye, or anything else. Fortunately, Jess had gone. As she zipped up her boots and shoved her arms into her coat, Rascal got up from her bed and came over to do a little dance at her feet. Instead of making her feel better, the enthusiasm only made it worse.

She texted a quick apology and explanation—okay, lie—to Lori as she walked to her car. There was no way she'd make it to even the tail end of the budget hearing at this point. Unless she went as she was. A glance in the rearview mirror revealed smudged mascara and a veritable bird's nest of hair. She was a mess, but she could tame her hair with a clip and do a patch job of her makeup.

She did a quick calculation in her head and steered her car in the direction of downtown rather than home. Unfortunately, an accident on Highway 25 had traffic snarled. The minutes ticked by, but she stubbornly refused to stop trying. It took her close to an hour to get even halfway there.

At that point, with the hearing officially over and absolutely no reason to be downtown at all, she gave up, pulling off the highway and into the parking lot of a drugstore. She contemplated punching the steering wheel but rested her head on it instead. What was she doing? Like, what the actual fuck?

It was one thing to go after Finn, to let her guard down and let her—clearly repressed—inner sex goddess come to life. But she was an adult. An adult with responsibilities and people counting on her and a whole agency to run. Those things didn't get to be put on hold while she went off on one sexcapade after another.

And then there was the whole matter of what she was doing with Finn in the first place. Fuck-buddy arrangement. Finn's words echoed in her mind and left a hollow feeling in her chest. So much for being in love. She picked up her head and swiped at the tears that had crept down her cheeks, then straightened her shoulders. Enough. Crying in a parking lot was next-level pathetic.

Like crying on the paramedic.

The thought left her in that strange bubble between a full meltdown and near-giddy giggles. *Seriously, Amelia. Enough.*

She put her car back in drive and started home. With practically no one heading that direction, it took a mere twenty minutes. Nana's car wasn't in the driveway and she said a prayer of thanks to the universe for small kindnesses. She went in and was showered, dressed, and on her way to work in under half an hour.

Still, by the time she walked into her office, it was close to noon. She was put together but otherwise utterly defeated. Lori ended a phone call and made a beeline for her. "Oh, my God. What happened? Are you okay?"

She pressed a finger to her forehead, right between her eyebrows, even though it would do little to ward off the headache she had brewing. "I'm fine. Frazzled and frustrated, but fine."

Lori's eyes narrowed. "Are you sure? You're never late and you never miss anything."

"I don't mean to be a jerk, but can we please not talk about it? It was a bad morning, but I'm fine and I need to focus on cleaning up the colossal mess I made."

Before Lori could respond, the door swung open and Anna and Paul—her assistant director and budget director—breezed in. Anna spotted her first. "Amelia. Thank God you're okay. We were so worried."

Paul nodded. "Lori told us you'd texted, but we were convinced something horrible happened. You never miss budget hearings."

The fact that everyone kept saying that was a testament to her generally stellar professional reputation, but today it only managed to make her feel like a heel. "I know. I'm sorry. How bad was it?"

The phone rang and Lori groaned before going back to her desk to answer it.

"Actually, we nailed it." Anna beamed.

"You did?" Both Anna and Paul were beyond competent, and she often joked they could run the place without her, but neither was keen on public speaking. They'd, individually and collectively, refused to do so unless absolutely necessary.

Paul nodded. "Anna did the pitch and she hit it out of the park."

Anna blushed but nodded her agreement. "And then the guy running the hearing—"

"Whitburn?"

"Yeah, that's him. He asked where you were."

Amelia groaned. "What did you say?"

Anna turned to Paul and gestured Vanna White style. Paul grinned. "I said that you were in a doctor's appointment that ran long and used it to bolster the request for additional Medi-cars."

"And they bought it?"

"Oh, they bought it all right." Anna did a little dance. "Twenty percent bump in our transportation budget."

She felt herself blink, not in disbelief exactly, but sort of. "Wow."

Paul's expression turned serious. "They didn't go for the increase to the activities budget, though. They said we should be maximizing the socializing that happens at meal sites."

That wasn't really a surprise. She'd asked for it in part as a buffer, giving them something to say no to and lowering the chance they'd slash something else. Nothing would be final until the budget vote, obviously, but by all accounts, today was a win. "I can't thank you two enough, not only for covering my ass, but for getting it done for our seniors."

Anna and Paul high-fived each other, then her. "We got your back, boss," Paul said.

Anna angled her head. "Are you sure you're okay, though? We were so worried."

She winced. She'd screwed up royally and made her staff worry. "I am. I'm going to ask really nicely not to talk about it, though."

Anna's hands went to her hips and she gave Amelia an incredulous look. "Would you let one of us get away with that?"

She tried to respect people's privacy, but the social worker in her usually had her needling—gently, of course—for thoughts and feelings. "How about I promise you both a pass next time you don't want to talk about something?"

Anna's worry lines deepened. "You don't have to do that, or tell us. But—"

"I'm fine. Promise."

"You're stubborn," Lori offered from across the room. She'd finished the call and resumed listening in. "But we love you."

"And not only as our fearless leader." Anna took her hand and gave it a squeeze.

Amelia nodded and mustered a smile. "Same."

"Glad we're clear on that." Paul folded his arms, clearly uncomfortable with the emotional display but trying.

She nodded again and, since she was on the verge of crying some more, retreated to her office. She rarely closed the door, but she did this time. Then she pressed her back to it and slid to the floor, hugging her knees to her chest.

She knew she shouldn't, but she pulled out her phone. Finn hadn't called or texted. Amelia hadn't really expected her to, but it didn't stop the wave of disappointment. She thought of the conversation she'd wanted to have with Finn—about how she'd tried to hold back but was falling for her anyway and didn't care. Now she knew she should have been more careful with her heart.

She took a shaky breath and felt new tears threaten. No more crying. She was at work. A shitty morning didn't absolve her of her responsibilities. If anything, it meant she needed to spend the rest of the day making up for her complete lack of responsibility that morning.

At her desk, she booted her computer and did a quick skim of her inbox. Not too many emails and no big surprises, nice considering she'd been out of the office all morning. She breathed a sigh of relief. The truth was, she loved her job. It wasn't exciting or glamorous, but she liked the work and knew she made a difference in people's lives—when she was on point and doing it well, anyway. And until this morning, she'd felt like she always gave her job her best.

Lately, though, she'd been focused a whole lot more on Finn and their budding relationship than her work. Missing the meeting brought that realization to a head in the worst possible way. But maybe she needed the reality check. She'd let herself imagine a future with Finn. The future she'd dreamed of with Veronica, only better. Unfortunately, she hadn't asked Finn what future she wanted.

She covered her face with her hands as Finn's fuck-buddy comment repeated in her mind. Hopefully this morning wasn't the finest hour for either of them, and the comment had more to do with being snapped at than Finn's feelings about where their relationship stood—and where it was going. She'd give them both some time, then she'd reach out to Finn. It wasn't like they'd had some knock-down, drag-out fight, right? Right?

She drew in a breath and straightened up, eyeing her inbox with resolve. After the morning she'd had, focusing on emails was a better pursuit than judging if dating Finn was a good idea or not.

CHAPTER TWENTY-SIX

Switching from working days to nights was never a picnic. But by day four or five, usually she'd gotten into the swing of it. Not this time. She annoyed even herself with all the grumbling she did. Toni blamed the bomb cyclone snowstorm that had hit their first night on, right at peak commute time, and then the extra shift they had to pick up, but it was more than all that.

She'd texted with Amelia but hadn't had time to meet up since their fight. All she'd done in the meantime was work, sleep, work out, and then hit repeat. In truth, she could have managed seeing Amelia but she hadn't wanted to. Not after being summarily dismissed as a waste of time—right after she'd decided to throw in all her chips and really go for the relationship. So much for trying to be emotionally available. When Amelia left, Finn had wanted to curl up in a ball. She'd apologized more than once about not setting an alarm but clearly the problem was bigger than that.

"What are you doing tonight?" Toni asked. "Hooking up with your cat lady?"

"We're going Christmas shopping." She wasn't sure what to expect beyond the shopping part. Would they talk and resolve things? Or were they about to end whatever it was they were doing?

"That's sweet. You two gonna pick out matching reindeer sweaters?"

"Well, I know I'm picking one out for you. I got my eye on one with little twinkling lights. You're gonna look hot. Hippie chick is gonna want to rip it right off you." Finn waggled her eyebrows. "What are you getting me for Christmas?"

"A case of kombucha."

"You wouldn't."

Toni grinned. "Oh, but I would."

"Maybe we should agree to skip presents."

"No way, boss. I want that reindeer sweater. And I already bought you the kombucha." Toni raised her hand. "See you in three days."

Finn watched Toni head for her car, then unlocked her truck. The wipers had frozen to the windshield, so she settled into the front seat with the defrost blasting and pulled out her phone. No new texts from Amelia, and no voice mails either, but there was one missed call from a number she didn't recognize in South Dakota.

After a moment of wondering who it might be, she decided to return the call. On the third ring, her sister's shaky voice answered. "Dara? You okay?"

"No." A stifled sob followed.

"What's wrong?"

"I think something's happened to the baby." Dara tried to go on but her voice broke and she started crying in earnest.

Dara wasn't a crier. If anything, she was too tough for her own good. As a kid she'd tried to brush off a broken arm just so she could keep playing ball with the other kids, and she'd gotten more than her share of bruises riding horses and dirt bikes.

Finn squeezed the bridge of her nose. Between the exhaustion and the trembling sound of her sister's normally strong voice, she was in danger of crying too. "Dara, talk to me."

"I can't feel him moving. He kicks, you know…" Dara took a shaky breath before continuing, "Yesterday he barely moved all day and then last night, nothing. I called the clinic and they said maybe I'm missing the kicks. Finn, I know something's wrong. And I had a little bleeding just now. Not a lot, but…Something's wrong, isn't it?"

"A little bleeding can be okay. It might only be the uterus thinning. But the baby should still be moving. Have you felt any contractions?"

"No."

"Have you called Mom? I know she's not a doctor but we both know how many calves she's delivered. And babies too."

"I don't want to talk to her."

Deciding who was more stubborn—her mom or her sister—had never been easy. No surprise that neither one had apologized about whatever had happened. "I know she can be difficult, but she knows a lot."

When Dara didn't answer, Finn knew it was a lost cause. She'd played the mediator between her mom and Dara countless times but decided not to get involved with their latest blowup— that was now over a year old. That fight had coincided with her figuring out that Nadia was cheating, and she'd been more focused on licking her own wounds than helping anyone else. But now a year later she didn't have a good excuse for why she was still in self-care mode.

"Where are you?"

"Rapid City. I've been staying with a friend…I dropped out of school. I know you wanted me to finish my AA but I couldn't swing working and studying after I got pregnant. I was too tired at night."

"It's okay, Dara."

"And my car's in the shop. And I lost my phone." A fresh sob rose up.

That explained why she hadn't responded to any of the texts. Finn closed her eyes. "When Dad told me you were pregnant, I tried calling you…" She should have tried harder to track Dara down, but none of that mattered now. "We need to get the baby checked out. You've got a doctor, right?"

"Sort of. I saw someone at a clinic last month. Finn, I'm worried. It was a lot of blood. What if the baby's not alive?"

"I'm sure everything's fine. A little bleeding can be normal." Finn swallowed against the lump in her throat. "Sometimes it only means you're about to start labor. And when babies move down toward the birth canal sometimes you can't feel them kick as much. How far along are you?"

"About thirty-six weeks. I think. I don't know exactly. I wasn't keeping track…God, I'm such a fuck-up. I don't even know who the father is."

"You're not a fuck-up, Dar. Or maybe we all are, a little bit."

Dara's muffled laugh was cut short by more crying. If only she were in South Dakota… Instead she was in Denver and couldn't do a damn thing to help.

Well, maybe she could do something. She squinted at the time and then scrubbed her face, trying to focus. Getting Dara to the doctor was first order of business.

"Listen, I'm going to get you a ride to the clinic. They'll put a monitor on and you'll be able to hear his heartbeat. If something's wrong, they'll keep you there. But it's probably nothing."

"Okay. *Okay.*" Dara was clearly psyching herself up for the worst news, and the possibilities gave Finn's welled tears an excuse to fall.

"Tell me your address—and I'm paying for the ride so don't argue. When you get to the clinic, call me if there's a problem. Someone'll let you use their phone if you explain what's going on. Probably we'll just listen to the little guy's heartbeat together, okay?"

"Thanks, Finn." Dara took a big breath and exhaled. "I didn't know who else to call."

"You can always call me. You know that."

"I should have already bought diapers."

"We'll have plenty of time to get those." Finn hoped this was a false alarm. And maybe exactly what Dara needed to make her realize she needed to be with family instead of a friend who she couldn't call in an emergency.

After she hung up, Finn went online to schedule a ride. She thought of all the messages she'd left for Dara after she'd heard about the pregnancy. And the texts and emails. She'd assumed Dara was simply busy doing her own thing. The way Dara always did. But Dara had no idea she'd even tried contacting her.

She rubbed her eyes, taking away the rest of the tears. She wanted to call Amelia and tell her what was going on, talk through the crazy idea she had of driving up to South Dakota to be with her sister. Her dad was right when he'd said she was the only person Dara ever listened to. Maybe in person she could convince her to move back to the ranch.

Finn considered for a moment and then rang Amelia. She waited until voice mail picked up but instead of leaving a message, ended the call. If the tables were turned, would Amelia call her to talk through a problem? She'd called after her breakup with Veronica, but she was stuck then and needed a ride.

As much as Finn had hoped they were building a real connection, the past week cast doubt on all that. For Amelia, their relationship—if she should even call it that—wasn't serious. It was still only about letting go and having fun. Maybe they'd had a few sweet, shared moments, but rebounds had plenty of those. Along with plenty of sex.

Finn woke to the sound of her phone ringing. She'd only been asleep for a short while, a few hours at best, and when she stood, the room swirled around her. Rummaging through the clothes on the floor, she found her phone. A familiar wave of nausea—thanks, sleep deprivation—told her to sit down as soon as possible. She plunked down on the bed before answering.

"Finn? They say I have to go to the hospital," Dara said quickly. "Something's wrong with the placenta. The doctor said it's detaching or something like that. Do you think it's too soon? Will the baby be okay? I asked the nurse, but she wouldn't tell me."

Shit. It could be bad. Very bad. How much oxygen was still getting to the baby? Finn straightened, fear making her wide awake. "Babies come early all the time, Dara. It's gonna be okay."

Even and calm, just like at work when things weren't going well with a patient. But Dara was her sister, not some stranger. "Do what they say and go to the hospital. I'm gonna call Mom. You need someone to be with you."

"Can you come instead? I know it's a lot to ask."

"I'll get in my truck now and head up." Finn had already started dressing, fishing out a clean pair of cargo pants and a flannel from the pile of laundry she hadn't gotten around to putting away. "But, Dara, I think you need someone there sooner. It'll take me at least seven hours even if I push it. Please let me call Mom."

Dara was quiet for a moment. Finn knew she was weighing how much she didn't want to be alone with how much she didn't want to swallow her pride. "Okay."

As soon as they hung up, Finn dialed the ranch then shot a text to Jess, thankful when she confirmed she'd be home to take care of Rascal. She hurried to pack, indiscriminately stuffing jeans, shirts, socks, and underwear into her gym duffel bag. She didn't stop in the kitchen for food—at some point in the drive to Rapid City she'd need gas and an excuse to stretch anyway—but she did take a minute to snuggle Rascal and promised a long game of catch when she got back.

The baby might not survive. She'd seen that tragedy unfold firsthand. If the placenta completely detached before labor and the baby didn't get oxygen… Finn stopped herself from finishing that line of thought. It was different when it was a patient she didn't know crying on her shoulder. Sure, she felt for them and she cried along, but this was her little sister.

Did Dara even want to be a mom? Probably her answer would be "not yet." But this—the placenta detaching, and Dara alone and scared—wasn't how Finn wanted the universe to decide things. And what if things went so bad that Dara's life was in danger?

Finn latched her seat belt and made a silent prayer she'd get out of the city before afternoon traffic started. But South Dakota and everyone who needed her was so far away. What was she doing living in Denver anyway?

CHAPTER TWENTY-SEVEN

Are you running late or are you not coming?

Amelia read the text she'd sent to Finn an hour ago. No reply. Not even a read notification. Finn had called that morning but hadn't left a message, and now Amelia didn't know if it was to chat or cancel or because something was wrong.

Although she hadn't been ready to talk to Finn for the last few days, she would have answered—if she'd heard it. Unfortunately, she'd been in the shower singing badly enough for Percy to come in and make sure she wasn't being murdered. Then when she noticed the missed call, she'd wanted to call Finn back but remembered she'd probably be sleeping after an all-night shift.

Still, knowing Finn had tried to reach her had cheered her up and made her want to fast-forward her day to the time when they were supposed to meet. She was tired of the avoiding and the meaningless check-in texts that felt hollow. She wanted to resolve things. Yes, she'd hoped Finn would have already apologized for the fuck-buddy comment, but she'd started it by being snippy in the first place. A short conversation would likely fix everything, she'd told herself, and then they could kiss and make up. Even mad, she'd wanted to wrap her arms around Finn and sink into her embrace.

Well, she had wanted to do that, but now her good mood and optimism were faltering. It was nearly four—almost an hour after Finn was scheduled to pick her up. Knowing Finn had switched back to nights and sometimes struggled to adjust her sleep schedule, she wanted to give her the benefit of doubt. But as the minutes ticked by, she succumbed to that horrible blend of irritation and worry. She didn't want to wish something bad to have happened, but Finn better have a damn good reason she hadn't bothered to show up or call.

"Is something wrong, dear?" Nana looked up from her knitting needles.

Nana knew very well something was wrong, since Amelia had told her she had plans to spend the afternoon with Finn and yet remained on the sofa, staring into space. "No."

Nana set the knitting firmly in her lap. "Let me rephrase. What's wrong? Did Finn cancel?"

Canceling would have been preferable to being stood up, honestly. "No."

"Did you cancel?"

"No."

Nana's look turned from one of concern to one of exasperation. "You don't have to tell me your personal business, but don't take it out on me either."

She hadn't told Nana about her fight with Finn or the work disaster that had turned out okay in the end. But she'd been surly and home three evenings in a row—a rarity these days—and was a pretty terrible liar on top of that. "Sorry."

"I'm not looking for an apology. I'm—"

Amelia's phone rang and vibrated in her lap. *Finn.* "I'm still sorry. Let me take this and I'll explain."

She got up and headed to her room, not wanting whatever conversation unfolded to do so with an audience. She swiped a finger across the screen as she closed the door behind her. "Hey."

"I'm sorry. I completely forgot about our plans." Finn's voice sounded far away and muffled, like she was driving.

"Did you get stuck at work?" The idea that Finn forgot their plans—again—irritated her. A little bit of her irritation faded at the idea of Finn pulling an extra-long shift, but still.

"No, no. It's not that. I'm on my way to South Dakota."

So, she was driving. And far away. "Is everything okay?"

Finn didn't answer right away, and worry bumped anger to the back seat.

"An emergency came up. I should have called you as soon as I started driving, but I was a little out of it…"

"Finn, are you okay to drive?"

"Yeah. I'm fine. It's my sister." There was a long pause and then Finn cleared her throat. "She's pregnant and not super tight with the rest of my family and needs a friendly face." Her voice had that fake chipperness to it, like she wasn't telling the truth.

"Is that really all?"

"Well…"

"You can tell me, you know." When Finn didn't immediately answer, she added, "I'd like you to be honest with me. These past few days have kind of sucked."

"Yeah." Finn sighed. "They have."

Finn's acceptance of that fact pushed her to say the rest of her thought. "I don't want to have the kind of relationship where we don't tell each other what's really going on."

"Me neither. Dara had some bleeding this morning. She went to get checked out and they think the baby's in danger. The placenta's detaching. She's on her way to the hospital now and she asked me to come."

The rest of her irritation faded, giving way to worry about a young woman she'd never even met. She also had the worry of what it meant that, without prodding, Finn wouldn't have told her what was happening.

"I really am sorry about missing our shopping date. Maybe we can get a redo when I get back?"

"I don't care about the shopping date. Your sister needs you. I get it." She blew out a breath. The problem was everything else.

"You're still mad."

"I'm not mad." She was, clearly, and she couldn't hide it.

"You are mad, and you have been all week, but I don't know what to do about it."

"Avoiding it seems to be the strategy you went for." She wanted to take back the words as soon as she heard them. "We both did," she added. "I'm not saying that now is a good time, but I think we need to talk about it. And what was said."

"I don't even know why you got so ticked off. I mean, I get that you were upset about missing the meeting and me forgetting to set the alarm, but…well, whatever."

"Don't say whatever." It would have been one thing for Finn to backpedal. Or even to defend that she didn't mean how the fuck-buddy comment came out. But that she wasn't even going to acknowledge that was the problem? Or that she couldn't see why that would have hurt? That's what did her in. "What are we doing, Finn?"

"Well, we aren't shopping. I swear I do feel bad about that. You know I'm shitty at keeping dates. Although this is kind of an extenuating circumstance."

The almost casual dismissal made her want to scream. Even with whatever Finn's sister was going through, she couldn't simply drop it. "I'm not talking about this afternoon. I'm talking about everything. What are we doing?"

Another pause before Finn eventually said, "We're having fun. Or at least we were until a couple of days ago."

"Right, because that's all we are. A good time." Amelia pressed her hand to her forehead. Was that really all they had? Crying about it wouldn't change what she was to Finn, but she couldn't stop the tears. "Maybe we shouldn't have this conversation right now. You clearly have other things on your mind. And you're driving."

"Hold on. There's a rest area. I'm going to pull over." The road noise quieted, then stopped. "You're the one who said you wanted—needed, even—to let go and have fun."

She had said as much, although she never, ever, said it was all she wanted. "And that's exactly what you wanted, isn't it? A fuck buddy." Saying it out loud made her heart hurt. "I wish you saying that hadn't hurt as much as it did."

"I don't remember saying that…but I wasn't really paying attention to what I said." Finn sounded both surprised and hurt, which made no sense.

"What the hell were you paying attention to?" She'd sat on the corner of her bed, but now she got up to pace. She could only get about three steps in each direction, which, along with Finn not answering her question, made her want to scream. "When I overslept and I was getting dressed, you said something wasn't part of our fuck-buddy arrangement. I don't even remember what you were talking about—coffee, I think. All I remember for sure was that comment."

"Yeah, well, I remember you not wanting to waste your time."

"Waste my time? What are you talking about?"

Finn didn't answer, and Amelia strained her memory to recall everything that had been said. She had been upset, and snippy. She also had a vague recollection of saying she didn't want to waste time talking. But that didn't warrant a fuck-buddy comment. Unless Finn had completely misunderstood what she meant by wasting time. "I get that you don't want to talk, but I need you to tell me what you mean."

"Amelia, I don't want to be a tool, but I don't think I can focus on this right now."

Finn was worried about her sister. She had to give her a break there. But her words stung all the same. "Okay. We'll talk when you're ready, I guess. I am sorry if I said the wrong thing that morning. It was a really important meeting." One Finn hadn't even bothered to ask her about afterward.

"I know. And you're still mad at me not setting the alarm."

"I'm not mad about that. I should have set my own alarm." What she was mad about was not being able to talk it out like reasonable adults, and even now they were talking circles around the problem.

"You're absolutely still mad. I can hear it in your voice."

"You know what? You're right. I am mad. About a lot of things. I like you, Finn, but…Does it even occur to you to tell me when something major is going on in your life like your sister being pregnant?" That Finn didn't think to confide in her was worse than the flip reference to their relationship.

"I—crap."

Amelia closed her eyes and willed tears away.

"I'm getting a call from South Dakota. I think it's my sister. I told her to call me when she got to the hospital. I gotta go."

The phone went silent, but Amelia stared at it for a long time. Percy's face reappeared and, eventually, the screen went black. When she looked up, the surroundings that had been so familiar felt suddenly stifling. She was basically living in her childhood bedroom with a girlfriend who didn't even think of her as a real girlfriend.

She'd asked Finn what they were doing when, really, she should have been asking herself. What the hell was she doing with her life?

She flopped back on the bed, not liking any of the answers she came up with. From the colossal mistake that had been Veronica to not having a place of her own to go home to after the accident. From hopping into bed with Finn to letting herself believe there was more to it than sex. Even her job—which she told herself was about helping her community—was also safe and easy, more like having comfort food for dinner than a strategic plan for a fulfilling career.

A light knock on her door pulled her from her wallowing. "Amelia?"

If it had been anyone but Nana, she'd have yelled at them to go away. Since it was Nana, she let out a big sigh and said, "Come in."

The door opened. "I heard your raised voice, then nothing, so I thought you might be ready for a friendly ear."

What would she do without this woman? "I'm not sure there's anything to talk about."

Nana let out a sniff and sat on the corner of the bed. "That seems unlikely."

Amelia sat up. "Finn completely forgot about our plans. I started out mad because this isn't the first time. But she's on her way to see her sister who's pregnant because there might be something wrong with the baby. So, I want to be understanding but I'm mad that it didn't occur to her to confide in me or even tell me. Or maybe more hurt than mad, but mad at myself for thinking there was more to our relationship than maybe there is."

Nana nodded. "That's a lot."

"I know." She flopped back once again, but immediately sat up. "I feel like I keep making mistake after mistake. Taking a chance when I shouldn't and not taking a chance when I should. Does that make sense?"

"It does. I think the thing with taking chances is that you don't know ahead of time if it's going to pay off or not. You trust your gut and go for it."

"Yeah." The comment made her think about how she'd taken chances with Finn in bed and how well things had paid off there. Taking chances with her heart was a different story.

"Have you told Finn how you felt?"

"Sort of?"

Nana shot her a stern, don't-BS-me sort of look.

"Every time I try to talk to Finn about feelings, she kind of shuts down."

"How many times have you tried?"

An innocent enough question, but it got her hackles all up. Because the truth of the matter was that she hadn't tried all that much. She liked Finn and worried about messing things up or, worse, scaring her off. Also, her track record on talking to women about feelings was perhaps even more dismal than her track record on dating generally. "I guess I could have more. It feels like Finn gets cagey when I try."

Nana lifted a shoulder. "Well, she did have her heart broken."

Did Nana know more about Finn's past than she did? She thought of the one time Finn had mentioned the ex she'd been planning to marry. Finn hadn't been exactly forthcoming with details, but she also hadn't pressed. "I had my heart broken too."

Nana rested a hand on her knee and looked her in the eye. "Did you, really and truly?"

So much for consolation. Amelia resented the question, but only because of the answer. "I guess my heart wasn't completely on the line to start with."

"Are you talking about Veronica? Or Finn?"

It hit her in that moment how much more invested she was in Finn than she ever was in Veronica, even without talk of futures or being exclusive or anything resembling a serious relationship. "I'm a complete idiot."

"You aren't." Nana's tone was firm.

"I'm pretty sure I am. I also have no idea what to do." And she had no idea when—or if—she'd hear from Finn again.

CHAPTER TWENTY-EIGHT

After all the stress of the night before, all the comings and goings of family and nurses, dawn was blissfully quiet. Peaceful even, despite the cold sterility of the hospital room. Finn must have dozed, because her arm complained when she tried to shift it, but she knew she hadn't truly slept. She couldn't. Not with a baby in her arms.

She couldn't look at him enough. Peach fuzz for hair, tiny little fingers curled into fists, and ridiculously cute cheeks. He was still soundly sleeping in the crook of her arm, exactly where the nurse had placed him hours earlier. Nothing was wrong with him. Amazingly, he'd been given a clean bill of health and now only needed to figure out how to survive the next eighty-odd years of his life.

"Good luck, little buddy. It isn't easy out there."

Dara murmured in her sleep and Finn looked up from the baby to her sister's face. Thin rays shined in through the cracks in the blinds, but even with the light Dara seemed a shadow of her old self. Seeing how pale she'd gotten, how ragged her voice sounded, and how terrified she'd been as they'd wheeled her into the OR for the emergency C-section, had cemented Finn's decision to stay. Not only for the night so that Dara wouldn't be alone in the hospital, but until she saw both Dara and the baby, who still needed a name, settled at the ranch. As long as it took to make sure they were both safe, she'd stay.

"Finn?"

"I'm right here." Finn reached out the hand that wasn't cradling the baby and her sister weakly squeezed it.

"Is he okay?"

"He's fine. Still sleeping. He's a perfect little baby."

Dara let go of Finn's hand and closed her eyes again. "Thank you for holding him. For being here."

A moment later Dara was back to snoring. Finn shifted the blue-and-pink-striped blanket-wrapped bundle from one arm to the other and then fished for her phone. In all the hustle and bustle, she hadn't had time to take any pictures. She knew her parents had gotten a few before they'd left last night, but she wanted one of her own. Stretching, she widened the crack in the blinds to let in more light and then snapped a shot right as he yawned.

Worried he'd cry, she quickly pushed the blinds closed. He opened his eyes and studied her.

"Sorry, buddy," she whispered. "You're really cute. I can't help it."

He yawned again but his eyes fluttered closed. After she'd rocked him back to sleep, she glanced at the picture she'd taken. She wanted to text the shot to Amelia but hesitated. They had a lot to talk about, she knew, and Amelia might not want a picture of a baby anyway. She deliberated for a minute and then hit the send button. Amelia was the only person she wanted to send the picture to, and that had to mean something.

A moment later her phone buzzed with a reply: *Glad everything turned out okay.*

Finn waited for Amelia to say more. She watched the bubble with the three dots blink for at least a minute before it disappeared. It was early. Maybe she'd started to type something and then fallen asleep. Or she didn't know what else to say. Finn didn't either.

"Women." Finn had whispered the word but the baby opened his eyes again. Softly, she added, "Someday you'll understand. Or maybe you'll fall for a guy. You can tell me if they're any easier to love."

* * *

"Wanna help me unload the truck?"

Finn nodded, happy for an excuse to go outside despite the snow flurries. The weather channel guaranteed there'd be a fresh blanket of snow by Christmas Eve, but it wasn't pretty yet. Just cold. She picked out one of the wool hats by the back door that smelled vaguely of cow manure and tugged it on along with one of her dad's jackets—a lined canvas Carhartt that once had been blue but was as gray now as her dad's beard.

Bundled up, they stepped outside, and the icy wind whipped in greeting. Dad tugged the tarp off the truck bed, exposing the firewood they'd picked up the day before. "You've been quiet this morning. Everything okay?"

Finn shrugged, pulling on a pair of leather gloves.

"I'll take that as a no."

"Take what?" She looked up from the logs and her father chuckled. "What?"

"You're distracted."

"Yeah...sorry." She'd gotten only one-word responses from Amelia to all the texts she'd sent over the past three days she'd been at the ranch. *How are you?—Fine. How's work?—Busy.* She hadn't called only because she still didn't know what she should say. "I'm kind of in a fight with my girlfriend."

"Kind of? Or you are?" Dad chuckled again when Finn nodded. "You know, your mom and I are either madly in love or fighting. Keeps things interesting."

Finn shifted a few of the split logs onto one arm and started gathering more. "You and Mom don't seem to fight much."

"Well, mostly we're madly in love." He tossed two more logs on top of Finn's load. "What'd you do?"

"Said the wrong thing. And didn't say anything when I should have." Finn thought back to how happy she'd been sitting across from Amelia their last night together. "I thought she'd know how I felt without having to say it."

"You're definitely my kid." He patted her shoulder. "I know it seems easier to not talk about problems, but they don't go away."

"Didn't even think we had a problem."

"Oh, there's always some problem. You should've figured that out by now. No relationship's perfect. You love her?"

"Thought I did." She shook her head. "No, I still do. But maybe I thought we had something when we didn't?"

"Or you just fucked up."

Finn couldn't help laughing at her dad's assessment.

"Ask what the problem is. Then deal with it. You have to be willing to take some risks. Put your heart on the line."

"Yeah...maybe." But that would only open her up to get hurt more. She stacked the logs she'd gathered and went back for another set. As she hefted more logs, her eyes kept roaming from the truck bed to the range beyond. She thought of the picture she'd shown Amelia and how different everything looked in the winter. Would Amelia even want to come visit a place like this? Would it only look cold and desolate to her?

"Hey, daydreamer, no standing around on the job." He tossed logs into her arms. "Gotta work fast or we'll freeze out here. Wind's not letting up."

They hustled and had the truck emptied in a half hour. By then, Finn was sweating despite the biting wind.

"I'm gonna head over to Ed's before the storm gets any worse." Dad latched the tailgate. "He's got a rocking chair he's selling."

"For Dara?"

Dad nodded.

"Want company?"

"Nah. What I'd like is for you to talk to Dara. Convince her to stay past New Year's."

Finn wondered what Dara was thinking even considering leaving the ranch then. She couldn't go back to work yet. And they all knew she was broke. "I'll talk to her. No promises, though."

"I think she wants to stay. Just won't admit it." He pulled off his gloves and got in the truck but didn't close the door. "Finn, one other thing. You might want to fix things with your girlfriend sooner rather than later. I know you like this one 'cause you're more than your usual level distracted."

"I like her a lot. That's the problem."

"Yep. Usually is."

After she'd waved him off, she headed back to the house. The sounds of little Elliot's cries filled the kitchen and she found Dara pacing from the table to the refrigerator trying to settle him.

"Give him here," Finn said, holding out her arms. "You're still supposed to be in bed. The doc said two weeks after a C-section."

"He won't nurse. I've changed his diaper, but he keeps crying." Dara handed Elliot over with a look of relief.

"Did you try singing?" Finn bounced on her toes until Elliot paused in his crying long enough to look up at her. "He liked when you sang to him last night."

"I've been singing all morning. I've run out of songs to sing." Dara dropped into the kitchen chair. "God, he's so cute when he's not crying."

"Did you hear Mom last night bragging about him to her friend on the phone?"

Dara smiled faintly. "She likes being a grandma."

"She does. And she's good at it. I know you don't want to talk about it, but you need to think about staying here and letting her help you."

"You're right. I don't want to talk about it."

Finn glanced down at Elliot, quiet now, and then over at Dara. "I'm going with Dad to pick up your car tomorrow."

Dara's brow furrowed. "It's not drivable."

"Is now. Carl replaced the transmission. He had the time to change the brakes too. Said the discs were about done for."

"I can't pay him."

"Bill's already paid. And don't think about paying me back. Since I didn't get invited to the baby shower, this is my present." There hadn't been any baby shower and Dara needed all the help she could get.

"Oh, Finn. Thank you."

"Welcome. Now, about you staying here for the year..." Dara started to protest but Elliot's cry stopped her. Finn waited till he'd settled back down before starting again. "You and Elliot will be better off here. You won't be able to work anyway, and you'll need to focus on him. At least for a few months. You'll have your car if you need to go somewhere."

"Mom and I—"

"Whatever that dumb fight was about between you two, you got bigger things to worry about now."

Dara leaned back in the chair, one hand pressing her head and the other on her belly. "It wasn't a dumb fight." Finn waited, and finally Dara continued, "It was about bison—and before you look at me like I'm being ridiculous, let me finish."

"You're not ridiculous. Stubborn, yes, but go on."

"Mom and Dad were selling organic grass-fed beef long before it was all the rage. You know that. But when I told Mom about my plan to bring in some bison, she flipped. She doesn't think I have any sense when it comes to ranching or the business of it—but I do."

"I could see bison here."

"Right? Bison belong in South Dakota. Reintroduction, with careful breeding, would be good for the bison. And the land. Besides that, it's money. We can still raise cattle, too, but if we got a little herd of bison going..." She stopped and shook her head. "Anyway, that wasn't really what the fight was about. Mom—and Dad too—treat me like I'm still a kid. They won't listen to any of my ideas and won't trust me taking care of anything. Even after I got their website up and got them online with all the ordering."

"So, the fight wasn't really about bison."

Dara dropped her gaze. "No."

"If you want to take over the ranch someday, you need to start acting like it."

"I try, but—" Dara opened and closed her mouth. "How'd you know I want to take it over?"

"It was more than the bison idea. You've always loved it here. More than any of us except Dad maybe."

"I feel like there's a *but* coming."

Finn hesitated. "Mom and Dad remember all the times you've gotten excited about something and then given up. They know you're full of fire and tough as anyone, but you don't always follow through."

Dara looked at Elliot and then at Finn. "You're right. That's how they see me. How you see me too, I guess."

"Nope. I know there's a hell of a lot more to the picture. You gotta have something you really believe in—and someone you don't want to let down—but then you do amazing things. If ranching's what you want to do, get the bison. Show everyone you can do this."

Dara seemed to take strength in Finn's words. "What about you? I know this place has always been in the back of your mind. You've said you'd take over when Dad gets too old."

"Yeah, I said it, but I don't actually want that. I'd do it for Dad and Mom, but this place…" She looked around at the kitchen she'd grown up in and felt the walls press in. "I love it here, in some ways. In other ways, it's never been the life for me."

"Your life's in Denver."

Finn thought of how Jess said she'd been living partly in both places. Maybe that was true. But if she could pick one, knowing the ranch would be taken care of without her, she'd choose Denver in a heartbeat. And Amelia was part of why she liked Denver more than ever. Colorado was as much home now as South Dakota. "Turns out I'm as much a city kid as a ranch kid. Go figure."

"I want to run this ranch, Finn."

"You'd be awesome at it."

"I think I needed to know you didn't want it."

Finn smiled. "You want to know the funny part? I think I needed to know that you did."

"I can only stay here if Mom starts treating me like an adult." Dara held up her hand. "And before you say it, I know. I have to start acting like an adult."

"This little guy will help you out there." Finn looked down. Despite the bundle in her arms, she felt lighter than she had in a long time. If Dara wanted to run the ranch, she didn't have to carry that obligation anymore. She could plan her future in Denver. Amelia returned to her mind. She wanted to see her now more than ever.

"I know I've messed up before, but do you think I can pull it off?"

"I do." Finn studied Elliot for a moment. "The question is, can I fix my mess-ups?"

"Does one mess in particular have to do with a woman named Amelia?" Dara picked Finn's phone up from the kitchen table. "Her texts keep popping up on your screen. She doesn't sound too happy."

Finn's stomach clenched. Before she could process what Amelia might have said or complain about privacy at the ranch being nonexistent, Dara continued, "She wants to know if you'd like her to take care of your dog. Your roommate has to go out of town for something and she's worried about Rascal going to the kennel."

It was sweet of Amelia to offer and would be a huge help. But from Dara's tone, she could tell there was more. "What makes you think she's unhappy?"

Dara scrolled through the texts and then cleared her throat. "'We need to talk about where things are going.'"

The tight feeling in Finn's stomach turned to full-scale nausea. "Oh."

"Yeah." Dara set the phone on the table. "But if she wanted to break up with you, would she offer to take care of Rascal?"

"She's a nice person. She might." Finn looked down at Elliot again. "Maybe you'll be braver when it comes to women and talking about feelings."

"I'll try and coach him." Dara stretched out her arms to take Elliot. "Now that you've worked your magic, I've got big things to plan for him and me. And you need to text Amelia."

Alone, Finn sat at the table and read through the texts. Instead of the one-word responses Amelia had sent all week, this time there were paragraphs. Tears welled but she brushed them away before they fell. Amelia thought things were over between them. She hadn't said it directly, but the gist of her message was clear.

Head spinning, Finn texted a thank-you for Amelia's offer to take Rascal and then a request to talk about everything in person. She stared at her phone as minutes passed with no response. Was it too late?

Jess was right. She'd held back from Nadia and she'd always dated women she could leave without looking back. But having one boot in South Dakota was only a good excuse for not getting hurt by risking too much. Her dad had been closer to the truth there. She might have thought she was in love before, but she'd never been willing to put too much of herself on the line.

Everything was different with Amelia. She wanted to take all the risks.

All the reasons why she'd worried about doing that before weren't as important as giving their relationship a real chance. She wanted to lay all her cards on the table. And she wanted to tell Amelia she loved her. As soon as she realized she needed to do exactly that if she had any hope of keeping Amelia, a plan formed.

For the first time, she didn't want to be in South Dakota for Christmas. She wanted to be with Amelia.

CHAPTER TWENTY-NINE

Amelia sat on the sofa cross-legged in flannel pajama pants and thick wool socks. Oh, and Finn's sweatshirt. It didn't smell like Finn anymore, but she couldn't seem to stop wearing it. She'd left only a week ago, but it felt like ages. Maybe missing someone and being mad at them doubled the sensation of time dragging.

She didn't want to be mad, but it was starting to feel like Finn was incapable of having a grown-up conversation about feelings or the future. Or maybe Finn was capable and simply not interested in having that sort of conversation with her. At least Finn had texted her more over the past few days. Most of it was little stuff—commentary about decorating the barn with Christmas lights for the cows and pictures of baby Elliot—but it helped her feel connected. And Finn wanting to include her gave her some small hope that they weren't on the verge of a breakup.

"Don't mope, dear. It's Christmas."

Amelia looked up and forced a smile. "Sorry."

Nana waved a hand. "Don't apologize. You're not bothering me any. But I hate seeing you so sad."

That was the problem. A tiny part of her was mad at Finn, but the much bigger part was sad. Sad because so many things about Finn were perfect. Sad because she'd let herself believe they had a future. Sad because texts weren't enough. They needed to talk. If they didn't, she had a sinking feeling she was about to start over at square one. Again.

"You're right. It's silly to be sad on Christmas morning. Especially one spent with my favorite person on the planet." She smiled with more feeling this time.

Nana tutted, clearly not impressed with the comment about being Amelia's favorite. "How about breakfast?"

"That's a fantastic idea. I'll take care of it since you'll be cooking up a storm later." Even though it would just be the two of them, Nana had bought a whole ham and planned at least half a dozen sides. Because tradition was tradition.

"Okay, dear."

It was hard to tell if Nana appreciated the offer or was merely humoring her. Either way, it would be good to get off the sofa and actually accomplish something. She shifted the afghan from her lap, settling it over a snoozing Rascal, who sighed but didn't bother to pick up her head. Neither did Percy, who'd curled up right next to her. If she'd been the superstitious sort, she'd have sworn the way the two of them got along—like long-lost friends who never wanted to part ways again—was a sign. Probably a good thing she wasn't, since all the other signs about Finn and her seemed to point in the opposite direction.

She headed to the kitchen and put in the cinnamon rolls they'd assembled the day before. Cinnamon rolls had been the traditional Christmas morning breakfast for as long as she could remember, only now Nana had found a recipe that could be made the day before and left in the refrigerator overnight before baking. By the time she had the frosting made, the aroma of sugar and cinnamon and yeast wafted through the kitchen.

They ate in the living room in the glow of the tree, and opened presents. She'd splurged and bought Nana an iPad, and was rewarded with a mixture of exclamations she shouldn't have and delight. Nana got her a pair of earrings and had knitted her the softest, most intricate scarf she'd ever seen. She wrapped it around her neck, not even minding that, paired with the hoodie, she looked downright silly.

She put on some music and they spent the rest of the morning lounging. Even as part of her longed for the magic of Christmas morning with kids, she couldn't bring herself to complain about this time with Nana. Something about it—joyful but calm—always seemed absent the years her mother joined them. It might make her a bad person to say so, but she preferred when work kept Miranda in New York.

She let her thoughts wander to Finn and wondered what a big family Christmas morning would really be like. Finn had mentioned fried bread and bacon. And stockings. Did the baby bring an extra layer of celebration to the holiday? From Finn's texts, she'd gathered that there was less tension now that Dara had agreed to move back home and start learning the business of the ranch. It was all great to hear, but Amelia couldn't help wondering if Finn was thinking about their future.

Did they even have one?

The sound of the doorbell yanked her from her ruminations. She looked at Nana with confusion. "Are you expecting someone?"

Nana shook her head. "Carolers?"

Rare, but not unheard of. She headed down the hall, patting at her hair and realizing it was a lost cause. Oh, well. Who stopped by on Christmas unannounced anyway? When she opened the door, she wasn't greeted by a cluster of people waiting to burst into song. It was Finn looking at her with that perfectly lopsided smile. In one hand she had a potted Christmas tree and in the other, a big poinsettia.

"Hi."

Was it possible for the heart to stop and race at the same time? She would have sworn that's what hers was doing. "Finn. I wasn't expecting you."

"Yeah…And I'm thinking now that I probably should have called in case you didn't want to see me."

Not seeing her had been the problem. But now that she was here, Amelia had a hard time getting a grip on the emotions swirling around inside her. Since big-picture thinking was definitely a lost cause, she settled on the logistics. "You didn't need to call. I'm guessing you're here to pick up Rascal?"

"I really appreciate you watching her, but that's not why I'm here. I wanted to talk to you. I've been doing a lot of thinking about us...You said we needed to talk in person, and I agree." Finn lifted the potted tree. "Also, I saw this and thought of you."

"Is that my very own Christmas tree?"

Finn nodded.

"That's sweet. The poinsettia is nice too."

"I was worried flowers and a tree might be too much, but I saw them and, well, thought of you then too. I also got you a wreath, but that's in the car because I felt silly coming up to your door with all three."

Amelia smiled.

"If now isn't a good time to talk, we don't have to. I just didn't want to let Christmas go by without seeing you."

She could take the comment a dozen different ways. "You drove all this way to see me on Christmas?"

Finn nodded, a sheepish expression on her face. "I wanted to say I'm sorry—I am sorry, I mean. That fuck-buddy comment was dumb. And I didn't mean it. I like you, Amelia. A lot."

It was too early for her heart to be dancing. They had a lot to talk about. But still. Finn had given up her family Christmas and driven who knows how long to see her. And the way Finn held her gaze, looking hopeful but nervous too, made it hard to hold back the words *I love you*. She stepped onto the porch and pulled the door closed behind her. "I want to invite you in because it's cold out here, but I also want to talk to you alone. And we have about ninety seconds before Nana's curiosity gets the better of her and Rascal realizes her mama is here."

"I'd like more than ninety seconds."

"Me too." No way could she say everything she was thinking in that time. "Thanks for apologizing. I'm sorry I was snippy and I'm sorry I blamed you for that morning."

Finn dropped her chin. "And the part about being a waste of time…I thought it over and I think maybe you meant that us talking right then was a waste of time. In the moment, I took it to mean you and me. Our relationship."

"I didn't mean that, Finn. Not at all." She couldn't stop there. "I know I said I needed to let go and be in the moment and just have fun and all of that, but that's not what I actually want. Not from a relationship in general and certainly not with you."

"I don't want that either. The more time I spend with you, the more I start thinking about the future and if—"

A sleek silver SUV pulled into the driveway, capturing both their attention. Amelia squinted at the figures behind the windshield. "Oh, God."

"What? Who is it?"

Before she could answer, the passenger door opened and out came Miranda. And from the driver's side? Veronica.

"What is she doing here?" Finn asked. It sounded more like an accusation than a question, but Amelia couldn't really blame her for that.

"I have no idea. But the woman she's with is my mother."

"Oh. Shit."

She could only imagine what was running through Finn's mind, but she didn't get the chance to find out. Or explain. Or assure. In a matter of seconds, both Veronica and Miranda joined them on the porch.

"Merry Christmas, Amelia." Miranda leaned in. It wasn't quite an air kiss, but it might as well have been.

"Surprise!" Veronica mirrored the gesture, which proved doubly disturbing.

The front door opened. Nana looked from Finn to Miranda to Veronica before turning her gaze to Amelia. "What's going on?"

Miranda, so used to taking charge, spoke first. "We decided to surprise you." She waved a finger between Veronica and herself. "We."

The gesture was clearly meant to dismiss Finn and, from the look on her face, Finn picked up on it. Amelia wanted to reach for Finn's hand, but she was still holding the poinsettia and the tree. "And Finn drove down from South Dakota."

Nana continued to look confused, but she opened the door wider and motioned for everyone to come inside. "Well, let's not sort it out on the porch."

The five of them crowded into the living room. Rascal, awake and realizing who at least one of the new arrivals was, leapt from the sofa and let out a series of excited barks. She raced over to Finn, bumping into Veronica in the process. Veronica squeaked and lifted her hands like she was under attack. Finn tried to calm Rascal down while Veronica whispered something to Miranda that sounded a lot like, *"She's Edith's pot dealer."*

"Coffee, anyone?" Nana asked as though the melee was the most natural thing in the world.

All Amelia wanted to do was grab Finn and drag her to the relative quiet of her bedroom, but they were literally separated by Veronica and Miranda. She tried to catch Finn's eye to convey, well, something, but Finn's attention was focused on Rascal, who'd yet to calm down. She turned to Veronica instead. "What are you doing here?"

"You wouldn't answer my texts, so I came here to convince you in person. I want us to have another chance. We were good together, Amelia. I know it and you know it."

There'd only been three texts, and her response to each had been clear, and yet the declaration didn't take her completely by surprise. It sure as hell surprised Finn, though, who jerked her head up and looked at Amelia with a mixture of confusion and betrayal.

"I told you it's too late. I'm with Finn."

It sounded more feeble than she wanted it to, but God, she so didn't want to be having this conversation, especially with an audience.

"Finn?" Miranda lifted both hands. "Who's Finn?"

Veronica jerked her head in Finn's direction.

"That's your girlfriend?" Miranda turned to Veronica and, with a barely lowered voice, added, "I thought she was over dating women who dressed like men."

Amelia had been embarrassed by her mom before, but she seemed to be trying to sink to a new low. "I can't handle this right now."

Veronica wrinkled her nose. "Why do I smell manure?"

Finn cleared her throat. "That would be my boots. I fed the cows before I got on the road this morning." She looked down at her feet, then at Amelia.

Amelia opened her mouth to say something, but no words came out.

Disappointment shone on Finn's face. "I'm going to take Rascal home and shower. I think I need it."

Nana frowned. Amelia already knew what side of the fence she was on, but it was reassuring to see. Even if everything else seemed to be falling apart.

"You'll come back for dinner later," Nana said. "You're not going to spend Christmas alone in your apartment."

Finn ruffled Rascal's ears. "Thank you for the invitation, but I think we're going to lay low tonight. You ready, girl?"

At the question, Rascal started to dance around. Veronica took a step back as though Rascal might pounce. Finn walked to the front door and Amelia fought her way through the crowded room to follow. How was it the one person she wanted to talk to was the one who wouldn't stick around?

She thought maybe Finn would say something about talking the next day, but she clipped Rascal's leash on and opened the front door. Amelia followed her out onto the porch, not sure what to say but knowing she didn't want Finn leaving like this. "Finn, wait."

Finn turned, but her face told Amelia she'd already checked out. "I guess my idea of surprising you wasn't so original after all."

She shook her head. "My mother has come home for Christmas exactly twice in the last ten years. I have no idea what got into her."

"Uh, I'm pretty sure it was Veronica. You didn't mention she's been texting you."

At the accusing tone, Amelia felt her frustration reach a breaking point. How was everything going wrong all at the same time? "I don't hide things, Finn, but we haven't been talking all that much."

Finn shook her head. "You're right. I wanted to talk in person—not on the phone—but I think now that was a mistake."

"Honestly, we needed to have a real conversation about us two weeks ago." Tears burned her eyes, but she didn't try to rub them away.

"And maybe now I'm too late." Finn looked between her truck and the house. "I shouldn't have shown up here unannounced. You've got enough on your plate today, but I still would like to talk later. If you want."

"Finn." It came out sharp. She meant to be conciliatory, but her frazzled nerves—and Finn taking off, once again—got the better of her. "I don't want you to leave."

"I need to leave. I need you to figure that out without me." Finn motioned to the house. "And depending on how it goes, I'd like to finish our conversation about us."

Even if logically she agreed that Finn didn't need to suffer through her telling Veronica off, or deal with the aftermath, she wanted her to stay all the same. She'd already figured the important thing out—she wanted Finn. And even if she knew it was too soon, knew they had things to work on, she was in love. Not halfway, not maybe, not if she let herself. She was completely and totally gone.

"Call me when you're ready. It'll be okay whatever you decide." Finn's expression was something close to resignation. "Come on, Rascal. Let's go."

Amelia's head was still spinning as Finn and Rascal headed down the porch steps. She'd parked on the street, so there were no cars to jockey. They piled in and, in a matter of seconds, were gone.

She let her head drop. How had that gone so badly?

The front door opened and Veronica popped out. "Oh, good. She's gone. Come inside so we can open presents and catch up."

As much as doing Veronica's bidding was the absolute last thing she wanted to do, standing outside without a coat and wishing for Finn to reappear wasn't solving any of her problems. She let Veronica hook her arm and sweep her inside, wishing the conversation she had to have about their relationship being over was behind her.

Inside, Nana shot her a questioning look. All she could do was shrug. She took the tree and the poinsettia Finn had brought to her room and then reluctantly joined the others to open presents—a cashmere sweater from Miranda that probably cost half her paycheck and a pair of fancy Bluetooth headphones from Veronica. "They're great for working out," she said with the enthusiasm she reserved for all things exercise.

Although she'd planned to spend the day in pajamas, she cited wanting to take a shower and escaped to the bathroom. It gave her a few minutes of quiet, but no answers. In her room, she paced back and forth in her robe, phone in hand. Should she text Finn? What would she say? She'd spent the last week sad and frustrated with Finn, and now she had the feeling she was the one needing to apologize. Maybe the universe was trying to tell her something if big problems were coming up before they'd even started calling each other girlfriend.

But even as that thought formed like a dark cloud over her head, a slew of good memories flashed through her mind. The way Finn held her hand the day they met. The afternoon of making pies with Nana. The way Finn asked her questions and truly listened to the answers. And the impossibly perfect way they fit together in bed.

Being with Finn was everything she wanted. Well, aside from settling down and starting a family. Though, to be fair, they hadn't managed to have that conversation. She'd been more focused on letting go and having sex at every opportunity than really getting to know Finn. But Finn had tried on her end.

Amelia thought of their brunch at the diner and how perfect everything had felt. Was it all only an illusion she'd created? Finn hadn't stayed to fight for her. Instead, she'd walked away and told Amelia to figure things out on her own. Maybe that was exactly what she needed to do. Even if she knew she wanted Finn, she didn't have much more of a plan than that.

Doubts danced at the edge of her imagination, but she couldn't stop thinking about the look on Finn's face as she'd held the poinsettia and the Christmas tree. She'd shown up to apologize even if she wasn't the only one in the wrong. She'd left her family Christmas to be with Amelia. She must have left the ranch before dawn. Not a fuck buddy kind of gesture.

She pulled on clothes and went to the kitchen to help Nana finish dinner. As much as she wanted to kick Veronica out of the house, she didn't want to ruin Nana's Christmas with more drama. "I can slice the carrots."

Nana nodded and handed over the knife, moving on to the mashed potatoes. Christmas music played but Amelia didn't sing along. She tuned the music out, along with the conversation Veronica and Miranda were having about some celebrity she'd never heard of. After the carrots, she moved on to green beans, and every time she caught Nana eyeing her with concern she did her best to smile—not that a fake smile would stop Nana from knowing exactly how she felt.

When they sat down to eat, Amelia didn't have an appetite. She looked around the table and felt sick. She couldn't keep pretending things were fine. Not even for Nana. She wanted to be eating Christmas dinner with Finn.

"Do you want a roll, dear?" Nana asked.

Amelia shook her head. If Finn had shown up at her place, there was no reason she couldn't show up at hers. It wasn't as romantic as Finn's driving hours to see her, but romantic wasn't the point really. She needed to fix things, exactly as Finn had tried to do that morning. "I have to go."

Miranda angled her head. "Go where?"

"To Finn's."

"Who's Finn?"

She had to stifle a laugh. Miranda had absolutely no clue what was going on in her life. "My girlfriend. The person I was talking to when you showed up."

"Oh."

More than the one-word response, her mother's disdainful tone said everything. Finn was not someone Miranda Stone would waste a moment thinking of. Finn was someone Miranda Stone would expect to get out of her way—quickly, without making eye contact. Miranda Stone, the woman the nation thought of as the sweet and pretty, wholesome next-door-neighbor type who shared healthy recipes and juicy but innocent celebrity gossip, wasn't sweet at all. Miranda Stone, whom the nation tuned in to watch every afternoon on the talk show "that no one could stop talking about," was in fact someone Amelia didn't even like.

Miranda Stone didn't show up for Christmas because she wanted to be with her loved ones. She was here to help Veronica, to some extent, but more than that she was here to help herself. Pictures of her looking beautiful at her daughter's lesbian wedding would surely boost ratings on the talk show—especially if the other bride was a gorgeous up-and-coming star. Those pictures would prove that Miranda Stone was as loving and motherly as everyone suspected.

But who had shown up to help when it really mattered? Finn. Finn was the one in the hospital room giving her a hug, the one telling her it was okay to go easy on her body, the one she could relax and be herself with, the one who had come for Christmas because she wanted to spend time with her.

Guilt at not defending Finn earlier mixed with guilt for not standing up for herself against her mother countless times. On the heels of that came anger. How had she not seen Miranda for who she truly was until this moment?

Nana, probably hoping to dispel the tension, asked Miranda about work. As soon as Miranda started relaying some disagreement she'd had with one of the writers for her show, Veronica leaned close to Amelia and said, "I get that we both needed a little spice during our break, but you could have done a lot better. She's not in the same attractiveness bracket as you are. Not even close. And she drives an ambulance for a living."

Rather than irritate her, the comment only drove home how misguided her relationship with Veronica had been. "I think Finn's sexy as hell. But you know what's more important? She cares about me. She's come to my rescue in more ways than one. And helped me realize when I can rescue myself."

Veronica rolled her eyes, Miranda looked confused that her story was being interrupted, and Nana only smiled.

"You go, dear," Nana said. "Talk things out and make them right."

Amelia got up and kissed Nana on the cheek. She might not be able to fix everything, but she damn well was going to try with Finn. "Thank you."

"You're leaving? Right now?" Miranda looked incredulous.

"I am. If I miss you two before you leave, safe travels back to New York." That might be overplaying her hand, but it felt good to say. "Oh, and Veronica, we're not taking a break. We're done. We were done months ago. But I'm fine with you and Miranda being friends. You're perfect for each other."

She tugged on her boots and put on a coat and scarf. She was halfway out the door when she remembered Finn's Christmas present. She snagged it from under the tree. Again, maybe overplaying her hand, but today was all about taking a chance.

CHAPTER THIRTY

Finn stared at the wreath hanging on the coatrack. She'd intended to place it somewhere more appropriate, but since getting home from Amelia's all she'd managed to do was take Rascal to the park, shower, and hold down the sofa. The wreath was officially the only Christmas decoration in the apartment and that made it all the more pathetic. A lot like her attempt to win back Amelia.

Rascal hadn't left her side, and Finn wondered if the clinginess was because she'd been gone for a week or if Rascal was worried about her. She stopped petting her for a moment and Rascal met her gaze. "What would you have done?"

One ear cocked up and then the other. She tilted her head from side to side and Finn couldn't help smiling. After a moment of clearly trying to understand the question, she gave up and pushed into Finn's palm, sneakily licking her fingers.

"Gross." Finn laughed, wiping dog spit on her jeans. "Yeah, I don't think licking her would work in this case, but thanks for the suggestion." She settled back on the couch and closed her eyes. "Why did I think it'd be a good idea to have a girlfriend anyway?"

Amelia's smile when she'd opened the door that morning had seemed genuine. She'd *seemed* happy to see Finn. More than that, her whole expression told Finn she'd made the right decision surprising her. Still, she hadn't been ready to kiss her—she'd held back, not even coming close enough for a hug. They needed to talk, though, so Finn hadn't worried about Amelia acting hesitant. It felt right to clear the air before they made contact. But then Veronica and Amelia's mom had shown up and the opportunity to fix things vaporized.

Amelia hadn't introduced her to her mom. She'd clearly been thrown by Veronica showing up, but the slight still stung. Although the fact that they'd been texting and Amelia hadn't said a word about it made Finn wonder how unexpected the visit had been. Had Amelia known Veronica wanted her back? More importantly, did she want to be with Veronica?

Seeing Veronica again and knowing she was trying to win back Amelia brought back the fear that what they'd had was only a rebound for Amelia. Besides all that, if Amelia had wanted someone like Veronica, what was she even doing with her? She was about as different from Veronica in every way imaginable. Veronica and Amelia's mom both looked like the type of people that belonged on a red carpet in front of flashing cameras, while Amelia was simply beautiful in a way only she could be—showstopping with no makeup and still in pajamas.

The phone buzzed and she scrambled for it, hoping to see Amelia's name flash on the screen. She didn't bother holding back a groan of disappointment when she saw the message was from her dad.

Dad: *How did it go?*

Not great. I'm home with Rascal feeling sorry for myself. Should have stayed at the ranch.

Dad: *Should have gone for a bigger tree.*

Finn couldn't help smiling. *It's not about the size, Dad.*

Dad: *LOL*

She loved that her dad knew to text that. He might look like a crusty old rancher, but he had his moments of being hip. The next text from him was a picture of the whole family crowded around the table. He'd taken the shot on Christmas Eve and Finn remembered wishing then that Amelia could be there. To feel what a big family Christmas was like. She knew Amelia would have been enamored with little Elliot too.

With a sigh, she tossed her phone on the coffee table. Maybe after she'd left, Veronica had convinced Amelia to give them a second try. Maybe they were kissing even now.

"Ugh. Stop, brain."

The last thing she wanted was to imagine Veronica and Amelia kissing. Okay, scratch that. The last thing she wanted was to imagine them having sex. Kissing was also down on the list, but the thought of Veronica taking off Amelia's clothes? Or slipping her hand over Amelia's body?

No. Just no. She couldn't believe Veronica had come back. Couldn't believe that Amelia was spending Christmas with her. And she'd let it all happen without even putting up a fight.

She should have stayed, should have pulled Amelia aside and had the conversation she'd come to have, but like a coward, she'd fled. If only it could be about the size of the damn tree.

Rascal let out a yip of excitement, hopped off the couch, and raced to the door.

"What's gotten into you?"

A moment later, Finn heard a tentative knock. She got to her feet, foolishly hoping it was Amelia. She couldn't help the hoping. But would Amelia really leave everyone and come over? Her heart pounded as she unlocked the door. Rascal spun donuts between her feet and the rug, annoyed that she was taking too long.

As if conjured by how desperately Finn wanted her, Amelia stood on the other side.

Finn felt shaky all over. Her heart still raced, and as much as she wanted to say a million things to Amelia all at once, she couldn't manage to say anything at all. Rascal let out a howl of delight, circled Amelia's legs, and then zoomed back to the couch, tail wagging furiously.

"Someone's happy to see you," Finn said, cautiously meeting Amelia's gaze.

"I was hoping more than one of you would be."

"Amelia, I…" Finn stopped. She opened her mouth to try again but the words caught. She wanted to apologize for leaving earlier but the words *I love you* pushed to the front of her mind instead. It was all she wanted to say. It wouldn't be enough, but could she start there?

"Can I go first?" Amelia took a deep breath. "I'd really like to kiss you before saying anything. That's what I wanted to do this morning, but we needed to talk and then…everything happened. But I should tell you that it's taking all I have to not step through this doorway and wrap my arms around you." She swallowed, seeming to barely hold back tears. "And to ask you to hold me forever because you always seem to make everything feel right in the world."

Forever. It took every ounce of Finn's self-control not to close the distance between them. "I'm sorry I didn't stay this morning. I should have."

"I was mad at you at the time, but it was the right thing to do. I had to deal with some things. On my own."

"How was Christmas dinner?"

"I left in the middle of it."

"What about your mom? And Veronica?"

Amelia shook her head. "I left them with Nana."

"It's Christmas, though."

"And you came to see me on Christmas." Amelia started to reach for Finn's hand but then stopped herself. "Finn, I never should have let you leave. Or I should have left with you. You have no idea how much I wanted to stop you. Everything happened all at once and then you were walking to your truck and I couldn't seem to say the right words."

Amelia pulled back her shoulders, straightening up. "You're the only one I wanted showing up on my doorstep. You're the one I wanted to spend Christmas with."

Finn let go of the breath she didn't know she'd been holding. "I'm sorry for what I said that morning you missed your meeting. And for what I didn't say. I should have told you how I felt about you."

"It's okay. I said some dumb things too. Mostly I was scared that this wasn't a big deal to you. That I wasn't important to you." She sniffed. "Wow, that's hard to say out loud."

"Funny thing is, I was scared of the same thing."

Amelia smiled. Not a big smile, but a tentative one that made Finn's heart ache.

"You're a big fucking deal to me."

"Thank you for saying that. Amelia, I—"

"Wait, can I keep going?"

Amelia reached for Finn's hand again. This time she didn't pull back, and as soon as their fingers entwined Finn felt her chest tighten with a rush of emotion. She squeezed Amelia's hand.

"I know I should let you talk," Amelia said. "And I promise I will, but I need to say everything I wanted to say before I lose my nerve."

Finn brought Amelia's hand to her lips and brushed it with a light kiss. She didn't want to worry about whatever else Amelia had to say. She wanted to simply trust the feeling of connection, the bond she knew they had. But what if Amelia needed to say that she couldn't handle being in a relationship right now? "Tell me."

"I don't want to be with anyone else, Finn. I want you. For more than sex—as much as I love that part. I fell for you before we even started sleeping together. And I think, as weird as this sounds, the amazing sex kind of threw us both off track."

Finn nodded. "I think you're right. I don't actually want to ask this, but…do you think we should stop having sex for a while?"

"Not on your life. But I need you to know that I love you for more than that."

"I love you too." Finn didn't need to say anything more. Everything Amelia said was all she needed to know. "Can we kiss now?"

Amelia stepped over the threshold and threw her arms around Finn, pressing their lips together. A full kiss that left no doubt of how much she wanted to be kissed back.

Finn pulled Amelia the rest of the way inside and kicked the door closed, not letting up on her lips. Minutes passed and still they didn't stop kissing. They should talk more. Figure out the next steps. But she couldn't bring herself to let go of Amelia. Not until she was sure all of this was real. Another kiss and then another.

When she finally pulled back, a little moan escaped Amelia's lips. Finn smiled. "I like kissing you too."

"I don't just like it—I love it. But what we have is about more than kissing."

"So much more." Finn wrapped her arms around Amelia. She was in love, so much that her chest ached to hold her even tighter. And Amelia loved her back.

* * *

Finn woke the next morning with Amelia nestled against her. Before opening her eyes, she snuggled closer to Amelia. They were spooning, but fully clothed. For the first time, they'd shared a bed without having sex. True, they'd given each other a massage without shirts on, but then they'd gotten into pajamas and simply cuddled until sleep took them. And it was perfect.

"You awake?" Amelia asked softly.

"Mmm. I'm pretending to sleep so you don't move."

Amelia turned onto her back and looked up at Finn. "I don't want to let you sleep in today. I've got plans for us."

"You've got plans, huh?"

Amelia shifted and kissed Finn's cheek. "Yes. And don't sound so surprised."

Finn chuckled. "I love plans. I want to hear all about them. But now that we're up and talking, Rascal's gonna need to pee."

Hearing her name, Rascal promptly appeared in the room. She cocked her head, looking between Finn and Amelia, then whined softly.

"Let's take her for a walk together," Amelia said, getting out of bed. "But I need to pee first."

"You don't have to come. Rascal and I have this down to a science."

Amelia was already to the bathroom door. "I'm sure you do, but I'm trying to walk more. And I want to be with you."

"Well, that I'm not going to say no to."

They bundled up quickly, throwing jackets over their pajamas, and Rascal herded them to the door. Finn loaned Amelia a hat and mittens, but outside the air had the bitter sting of December, bone dry and frigid.

"You sure you don't want to stay inside?" A walk at seven in the morning was never a picnic.

"I want to be with you."

Finn smiled. "So you've said. But I don't want you getting frostbite."

Amelia laughed. "I was born here. I can handle the cold. When I was a kid I used to refuse to wear pants unless it was below zero. Paraded around in shorts and wouldn't admit to freezing even if I was covered in goose bumps."

"So you were stubborn then, too, huh?"

"Oh, I was worse." Amelia hooked her arm in Finn's and then stepped closer so their shoulders bumped. "You're lucky you met me now."

"So lucky." Finn's chest felt tight with how true the words were. They crossed at the intersection and Rascal pulled toward the park as if knowing she'd get her way this morning.

"How was South Dakota? I meant to ask all about your sister and the new baby yesterday but then everything went sideways."

"I like you sideways. Actually, I like you all the ways." Finn smiled at Amelia's eye roll. "Little Elliot is adorable. And Dara's getting used to being a mom. I think she'll be good at it once she stops fighting my parents and accepts a little more help." She paused. "Christmas Eve was nice, but all I could think of was how much nicer it'd be if you were there."

"Maybe next year."

"Really? I'd love for you to come. Almost as much as I love that you're thinking of next year already." She thought of all the things she'd wanted to tell Amelia yesterday. "Family's important to me and I know we're still figuring things out, but I want you to meet everyone. Would Edith come too? I don't want her to be alone on Christmas."

"I love that you think of everyone." Amelia kissed Finn's cheek. "Nana would love to come. She came from a big family, too, and I know she misses it."

They'd reached the park and Finn bent to unclip Rascal's leash. No one else was out in the cold and Rascal took off running as if she had no intention of coming back. Fortunately, Finn knew better.

Amelia had turned to look at something across the street and Finn followed her gaze. "What is it?"

"Oh, I'm always checking out houses with for sale signs."

Since it was across from the park, Finn had noticed the green bungalow often enough. Over the past year it had fallen into disrepair. The once tidy yard passed the summer unmowed, weeds sprang up in the cracks on the walkway, and now it was obvious that the paint needed a touch-up. Even the porch swing looked sadly unloved with one broken chain. "I've always liked that house. It's a perfect spot. Right by the park. The old couple who used to live there moved out a while ago—I think to a retirement home."

"I bet they were sad to leave."

Finn had had the same thought.

"I'd like to live in a little house like that someday."

"Me too. I've got a down payment saved up, but..." Finn glanced at Amelia, wondering if she should tell her the rest of her thoughts. "I've held off buying a house here because I kept feeling like it didn't make sense."

"Why not?"

"Always figured I'd move back to the ranch. Back home." Before she could go on, Rascal appeared with a ball in her mouth. She dropped it at Finn's feet and her whole body wiggled with triumph. Finn tossed the ball and then returned her attention to Amelia. "I did a lot of thinking when I was in South Dakota. I love the ranch, but I don't want to live there—and I don't want to be a rancher. I like being a paramedic."

"You could do your same job in South Dakota."

"Wouldn't be the same. Besides, turns out I like Denver, and I like some people who live here. A lot, actually."

"You do, huh?" Amelia smiled. "I like knowing that."

Finn whistled and Rascal's head popped up from a mound of snow she'd disappeared behind. The ball, however, was missing. "I do want to buy a house someday. With a big bedroom to share with someone I like." She sidled up to Amelia and grinned. "And a doggy door for Rascal. And a big yard for kids to run around in spraying each other with the garden hose."

"Kids?"

"Why do you sound surprised? I like kids. Two or three would be nice, but I'd settle for one. Elliot convinced me babies are pretty cool, too, and most of the time you start there." Finn smiled at Amelia's narrowed gaze. "What?"

"Finn Douglas, you wait till now to tell me you want kids?"

Finn chuckled at Amelia's admonishing tone. "I've always wanted kids."

"Why didn't you say so?"

Finn cocked her head. "Why didn't you ask?"

Amelia opened and closed her mouth. "You're right. I should have asked."

"Well, we have time for lots of questions now."

Amelia slipped her arm around Finn and relaxed against her. "You're perfect, you know that?"

"Not perfect. But you make me better."

"We make each other better." Amelia sighed softly as Finn wrapped her in a hug. "Maybe we're not perfect, yet, but this feels perfect."

"It does. And I love you."

Amelia smiled. "I love hearing that. Also, I love you back."

EPILOGUE

Amelia closed one eye and surveyed the contents of the U-Haul. A bigger truck, but even fewer boxes, bags, and pieces of furniture than the last time she'd loaded a moving truck. Of course, many of her things had migrated to Finn's in the last few months. They'd load that stuff when they got to her place. And the new furniture they'd bought would get delivered later in the week.

She straightened her ball cap, adjusted her ponytail, and grinned. She was a homeowner.

Well, half-a-home owner. Finn's name had been next to hers on the thousand or so forms they'd had to sign at the closing the week before. After months of looking, they'd finally found one they both loved and could afford and took the leap.

Buying a house together managed to feel surreal but also like the most reasonable and natural thing in the world. Kind of like their relationship. There were moments it still amazed her they'd found each other, and others where she couldn't imagine life any other way.

"Is that everything?" Finn came around the back of the truck to join her.

"It is." She folded her arms. "For being such a girl, I don't have a lot of stuff."

Finn raised a brow. "My closet would beg to differ."

"Ha ha. Aren't you glad we're about to double our closet space?" The midcentury craftsman they'd settled on didn't have a ton of closets, or square footage for that matter, but it was a massive upgrade from their current digs. And with three bedrooms, it would be just the right amount of space to start a family.

Finn's arms came around her and pulled her close. "I'm mostly excited to have a place where I can have you all to myself, anytime I want."

Amelia blushed at the suggestive tone. It didn't seem to matter how long they'd been together or how often Finn still wanted her, the effect Finn had on her remained the same—turned on in two seconds flat and slightly embarrassed by that fact. "You have a one-track mind. We have work to do. And besides, Nana is waiting inside with breakfast."

Finn released her, but not before kissing her long and slow. Turned on, yes, but Finn also still managed to make her weak in the knees. "Let's go. I'm starving."

She couldn't help but laugh. "You're always starving."

It was a good thing Finn had a healthy appetite because Nana, as usual, had made enough food to feed at least a dozen people: eggs and bacon and hash browns, as well as cranberry-orange scones and fresh fruit. She'd also made a batch of brownies—sans pot—for them to take to the new house. "In case you need a boost later."

"You're a goddess." Finn took the Tupperware from her and kissed her cheek. "And we'll see you tomorrow, yes?"

She patted Finn's cheek. "I'll bring Rascal and Percy over at lunchtime and I'll pick up sandwiches."

It was the compromise they'd reached to prevent Nana from overdoing trying to help with the actual moving. It also seemed safer, considering Percy's last adventure in a U-Haul.

Amelia put a hand on her shoulder. "I promise there will still be plenty to do."

Nana lifted her other hand so she could pat their cheeks in stereo. "I'm not worried, dear."

They headed back out to the truck, but both paused. She looked at Finn. "So, who's going to drive?"

Finn looked at her with something resembling alarm. "Um."

She put her hands on her hips. "The accident wasn't my fault, if you remember."

"Absolutely wasn't. You totally can drive."

She shook her head and laughed. "You're cute when you're squirmy. I was just trying to decide if it would be bad luck or good. I mean, it is how we met."

Finn fished the key from her pocket and held it out. "Not that I'm glad your broke your leg or anything, but I do consider it the luckiest day of my life."

It had felt like the unluckiest at the time, but given how everything turned out, she couldn't disagree. She took the key. "I love you, you know."

"I love you too. But don't hit anything. There are plenty of paramedics out there who are hotter than me, and if we end up in an accident...well, I'm not sure about my chances."

She bumped her hip to Finn's before heading around to the driver's side. "Trust me, your chances would still be very good."

They drove over to Finn's and, with the help of a few of her work buddies, got everything loaded in a couple of hours. The same group, plus Cody and Jess, showed up at the house to help them unload. By the time they were done, her arms ached and she was definitely in need of a shower. But she wouldn't have had it any other way.

She flipped on a few lights against the approaching dusk and stood in the living room, surveying the random pieces of furniture and stacks of boxes. "I think that went well."

Finn crossed the room and wrapped her arms around Amelia's waist. "Agreed. Welcome home, Ms. Stone."

She smiled. "Home."

"What do you want for dinner?"

They'd not even begun to unpack the kitchen. And other than the pan of cinnamon rolls she'd made to bake in the morning and the coffee she'd swiped from Nana's pantry, there wasn't a lick of food in the house. "Pizza?"

"Mmm."

"I love that you love pizza as much as I do."

"I do." Finn nodded. "But I was mostly thinking about having my way with you against the kitchen counter while it got cold."

She smiled at the memory of their first real date, or what was supposed to have been their first real date. "Maybe we could do pizza, then shower, then...other things."

Finn tutted. "So practical."

"One of us has to be." The smirk would get her into trouble later, but it was exactly the kind of trouble she craved.

"We'll see about that."

Despite the moving grime and the sheer exhaustion, her body responded—more promise than threat. It didn't seem possible to want Finn with the same ferocity as when they'd first met, but she'd swear she wanted her even more.

Finn ordered the pizza and opened a bottle of wine. When it came, they sat on the floor and used a cooler as a makeshift table. "Maybe we shouldn't have bothered with the dining set," Finn said after her first slice.

"How would we have Thanksgiving without a table?" They'd convinced Nana to let them host, and to join them in South Dakota for Christmas. Nana wouldn't admit it, but Amelia thought she might be relieved to shift into guest mode.

Finn nodded, a serious expression on her face. "I suppose you're right. I'm still more excited for the sofa."

As much as she was looking forward to a real table and chairs—of her very own—she was definitely looking forward to the cuddle-up-and-take-a-nap sectional more. "Same."

Finn straightened. "I think now's the right moment to give you a little housewarming present."

"You got me a housewarming present?" She loved Finn's tendency to spoil her, but it made her worry sometimes that she was dropping the ball. "I didn't think to get you something."

"You promised me cinnamon rolls in bed. That's the best present ever."

She laughed because it was a sweet thing to say, but also because she didn't doubt Finn meant it. She was a sucker for homemade cinnamon rolls. "Okay, that's fair. Where is this present?"

Finn got up and went to a pile of bags and boxes in the corner. She unzipped her overnight bag and took out a small box wrapped in red and green. "I actually got it for you for Christmas last year, but I chickened out giving it to you then."

Amelia looked at the box, then at Finn. "Chickened out, huh?"

"Well, if you recall, things were touch and go that day." Finn handed her the box.

"That's fair." Now that almost a year had passed, she could laugh over how comically bad their timing had been. But it had worked out in the end. Not because of any accident, but because they'd both decided they wanted it to work. They'd put in the time and the work, and she loved their relationship all the more for it.

"Go on, open it."

"Okay, okay." She smiled at Finn's impatience. Under the wrapping, the box was brown and nondescript. She removed the lid and tugged at a loop of ribbon poking out the top. It came loose from the tissue paper, and she smiled as soon as she saw what it was—a tiny U-Haul truck that had been fashioned into a Christmas tree ornament. "Where on earth did you find this?"

"I was poking around a vintage shop looking for something for Jess. Obviously, this one reminded me of the day we met."

"It's so cute." Actually, it was more than that. It was a perfect reminder of something she once thought she'd want to forget. As it turned out, the worst day on record was also one of the best. She looked at the ornament, then back at Finn. "Why did you chicken out?"

"Because there was more to it than an ornament. I wanted to give you that and then ask you to move in with me."

Amelia's brain went back to the day everything went wrong. *Christmas.* So much right had happened since, but she could easily recall the worry and frustration she'd felt then thinking Finn wasn't as serious about their relationship as she was—and thinking that it all might end any moment. "You were thinking about moving in together at that point?"

"I mean, I knew it was a little premature, even for you." Finn angled her head.

"Hey, now." They'd been together long enough that she didn't mind the teasing.

"In my heart, I wanted to give you something else too. But I knew we weren't ready." Finn reached into her pocket and when she pulled it out, light sparkled on the most gorgeous emerald-cut diamond ring.

Amelia's heart leapt to her throat as Finn dropped down on one knee.

Finn looked up and met Amelia's gaze. "Wow. I didn't think I'd be this nervous." She smiled and then took a deep breath. "I'm not sure if you're ready, but I am. You make me happier than I ever thought I'd be. You're the best thing in my life and I want to be the best thing in yours. Will you marry me?"

Finn was serious. There was no doubt in her eyes. And Amelia couldn't remember the last time she'd felt so flooded by happiness. Being with Finn was everything she wanted. She held out her hand, aware of the press of tears but not caring. "Yes."

Finn slipped the ring over her finger, her own hands shaky. "I'm glad you said yes. I just realized this whole buying-a-house-together thing was going to be awkward if you turned me down."

Amelia laughed, tears streaming down her cheeks now. "I love you so much."

"Enough to marry me?"

She nodded. "And then some." The next thing she knew, Finn was gathering her up in her arms.

"It was too soon before, but I wanted to think maybe we'd get there. I just didn't want to jinx it by giving you the ornament and pretending it was only a joke about how we met."

Amelia pressed a finger lightly to Finn's lips. "I love how you're always planning ten steps ahead. And that I'm part of your plans." She replaced her finger with her lips and melted into a perfect kiss. When she pulled back, Finn's smile was as wide as her own. "You're perfect."

"We're perfect for each other."

It had become a bit of a thing with them—calling each other perfect but both finding a certain discomfort with the word. She pulled Finn into another long, slow kiss. "Perfect for each other."

Bella Books, Inc.

Women. Books. Even Better Together.

P.O. Box 10543
Tallahassee, FL 32302

Phone: 800-729-4992
www.bellabooks.com